Call to Arms

Modern LGBTQ+ fiction
of the Second World War

An anthology from
Manifold Press

Published by Manifold Press

E-book ISBN: 978-0-9957125-1-5
Paperback ISBN: 978-1-908312-59-4

Proof-reading and fact checking: F.M. Parkinson

Editor: Heloise Mezen

For further details of Manifold Press titles both in print and forthcoming:
manifoldpress.co.uk

All proceeds from this book
will be donated to the British Refugee Council
(Registered Charity No. 1014576)
to help further their work in
Supporting and Empowering Refugees
refugeecouncil.org.uk

Table of Contents

Introduction

"I don't mind doing that," I said as we discussed future projects at Manifold Press's Retreats for You weekend; and so was born this anthology. It seemed a natural progression from its companion volume, *A Pride of Poppies*: from one World War to the other.

There have been differences, of course, and this has been reflected in the stories. For a book about a war there is remarkably little combat. I wonder whether it reflects two things: first, the feeling that love is something which has to be sought in the quiet times, however much it may be born under fire; second, not so much the experience of the authors as their experience, at one remove, of the Second World War and its history. My parents were evacuees, my grandparents served in the armed forces or in the voluntary associations supporting the Home Front. I would hazard a guess that the same is true for most of the contributors, and that their work refracts the light of other histories, shining it on the different ways of life and love which make up the stories in this collection.

The stories of *A Pride of Poppies* were arranged in chronological order and, after some deliberation, I decided to follow this lead in *Call to Arms*. Some stories had specific dates, some could have happened within a wider period and so could be shifted around; this was useful, as I also wanted to try to vary the tone as much as possible. There were surprising coincidences: names, places of origin, pigs (of all unlikely things) and Gilbert and Sullivan – but in the end I felt that each story was individual enough to stand on its own merits. It is perhaps inevitable that with a Europe-centred group of authors the stories are mostly set in Europe, although the reader is taken to China and Brazil by Barry Brennessel and Sandra Lindsey respectively.

One of the things I noticed, as I shifted the stories to and fro, was the emphasis on movement: escaping, invading, sometimes having one's movement entirely restricted. The desire, however, was always the same: to be home, or to be safe, and to have someone to be safe with, no matter how dreadful life might be until that happened. Unlike medieval wars, where armies moved across an ordinary landscape, causing havoc, maybe, but rarely uprooting the local population, modern wars have resulted in vast shifts of civilian populations bombed out, expelled, forcibly resettled. According to UNHCR, the UN Refugee Agency, there are at present 65.6 million forcibly displaced people worldwide; some calculations put the number of Europeans alone displaced by the Second World War at 60 million. Under the circumstances it is fitting, I hope, that the proceeds from *Call to Arms* will be donated to the Refugee Council. You can read more about their work at refugeecouncil.org.uk.

Mrs Beeton, in the preface to her *Book of Household Management*, said: "I must frankly own, that if I had known, beforehand, that this book would have cost me the labour which it has, I should never have been courageous enough to commence it." At times I have felt the same! I am extremely grateful to the team who supported me. Thanks are due to many: to Mick Forsyth and Alex Woolf for putting me in touch with assorted contacts; to those who, one way or another, have helped the authors with research and advice; to Fiona Pickles and Julie Bozza, editors at Manifold Press, for being brave enough to entrust me with this project; and particularly to F.M. Parkinson for her meticulous and speedy proofreading skills.

Finally, of course, I owe a huge debt of gratitude to the authors. They have tolerated my dilatoriness in the matter of communication, responded cheerfully to my editorial suggestions and put in the necessary hard work, late hours and sheer inspiration to produce the book that is now before you. THANK YOU ALL VERY MUCH!

An Affirming Flame

Jay Lewis Taylor

"We're so sorry you're leaving us, Herr Lawson," Gisela Albrecht said, in German, and from the other side of the room Jutta called out, "You forgot! We're not supposed to know."

"English, if you please, ladies," Patrick Lawson said, and both of them jumped up and ran towards him, their shoes pattering on the fine carpet.

"You have been so good a teacher," Jutta said. "We will miss you."

"I hope we have been good pupils," Gisela added, smiling at him. She smiled a good deal; smiling showed off her dimples, and Patrick suspected she knew that. At any rate, he had caught her several times improving them with the point of a pencil when she should have been studying the pluperfect forms of English verbs.

"Sadly," he said, "you have been terrible pupils, of course." At which both girls burst into peals of laughter. "Why were you not supposed to know?"

"Oh," Gisela said, "politics. *You* know what Father's like. He wants to protect us." She shrugged. "I don't know from what. I can read the papers, and I can see what's on the street." She clambered on a chair to reach the windowsill and sat there, swinging her feet.

Jutta sat on the chair Gisela had used for climbing and said, "We have tried to think how you could properly stay here, but it's difficult. How old are you?"

"Jutta!" Gisela swiped one hand at her sister's blonde braids. "Don't you dare."

What can the little minx be thinking? "I am twenty-six," Patrick said, cautiously.

"Oh, well. That's no good, then." Jutta pulled one braid round her shoulder and sucked the end of it thoughtfully. "You are too old. I thought you were. Gisela is almost sixteen, so – "

"*Jutta* – I *told* you – " But Gisela was blushing.

He turned away, too late; Jutta said, "He's laughing. You're angry, Patrick?"

"I'm not angry," he said. "But your mother and father would be. Respectable girls like you, throwing yourselves away on a poor English musician."

The sunlight was very bright; Gisela slipped down from the windowsill, and drew the net curtains across. Shadows dappled the room as a breeze moved the linden branches; from outside the noise of feet and hooves and the occasional car intruded on the silence.

"So, you are right I think," Jutta said. "It is a pity. But, when do you leave? I hope we will have some time to play our new piano for you." She tugged at his sleeve. "Come see it, Patrick, it's beautiful."

Unwilling to dampen her enthusiasm, he let himself be dragged into the music room. Yes, the piano was beautiful; and he recognised it. Something tightened at his heart. "But isn't that – "

Jutta took no notice, but bounced onto the piano seat and began playing, enthusiastically and inaccurately, Beethoven's 'Für Elise'.

"Yes," Gisela said quietly. "It's from the Hirsches. They are leaving tonight. We are not supposed to know that, either."

"*Damn*," he whispered, remembered himself, and said, "All of them?"

"Yes. They have family in America, you know? Somehow they have a ticket from Hamburg." Gisela winced as Jutta played a wrong chord, and said, "I shall miss Debora."

"I must – " he said. And then: "If I go out – "

"We will be fine," she said. "Good English, no? We will be fine. Margrit is in the kitchen and I will look after Jutta. You go out and say goodbye to them, Mr Lawson. Don't forget that Mama and Papa will be back in an hour, and there is the farewell dinner for you."

He nodded and ran downstairs. In the hall, he took his hat from the stand, and slipped out by the tradesmen's door. The water cart had passed by a while ago, and the scent of lime-blossom, wet dust and petrol hung in the air. Patrick avoided the streets of grand shops, where empty windows had yawned like missing teeth for eight months now, and made his way along alleys and side streets until he reached a taller, narrower house where the windows at ground level were curtainless. For a moment he thought he was too late, until he saw a movement behind glass, a bare arm pointing: Debora, in a summer dress. Two houses along was another alley. He went down that, turned a corner, and so came at the Hirsches' apartment from the side.

The railing on the back steps shifted a little, as it always did when anyone leaned on it; at the sound the door opened, and there was Debora.

"I can come in?" he asked in German, taking off his hat.

"Ja, herein," she said. "I thought you would be here as soon as you heard the news. I will tell Felix. Stay there." She closed the door behind him and went out noiselessly. All the people he knew were walking quietly today, he thought: the girls at the Albrecht house, and now Debora. Only the strangers and the horses on the road made a noise; as if they were real, and he and his friends were walking in a dream. Patrick shivered, although the scullery was very warm. It smelt of damp and soap flakes, and the paint was flaking from the walls.

"Pat."

He looked up. Felix stood there. Not the dapper, elegant Felix of Patrick's first year at the Konservatorium, before Felix had been forbidden to attend, and the Hirsches had been forced to move house; not even the Felix who had kept his charm and self-possession through the hard times. This was someone older, dusty and dishevelled and not entirely in control. His lower lip was split, and there was a bruise on his left cheekbone.

Patrick's mouth dried, suddenly, as if the blow had been aimed at him. "What happened?"

"Reb Issachar, someone lay in wait for him." Felix pumped water into his cupped hands, and wiped his face. "I started in to help, but there were too many, so he ordered me to get away. I was never so glad I can run fast."

"And he?"

"I don't know." Felix stood still, hands over his eyes. "I don't know."

Words fell silent on Patrick's lips. At length he cleared his throat and said, "I heard you were leaving."

"Yes." Felix looked up and smiled a slow, difficult smile. "I'm sorry you didn't hear it from me. There were too many people in earshot, last time we met."

"I understand." He turned his hat in his hands. *Why are there no words?* "It'll be the Sabbath. Once the sun sets." A pointless thing to say, because who would know that better than Felix and his family?

"I know. All the more reason to go. They'll expect us still to be here tomorrow. And – for reasons of saving life – well, you know. Our ticket is for Monday. Third of July, I've been saying that time and time again, like a spell. Third of July, nineteen thirty-nine, we'll be gone." Felix was still looking at him, intently. "I've been clearing out. I helped move the piano earlier. We can hardly carry that on board a steamer."

"That was how I knew. Because of the piano. Gisela told me." Patrick glanced up, saw the expression in Felix's eyes and looked away again.

"We're not supposed to take anything with us," Felix said. "But I'm not leaving my flute behind. I'll hide it, somehow. And – and if when we get to America I have to play on the streets to earn a living – well, at least I'll be able to."

Patrick put his hat down on the edge of the stone sink. "Oh, Felix – "

"Hush," Felix said. "I know. I know." *Ich weiß:* soft whispers of vowel and sibilant. The two of them stepped forward, and Patrick leaned into the embrace as he had so often before, while Felix, taller by six inches or more, wrapped his arms round Patrick's shoulders and whispered endearments into his hair.

After a few moments they broke apart. "I'm sorry," Patrick said. "I should be making this easier for you, if I can. Not harder."

"No matter." Felix caressed Patrick's face. "You always knew there would be an end. When you went back to England, if not before."

Patrick nodded. "And at least you knew that too. Not like Dieter."

Felix threw back his head and laughed. "Indeed. Poor Dieter. He is besotted, you led him on so."

"Nonsense!" But the response was half-hearted.

Felix shook his head. "Only you could get away with having two lovers at once, Patrick Lawson."

Patrick reached out again, and held him close. "I didn't mean that to happen. *You* know. I couldn't push him away. It would have been like smacking a puppy."

"Puppies grow up, and learn to bite. It's as well he left, perhaps." Felix rested one hand on the side of Patrick's neck, under his chin.

"It doesn't seem fair. He had such a hard time, what with his father, and having to give up his studies. I'm sorry he left."

"I'm not. He was very drunk, the night before he went back to Gildehaus. You were out somewhere, so he came and found me instead. And told me, in considerable detail, about his first time with you."

"Oh." Patrick pushed his face into Felix's shirt, but the white linen did nothing to cool his blushes.

Felix's voice was dry, but still affectionate. "I didn't tell him that you learned most of it from me. Poor Dieter, eating his heart out in a railway office to make a living now, and playing piano in the café at weekends because that is all the music work he can get."

"I didn't think you liked him so much."

"I don't. But I have a fellow feeling, since I may be in the same position before long." Felix held him close for a moment, then said, "Enough. You must go, but before that I have something to give you."

"Not anything you're going to need," Patrick said.

"Nothing like that." Felix was digging deep in his pockets. "Where – ah. Here it is." He held it out to Patrick: nothing but a thin sheaf of paper, it seemed, a few pages folded in half. Patrick unfolded it, read it hurriedly, and said, "You wrote this?"

Felix nodded. "Yes. You can play the violin part perfectly well without the piano. And the accompaniment without the violin, come to that." He paused a moment and said, "It's for you. I'd like to call it 'Für Patrick'. If you don't mind. It's a copy. I have the original."

"*Mind?* Oh God. Thank you, Felix." His heart ached. "I wish I had my violin here. Then I could play it for you."

Felix turned his face away, and shrugged. "I should know what it sounds like by now."

"But I *want* to." Patrick thought for a moment. "The Albrecht house, you know which is my window?"

"I do – Juliet." Felix pulled away, laughing, as Patrick swung a fist at him. "All right, Pat. Sorry. Yes, I know your window."

"I'll be there at ten o'clock. Maybe you'll be outside, maybe not. I'll open the window."

"Very well." Felix handed him his hat. "I can't kiss you goodbye, my mouth hurts. But I'll say shalom, in case I don't see you tonight, after all."

Always before, it would have been shalom lehitraot – until next time. Patrick nodded; he could not say anything for a moment. He reached back and opened the door, letting in the noise of the city. Still no words. He cleared his throat. "Shalom, Felix. And thank you."

"Thank *you*, Pat, my small friend. Go home and make music for us all."

He stepped out of the door, backwards so as not to turn away. "You have my address in England?"

"I have it. I'll write from New York." Felix smiled at him. "Go away, you idle brat. You have a dinner to eat before you think about playing that piece for me."

"I'm going," Patrick said hastily, and took the steps two at a time. As he swung round the corner of the wall into the narrow passage between houses, the door closed.

Back in the music room at the Albrechts' house he took the sheets of paper from his pocket and propped them on a stand; tightened the bow of his violin, and gave it a stroke or two of rosin. The violin, glossy as a horse chestnut in its velvet scarlet case, lay ready, but he waited for a moment, looking over the music again, before taking the instrument up, lifting the bow and beginning to play.

It was in E major, with four sharps, but the tune was deceptively simple, lilting like cool water. He played the violin part through once, and then again, a little faster.

A cooler draught of air made him look up. Gisela had come in, leaving the door open. "Das klingt gut," she said, then remembered herself and went on in English. "Lovely. May I look?"

His first instinct was to say "No", but good manners forbade that. Instead he stepped back, wordlessly, and gestured with his bow. His head was too full of music and Felix for him to speak.

Gisela, already dressed for dinner, took the sheets of paper from his music stand and stood looking at them. Presently she said, "I think I could play the piano part. If you would like."

"Can you? Please do."

She sat at the piano, and rested the score in front of her. Slowly at first, stumbling a little, she started to play the accompaniment; not the same as the violin's tune, at all, and yet there was a relationship. She played it through several times, watching the music intently. Then she sat up, smiling at him. "So. I think perhaps we may play it together?" She held her hands close above the keyboard.

"We can but try." He fitted the violin under his chin, where Felix's hand had rested that afternoon. "A count of two. One, two – "

Outside, the sunlight was deepening to gold, the breeze rising a little and stirring the light curtains. They played the piece through twice, Patrick simply saying, "Again," as they reached the end the first time. The sound of the two instruments flowed, blended, drew apart. Leaf-shadows danced across the room.

Afterwards they were silent, not looking at each other. Gisela spoke first. "Is there no chance that you will stay here, Mr Lawson?"

"None, Miss Albrecht. Forgive me."

"Oh, there is nothing to forgive. I suppose you are in love with Debora."

He shook his head. "I don't think this is a good time to be in love with anybody."

"No." She stood up from the piano stool. "You are quite right, as ever. Hurry up, Mr Lawson. You have not changed for dinner, and Margrit will be offended if you are late for her good cooking."

Dinner – a lavish, formal meal in honour of his own forthcoming departure – was hard work. He had always enjoyed dressing formally, playing up the effect of his looks as only a half-Irish black-haired blue-eyed musician can; but it had been better when there were friends to admire him. Here, the Albrechts, kind as they were, put him at the head of the table like an exhibition piece, while Jutta at the far end chattered like a jay, and Gisela, halfway along, had an odd brittleness in her laughter that sounded wrong, coming from a sixteen-year-old. She caught his eye now and then, smiling. Her cheeks were flushed with the heat, and he thought that she might have powdered her face. She had not done that in all the time he had been in Berlin.

He was at ease with the other guest of honour, an old man who had taught Frau Albrecht to play the piano in her young days; but the rest of the company consisted of couples richer than the Albrechts and less kind. Patrick was glad that he was not seated among them, as he would have been at any other of the Albrechts' numerous dinners. Tonight, when he was eager to be gone, the guests stayed on long after the dessert of berries and cream had been eaten. At last, when the clock struck quarter to ten, Patrick pleaded a headache and retired upstairs.

His room was high, under the eaves, and warm with the heat of the sun on the roof all day. He opened the window and leaned out. The scent of roses drifted in on the night air, but nothing else was to be heard. There was nobody under the rosebushes, nobody in the shadow of the wall. The moon was almost full, and the garden under its light had an icy, colourless look; when he laid 'Für Patrick' on the windowsill, there was light enough to read it by. Patrick took off his bow-tie and loosened his collar before settling the violin under his chin again, and beginning to play.

He had meant to play the tune through twice, as he had with Gisela at the piano; but his throat was tight, and he needed to swallow. It was all he could do to play it once; he let the last note die away and his hands fall, and stood in the window, breathing hard.

After a moment there was a movement under the leaves of the lilac tree, where the blossoms had browned and fallen weeks ago. Felix stepped out into the moonlight. He stood for a moment looking up at Patrick's window; Patrick lifted one hand, both in greeting and farewell.

Felix took off his hat, and bowed, his face a white glimmer under the moon. He stepped forward. For a moment he paused, picking something from one of the plants close under the window, then turned and was gone. Patrick knew which plant it was; Felix had taken a sprig of rosemary with him. He stared into the light and shadow, but there was no more movement. After a long while he turned the screw to loosen his bow, opened the case and stowed violin and bow in their place once more. The score he pushed into a pocket in the lining before closing and locking the case.

Then, slowly, he undressed and went to bed.

By Monday night everything was ready, except his mind. He had been planning his departure for months, but now that it came to the point he did not want to leave, though leave he must, since he had a ticket for the early train. His books and scores he had sent ahead, and he would travel with nothing but a change of clothing, a few essentials, and his violin. He lay in bed, staring at the ceiling. *What have I forgotten?*

He had forgotten to wind his watch, and to set his alarm clock, so that the luxurious half-sleep of a summer's morning gave way to panic at Margrit's knock on the door and her enquiry, "Herr Lawson, schlafen Sie noch?"

Half-washed, unshaven, shrugging his jacket onto his shoulders, he ran downstairs and wolfed the breakfast that she had put ready for him, before catching up haversack and violin from the corner where he had left them the night before. He had said goodbye to the family then, rather than expect them to leave their beds so early, and there was only Margrit to kiss him on both cheeks and speed him on his way with a cry of "Gute Reise!"

The city suburbs were washed pale with early light, the dawn chorus giving way to the everyday business of birdsong. Dodging the few people already afoot, pausing to strap his hat into his haversack rather than risk losing it as he ran, Patrick took as direct a way as he could to the station, hoping against hope that the train might have been delayed.

He was still quarter of a mile away when the whistle and the plume of steam advertised his failure. He stopped, whooping breath into his lungs, and opened his mouth to swear. Then he set down his baggage and reconsidered.

There was no need for him to be back in England by a certain time. The ticket had cost a great deal, true, and he was not sure if it would be valid for any other train, but he could afford another. Even if he missed his scheduled ferry, that was hardly the end of the world, although it would mean one more expense on top of the other, and his uncle would not be best pleased.

What rankled most was that things never went wrong for him, Patrick Lawson. He had become accustomed to everything happening as he wanted; it had not seemed too much to ask of a world where war had left him fatherless when he was three years old, and influenza had taken his mother two years later.

After a moment more he realised that his anger was not about missing the train, nor about his own stupidity in forgetting watch and alarm, but about Felix and Debora and their family. He had read things in the papers, he had heard things on the streets, but the slow decline of their fortunes had seeped into his mind as if it were almost inevitable, not so very bad after all, because they themselves seemed to make nothing of it.

I should have realised sooner. It should not have taken a bruise on Felix's face to bring it home to me. That half hour with Felix in the damp warmth of the scullery was vaguely dreamlike now, as if he had been drunk at the time, although he had been stone cold sober that day, until dinner. *Oh dear God, let them be safe. Let them be safe.* Patrick took a deep breath, picked up his haversack and violin, and walked on towards the railway station, under a sky still white with before-dawn light.

There was a train standing at the platform. Patrick had studied the Kursbuch intently before buying his now-useless ticket, and knew that this was no regular service. All along the platform were adults and children, but only the children were climbing aboard. It was very evident that farewells were being taken. And everywhere, watching, there were soldiers.

Patrick's first impulse was to turn away; and then – *I should have realised sooner.* He turned back, and almost at once heard an English voice. A woman's voice, quavering slightly.

"Betty, what are we going to do? I can't make the man understand."

The reply came, like the question, from behind a line of uniformed men. "Isn't Mr Sachs here? He said he would help."

"But – I can't – "

"Oh, stand firm just for a moment, Jean. Let me look. Let me *think*." Her silence was interrupted by an impatient question in German, and the invisible Betty muttered, "Oh, do be *quiet*, you big bully."

Patrick stepped forward. "May I help, ladies?" he said, projecting his voice a little. There was a quickly-stifled gasp of relief.

"You most certainly can, young man." The rank of uniforms broke to reveal the two: tweed-suited, sensibly shod, between middle-aged and elderly, wearing the sort of hat that could only be worn by Englishwomen bent on good works. "Are you by any delightful chance English?" the taller and stouter of the ladies asked.

"I am, madam."

She beamed on him. "Splendid. If you are also, perchance, able to speak German, then be assured you are the answer to a maiden's prayer."

There's always a first time. He tried not to smile as he answered, "I speak German tolerably well, I believe. What's the problem?"

"We're with these children, as you see, and a Mr – I suppose I should say Herr – Josef Sachs was supposed to be joining us as a translator. I can't find out what's happened to him." She held out her hand. "I'm Betty Tolworth, and this is Jean Fairhall, both of us from the Society of Friends – Quakers, you know."

He set down his things, and shook hands. "My name is Patrick Lawson. Is it just you and the children, then?"

"Oh, no, there's Miss Vavasour too. She's not one of us, not a Friend, you understand, but she's wonderful in a crisis, she just looks at an official and he quails, so a useful person to have in the offing, as you might say. I believe she's gone off about a problem with some passports." Betty Tolworth rummaged in her bag. "But I digress. If you would be so kind, dear boy, as to establish from somebody why Herr Sachs isn't here, then I can tell Miss Vavasour. Jean, dear, would you like a sugared almond?" She held out a neat, white paper bag.

"Oh, Betty, really – all this, and you offer me sugar?" Gloved fingers hovered, all the same, over the dragées.

"Sugar is good for morale. Go on." Betty waited for Jean to choose, took a pink one for herself, and said, "Young man – Mr Lawson, was it not? – one for you?"

"Perhaps better not until I've made my enquiries, Miss Tolworth." He looked down, checking that his violin was safe.

"Mrs, but never mind. We'll look after your things, don't worry."

"The violin stays with me, but thank you." He smiled at her, eliciting a startled blink in return, and turned away, looking for the right person to talk to. At length, after being passed from office to office, he asked the question for the fourth time.

"Sachs? Josef Sachs?" The laughter was scornful. "Jude. Was erwarten Sie?" The official shrugged, and turned away.

Patrick stared at him, thought about a retort, decided otherwise, and returned to the platform. It was quieter than it had been now that the children were on the train. The last of the parents were being hustled away, and a few soldiers stood idle at the gates. The engine was hissing quietly, and the two Englishwomen were nowhere to be seen; another woman, tall and slim, was standing on the platform.

"Hurry!" she called, and he lengthened his stride. "Any news?"

He shook his head. "Nothing good."

"Damn. Do you want a free ride to England? I need someone who can speak German, and Betty says you can." She picked up his bag. The engine let out a demented shriek and vomited steam across the platform.

"Yes!" he shouted.

"Get on, then!" She climbed in at the other end of the carriage. A station guard closed the door on her. Patrick hugged the violin to himself with one arm and leapt for the last open door just as the man took hold of it. He caught the heel of one shoe as it slammed, only pulling free when he flung himself forward and down, landing with the violin pressed uncomfortably into his ribcage.

For a moment he lay getting his breath back, then scrambled to his feet. The carriage was full. On each long seat there were three, sometimes four children, sitting straight, or feet tucked under them, or in the case of the smaller ones lying down with their head in another child's lap. Some young, some older, some dark, some fair, some excited, some with the traces of tears smudging their cheeks. Nearly all of them were wearing too many clothes for a summer's day, and most of them were clutching something: a cloth rabbit, a book, a pair of ice skates for which there could be no possible use yet.

At the far end of the carriage, just turning to walk towards him, was the tall woman who had offered him a place on the train. He stepped forward, and she waved him back. Behind him someone tugged at the tail of his jacket; he turned, and saw where two girls had squashed together to leave him a place.

"Danke," he said, smiled, and sat down.

"Bitte." They smiled back at him, and settled down together, playing a game of cat's-cradle, heads close, voices murmuring softly.

The tall woman stopped in front of him. "Here's your bag, and thank you. I never heard your name, and I'd as soon not trudge down the far end of the train to ask Betty."

"Patrick Lawson, ma'am." He undid the catch on his violin case.

"And I'm Celia Vavasour. How did you come to be in Berlin?"

"I was a student at the Konservatorium," he said, "and I taught English. I should have been coming home by the express, but I missed my train." He shifted along a little. "Do you want to sit down?"

"Just for a few minutes." She did so, and a hint of Chanel no.5 drifted through the air between them. "Were they able to tell you anything more about Josef Sachs?"

"They may have been able, but they didn't. All I could get out of the one man who would say anything was along the lines of he was Jewish, so what did I expect?" He opened the violin case and stared at the instrument, as if he could read the future in the gleam of polished wood.

After a moment's silence Celia Vavasour said, "That sounds – unhopeful."

"Yes." He looked at her. "Do you really need a translator?"

"Probably. My German is basic to say the least, and if any of the children

14

has a problem I'd like to be able to help." She sighed suddenly, leaned back and made a move as if she would have rubbed her eyes, but stopped, and fidgeted with the finger-ends of her gloves. "Ah, etiquette be damned. I'm taking these off." A few seconds later the gloves were off; a quick rub of her eyes, and she said, "We may be in for a long journey. I gather we're likely to be shunted into sidings whenever they need to let a train pass."

"Who are the children?"

"I don't know, not exactly. But they're all Jewish. Some of them, their fathers have been arrested. Some of them have no parents. Some of the boys are old enough for Hitler's people to be looking at them for the labour camps any moment now."

Why didn't I know these things? he asked himself. Soon enough the answer came back: *Because you didn't want to.* How come Felix had not been picked up? *I suppose I'll never know.*

"You're very quiet," Celia Vavasour observed. "If you don't like being on a train full of – "

"No, it's not that. I have a good friend, he's Jewish. I was just worrying about him." For a moment he put his hand on the velvet lining where 'Für Patrick' was hidden, then said, "Do you think the children would like a tune?"

"I'm sure they would, eventually. Let's save it till the excitement has worn off, and they need something to listen to." She rose to her feet. "I'm very pleased to have you aboard, Mr Lawson."

Beside him, the girls murmured and whispered over their game of cat's-cradle.

It was night. Patrick had no idea of the time; although the moon was high, it was too dark in his corner to see the dial of his watch. And it was quiet, so quiet that he had, earlier, been able to hear clearly a child's stifled sobs at the far end of the carriage. He had gone to investigate, but one of the older girls had waved him back, and he had left her to deal with the problem. Whatever that had been, the weeping had stopped, eventually.

For about the fifth time since the journey had started the train was at an unheralded, unexplained standstill. They must be a long way across Germany, Patrick thought, shifting his coat behind him, where he had pushed it, rolled up, in the quest for more comfort than the floor and side of the carriage gave. They were beyond Hanover, where more children had boarded, and should have been at Osnabrück by now. He had seen Miss Vavasour occasionally, but Betty Tolworth and Jean Fairhall were in the middle and the other end of the train; there were other adults with the party, in other carriages.

Patrick's shoulders ached a little from hours of work at the violin; he had moved from carriage to carriage, playing almost non-stop anything that the children asked for, if he knew it, and other tunes besides.

He lifted his head at the sound of footsteps and saw a tall shadow with a night light burning on a saucer in one hand, and a small child asleep in the crook of her other arm: Celia Vavasour, unlikely Madonna. She folded down beside him on the floor, bolt upright with her back against the wall. "Are you sure you're comfortable there? You needn't have moved."

Patrick indicated where he had been sitting before; the two girls were curled up asleep, one with string still looped round her fingers. "If I sit here, they get to lie down. I'm tougher than they are."

She glanced down at him. "May I say that you don't look very tough?"

"Still tougher than an eight-year-old."

She nodded. "Kind of you, all the same. What did you say your surname is?"

"Lawson."

"Any relation to the Suffolk Lawsons?"

"Not so far as I know." After a moment he added, "My mother's brother lives in Cambridgeshire, but he's not a Lawson, of course."

"Ah." She set the night light down on the floor and rested the child on her other arm. "Ouf, I never knew something that looks so angelic could weigh so much. Would you like a cigarette? I don't smoke, usually, but it's something to do that isn't screaming."

"I would," he said, "but better not in here, two of the children have been sick already. I'll lean out of the window at the end of the carriage. Thank you, Miss Vavasour."

"Celia will do," she said, and leaned sideways to extract a cigarette case from her jacket pocket. "Here, take a couple."

"One will be enough, thanks." He tucked the cigarette behind his ear, pocketed the lighter that she handed him, and walked along the carriage to the door. All the doors had been locked before the train left Hanover; the windows, however, could still be opened. He unhooked the strap that held this one closed, and lowered it carefully; to let it go was to make the window drop with a crash, and wake every child within earshot.

It was a long time since Patrick had smoked, not since Felix had given up – had had to give up, he realised now; it was an expensive pleasure. The taste of the smoke in his mouth, the warm feel of it in his nose and throat and lungs, took him back with a vivid flash of memory. Himself, curled up on the hard bench of the beer cellar in Französischestraße, with Felix's arms round him and Dieter practically sitting in his lap.

There was mist over the fields; squares of light gleamed from a few distant windows, and above the mist and farther still there were stars shining. He breathed out, and a cloud of smoke floated upwards and was gone. Patrick made the cigarette last for a long time, and eventually stubbed it out against the window glass, making sure it was completely extinguished before he dropped it to the track bed. He did not want to return to his place in the carriage, and stayed where he was. Presently he realised that in the darkness of the ground – field, meadow, pasture? – across which he looked, something was moving. Too tall to be a sheep, too thin to be a cow. He struck a flame with the cigarette lighter in an attempt to see, and heard a quiet noise of satisfaction. A woman was walking towards him, faster now that there was light to steer by. She had a shawl round her shoulders, and her arms were full. She walked straight, silently, to the door of the train where Patrick leaned on the window, and looked up at him.

"Bitte," she said.

"Was wollen Sie?" he asked cautiously, closing the lighter and putting it back in his pocket.

"Bitte," she said again, and then in English, "take her, please."

Incredulous, he looked down at what she held in her arms. A child's face, pale and with a steady gaze from dark eyes, looked back at him; he could not tell her age. Automatically he shook his head. "I can't – "

"You *must*. Please. She is not safe."

Questions blundered to his lips. "Are you English?"

"Nein. I speak it." The train hissed slightly, as if a serpent woke. He felt a jolt run through him as it shifted on the rails. The woman said, "Geh jetzt, Lotte. Gott segne dich," and lifted the child high towards the open top of the window. Patrick stepped back, uncertain, and the child reached towards him through the window. "Bitte. Save her," the woman said. "Bitte."

I couldn't help Felix. But I can help here, now ... He took the child as carefully as he could. "Her name? Her age?" His German was deserting him.

"She will tell you. Thank you. Danke." And as the train moved, at last, jerkily, from where it had stood for so long, the woman stood back and let fall her arms. He peered out of the window and saw her standing, watching, receding into the distance.

Celia Vavasour had moved on while he was smoking, so he sat down in the place she had vacated, tried to make the child comfortable, and talked to her.

In the next half hour he discovered that her name was Charlotte Hoffmann, but everyone called her Lotte; that she was ten years old and small for her age, and that she could speak some English. The woman who had brought her to the train was not her mother, but a family servant. Her parents both lived in Osnabrück, where her mother worked in a hospital and her father was a government official. She would not say whether or not she was Jewish; there was no cross or Star of David round her neck. She sat very quietly and still, legs curled round awkwardly, and shook her head every time he asked if she would like to walk along the train. In the end he fell asleep with her on his lap.

He slept all through the stop at Osnabrück, when they took on more children still. It was past dawn when he woke. His trousers were uncomfortably, warmly, damp. After a moment, grimacing, he realised what had happened. Lotte's face was hidden in her hands; he thought she might be crying.

"Wein' doch nicht," he said. "Don't cry. I'm not angry." He hugged her. "You couldn't help it."

"Ich wollte Sie nicht aufwecken," she whispered.

"Well, wake me next time, and we'll go for the bucket."

Lotte shook her head, and said nothing more. He was too tired to argue; sighed, settled her on his lap again, and leaned back against the end of the carriage. In front of him there was movement; one of the cat's-cradle girls was awake, sitting up and rummaging in her suitcase. Presently she nudged Lotte with one foot. "Nimm, bitte." A small, white pair of knickers changed hands, and was received with a murmur of thanks; presently he realised that Lotte and the girl were whispering together, watching him.

"Shall I look the other way?" he said, amused, and did so until one of

18

them said, "Danke, mein Herr."

"Patrick."

"Patrick." They giggled.

The door at the far end of the carriage opened, and Celia Vavasour slid through, a cup in each hand. "Coffee, Mr Lawson, I don't suppose it's very good, but – what the – " She stopped short with an obvious effort. "My apologies. How did we acquire an extra passenger?"

"Through the window. She was in danger, or so the woman said."

"Jewish?"

"Not as far as I know. But there must be something."

She handed him the coffee. "I'm sorry, Mr Lawson, but that was just plain lunatic of you."

"What could I do? The train moved off. And be careful, she speaks some English." He breathed in the steam and the coffee smell, almost as stimulating as drinking the stuff. "Thank you for this."

"I wish I could thank you for *this*," she said a little drily, "but I fear we may be in for some difficulty."

She is not a 'this'. "Her name is Lotte Hoffmann," he said. "And if I may call you Celia, you can call me Patrick."

"Oh." Celia, taking care to hold her coffee level, sat on her heels in front of Lotte. The two stared at each other.

After a moment, Lotte said, with some care, "Good morning, madam."

"Why – good morning, child," Celia said, and smiled suddenly. "Don't worry. We'll look after you."

Lotte smiled, the smallest, most hesitant of smiles. "Thank you."

They were almost at the border now; looking from the window as the landscape passed smoothly and slowly beyond the glass, Patrick saw 'Gildehaus' painted on a sloping roof; his mind latched on to the name, he could not remember why. Not long afterwards they reached the border station and halted amidst steam, the clanking of iron, voices. The children who had been dozing sat up; the cat's-cradle girls brushed each other's hair and put in fresh ribbons. They brushed Lotte's hair too, and it was then, as she leaned on the bench for them to do this, that Patrick realised why she had not accepted his offer to walk with her along the train. Even though she was standing, her legs were not straight; she was poised on her toes, heels not touching the ground, knees turned inwards and bent in front of her.

As Patrick watched her Lotte turned round, eyes down in concentration and one hand gripping the corner of the bench, the other reaching for nothing as if to steady herself. Patrick reached out. "Komm, Lotte," he said, and went on in German, "if I hold both of your hands can you walk?"

"Ja." She was pink, whether with embarrassment or effort he could not tell. "Aber nicht jetzt."

But not now. Fair enough. "Stimmt," he said, and smiled back as she smiled at him.

The door at the far end of the carriage opened, and when Patrick looked up he saw a face he knew, and remembered. *He went back to Gildehaus … eating his heart out in a railway office … poor Dieter,* Felix had called him … Dieter Koch.

Celia was at Dieter's back, evidently using her extra height to read, over his shoulder, the papers on the clipboard that he was holding. Dieter himself had his head down, and kept pushing his spectacles irritably up his nose; he was asking questions, ticking names on a list, and – *Lotte won't be on any list.*

They were in the last carriage. The door behind him was still locked. It was too late for Patrick to leave without being noticed, and in any case there was nowhere to go. He pulled Lotte closer. "Your name is Charlotte," he whispered in her ear, using the two-syllable, English pronunciation. "Speak English. Pretend to be sleepy. Understand?"

"Yes," she whispered back.

"Good girl." He helped her to sit down.

Dieter was half way along the carriage now. He paused to turn a page, looked up, and saw Patrick. His eyes widened and his mouth dropped open a little, until he recovered himself, and put on what Felix used to call his 'offended infant Schubert' expression; Patrick might have laughed at the memory if his nerves had not been so tightly coiled inside him. Dieter continued, nearer, nearer, ticking his list as regular as a metronome, and eventually stopped in front of Patrick, looking down.

"Patrick," he said. "I did not expect to see you here." As ever, his English was precise, hardly accented.

"I didn't expect to *be* here," Patrick answered. "Missed my train. I'd forgotten you lived in this area. How's things?" He smiled up at the serious face above him.

"Things? I – oh, I am doing well. Thank you." Dieter turned back to the beginning of his sheaf of papers, and leafed through it again slowly. "This child cannot be on my list. I have no more names. Indeed, you are not on my list. I should not let you leave."

"Do you have Josef Sachs on your list?"

"Not now," Dieter said.

Patrick dropped his gaze; then he dug his wallet from his haversack and opened it. Lotte, who had been asleep – or pretending to sleep – on his lap, stirred, shifted herself and curled up on the floor. "Tickets, see? I'm not travelling for free, even though I'm on the wrong train. The ladies are friends of mine and wanted help with their German."

"I understand. And I understand that you want to help. That is like you. I'll put you on the list." Dieter wrote, and for a moment smiled. "But not the child."

His heart beating painfully, as if it would block his throat if it could, Patrick said, "She's mine."

Dieter laughed, as if at a child's stupidity, or as if he had not properly heard what Patrick had said; but the laughter cut off short as he looked into Patrick's eyes. Stared. "Don't lie to me, Pat."

"I'm not," he said, hoping that his voice did not reflect the dryness in his throat. *It wouldn't be the first time.* His outstretched hand was shaking; his ticket was uppermost in a small collection of scraps that might have been anything. *I hope Dieter doesn't ask to see Lotte's.* He could pretend to have lost it, of course, and buy another, but – *I hope …*

"But – " Dieter stepped back. "Let me look at her." Behind him, Celia Vavasour was standing very still, mouth a compressed line of red lipstick, eyes alert.

Patrick shook Lotte's shoulder. "Charlotte, love. Wake up."

If she was not asleep, she acted waking very well, and sat up, clinging to Patrick's right arm. "Daddy?"

For a moment his heart clenched. "My friend Herr Koch, Dieter that is, wants to say hallo." He looked up at Dieter. "She is rather shy; I'm sorry."

"Hallo, Mr Koch. Dieter," Lotte said, and hid her face on Patrick's shoulder. He put one arm round her.

After a moment Dieter said, "I have remarked upon the colour of your eyes often enough, I believe."

"Indeed," Patrick said. *Turn on the charm. Or has it left me in the lurch?*

"The child's eyes are brown."

Keep smiling.

Celia Vavasour said, "She takes after her mother," and when Dieter turned round, laughed. "No, don't look at me, please. True, my eyes are brown, but I'm far too old to have a child that young, and when you force a woman into admitting that she's old you have made a big mistake, Mr Koch. Patrick is my son-in-law. He said we were friends, didn't he?"

Dieter glanced at her hands, still gloveless. "*Miss* Vavasour. You don't have a wedding ring."

"We all make mistakes, Mr Koch. I too." Celia paused. "Don't make another one, please."

For a moment Dieter turned and looked up at her; she was several inches taller. Then he turned back, eyes on Patrick, imploring. "*Pat*," he said. "Really? True?"

Patrick nodded. "I'm sorry." And even as he thought, *That is the face of a man whose dreams are falling around him* he heard Felix say, in his memory, 'infant Schubert', and tried not to laugh.

Celia Vavasour took the pen from Dieter's hands. "I'll write it for you, Mr Koch, shall I?"

"No," he said, snatching it back. "I will do it. Her name, Patrick, please."

Patrick could barely speak; he wondered that Dieter did not hear the tension in his voice. Perhaps the sound of falling dreams masked it. "Charlotte Patricia Lawson. Thank you so much."

"It is done," Dieter said. "Excuse me, Miss Vavasour." He pushed past her, walked to the other end of the carriage with his head up and his back straight, and left the train.

Within the hour they were at Oldenzaal, the first station across the Dutch border. The doors were unlocked to cheers and cries of welcome; they could leave the carriages unchecked, unhindered, although with two hundred children and one station they had to be orderly. There were no soldiers. On the platform were tables laden with food and drink: plates piled with salt beef, pickles, bread; jugs full of coffee and lemonade and soda water, and everywhere the glint of Star of David pendants worn by the women who dished out the food.

Once they had eaten, Celia said, "We have another hour or so here. Baths. Laundry. You and Lotte need them if I don't. Come on, I'll find someone." She ducked. "Another photographer, I don't *believe* it."

Clean and refreshed, although his trousers were still faintly damp from the steam press, Patrick boarded the train and sat in the same seat as before. Presently Celia and Lotte arrived, Lotte holding determinedly to Celia's hands above her and walking one careful, lurching step at a time.

"They've given me a cushion for her," Celia said. "These people are so delightful. It's a huge relief. I know I've done the right thing at last." She dragged the cushion round – it had been slung at her back – and set it down. "There you are, Lotte."

"Don't you always?" Patrick said.

"Be amused if you must, but I'm never so sure of myself as I seem, believe me." Celia sat down on the other side of him from Lotte, and whispered, "She really is quite crippled, the poor little thing. I wonder if her parents didn't just give up on her. They can't be poor, her clothes are good material. And learning English, too."

"Maybe they had to," Patrick said. "If my friend can be thrown out of music college for being Jewish, why not discard a child for being – what she is? It makes as much sense – which is none – either way." He put his hand out to feel the familiar rough-smoothness of his violin case. "I don't know what's come over me. I wouldn't have given a damn three years ago. A year ago. Please don't say anything."

Celia patted his hand. "I won't, then. But you'll be glad to hear that we're well on time for the noon ferry."

The welcome and the gifts were the same everywhere they stopped. The children grew livelier, even mischievous at times, as the train rattled and lurched from Oldenzaal to Rotterdam to the Hook of Holland. It was almost impossible to sit comfortably on the floor, although Lotte seemed happy enough on her cushion. Patrick, on the other hand, accepted an invitation from the cat's-cradle girls, sisters called Miriam and Anna, to sit on the bench next to them.

The ferry crossing lasted six and a half hours; the sea was blessedly calm, and the children ran around in the sunshine under the benevolent eye of Mrs

Tolworth and Miss Fairhall, and the slightly more sardonic one of Celia Vavasour. Patrick was introduced to the men and women who had travelled in other carriages. Most of the older boys, and a few girls, disappeared under crew supervision into the engine room and steerage, while the remaining girls mothered the younger children, or sat and talked with the boys who preferred not to explore.

Disembarkation at Harwich meant a short walk inland; Patrick, suddenly so exhausted that he hardly noticed where they were going, carried Lotte. They dined in a hall that smelt faintly of mutton and boiled cabbage, and he ate what was put in front of him without really thinking about it. Celia, on her way past behind him, paused with one hand on his shoulder. "I don't suppose you're up to playing the violin after dinner?"

"I'm afraid not," he said. "I feel as if I haven't slept for weeks. I know it's only been one night on the move, but – I'm sorry, I can't."

"It's no matter," she said, gently.

"Will Lotte be all right here?" He laid his knife and fork down. "I wish I could give her a home, but – well, how could I?"

Her grip on his shoulder tightened. "I'll make sure she's all right. Believe me."

"Thanks, Celia. Ah – I'm not too badly off. Let me know if you need anything."

She stooped and kissed his cheek then. "Thank *you*, Patrick. You're a darling. But I'm stinking rich, and if you can offer to spare something, I most certainly can. Don't worry. Go to bed."

Patrick nodded, got to his feet, picked up his haversack, hat and violin from where he had left them on an empty chair, and walked away from the tremendous, overwhelming chatter of freedom.

The curtains, thick and dark, kept moonlight and sunlight out of the little room with its two beds very effectively. Patrick woke from uneasy dreams on a hard mattress and saw, in the dimness, a slim, dark man bending over him, one hand at Patrick's shoulder as if to shake him awake.

"Felix," he said muzzily, took the hand and pulled him into an embrace, fingers linked at the back of the dark woollen coat. He turned his face sideways, feeling the soft, short hair brushing on his cheek, smelling –

This was not Felix. He let the man go at once. "I – I'm sorry. I thought you were – "

"Felix," the man said quietly. "I'm sorry I'm not. My name is Mark Berridge, from the Society of Friends. My wife and I have been on the team to cook breakfast here since the children started coming through last December." He stepped back. "I was checking the rooms to see which needed cleaning; wasn't expecting to find anyone in here, let alone anyone English. Would you like some breakfast?"

"I wasn't meant to be on that train, or that ferry. I missed mine, and Miss Vavasour said I could help her." Patrick lay back, blinking. "Lotte! Is she all right? A little girl … " His voice faded away. There were so many little girls.

"The lame child? She went off with Celia Vavasour, very happy," Berridge said. "I don't think you need to worry. Tell me about yourself."

On his feet, Patrick tried to straighten out his clothes. "My name is Patrick Lawson, and I'm a violinist and an English teacher, neither with any great success. And I would love some breakfast."

Mark Berridge smiled. "This way, then."

The canteen was almost empty; it was later in the morning than he had thought. "Holiday camp taken over for the duration," Berridge explained. "Tea or coffee?"

"Tea, please, as strong as you can make it, and no sugar." Patrick sat down and reached for a bowl and a box of cornflakes. "It's all right for me to help myself like this?"

"Of course. What else would you like? Owing to a, um, misunderstanding with our temporary caterers, we have a distinct surplus of bacon. If you'd like bacon and eggs, or a bacon sandwich or twelve, I'll ask Anne to make some up. Unless – "

"Bacon and eggs will be wonderful. Thank you."

They arrived before very long; Berridge set the plate in front of him, and sat down opposite. "Tell me to go away if you don't want company."

Patrick, mouth full, shook his head, swallowed hastily, and said, "I mean, don't go away. That's fine. Your wife should get a hotel to take her on, I've never had a breakfast like this."

Berridge laughed. "We do well enough here, Anne and I," he said. "I'll make some toast when you're ready."

Once Patrick had eaten enough, they went outside and sat on the low wall at the edge of the camp, beyond the bowling lawn. Patrick tugged his hat down a little at the side, to keep the sun out of his eyes. Ships, dark against the reflected light, trailed ragged clouds of smoke across the rough glass of the sea.

"Shotley behind us," Mark Berridge said. "Walton Backwaters on the far side of the Naze to your right. Felixstowe on the other side of the Stour and the Orwell, to your left."

Felixstowe. Felix. Patrick clenched his hands in his lap. *Dieter.* All at once he was shaking, trying not to weep, not to break down in front of this stranger. The double tune of 'Für Patrick' danced through his mind.

"Patrick?"

"I – I'm all right."

"I don't think you are, you know, but I'll leave you alone if you want."

Patrick shook his head. "Don't go, Mark. I can call you Mark?"

"Of course you can." Mark sat very still and quiet, his face tilted to the sunlight.

Patrick said, "My two best friends were in Germany. I think I've lost them both. One has gone to America, and the other … "

Eventually Mark said, "The other?"

The noise of sea and wind and distant engines filled Patrick's head. Children and seagulls laughed, sparks of sound in the bright air. "What would you think of a man who destroyed his friend's dreams for the sake of an unknown child?" he asked, and buried his face in his hands.

"For the life of the child?" Mark asked.

"Maybe. I don't know for sure."

"Hm. I would say that life is better than dreams, and that the man did the right thing." Mark paused. "You?"

"Yes." Patrick lifted his head, and breathed deep.

"And will the friend live?"

"I dare say," Patrick said. "He likes his little tragedies. I'm sorry, that wasn't kind of me."

Mark nodded. "When you only have dreams, even small tragedies loom large. But you still did the right thing."

"Thank you," Patrick said. He put his hand down to touch his violin case again, as if it were a talisman. *I suppose I ought to think about leaving, soon.* "I hope so." He lifted the case to his knees.

"Anne and I will be around for a while. Come and find us when you want to go to the station." Mark's feet crunched on gravel, then were silent on the lawn.

Patrick stayed where he was, hands on the clasps of the violin case. For a moment he thought of taking his violin out and playing something, but that was the kind of Goethian gesture that Dieter would have made. Not for him. He closed his eyes, trying to remember what his plans had been for his first week back in England. *Visit Uncle Edward. Go and see whoever is the director at the Royal College of Music now.* To those he added more. *Find out where Celia Vavasour lives, if I can, and write to Lotte. Hope to have a letter from Felix.*

Patrick wished there was more than hope; but if that was all there was, it would have to do. He opened his eyes again. In front of him the sunlight still danced on the waves. *I can do more than hope.* He got to his feet, picked up his belongings, and walked back across the lawn.

Ironic points of light
Flash out wherever the Just
Exchange their messages:
May I, composed like them
Of Eros and of dust,
Beleaguered by the same
Negation and despair,
Show an affirming flame.

W.H. Auden
September 1, 1939

Author's Note

This story was inspired by several things: the Kindertransport, which brought Jewish children from Hitler's Germany to Britain; Aktion T4, the modern name for the programme of mass murder of disabled adults and children by 'euthanasia' in Nazi Germany; and the attempts of the British government in 2016 to limit the numbers of unaccompanied refugee children entering the UK.

Acknowledgements

Acknowledgements are due to: Daniel Cesarani of the Wiener Library, and Jeanette Rosenberg, for helping me with information about the Kindertransport; to Cath Senker for sensitivity reading and corrections to my German; and to Garrick Jones for attempting to keep me on the straight and narrow about music. Any mistakes remaining are entirely my own.

Extraordinary Duties

Elin Gregory

A warm spring day in early April and how better to spend it than looking for a man? Charlie Cruickshank stepped out along Eastbourne promenade, swinging his cane, enjoying the warmth of the sunshine and feeling very pleased with his little part of the world. He didn't think he could be blamed for that, despite the current unpleasantness over the Channel. Morale was important and, if the rumours about what had happened in Narvik were correct, would become even more so as the months passed. Not that the general public were privy to the same kind of intelligence as Charlie. Oh, dear me, no. And just as well too. But that knowledge, and the responsibility offered to him by friends of friends in high places, had led him to his walk along the prom and his search for a man.

There had been times when Charlie's searches had been on pleasure bent – a phrase that had always made him smile. In '16, there had been one book-strewn corner of a certain officers' mess, well removed from the bar and the piano, where the more serious types congregated for quiet, earnest conversations about strategy, or logistics. Two men with their heads together over a copy of *Principles of Military Movements* could be talking about something else entirely and no one the wiser. Post-war, there had been certain pubs, certain cinemas, and music halls, where one could find what one wanted, even sometimes for free. It had been a wild time when it was easy for a man, inspired by the Bright Young Things, to be led astray. Coming home to Eastbourne to recuperate, he had been lonely and frustrated until he discovered peace in embracing more domestic pleasures with exactly the right person. It had all been such fun, but today he was in search of something – someone – equally special but in a different way.

He checked his watch and left the windy sunshine of the promenade to cut through a smaller street lined with guest houses. Compton Street opened out to left and right offering the grocers and butchers and outfitters who provided all the nuts and bolts of everyday living. With a bit of luck, it was here that he should find what he was looking for.

Charlie paused to let a couple of sailors pass, bell-bottoms flapping in the sea breeze. He tipped his hat to them with the respect of a man too old to fight, envying their youth and brand new uniforms, and they smiled and nodded an acknowledgement. Then he strolled on, keeping his eyes peeled. It wasn't long before his attention was caught by two dogs waiting, patient as statues, outside a chemist. One was the shaggy grey-and-white local breed used for herding and guarding, but the other was tall, more sturdy than a greyhound but with a similar leggy arched build and a wiry golden coat brindled with black along his back.

"There you are," he said, because he'd had his eye on this specific man for some time and wherever the dogs were, their master wouldn't be far away.

Rather than make a direct approach, Charlie paused by the safety-taped window of a clothier and feigned interest in a display of summer shirts and collars. From the corner of his eye he observed the dogs, the grey one curled nose on paws, and the other upright as a statue of Anubis. On guard, obviously. Charlie approved of that. He'd had subordinates, both private and commissioned, who showed less care for their surroundings.

The chemist's doorbell jingled. Both dogs jumped to their feet, heads low, tails wagging, to greet their master. There he was, calling a farewell over his shoulder, then closing the door and stooping to greet his wagging attendants. Sam Hobb in an old gaberdine coat and soft hat, not long past thirty, brown of hair and face and eye, broad in the shoulder and short in the leg, particularly on the left where the built-up sole of his polished brown boot gleamed in the sunshine. Plain as bread and cheese, and just as wholesome, with a faint whiff of wintergreen oil and a strong and sturdy build that could have shown promise – if Charlie had been searching for a distraction. As it was, he had other things on his mind.

Charlie watched, wondering if Hobb would turn towards Charlie and continue his shopping, or turn the other way to take the lane west out of town and a two-mile walk home. There was a stick in Hobb's hand, held below the distinctive tight curl of the shepherd's crook, but was it a tool of his trade or a necessity?

Hobb turned west and Charlie grinned at the shirts in the shop window, tipped his hat to a more pleasing angle and followed. Soon he was hurrying. Hobb might have been lame but he covered the ground fast with long lurching strides, the dogs keeping close to his heels. He only paused once and that was to draw aside as three soldiers in brand new battledress came out of a café and took up the entire pavement. One glanced at Hobb and curled his lip, another muttered something about *he'd* thought all able-bodied men were in uniform, the third said nothing as they shouldered Hobb into the gutter. But as they passed Charlie, leaving him a decent amount of space as befitted the rank suggested by his well-cut tweeds and gold watch chain, he heard the third man say, "Gotta be fair, farming's a reserved occupation, innit," drawing sneering guffaws from his fellows.

Sam Hobb had walked on, his only reaction to their laughter a reddening to the sun-browned back of his neck. Charlie observed it for a moment, then hurried to catch up. "I say," he called. "Hold on a moment, will you? Yes, you there, with the dogs … "

Hobb slowed, then turned and levelled a wary glare at Charlie who swung his cane and gave him the type of smile that his friend had described as typical of an affable silly-ass. "My goodness you do go at a rate." Charlie puffed up to him and leaned on his cane. "Must be all that fresh air, what?"

Sam gave him the look of a man who was not prepared to waste his time for much longer. "Mr Cruickshank isn't it? From Eastdean?"

"Yes, that's right. You have a good memory." Charlie had taken pains to introduce himself a week or so ago, arranging a 'by chance' meeting while hiking across the farmland to the west. "And you're Sam Hobbs, no, Hobb, shepherd up at Withybush."

"That's right. Can I help you?" Hobb asked.

"Well, I hope so. Firstly, I wondered about your dog, the brown one. I didn't get a good look at him last week and I don't recognise the breed."

"You wouldn't. He don't come from round here." Sam Hobb's voice was deep with a softer burr than the locals'. "Where I come from we call 'em Hillman dogs, use 'em for the sheep and cattle. Nothing better on rough ground, but he's five – getting a bit old for hill work now – so I brought him south with me."

"Ah, I thought that wasn't a local accent. Herefordshire? Or a little further west?" Charlie inspected the two dogs and nodded, then turned his attention to the man and gave him a similar smiling inspection. Hobb raised his eyebrows and Charlie allowed his smile to broaden. "I wonder – there is another thing I'd like to put to you. Would I be holding you up if we took a few minutes to discuss it now?"

"Well, I do need to get back." Was Hobb's suspicious expression thawing a little? Charlie fancied it was.

"Surely you could spare me a few minutes?" Charlie offered his hand to the Hillman dog to sniff but it turned its head in disdain. "My goodness, spurned! My overtures of friendship have been spurned. The least you can do is make it up to me – perhaps over a cup of tea?"

Hobb snorted a laugh but Charlie was pleased to see a spark of interest in his eyes.

"I can spare a little time," he said. "What is it?"

"I'd prefer not to discuss my proposition so publicly, if you don't mind."

Their eyes met and Charlie saw understanding dawn. Hobb used his free hand to take off his hat, pushing back the oak-brown strands that flopped over his forehead with the back of his wrist. "Well, you're a bold one, Charlie Cruickshank," he breathed. "And I think you could be a lot of trouble. What did you have in mind?"

Charlie smiled at that and after a moment so did Hobb, disclosing even teeth marred by a chipped incisor that coincided neatly with a scar on his lip. The smile had been worth the wait and Charlie felt sad that he was about to surprise Hobb in a way he didn't expect.

"There's a tea shop at the top of the road. Not at all fancy but they made a decent scone before the war," Charlie pointed to the sign. "My treat."

The tea shop was, as Charlie said, quite ordinary, but the service was excellent. Larry, the waiter, was one of Charlie's boys, so Charlie expected the prompt attendance, but he was surprised that the lad also knew Sam Hobb.

"Of course you can bring them in, Sam," Larry said of the dogs. "They're no trouble. Just come and sit over here and they can lie down by the window." The table was also one where they'd be unlikely to be overheard. "A pot of tea for two? I can do you some toast?"

"Just the tea for me, thank you," Hobb said, so Charlie followed suit.

With their cups filled and steaming, Charlie broached his subject. "Not looking too good across the Channel, is it?"

Hobb sipped before he replied. "I reckon we're in for a long haul again. I was too young for the last lot but my brother and my uncle went. Came home too. They were lucky." His weather-tanned face reddened a little and he said, "I would go if they'd let me."

"I have no doubt of that," Charlie assured him. "It must be hard to be faced by the kind of thing I saw out in the street. Such a pity that some people equate the possession of a uniform with thuggery."

Hobb snorted. "Well, it certainly don't incline people to chivalry. I think all those were dead by '18, poor sods. We had a doctor in our parish. Lovely man, kind word for everyone. Lasted less'n ten minutes on the front line. His sergeant said, 'We have to be careful here, sir,' and he said 'Why's that sergeant?' and looked an' pow! Sniper got him right between the eyes. My brother saw it. Said it broke his heart. You need thugs to deal with that kind of thing."

"Maybe so, but there are other ways of serving."

"That's what I thought." Hobb put his cup down and leaned forward on the table. He looked like a man about to impart confidences, exactly as Charlie hoped. "I went off to the recruitment office in Hereford. I'll do anything, I said. They took one look at my legs. Unfit for purpose, they said. They wouldn't even let me go down the pit."

"So you came south, with your old dog, to free another man to fight? That's commendable."

"The doctor's widow put in a word for me. Her family came from Seaford." Hobb turned the cup on the saucer. "Farmer Nicholls was lucky to get me, did he but know it."

"So I've heard," Charlie grinned at him. "Rumour has it you're good with the sheep, can handle horses, and are a better than fair mechanic. Nicholls must be rubbing his hands with glee, but you're not working every hour of the day, are you? You do have some free time?"

That wary look had come back with maybe just a touch of interest. "Free time, yes, but the job comes first."

"Shall I freshen the pot, sirs?" Larry was back with a jug of hot water, and Charlie very deliberately allowed Hobb to see him appreciating the view as the lad walked away.

"I can think of several things an intelligent grammar school boy with a flair for initiative could do for me," Charlie said very quietly.

Hobb leaned across the table, voice icy cold. "Larry's got a sweetheart called Mary who works as an usherette in the Royal. They're both nice children saving up to be married. He'd be in the forces himself if he hadn't took sick last winter. And his ma and pa are friends of mine so I suggest you save your nonsense for them as wants it."

Dammit, there it was – the fire Charlie had been told to look for, smouldering away under that stoic countryman's expression and shabby clothes. It was the most exciting thing he'd seen that week.

"I was referring to you," Charlie said. "Yes, Mr Hobb, I made enquiries. Scholarship boy, weren't you? That can't have been comfortable yet you still attained your Higher School Certificate with no difficulty. You were bright but went back to the farm. Why's that, I wonder?"

Hobb, who was red-faced and had been trying to get a word in, shut his teeth with a snap and gritted through them, "Da didn't mind school when I was a kid, and he was proud of me getting my Higher, but after that I needed to work." He paused and gave Charlie a bleak stare. "Shepherding's lonely work, but I'm out of temptation's way, and it gives me time to read."

"I admire that," Charlie said. "Not the reading but staying out of temptation's way. I've always been so awfully bad at that. Yes, I do have a proposition for you, but probably not the one you expect. I'm wondering just how serious you are about serving your country."

Hobb was surprised into a loud "Ha!" of laughter then dropped his voice to an urgent whisper. "Are you *twp* or weren't you listening?"

"Toop?"

"Daft. Stupid!"

"Not the least bit daft, thank you, and I was listening," Charlie said. "I'm just not sure yet whether you really want to be of service or you just want the uniform."

"Fuck off, Cruickshank," Hobb snarled. "You know what I found myself doing last time I was in town? I was exaggerating my fucking limp out of guilt, that's what. You show me a way to serve and I'm your man."

Charlie leaned on the table too. "Well, then, I have a friend, who is a friend of a man named Fleming. Odd character, travel writer by trade but he has this amazing imagination. One of the stories he's managed to sell to the War Office is that it's all very well going into a war hoping for the best, like we did last time, but it's a stupid man who doesn't prepare for the worst. For the past six months, all over the country, we've been putting measures in place."

"Like the Observer Corps and the Local Defence Volunteers?"

"That's been part of it, yes, but we've been doing something a lot less obvious than that. Preparing for a successful invasion."

"Now that is *twp*." Hobb glared at him. "It'll never come to that."

"Well, obviously, but you don't leave your flock unattended all the time, do you? I mean it's unlikely they'd all scamper over Beachy Head if they were left to their own devices but … "

"All right, I take your point. Hope for the best, prepare for the worst. So where do I come in? The LDV weren't keen on having a cripple in their ranks either."

"More fool them." Charlie took a packet of Capstan from his pocket and offered them to Hobb who declined. "No, what we want is much less obvious. We have teams in place, so if the worst happens they can retreat to prepared positions and take up arms to hamper the enemy's advance. Guerrilla fighters, trained to sabotage roads, rail and airfields, destroy supplies and kill troops. Their training, which has already started, is nothing like that of the LDV. But it's become clear that they can't operate on their own. Each of these groups will need to be self-sufficient and for the most part operate on their own initiative, but they will need to be kept informed of what's going on, of opportunities to ply their craft, of reasons to be extra cautious. To supply this intelligence we will need messengers."

As Charlie had been speaking Hobb's scowl had eased into a thoughtful frown, so Charlie wasn't surprised when Hobb filled in the rest himself.

"You'll be needing men with a good reason to be out all hours of the day and night. Men who can go anywhere, pretty much, who really know the ground." Hobb sighed and continued without a trace of bitterness. "And if he's a cripple? All the better. They might look twice at him. But the second look will be a sneer."

"I wouldn't have said that." Charlie smiled. "But, since you bring it up, that is probably another advantage."

"That'll be a first."

Charlie nodded. "I can imagine. Well, no, I probably can't. Do you mind me asking what the problem was?"

"Got run over by a cart when I was fourteen. Broke both legs, load of ribs, my right arm. The left leg was the worst. It didn't heal well." Hobb frowned down at his foot. "I get around all right. That's why Da didn't mind the schooling." He glanced at Charlie and let loose that impish smile again. "Silver lining, eh?"

"Indeed. And may I say I admire your attitude? Now, here's the bad part of my offer. Should the worst happen and the invasion goes ahead, your job would be incredibly dangerous. You would be exposed and, I'm sorry to say, expendable."

"You don't believe in dressing things up, do you?" Hobb grinned.

"Well, no, I don't. I'd sooner tell you now than have you work it out yourself later and panic. And it's a lonely job, too. You would have contacts – I'll be one of them – but mostly it would just be passing messages. The messages will be encrypted and the drop-off and pick-up points won't be manned. You'll also be trained to use a radio in case one of the regular operators is taken ill. We'd provide the set and you would need to find a safe place to hide it. In addition to all that, you would be operating under extreme secrecy. Nobody would be able to know what you're up to. You have to be prepared, in fact be able, to lie convincingly and mislead even those closest to you. Nobody can know and we will expect you to sign a very severe document to ensure that the secret is kept, for ever, if necessary. What do you say, Sam Hobb? Do you think you could lie for King and country?"

"Do I get time to think it over?" Hobb asked. "Because Farmer Nicholls might be a grasping bugger but he pays my wages and I wouldn't want to let him down. That would cause talk, and I don't think that would be good, would it?"

"No, it wouldn't. I'll just say that some of the men I've been dealing with have been training for four months now and none of them have missed a day's work or given their workmates or families cause to wonder. You fit your new extraordinary duties in around your ordinary ones."

"I must admit I like the sound of extraordinary duties," Hobb said. "I don't need to think it over. Of course I'll do it."

"Then I will be in touch."

Hobb's tea was finished and he refused a refill. Charlie made no attempt to detain him because they had said what they needed to say and, as Hobb admitted, those sheep wouldn't herd themselves.

Once Hobb resumed his hat and coat and called his dogs to heel he shot Charlie a last quizzical glance and said, "I must admit you surprised me. Shocked me, even."

"I'm sorry," Charlie said, then added, because he couldn't resist it, "are you disappointed that the proposition wasn't more – "

"Personal?" Hobb sighed. "As I said before, it's a lonely job but I prefer to stay out of temptation's way."

"But you were tempted," Charlie said with a delighted smile.

Hobb blew out a long exasperated breath. "Bold and trouble." He grinned, his plain face lighting up. "I'll be expecting to hear from you, then. Good morning, Mr Cruickshank."

Off he went, striding along the street with the gaberdine coat flapping around his legs and the dogs loping alongside. Charlie watched him go, then went home.

That night he served up a rabbit pie to the man who, as far as the neighbours were concerned, rented half Charlie's house to augment his pension. As they sat to eat Charlie said, "You were right about Sam Hobb."

"In the chemist buying wintergreen?" Doctor Marriott gave him a beaming smile. "You owe me a tanner. And the rest?"

"Lonely, fed-up, fit as a butcher's dog and ripe for trouble. He agreed with only the barest hesitation."

"Then you owe me two bob." Marriott nodded with satisfaction. "Not that I know what you want him for, of course."

"Well, no, of course not. It's all secrets, isn't it?"

They exchanged knowing glances, two men too old to serve their country openly, just as there were so many other things they couldn't do openly, either. They, and Sam Hobb, were very good at keeping secrets, just one of their many qualifications for carrying out extraordinary duties.

Author's Note

This story is dedicated to my betas, with many thanks *kisses*, and to the men of the Auxiliary Units who were, thank goodness, not called upon to fulfil their destiny, but managed to have a lot of secret fun while they waited for the invasion. Sam Hobb will be back in his own story, when I get a chance to redraft it.

The Boy Left Behind

Eleanor Musgrove

"Rosie, you look fine – you look beautiful, same as always. Please, just put your shoes on and get your gas mask – we're going to be late."

"We won't be late. It's not that formal, it can't be."

"Still, I'd rather not risk it if possible. The sooner we're there, the better chance we have of being able to help."

"All right, Henry. I'll be ready to go in one more minute. I want to look presentable."

Henry was less worried about looking presentable. She had long since resigned herself to being 'the strange girl in the trousers' – or, more accurately, the strange woman in the trousers. Henry had never really felt like a girl, but now she had become too old for anyone to make that mistake. She had always been a boy, really, in her heart, in all the ways that mattered most to her – but the world would always see her differently.

The exception, of course, was Rosie. Rosie had been her sweetheart since they'd first worked together to keep Dixon's farm going through the first war, and she had been completely understanding when Henry had explained that she was a man in a body that didn't fit quite right. In fact, Rosie had been relieved, because it had helped to settle her nerves about being attracted to Henry in the first place. From that moment on, they had never looked back. Well, that wasn't true – they'd had arguments, and doubts, and fears, but they'd come through them all and now they would come through this new war together.

"Come on, Henry, hurry up – we don't have all day, you know!" Rosie laughed and tugged at her hand on the way past, half-dragging her down the road towards the village hall.

Rosie had inherited the house they now lived in from her parents – it was small, but quite big enough for the two of them to have a room each for appearances' sake. They had a good life; they kept themselves to themselves, for the most part, but they weren't without friends and they both worked hard at things they enjoyed. Henry worked as a clerk, filing paperwork at the only large factory within walking distance, and Rosie had been a teacher at the village school for a few years before taking a job at the little cottage hospital on the edge of town. She cleaned, she cooked for the patients, and she did all the other vital jobs that the doctor and nurses were too busy to carry out. Then, when she got home, she always insisted on helping Henry with their own housework, too. Their weekends were partly devoted to tending their vegetable garden and partly spent together, relaxing after a hard week's work – unless, of course, Rosie was needed urgently at the hospital.

They were very happy together, and Rosie never seemed to mind that Henry wasn't quite the same as any of the other men who'd fallen for her beauty and kindness over the years. Henry, for her part, had no regrets whatsoever about refusing to surrender her comfortable trousers and dependable pullovers when the men came home from the war – well, that wasn't quite true. She did have one regret, and that was that no matter how hard she tried to be like all the other men in the village, she couldn't give Rosie a child. However much they both pretended that they didn't mind, the truth was that Rosie would have loved to be a mother, and they both knew it. Henry would rather be a father, but she would take being a mother at a push. Unfortunately, however, it was out of the question. For a while, when they were younger, Henry had lived in constant terror that Rosie would come to her senses and leave her for a man who could give her the family she deserved, but they had been together for over two decades now, and Henry could trust that Rosie only wanted *her*, for whatever mad reason that might be.

This – the meeting they'd been on their way to when Rosie had been called in to the hospital in a hurry, and which they were now setting out for once more, kicking up fallen leaves in their haste – was their chance, not to be parents, but to give a child a safe and loving home for a little while. The major cities of Britain had become dangerous places to be, and children were being sent out by train in every direction, evacuated to the country for their own safety. They would need to be billeted with local families, and even single people, and there was a troop of young evacuees arriving in the village that very day. It all seemed a bit strange, to Henry, this 'first come, first served' approach to allocating children, but everyone was expected to do their bit and she hoped, just this once, that the unique challenges of their relationship – of their life together – wouldn't stand in their way.

When they arrived at the village hall, however, the light was already fading from the sky and the doors were closed. Henry pounded her fist against the wood, hoping against hope that they weren't too late. To her relief, the door swung open.

"Yes?"

"Are we too late?" Rosie laid a hand on Henry's arm, and she hurriedly modified her question. "I mean, do any more children need homes?"

"With you?" The billeting officer looked them up and down with a disapproving look they were more than used to, then stepped aside with a sigh. "You'd best come in."

Inside, it was dark – not only in the tiny entrance hall, where they might have expected it, to ward off the ARP wardens, but also in the larger main room. Only the last faint light of the sinking sun came through the windows to illuminate the shadows of furniture – a small upright piano and several stacks of chairs. The billeting officer, whom Henry vaguely recognised from church, cleared her throat, and part of one of the stacks of chairs leapt to its feet, revealing itself to be a young boy.

"Sorry, missus. You didn't half frighten me."

"There's nothing to be frightened of. Well?" She turned to Henry and Rosie, her tone officious. "Will you be taking him or not? He's the only one who's been left behind, so those are your choices."

Henry turned to Rosie, completely nonplussed. Taking him? They'd barely even seen his silhouette, and now they were just expected to take the boy home? Perhaps if they'd tried for an evacuee the previous year, they would have expected this, but it had taken too long to work up the courage. Rosie shrugged, then took a few tentative steps forward.

"Hello. I'm Rosie, and this is Henry. Who might you be?"

"Tom. Er, Thomas. Thomas Atkins. It says on my label." He made a vague gesture towards the front of his coat.

"Well, it's nice to meet you, Thomas. May I call you Tom?" A shrug. "I hear you're in need of a place to stay." He shrugged again. "Would you like to come and stay with us?"

There was a long pause before the next shrug. "No one else wants me, missus. Are you sure you do?"

"Now that doesn't sound right at all." Rosie held out a hand, an offer of peace. "Do *you* want *us*?"

"Don't know you," Tom pointed out, but after another moment, he took her hand and shook it. "It's not half cold in here, though. 'Sides, won't be for long. Same as last year."

The billeting officer – Mrs Pearce, Henry remembered at last – had them write down their names and address, assured them that she would call in when she had a chance and check that they were all settled, and shooed them from the hall. Outside, with a glance up at the ever-darkening sky, Henry turned to Tom.

"Can I take that bag for you?"

"No thanks, mister." The boy's tone was polite, but he clutched his possessions tight against his chest and took a step back. "I'm all right."

"All right," Henry nodded. "It's good to meet you, Tom. It's only a short walk to our house, don't worry – and the sooner we're home, the sooner we can get warmed up."

"We've got milk at home, and there'll be more in the morning," Rosie assured the boy, "so I'll warm some up when we get home."

"Thank you." That sounded softer, warmer, more heartfelt than anything else Henry had heard the boy say.

By the time they got halfway home, Tom was clearly struggling with his bag, but he hadn't uttered a word of complaint.

"Thomas," Henry asked, trying to imitate the gentle tone Rosie had used, "are you sure I can't help you with that bag? I promise I'll give it back to you as soon as we get home."

Tom paused in the middle of the street. "And you won't look through my things?"

"Promise I won't," Henry told him. There was a tense moment in which Henry thought Tom was going to push on and hurt himself, but then he swung the bag down onto the ground.

"Thanks, mister. My arms aren't half sore." Henry was taken aback by the *mister* – Tom had said it before, too, she realised – but didn't question it. Instead, she swung the bag up into her own arms and followed as Rosie began chatting quietly to Tom. Rosie had always known what to say to youngsters.

Henry, having returned the boy's bag to him on the doorstep, beat Rosie to the stove in the end, letting her fuss over Tom – getting his coat off him, showing him up to the spare room that was, in theory, Henry's own – while Henry set out mugs and heated the milk for an evening drink. Usually, she and Rosie would have a cup of tea, but it seemed best, somehow, for them all to share a drink together on their first evening – and Henry had never liked tea much as a child. After a moment's pause, during which she could hear Rosie explaining where everything could be found, Henry decided to make a couple of rounds of sandwiches for them all to share. She couldn't imagine that jam would be unsuitable fare for a growing boy, so she opted for that filling.

Rosie had impeccable timing: the two came back downstairs just as Henry finished serving their small meal.

"I didn't know how hungry you might be, Thomas, or how tired," Henry explained, "but I expect you could fit in a sandwich before bed."

"I haven't eaten since this morning," Thomas confirmed, then looked up at Henry and faltered. "Sorry, missus, I thought you was a bloke."

"I'm quite happy to be called 'mister'," Henry told him, "despite appearances."

"Oh." The boy frowned, then stuffed an entire jam sandwich into his mouth as if he expected it to be taken away from him. It was a few moments before he could speak again. "Why?"

"Well." Henry had to think about it; she'd never really had to explain herself to a child before. Their parents tended to do it for her if necessary, for better or worse. "I suppose I just like it better."

"Oh." Another half a sandwich was summarily devoured. "But you're a lady."

"On the outside, yes."

Out of the corner of her eye, Henry could just see Rosie watching the exchange with obvious concern. If Thomas reacted badly to the unusual dynamics of their home, this wasn't going to work out. If he wanted to leave them, they would have no choice but to let Mrs Pearce find him another temporary family. Henry wasn't sure whether that would upset her or Rosie more, but they'd both be devastated. Here, for however long it lasted, was their chance to look after a child as if he were their own, and she couldn't bear to think that it might be snatched away.

Thomas held eye contact with Henry for a long moment, then looked back down at the remains of his sandwich.

"You're barmy. Do you have any more jam?"

The words stung, but at least the boy seemed more concerned with sating his hunger than with running back to the billeting officer. Henry would count that as a victory, for now.

"We do, actually, Thomas. Let me get you some," Henry offered.

"You can call me Tom, missus. Er. Mister? Er. Thanks. I'm not half hungry."

"How old are you, Tom?" Rosie had always had a way with children, and she hadn't lost her touch. Tom, who'd been shooting wary glances around the room since he'd first sat down in it, opened up to her with a sudden, disarming smile.

"Ten, missus. Nearly eleven."

"Nearly eleven! Well, and here I thought we'd have a little boy staying with us. I wasn't expecting a grown-up, were you, Henry?"

"I wasn't," Henry agreed, trying to maintain a solemn expression. "Still, I suppose we'll have to make the best of it."

"I'll be good," Tom promised, "you won't be sorry."

"Henry's only teasing – we're very happy to have you. Now, grown-up or not, I think it's time for bed, don't you? Are you too old for someone to tuck you in?"

"Nobody's tucked me in in years, missus, I'm much too old for those baby things."

"Fair enough." Rosie shrugged, as if to say that she'd expected as much. "Well, I'll – "

" … Would you, though? I'd … I think I'd like it. Just this once."

"Of course. Lead the way, if you remember it."

"Coming, miss- mister?" Tom pulled a face as he spoke, but Henry was just grateful that he didn't seem to be planning to cause any undue trouble.

"If you like."

Once Tom was settled and safely tucked into bed, his door left slightly ajar so they'd be able to hear if he needed anything, it was Rosie and Henry's turn to get ready for bed. As usual, Rosie unbraided her hair and then sat still in front of the mirror so that she could watch Henry brushing it out, a ritual they had both loved for many years now. This was when they could really talk, an intimate space just for them. Tonight, of course, their talk was mostly of Tom.

"I'll talk to my manager tomorrow," Henry promised, "and see if I can take a few days off to get him settled. The arrangements for school shouldn't take too long, should they?"

"No, they shouldn't. I'll ask too, and between us we have a decent chance of being able to look after him. But tomorrow's going to be a problem, isn't it? There's nobody to watch him while we're both working – "

"Actually, I thought I might ask Peter."

"Peter?" Rosie turned to look at Henry over her shoulder as she took back the hairbrush. "Are you sure he can manage?"

"Honestly, I think he might be glad of the diversion. It's not good for him to spend too much time in his own head."

"And he won't … *mind* … if the boy gets noisy?"

"I shouldn't think so. We have to try, at any rate. It would break his heart if we didn't ask."

"Hmm. Well, I suppose we'll find out in the morning. Come on. Bedtime."

The next morning, Henry rose early as usual and headed down to see to her vegetables before work, leaving Rosie slumbering peacefully. She came back indoors before it got properly light and decided to pop her head round the door of the room where Tom was sleeping. At least, she'd thought he was sleeping there, but as her eyes adjusted to the darkness, she realised that the bed was empty.

"Tom?" She'd have seen him if he'd been in the kitchen – if he'd been anywhere, really – and surely he couldn't be old enough to go out and play on his own in the grey light of dawn? "Thomas? Tom!"

"Miss? Er … I mean, er, mister?" A sleepy voice emerged from under the bed, shortly followed by a sleepy boy. "Am I in trouble?"

"You – no, you're just not in bed, I was worried."

"Safer down here, mister. If the bombs come."

"Ah. Good thinking, but they're not likely to bomb us out here. You can sleep in the bed, I promise."

Tom looked at her thoughtfully for a moment, apparently trying to decide whether she was lying. " … Thanks, mister. But I'm awake now. Can I come downstairs with you?"

"Course you can. And I thought maybe later you'd like to come and meet my brother. I'm hoping he'll help keep an eye on you now and then, when Rosie and I are both hard at work."

"Is your brother like you?" Tom's eyes were wide, and it didn't take long for Henry to work out what he was getting at.

"Peter? No. No, he was born a boy, just like you were. He's got a big bushy beard, too, if he forgets to shave it. But we do look a bit alike."

"How come you dress like a man, mister? And ... and you don't mind me calling you mister?"

"Being a woman never really felt right. Does that make any sense?"

"Like how my mum supports Arsenal but I like West Ham more, but sometimes she says I should cheer for Arsenal anyway and it makes me get a horrible feeling in my tummy?"

"Er ... a bit like that, I suppose. You're cheering for Arsenal, but really, deep down, you know you're a West Ham fan."

"Yeah! That makes sense."

"So ... for me, men's clothes are like ... a West Ham kit. They feel better, because I know I'm really a man, whatever people think."

"Cor. So you must be really clever, working all that out."

"It took a while. It wasn't until the last war that I really had a chance to find out how a pair of trousers made me feel."

"That's all right. It took me three years to get the hang of sums proper. How come your brother has time to look after me? And I am big enough to play by myself, you know."

"I'm sure you are, but you don't know your way around yet. Besides, I was hoping you might help me out by keeping an eye on Peter. He gets lonely, sometimes."

"Is it because of the last war?" Tom didn't miss a trick; Henry would have to stay on her toes around him.

"Yes. He was hurt, quite badly. And he was scared, too."

"Scared? Grown-ups don't get scared of nothing. And neither do I."

"Of course grown-ups get scared, sometimes." Henry refrained, with difficulty, from pointing out that the boy had been hiding under his bed just ten minutes earlier.

"Maybe it's just grown-ups in London, *they* don't get scared. But it's all right if your brother's a scaredy cat. I'll look after him for you, mister."

"Thanks, Tom. But will you help me out, pretend it's you who needs looking after? And, er, don't call him a scaredy cat."

"Course not, mister. I've got manners, you know."

"Of course. Well, shall we go and knock for Rosie before we start breakfast?"

"I'll knock!" And Tom hared off, out of his new bedroom, to start hammering on the door of Rosie's.

Peter was expecting to see Henry and Rosie that morning; he wasn't expecting the jittery ten-year-old trailing in their wake.

"Henry. Rosie. It's good to see you. Is this boy following you?" His tone was light, but his face betrayed his confusion.

"He's staying with us, Peter. This is Tom, he's come from London."

"An evacuee?" Peter looked him up and down, appraising him. Henry held her breath, awaiting his judgement, and her heart ached. She would never have worried about her brother's reaction before the war. As it turned out, though, she wasn't giving him enough credit. "It's a pleasure to meet you, Tom. I hope you don't mind if I shake the wrong hand."

"That's all right, mister, my friend's in the Wolf Cubs and they always do." Tom offered his left hand without hesitation, though his gaze lingered on Peter's empty right sleeve for a few moments more. Peter noticed, of course, but he was more than used to children eyeing his lost limb, just as most children accepted it as little more than a minor curiosity. Heaven knew they'd seen enough men scarred from battle.

"It's all right, you can ask," he told the boy in his low, gruff tones. "I lost it at Messines during the Great War, and it got so muddy I didn't bother picking it back up."

"Came home without it, daft beggar," Henry teased fondly, glad that they could finally begin to laugh about it, "but the important thing is that you came home."

"I did. I was very lucky."

"You must have been proper brave, mister." Tom was looking at him in absolute awe, and Peter shifted uncomfortably, a shadow passing across his face.

"No. No, I had very brave friends. I just did what I had to. You can call me Peter, you know. You're not calling this pair *Miss*, are you?"

"He's calling Henry *Mr*, actually," Rosie told him quietly, and a warm smile spread slowly across Peter's face.

"You, young Tom, can stay around here just as long as you like." He beamed proudly at him, then looked up at the two women. "Do you have to work today?"

"I'm afraid so. We weren't sure if we'd have anyone to look after today, so we couldn't ask for any time off." Rosie was obviously reluctant – Henry understood, because she would rather get to know their new charge, too – but it couldn't be helped.

"Would you mind – ?" Henry began, but her brother was speaking too.

"He can – " Peter faltered, then pressed on as Henry fell silent. "That is, would you like to spend the day here, Tom?"

"All right." The boy sounded casual, but they could all see the tension in his shoulders; nerves, that was all. Henry couldn't blame him for being anxious at the thought of spending the day with a stranger before going home with two more, but Tom bravely cast around for something grown-up he could say. His eyes settled on the chessboard tucked into the top shelf of Peter's bookcase.

"Do you play chess?"

"I do." Peter seemed surprised. "Do you?"

Tom shook his head. "My teacher told us about it, but then we got sent away. She said it was a game for grown-ups. Is it hard?"

"It can be," Peter told him, "but don't ever let that stop you from trying anything. I'll teach you."

By the time Rosie and Henry left, Peter was directing his new friend to his chess set's place in the cupboard his wireless sat on. Tom was almost entirely inside the cabinet, though he did pop his head out to give them a cheery wave of farewell.

Henry's mind was only half on her filing as she worked in the factory that day. She couldn't help but wonder what her brother and her new charge were doing. Peter had seemed to be in a good mood – she often thought that company helped him when his view of the world got dark – but he did get anxious, often, or melancholy, and she worried that the lively ten-year-old she'd hardly got to know would trigger one of his rough spells. She wished she could have taken a day off of work to keep an eye on Tom, to help make sure he settled in properly, but there was a war on and she couldn't justify arranging to take leave just because she hoped she might have an evacuee placed with her. Her manager, however, was understanding.

"Well, of course you can't let one of those city children wander around unsupervised. Who knows what havoc he'd cause. You can take tomorrow off to make arrangements – and to make sure he knows the rules."

"Thank you, sir. And, er, when school starts – "

"You can leave early to collect him, but you'll need to make up the hours. Perhaps you could come in early, or come back after he's safely in bed?"

"I could come back an hour or two after I left, actually, sir. Rosie will be home from the hospital, and she can take over."

Her manager sniffed dismissively – he preferred to ignore the existence of Rosie and of the rumours surrounding their relationship – but he agreed to the plan. Henry would be given a key, on the strict understanding that she was to stay away from the factory floor, and she could make up her hours after dark, signing in and out with the nightwatchman.

Until the evacuees were settled into school, though – and that could take days – she was hoping that Peter wouldn't mind helping to look after Tom. He'd been happy enough to take him for that first day, so everything rested on how well that day had gone. It was a rather anxious Henry who arrived at Peter's home that evening, and that anxiety only increased when she knocked on the door and noticed how quiet the house was. All became clear when Peter opened the door and immediately let go of it to place a finger on his lips.

"He fell asleep. Under the table, actually. And I don't think he likes chess as much as he thought he would, but then he's still learning."

"Perhaps I'll teach him to play draughts. It's simpler to start out with."

"Well, I couldn't move him anywhere more comfortable, so I thought I'd better let him sleep. Do you want to wake him up?"

"Only if you want us to leave. He'd probably have got confused if you had moved him."

"Well, if you're staying … Tell me about it all. I saw you two days ago and there was no mention of an evacuee."

"We weren't sure we were going to go. And then we were late, and the hall was dark … "

The story wasn't as long as Henry had remembered it being, in the end.

"And that's how we met Tom."

"I see." Peter looked troubled; the nervous tic in his left hand gave him away. "He doesn't have a problem with the way you and Rosie are?"

"I'm not sure he's worked it all out yet," Henry admitted, "but Rosie showed him round upstairs, so he knows we share a bedroom – "

"Cos you're her feller," a voice declared groggily from under the table, and Henry ducked down to meet Tom's eyes. "Right, mister?"

"Er … yes, but we don't tell everybody that, all right?"

"Gotcha. I don't really understand it, but it's all a bit peculiar around here."

"It is. Are you finished sleeping now?"

"I get a choice?" Tom seemed completely bewildered.

"Yes – but perhaps you could – Oh, never mind, he's asleep again." Peter made a gesture of frustration with his arm, but he was almost smiling as he settled back in his chair. "Still, you see? He's more observant than you'd think. He had some questions, earlier. About you, mostly."

"What sort of questions?"

"He was confused. But the more we talked about it, the more he understood it. Then he wanted to know what Rosie thought about it all – I did my best, but I don't know what she's thinking, taking up with the less handsome brother – "

"Hey!" Henry swiped playfully at him, and he scrunched his face up in mock terror.

"No, help, don't hit the invalid!" For a moment, it was like having a glimpse of her brother as he was before the war, but then she reached out and touched only air where his arm had once been.

"Sorry," she mumbled, "but … what did you tell him – about Rosie?"

"Just that she loves you, and you her. And then he asked the really tough question."

"What did he ask?" What sort of mortifying revelation had Peter had to make on her behalf, or what complicated facet of their relationship had Tom wanted to understand in detail?

"He asked if I knew why aeroplanes stayed up. I'm afraid I had to tell him I hadn't the faintest idea, and he did me the great kindness of explaining to me the little bits he knows. He's quite clever, actually."

"It sounds as if he did you some good."

Peter bristled slightly; he didn't approve of her 'fussing over him'. Still, the tension didn't last. "Perhaps he did. If he ever needs somewhere to spend a day, I suppose you could send him over. If that would help you?"

"Thanks, Peter. That would be lovely. Or you could visit us, perhaps? Get out of the house for a while."

"Maybe. Speaking of getting out of my house, don't you think it's time you removed that boy from the floor?" He said it with a smile, but he had a point; Tom couldn't be comfortable under the table, sound asleep though he seemed. There was just one more point Henry wanted to clarify.

"And he didn't give you one of your turns?"

"No." Peter shrugged his shoulder. "He cheered me up immensely, actually. I really do hope you'll let me borrow him occasionally."

"He's not a library book. But I'll suggest he visit." She ducked back under the table. "Tom? Wake up, it's time to go."

"Hm?" Tom unfolded himself from the little ball he'd been curled up in, stretched, and blinked at her as if trying to get his bearings. "Where are we going?"

"Home. Home here, I mean, not in the city. Rosie should be home very soon."

"Hm. All right. I'll be seeing you, Mister Peter."

"See you soon, Tom."

When they arrived home, Tom was still groggily enquiring about a return visit to Peter's house on another day. The two seemed to have got along splendidly, which was a relief to Henry. The following day would be devoted to just the three of them, assuming that Rosie had got the time off she had asked for, and then they could get on with being a temporary family. Henry deliberately wasn't thinking about the day Tom would have to return home to his real mother; she'd already grown attached to the lad.

"There you are! I thought you'd both been eaten by a cow. Did you have a good day with Peter, Tom?"

At Rosie's enquiry, Tom perked up considerably. "He taught me chess! But I'm not very good at it. So we played cards, but I think next time somebody else should hold his cards because I could see them when he put one down."

"Ah. Yes, he does have that problem." Henry grimaced, remembering the time her brother had bet all his socks on a poker game in his former convalescent home and sheepishly had to ask her for some new ones. "He should put them face down on the table, really, but he forgets."

"Well, we both have some time to spend with you tomorrow," Rosie promised him, "so we can do whatever you like. Even play cards, if you like."

"Can we go exploring? I've never been anywhere like this."

"Of course we can. That's settled, then."

Later that night, they tucked Tom into bed – he seemed to have forgotten that it had been *just this once* the previous night – and assured him that he was just as safe on top of the mattress as under it. Henry was the last to leave the room, and he called out to her as she left.

"Sorry for calling you missus before, mister."

"You don't have to apologise for that, Tom. Sleep well."

The apology was unnecessary, but Henry could feel the child's acceptance warming her heart all the way back to her own bed.

Author's Note

You can read about the beginning of Henry and Rosie's relationship in Manifold Press's World War I anthology, *A Pride of Poppies*.

The Man Who Loved Pigs

Megan Reddaway

London, September 1940

Michael Bernsey made his way to the bar of the Rose and Thorns in Soho and waited, tapping his fingers lightly on the wooden counter. There was a fair crowd in here tonight – more than he'd expected, given the bombardment London had suffered in the past few weeks.

"Well, hello." A sharp-eyed, grey-haired barman stood facing him with folded arms. "It's been a while. You must be busy with whatever it is you do."

Mike didn't answer the implied question. He was a wireless operator with the Security Service, but nobody here needed to know that. "A pint of best, please, Percy."

The barman took a glass mug from the shelves behind him and pulled on the pump. Mike half turned to reach into his pocket. His gaze swept over the other customers. Mostly male and mostly in civilian clothes, like him. A fellow didn't want to advertise his rank and service in a place like this.

Mike wasn't altogether comfortable here. He had to fight a constant urge to look over his shoulder like a little boy sneaking into the larder for a forbidden slice of cake. He didn't find it easy to make conversation with strangers, either. But he craved the company and felt more at home here than anywhere else – anywhere else that didn't offer a wireless he could tinker with, anyway. So whenever he was in London, which wasn't so often since war broke out, he'd sooner or later find himself in the Rose and Thorns.

His eyes were caught by a young man standing alone with his back to the wall. He wore a creased civilian suit and had mid-brown hair that might have been curly on top if it hadn't been oiled down. He held his full pint in both hands and glanced around wide-eyed from time to time in a way that was – well, it was damned attractive.

Percy set the full glass on a towel to catch the foam running down the side. "Got your eye on that? From the Midlands by his accent, and so green he comes in and asks me for 'a beer'. Only foreigners do that, as a rule.

Anyone else knows what they want – a pint of mild, a half of stout, a light and bitter." Percy leaned his elbows on the counter. "I wondered if he might be under eighteen, but he showed me his card and he's code A."

Code A on the national registration card meant over twenty-one. He wouldn't be much over, Mike thought – twenty-two or twenty-three, at a guess. Two or three years younger than Mike.

"Do you think he's wandered in here by mistake?" Mike asked.

"No, he knows what's what. 'Are you sure you're in the right place?' says I. He has a good look round, then he says, 'Oh yes, I think so. I'm hoping to make a friend,' and he gives me a wink."

The young man looked up. His dark eyes met Mike's with a flash of interest. He looked away shyly, and returned for a second look. When he saw Mike was still watching him, his lips parted and flickered into a smile. With his round cheeks, it gave him the look of a mischievous imp.

Conversation wouldn't be difficult with him. Mike had to get over there before anyone else decided to be the fellow's friend. He pushed off from the bar.

Percy called him back. "Oi! That's sixpence."

Mike fished in his pocket and dropped a coin into his hand. "Thanks."

His name was Eddy. "I grew up at Heybourne in Warwickshire," he said in answer to Mike's question. "On the River Dene, that joins the Avon near Stratford."

Mike didn't know the area, but Eddy made it sound pretty. "And what brings you here? Are you stationed in London?"

A tiny crease appeared between the wide brows. "Stationed? No. I'm a farm worker. I'm not in the army."

Then he was older than Mike had thought. To escape conscription, agricultural workers had to be at least twenty-five at the start of the war.

"Do you enjoy it?" Mike asked.

Eddy's eyes shone. "I love it. I like to be outside and to work with animals – the pigs especially."

Mike laughed and moved an inch nearer. "You like pigs?"

Eddy bit his lip. "I love them. I know it's funny, but I do. They're intelligent and affectionate – like dogs, almost. They're not the dirty, smelly, greedy creatures that city people think."

"I'll take your word for it. I'm not a city person, really. I'm from Kent. So is it your first time in London? How did you hear about the Rose?"

I'm asking too many questions, Mike thought. Most men didn't like it – blackmail was always a risk. But Eddy didn't seem to mind. He was still smiling, and his eyes were bright.

"I didn't. I was here since … almost a week, and I didn't think I'd find a place like this. But I heard something about Soho, so I came and walked around until I seen someone who looked the right kind of man, if you know what I mean. I followed him, and he came in here."

Mike supped his beer and moved a little closer. "You've been in London for a week? You'll have been in the air raids, then. I've just come up from my base. I haven't been through one yet."

"You won't have long to wait. They come every night. I was frit at first, but you get used to it. Do you think there's a shelter here?"

Frit – Mike grinned at the dialect word. "I expect they use the cellar."

Eddy grimaced. "I hope no bomb hits it. I don't want to die by drowning in this beer."

Die? Mike had never felt more alive. "Do you want to come outside?"

"Outside?"

Heat rose to Mike's cheeks. He hadn't meant to say that, not yet, but it was too late to go back on the invitation now. "For a walk and perhaps … "

"Oh!" Eddy's face came to life. "With you? Yes." He turned to put his glass on the table. It was still full. Mike had almost finished his.

"Sorry, you're still nursing that pint. We don't have to go this minute, if you – "

Eddy made a face. "I don't like the beer. Let's go."

The blackout made it easy to be sure they weren't followed, but it had its own risks – getting lost in the alleys, tripping over a coalhole cover or a dustbin. And you never knew when a nosy ARP warden might shine his torch round the corner.

But when Eddy pressed up close against him, Mike forgot everything else. Eddy might have been a stranger to London, but he wasn't a stranger to love. Mike didn't have to ask anything twice. Didn't have to ask at all, most of the time. Eddy satisfied needs that Mike hardly knew he had – needs that went beyond the physical. They fitted together.

Afterwards, Mike straightened his clothing in silence. Now they'd go their separate ways. Usually he was glad of that, but he didn't want to let Eddy go so soon.

Shall I invite him back to the hotel now? Perhaps not. Men sometimes told Mike he was too intense. He could ask to see him tomorrow, though.

"Would you – "

An ear-splitting wail drowned his words – the siren. Good God, it was so loud a man couldn't think. He'd never heard one so close. And it wasn't just one. Another farther off and another, all over London.

The noise rose and fell away, then rose again to deafen him. As the shriek faded for the second time, Eddy took his hand.

"Come on! The shelter. Where's the main road?"

Mike had no idea. He was in a London he didn't know any more, a London that had bared its teeth like a roaring wild animal. He couldn't see a thing, and he'd lost his sense of direction. He didn't even remember how they'd got here. Everything from before Eddy touched him was a blur.

He led Eddy in a straight line, or as close to it as he could, and in a minute or two they emerged onto a street. Instinct made them drop each other's hand, not that anyone could have seen. The darkness was total, the buildings unrecognisable. The bombers didn't only come on clear nights.

"I hear people down here," Eddy said, pulling to the right. He trailed a hand along the walls of the buildings to avoid stumbling off the kerb. Mike let him lead. Eddy might be in London for the first time, but he'd been here for a week, and this dark, wailing city was more familiar to him than to Mike.

When they reached the end of the road, Mike knew where he was. "This is Oxford Street. We're a long way from the pub."

"We'll go to the tube," Eddy said.

"Isn't it illegal?"

"Everyone goes there. The police don't stop you."

Mike hooked his elbow through Eddy's, determined not to lose him.

It was the strangest night he'd ever spent with a man. They bought platform tickets and picked their way through the bodies until they found a place where they could wriggle between other people's blankets to lie side by side on the cold, hard floor.

Most people had bedding. Some had food or hot drinks in thermos flasks.

Mike and Eddy had nothing. All the same, Mike wouldn't have swapped his place beside Eddy on the cold station floor for any other place in the world.

"Tell me about your farm in Warwickshire," he whispered.

Eddy inched closer. "We had nearly a hundred acres. Cattle, mostly, but my responsibility was always the pigs. It's beautiful there. I wish you could see it. So green and lush around the river, and then you go up a little hill and you can see for miles. And it's so quiet! No noise but birds and insects, and sometimes a cow."

Mike pictured Eddy walking through deep green fields in golden sunlight, pushing a rebellious lock of curly hair from his eyes. "You said 'had'. 'We had nearly a hundred acres.' Is it gone now? Sold?"

Eddy didn't speak for a moment. Mike felt his tension.

"It was never … it didn't belong to my parents. I haven't been there for a long time." Another pause. "My mother died when I was little."

"Do you have brothers and sisters?"

"No."

"Like me," Mike said. "Except my father died, not my mother. He was killed in the last war, when I was a baby."

"Did your mother marry again, like my father?"

"No. She once told me she didn't think it would be fair, with so many men gone. She'd had her romance, and she had a baby. Some other girl should have a chance."

Eddy's eyes crinkled. "That's so British. Like making a queue."

Mike felt himself smiling again. Eddy made him want to smile all the time. "Yes, she thinks the supply of men is rationed – one per person per lifetime."

Eddy moved his hand nearer, and one finger stroked Mike's wrist. "I think I had my share tonight."

"No, you have plenty more coupons. I'll stamp your ration book any time you like."

Eddy snorted. The woman beside them shushed them, though they couldn't have been making more noise than her knitting needles.

When the all-clear sounded and they made it up the steps to the street, it was getting light. In other parts of the city, people lay dead or dying under piles of rubble, but the only sign of the bombing here was a hint of dust in the air.

Mike stopped on the wide pavement and yawned. "I can't believe the way everyone comes out and gets on with their lives."

Eddy spread his arms and tipped back his head. "Splendid, isn't it? Hitler thinks he has crushed Britain and he can walk in any time, but the people here are ready to fight to the bitter end."

"Perhaps the end won't be bitter."

Eddy dropped his arms and looked at Mike quizzically. "What do you mean? You think Britain and its empire can win alone?"

"Yes, with the right" – *information*, no, he mustn't say that – "attitude, which we have. Don't you think so?"

Eddy looked stunned, as if the idea were new to him. Then he gave a great laugh. "Of course! Of course I do."

His smile was like the sun coming out. Mike didn't want to let him go. He said, "I have a hotel room back near the pub. It's the kind of place where they don't mind two men sharing. Do you want to come and get some sleep?"

"No, I must look for work. I need a new job." Eddy's face burned with enthusiasm, as if shovelling hay and feeding pigs was the most thrilling work in the world.

Mike would have done anything to have Eddy in his bed for the day, but he didn't want to be the man who acted as if he owned somebody after one night. He kept his voice casual. "How about this evening, then?"

"Yes, I'd like that."

"At the pub at seven?"

Eddy nodded, but would he be there, or was he just being polite? Then he said, "What's the name of the pub?"

He intended to come. He wouldn't have asked otherwise. A weight lifted from Mike's chest, and he grinned. "The Rose and Thorns in Dean Street."

"The Rose and Thorns. Perhaps at six instead of seven, because of the air raids?"

"Good idea. Six o'clock."

"And if the air raid starts earlier, I'll come at the all-clear."

Eddy moved closer and brushed dust from Mike's shoulder. For a moment they might have been the only two people on earth. This, here, now, Mike thought – this is paradise.

But a pair of shopgirls on their way to work stared, whispered, and giggled. It broke the spell. Eddy stepped back, and the two men went their separate ways.

Walking to his hotel in the grey light of dawn, six o'clock seemed centuries away. But the thought of it was like a hot-water bottle hugged inside Mike's coat, warming him through the day.

Eddy was waiting outside the pub, leaning on one of the wooden columns that flanked the closed door. His eyes brightened at the sight of Mike, but his mouth turned down in a mock frown. "It's closed today."

Mike checked his watch, though he knew exactly what the time was. He'd spent half an hour walking round Soho to avoid being too early and the last five minutes hurrying to avoid being late.

"It's not quite six. Are you used to earlier hours? No, you're not a drinker at all, are you? I forgot."

Eddy's eyes had the look of a startled rabbit. Before he could answer, a crack near their heads made them both jump. But it was only the landlord pulling back the bolts to open the door.

At the bar, Eddy ordered a gin and tonic and turned to Mike. "For you?"

"I'll have a pint of bitter, thanks. I'll get them, if you're between jobs."

"I have money." Eddy waved a ten-shilling note.

They didn't stay long. Eddy liked the gin and tonic all right and might have had another, but Mike didn't want to waste time in the pub, with German bombers likely to cut their evening short.

He took Eddy back to his hotel. His room was bare, functional, and none too clean, but someone had been in to straighten the bed and draw the blackout curtains in Mike's absence. Mike closed the door and leaned against it in the darkness, pulling Eddy to him.

He jerked awake at the first wail of the sirens, heart thumping in fear. His body was curled around Eddy's back, their legs tangled in the bedclothes and Mike's arms gripping Eddy as if to protect him from the bombs.

Eddy stirred, turned over, and snuggled his head against Mike's shoulder.

"We should go to the shelter," Mike said, but he didn't move.

"Where is it?"

"Under Soho Square. Not far."

"Let's not. Let's stay here," Eddy mumbled.

"Isn't it the worst place to be, at the top of a building? What if there's a fire?"

"You're very … you like to follow rules."

Mike took it as a criticism. The sirens were still going, making him tense. *Frit,* as Eddy had said. "If you mean I'm law-abiding, there's nothing wrong with that. My work is technical – things have to be done by the book."

Eddy moved, so his thigh pressed against a certain part of Mike's anatomy. Mike groaned. "Bloody hell, that feels good."

"You still want to go?" Eddy teased.

"I suppose we'll be all right. There's a fire escape on the landing. Do that again."

Eddy did it again. Then he did other things.

I'll never forget this night, Mike thought – if I live through it.

Then he stopped thinking coherently for some time.

He got up afterwards and stumbled along the landing to the WC. When he came back, Eddy was standing at the window with the curtains pulled back. A flash outside lit his face as he turned. He beamed like an excited child on Bonfire Night. "Look at this."

Mike's nerves went on red alert. "You're crazy. Come away. If the window blows in, the glass will cut you to ribbons."

Eddy didn't move. Mike went over and put his arms around him, meaning to pull him back to the bed.

He was caught by the view. Fires burned red and yellow in the distance, clouds of smoke hanging over them like malevolent genies. People must be dying there, but the sight had a terrible, fascinating beauty.

Then there was a flash of white light and a thud. Eddy moved fast, dragging Mike away as the window rattled behind them. He bumped into the bed and fell onto it, pulling Mike down with him.

Eddy gave a gulping laugh. "That was close."

"Yes."

"We'll go to the shelter now?"

But this time it was Mike who didn't want to. He'd heard it was as dangerous to walk through the streets as to stay where you were, once the bombing had started. Besides, the near miss made him feel invincible, as if the two of them couldn't be hurt inside their bubble of love.

He went back to the window. It hadn't broken. A new fire burned outside, but it was farther off than he expected.

"Michael, don't stand there." Eddy sounded worried.

"I'm just closing the curtains. We can move the bed to the far wall and pull the blankets over our heads."

"You want to stay here?" Eddy hesitated, then laughed. "All right." He helped Mike drag the iron bedstead across the floor.

Mike straightened the counterpane and sat on the edge of the bed. "You called me Michael. Nobody calls me Michael except my mother."

Eddy settled beside him. "Do you mind?"

"I like it."

"Michael, like the archangel, because you take me to heaven." Eddy stroked soft fingers down Mike's cheek. They kissed, a long, slow, tender kiss, and Mike felt Eddy relax. Silence reigned outside, as if the bomb that almost broke their window had been the enemy's last shot.

"Touch me like you did the first time," Eddy whispered.

The anti-aircraft guns roared, but Mike barely heard them.

He woke in daylight. He was alone under the blankets. The all-clear had sounded hours ago. The bed had been full and warm then.

Certain parts of him were sore from overuse, but he didn't mind. It reminded him of what he and Eddy had done to cause it. He pushed back the covers and sat up, missing Eddy already.

But Eddy was there, fully dressed, sitting at the rickety table near the open curtains. He hadn't left. Thank God. He turned around and gave Mike a smile. "Good morning."

Mike rubbed his face to wake himself up. "What are you doing?"

"Writing to you. I must leave. I found a job."

"You didn't tell me last night."

Eddy's smile faded. He put down the pencil. "You said you're going to see your mother."

"Not until tomorrow." We could have had another day, Mike thought. Another night. But why should Eddy turn down work when Mike could only offer him twenty-four hours? He tried not to mind. "You fixed that up fast. I thought you were still looking."

"I saw an advertisement and telegraphed. They'll give the job to the first man who comes. I could have gone yesterday, but I wanted this night with you."

Mike felt a little better. "I suppose I'll have to let you go."

"Farming's important, isn't it? Feeding people?" Eddy sounded anxious, as if he wasn't sure he was doing the right thing.

He probably gets some stick for not being in the army, Mike thought.

"Of course. It's vital."

"How far is Whitstow?"

"Whitstow in Cambridgeshire? I don't know – a couple of hours on the train, I suppose, if it isn't delayed. I think you go from Liverpool Street. Have you got time for breakfast, or at least a cup of tea? There's a café between here and Leicester Square."

"All right."

"Give me two minutes to get dressed."

Mike went to the WC and splashed water on his face in the bathroom, hurrying in case Eddy changed his mind and disappeared.

The café was busy. They had to share a table with two other men. Eddy asked for coffee, but the waitress said they didn't do coffee until lunchtime. Over tea and toast, Mike rifled his pockets for paper and wrote down his mother's address.

Eddy held it between his fingers as if it might bite. "I'm no good at spelling."

"I don't care. You don't have to write much. Just a postcard or something to let me know how you get on?"

"All right."

They shook hands on parting. Eddy held Mike's hand a fraction longer than other men might and smiled into his eyes. Then he was gone.

Mike's feet dragged as he went back to his hotel. On the desk he found the note Eddy had begun to write on the back of a receipted bill.

Dear Michael, I have a job

That was as far as he'd got. The writing was neat and clear. The curving line of the capital D came around into a loop at the bottom, as if he wanted to give it a little bit extra.

The room looked shabby and lifeless without him. The city Mike had always loved seemed dusty and dull. A piece of his heart had been cut away and gone with Eddy, leaving him with nothing but this scrap of paper. He tucked the note into his pocket.

Buckinghamshire, October 1940

Captain Bob Carter stuck his head round the door. "The Chief's here."

Mike put down his headset and went out of the back bedroom that was their wireless room. From the outside, this looked like any other house in its suburban street. The neighbours believed it was a billet for officers with desk jobs at the local army base. In fact it housed a middle-aged Dutch-German spy whom the Germans had blackmailed into coming to Britain by threatening his wife and children. He'd been caught within hours of landing, interrogated, and converted to the British cause. Carter was his case officer. Mike was his wireless operator, sending messages to Germany in imitation of the agent's 'fist', his signalling style, and listening for replies.

Carter split his time between this case and another, but Mike and two guards lived here with the agent. Mike slept on a narrow bed crammed into the wireless room. A local woman came in and did for them, producing meals from their rations and keeping the place as clean as she could: Mike wouldn't let her in his room in case she threw away some vital component.

He ran down the stairs after Carter, straightening his uniform as he went. The Chief was in the front room, a wiry man in his late forties who'd been in intelligence since long before the war.

"Close the door," the Chief said, when Mike and Carter came in. "Any luck?"

Mike shook his head. The Abwehr, the German intelligence service, hadn't answered any of their messages for weeks. Mike had signalled that the agent had no money for food and lodgings, and finally, last week, that if the Germans couldn't find a way to pay him, he'd have to dump the wireless and tramp round looking for casual work. Generally the Germans supported their agents; they'd send cash through someone else in the network, who had so far always been one of the men known to the British, or they'd drop a new agent with money for the existing man. That was ideal. Then MI5 could pick up the new arrival. But this time it hadn't worked. There'd been no response, not even an acknowledgement.

The Chief walked to the window and sighed. "All right. We'll have to face it – this one's a dead duck. We'll intern your man. The Abwehr must have cut him off. Either they've rumbled that he's working with us, or something's happened to the officer running him. That's where we have the advantage over them."

The Chief turned his steady gaze on each of them in turn. "An Abwehr officer's status depends on the success of his agents, so he guards them jealously, not letting anyone else near them. In this service, that doesn't happen. We work as a team. Our aim is to catch every spy they send and convince at least half of them to work for us instead, and we'll do it. We'll do it because there isn't a single man on my watch who'd put personal considerations before his duty to his country. Because of men like you, we're going to win this war."

Mike straightened his back. Another CO might have ripped into them, assuming one of them had made a mistake that alerted the Germans to the fact that their agent had changed sides. Instead, the Chief made them feel proud.

"I've got something else for you." The Chief took a few papers from the briefcase he'd put on their dining table, handing them to Carter. "We haven't found him yet, but we've named him. This is Agent Piglet, an unknown maverick writing letters in secret ink. The censor caught this one, but it may not be his first. The cover letter is in fluent English, with the kind of spelling mistakes you'd expect of a farm worker. Yet the coded message is in perfect German. No errors there."

When he said 'Piglet' and 'farm worker', Mike thought of Eddy. Any reference to pigs or farms made him think of Eddy. His mother had sent on a letter last week. It said only that he'd got the job and would write again when he had a few days' holiday and could get to London. There was no return address. Mike had read every word three times, then refolded the single sheet and put it in the box where he kept his mother's weekly letters.

Carter passed him an envelope addressed in neat block capitals to Miss M. Sousa at an address in Lisbon.

"Portugal again?" Mike said.

"Yes, it's becoming quite a hive," the Chief replied. "Spies, diplomats, black marketeers – they tell me you can't cross the street there without someone trying to sell you information. Inevitable, I suppose. It's the only neutral country in Europe that everyone can reach. Spain's in a mess, Sweden and Switzerland are too close to Germany, and Ireland's too close to us."

"Is there a Maria Sousa?" Carter asked.

The Chief took out his pipe and tapped it into an ashtray. "Yes – a little old lady in a black shawl. I don't suppose she's ever met our Agent Piglet. A lot of people come and go at that address."

Mike peered at the photograph. The postmark was Norwich. The skin on the back of his neck prickled. How far was Whitstow from Norwich? Not far, surely. It must be the next county.

The Chief went on, "We think he's lived in both Britain and Germany. Most likely he spent time here as a child and went to Germany for his upper school education. Then he might speak English like a native but write German better."

What had Eddy said about his farm in Warwickshire? 'I haven't been there for a long time.' But not because he'd been in Germany. Of course not.

It isn't Eddy – just because he's always on your mind. Think how many farm workers there must be in East Anglia.

The Chief fished in his pocket for tobacco. "It's awkward, because we rely on the public alerting us to foreigners acting suspiciously. If he sounds English, he'll be hard to spot."

Eddy sounded English. No, Eddy *was* English.

Stop thinking about Eddy.

Bob Carter held out the next document to Mike – a photograph of the unknown agent's cover letter.

"Dear Maria," it began.

It hit Mike like a bucket of icy water. That capital D – clear and round, with an extra loop at the bottom end of the curve, as if the pen didn't want to stop.

Dear Maria. Dear Michael. The same hand.

Mike blinked and rubbed at one eye as if trying to see through fog. He kept his head down, pretending nothing was wrong, hoping the others couldn't hear the pounding of his heart. To him it sounded as loud and treacherous as a drum. He forced himself to concentrate on the letter.

Dear Maria,

I hope you and your family are well. I am thriveing here. The Farmers Wife is fair with the meat and dosent give it all to the Farmer as I hear they do on some farms. I don't like to think of our Pigs being made into bacon, but I must confess I eat it as gladly as anyone.

Betsy farrowed last week and the little ones are doing well. They are growing fast and none have died. It does my heart good to see them take her milk so eagerly. They bump heads and squobble, and the strongest would push out the weakest if they could, but I make sure every one gets a share. Like the Goverment, I impose Rationing.

Yours always,

[indecipherable signature]

Yes, this was Eddy. Mike seemed to hear his voice speaking every word. The letter tugged at his heart, as if Eddy had written it for his eyes alone.

"Could – " Mike's voice came out as a squeak. He cleared his throat and began again. "Could the letter be innocent, and the German code's been added by somebody else?" The treated secret ink showed faintly between the lines, a long string of tiny, apparently random capital letters. There wasn't a single D. He glanced again at the envelope. None in the address, either.

The Chief shook his head. "We asked a handwriting expert."

Mike nodded. It had been a faint hope. So many things fell into place. Eddy's hands were soft – too soft for a labourer's. And there were things he didn't know, like the pub being closed in the afternoon. Words he'd hesitated over. And what had Percy said? *He came in and asked for "a beer". Only foreigners do that, as a rule.*

Eddy was a spy.

Mike felt sick. He'd spent two nights with him and never guessed. How could he have been so stupid? It hurt his pride, and more. It hurt that Eddy had deceived him. He'd fallen for Eddy – he'd fallen far and fast – and Eddy had made a fool of him.

Mike had always despised those men who spilled secrets to the Mata Hari type of female agent. And here he was, tricked in the same way – or worse. If this came out it would seem even more shameful because he was queer, seduced by another man.

No, it wasn't like that. Eddy couldn't have known who I was. He didn't approach me. He didn't ask about my work, and I didn't tell him.

It was real. The attraction between them had been real. And Eddy might have all kinds of reasons for doing what he did. Perhaps they'd threatened his family, like they had with the man upstairs. It didn't mean he was a Nazi. Hang on to that, Mike told himself.

Carter asked, "Do you think he's a British fascist?"

The Chief puffed a cloud of smoke from his pipe. "No, we know where they all are – the party members, anyway. I think he's German, or how would his written German be so much better than his English?"

Carter passed Mike another two pages – the message decoded in German, with a typewritten translation.

Heil Hitler.

I have still not been able to repair my wireless.

I went to RAF Coltishall today. There is a new anti-aircraft battery one mile to the north of the base, in an open field on flat land.

Coastal defences are strong. The beaches are mined, and I have heard rumours that the navy can set the sea on fire, using oil on the surface of the waves. There are many troops stationed at the coast. It is difficult to approach, even from within England. They expect an invasion and are prepared for it.

Morale in Britain is low and still falling because of the successful bombing of London. Large parts of the city have been destroyed, much more than they report in the press. I believe this war will be won in the air.

You asked me to report on the weather. This week has been dull and often wet. Barometric pressure is consistently low.

There has been no change to food rations as far as I know, but all food is bought by my employer's wife, who holds my ration book.

To victory.

Mike glanced over it, taking in very little at first. The opening *Heil Hitler* made his stomach churn.

The Chief had paused to relight his pipe. "The interesting thing is, there are no guns north of Coltishall. That's why I said Piglet was a maverick. God only knows what he's up to."

Hope flared in Mike's heart. "You mean he's deceiving them, sir? He's on our side?"

"Perhaps, Bernsey, but we can't be sure. He may have mistaken another base for Coltishall. And even if he's trying to help, his clumsy attempts to misinform the Germans might clash with our own better-planned campaign. We can't be sure they'll think he's the one who's gone off the rails. They might stop trusting any of the agents. This could be why your current case has collapsed. We have the Lisbon address now, so we can intercept any more letters he writes, but he might get his wireless working, and then where will we be? We need to find him."

The Chief went on to talk of practicalities. They'd asked the Ministry of Agriculture for lists of farm owners and labourers, but there were no new employees whose background didn't check out.

"The farmer may not have declared him, for reasons of his own. Not entitled to employ him, probably. We could send the police to every farm in the east of England checking identity cards. If we're lucky, he'll have one of Snow's machine-folded forgeries. But it's possible he has a genuine card, or he's not on a farm at all. All that about the pigs might be hokum – though there can't be many Germans who'd know a word like 'farrow'."

The Chief took the papers out of Mike's hands. "Anyway, I'd prefer to avoid a fuss. Large-scale inspections cause talk. If the public get to know, we'll have to prosecute him, and you know how I feel about prosecuting spies – the only good spy is a living spy. They're full of useful information, some of which we might not know we want until after they've been executed."

"Surely, sir – " Mike couldn't go on. His lips were numb. He was numb all over. Eddy, *executed?*

"Oh, if he meant to help us, he shouldn't get the death penalty. But the courts are unpredictable, and the public does love a good spy-hanging. So I'd rather keep him under our hats if we can."

Mike had a long argument with himself that night.

You can't inform on him. If he's caught, he might be hanged.

If we find him ourselves and arrest him quietly, it needn't go to court.

You can't be sure. Eddy may be afraid to tell the truth. If the Chief thinks he's lying, he might sacrifice him. We have to give some of them up. The public need to know the spy threat is real.

But is he any safer where he is? What about the Abwehr? What if they realise he's lying to them? They might drop another agent with instructions to kill him.

If British military intelligence can't find him, nor can one German agent working alone.

The Abwehr will know the name he's using. That would make it easier. He'd be safer in our custody.

But he'd find out you'd betrayed him. How would that feel?

Round and round in circles, until Mike got out of bed and went to the window.

What had the Chief said? "Not a single man in this room would put personal considerations before his duty to his country."

Was he wrong? Was there one man in the team who'd put his personal feelings before his duty? Was Mike that man?

Without meaning to, Eddy could blow the whole double agent network, a network that could save hundreds or thousands of lives by sending Hitler's generals false information about troop movements and shipping routes. They had to stop him.

That was why Mike had felt so bad. He'd known deep down that he'd have to tell the Chief that he'd met the agent they were calling Piglet. He couldn't live with himself if he didn't.

Cambridgeshire, October 1940

Mike checked the speedometer. It was easy to go too fast on the long fenland roads with their straight lines and sharp corners.

Bob Carter sat beside him. If someone had to be with him, Carter was better than most. He outranked Mike, but Mike knew him well enough not to have to say "sir" in every sentence.

Mike had thought of asking to be left out of it. The Chief might have agreed. So many farms had land girls now, they could probably have found him from Mike's description. But Mike would know him on sight. Nobody else would.

And if Mike hid in the background now, he'd have to stay hidden. If he ever saw Eddy again, the secret would lie between them, poisoning their friendship. This way, everything would be above board. There might be some chance of forgiveness later, when it was all over.

"God, this place is bleak," Carter said, staring out at flat fields under a grey sky. "If he's all the way out here, it's a hell of journey to Norwich to post a letter. I don't suppose there's a bus."

"He might have the use of a bicycle." Mike imagined Eddy cycling down this road, carefree as he'd been in London. He'd whistle as he went, Mike thought, or sing. The picture stabbed at Mike's heart.

I don't want to do this.

Carter looked down at the map on his knees. "The next one's not far now. We're getting through them at a good lick. What do you say to a spot of lunch after this, if we can find a pub?"

"Suits me."

The farmhouse sat like a dirty white toad in the patchwork of fields and drainage ditches. The farmer came out to meet them at the open gate. Carter consulted his list and showed his hastily-arranged Ministry of Agriculture pass.

"Mr Hawkey? We're doing a pig survey, if you wouldn't mind giving us a moment of your time. How many pigs do you have at the moment?"

The farmer squinted at Carter's pass. "Four sows, one gilt, and eleven piglets born at the beginning of the month. I won't be keeping those."

Betsy farrowed last week. The dates fitted. All the hairs on Mike's arms stood on end.

Carter's voice sharpened. "We'll need to see them, and I'd like a word with your pigman."

The farmer scowled. "I don't have a pigman for five sows."

"What help do you have? According to our records, your land girl left in August. Did you get a replacement?"

"Not from the Land Army."

Mike blurted out, "Don't you have a young man working for you?"

Farmer Hawkey crossed his arms. "And why shouldn't I?"

Mike's heart thudded. Eddy was here, he was sure. In a moment Mike might see him. It didn't seem real.

His voice didn't sound like his own as he gave the farmer the cover story for the arrest. "We have information that he's lying about his age. He's under twenty-five. He should be in the forces."

"I don't know anything about that. His papers were all in order."

Carter cut in smoothly. "Nobody's suggesting it's your fault, Mr Hawkey. You won't be in any trouble. Be a good fellow and let us speak to him, will you?"

"I suppose you'd better come in," the farmer muttered.

Mike's pulse raced as they walked along the side of the house. Then the yard opened out, and on the far side, facing away from them, leaning over a low wall, was Eddy.

All Mike could see was a back view of boots and dirty overalls. It could have been anyone, but Mike's heart knew him. His skin knew him. Every inch of him knew Eddy.

Carter spoke a word to Hawkey, telling him to keep back. The less the farmer overheard, the better.

Something alerted Eddy – their steps or Carter's voice. He straightened up and turned round, freezing at the sight of their uniforms. A second later he recognised Mike, and a smile of pure joy flashed across his face. It was like a knife in Mike's chest. How could he have informed on this man, a man who'd been his friend and more? The police would have found him sooner or later. Mike hadn't needed to be involved.

Eddy's smile faded fast. He took a couple of steps towards them and stopped, his expression guarded.

"This is our chap, is it?" Carter said. "Looks like he knows you."

"Yes. Perhaps if I could have a word with him on my own … " Mike started walking.

"I think I'm supposed to prevent that kind of thing," Carter said mildly, keeping pace with him.

Eddy's eyes shifted from Mike to Carter as they came closer. His shoulders were tense, and his breathing was quick and short. He didn't speak, and Mike couldn't.

Carter said in a low voice, "Captain Robert Carter, Military Intelligence, Section Five. Best for you if we keep this as quiet as we can. We'll need to see your identity card, please."

Eddy took a step towards Carter and raised his hand as if to take the card from a pocket. Instead, he punched Carter in the stomach and ran.

Carter doubled over. Mike went after Eddy without thinking twice. He caught him before the far gate, grabbed his arms, and twisted one of them behind his back. Eddy bent, panting, his back pressed hard against Mike. Mike's body responded as if they'd been alone, heat rushing through him.

Mike pulled his hips away. "I'm sorry I had to do this. Don't run. Don't fight. We're not the Gestapo – tell the truth, and nobody will hurt you. Honestly."

"*You're* bloody hurting me," Eddy gasped.

It did sound as if he was in pain. Mike moved his hand down an inch or two, so the armlock wasn't so tight, but he kept a firm grip on Eddy's wrists.

Eddy relaxed a little and raised his head. "Did you know all the time? Did you follow me to the pub in London?"

Mike winced. Did Eddy think everything they'd done together was a lie? "Of course not."

"So why are you here?"

"Your letters to Portugal."

They couldn't say any more. Carter had recovered from the punch and caught them up.

"Nice work, Bernsey. Keep holding him – I seem to have left the handcuffs in the car. Don't flinch like that, Piglet, I'm not going to hit you. Don't go for me again, though. You pack a hell of a punch. Now, where's your identity card?"

Mike was still holding his arms. Eddy indicated with his chin. Carter unbuttoned the pocket of the shirt Eddy wore under his overalls and pulled out the card.

"Well, well. Edward Roberts, is it? I don't think so, pal." Carter turned the card so Mike could see. It had the telltale signs of a forgery – machine-folded, and all the information in Eddy's own writing.

"What's your real name?" Mike asked.

"Edward Roberts," Eddy insisted.

"Come on, man," Carter said. "This card screams 'Made in Germany'. *Wie heißen Sie?*"

Eddy's mouth tightened. "Edgar Keller."

"That's better," Carter said. "You're under arrest, Keller. Where's your room? We'll take you to fetch your things. You won't be coming back here."

"Can I say goodbye to Betsy?"

"Who's that? Farmer Hawkey's daughter?" Carter raised one eyebrow at Mike.

"The sow," Mike said. "In the letter, remember?"

"He wants to say goodbye to a pig? Good God, is this the best the Nazis could send us?" Carter shook his head in disbelief. "All right. No, not inside the pen." Eddy was trying to climb in. "You might have a gun hidden in there. You can wave to her from here."

Eddy leaned in, clicking his tongue. The sow pricked up her ears and tried to turn behind the rails that stopped her squashing her young. A couple of the piglets ran to him. Mike released one arm. Eddy reached down and tickled their heads, whispering to them. When he straightened up, his eyes were brimming with tears.

Mike had to look away. If only they could take the car and drive out of this war, just the two of them. He wouldn't even mind two or three piglets coming along.

Eddy's room was almost bare. Mike did the packing, taking a battered suitcase from the top of the wardrobe. Carter told Eddy to sit on the bed.

"Any weapons?" Carter asked. "Better tell us now. We're going to find them, anyway."

Eddy shook his head.

"Cyanide, for killing yourself in this very situation?"

"I threw that away."

Carter lit a cigarette and turned to look out of the window, as if to give them privacy. Good of him, Mike supposed, though he yearned to be truly alone with Eddy, to explain.

He stuffed a pitifully small collection of clothes into the suitcase. In the underwear drawer he found a beer mat like the ones at the Rose and Thorns. A souvenir? He lifted his eyes and saw Eddy watching him, his face expressionless.

Mike slipped the beer mat into the case. He felt he was putting his heart in with it.

"So you're German, are you? Not from Warwickshire," Mike muttered.

"I only said I'd lived in Warwickshire. I didn't tell you any lies."

Mike would have felt better if he had. Then the betrayal wouldn't have been one-sided.

"I was born in Berlin," Eddy said. "My father is German. My mother was half German, half Danish. She died when I was seven, and I went to live with her Danish cousin, who'd married an English farmer. I travelled to England with strangers." Eddy wrapped his arms around himself like a small boy feeling the cold. "I was terrified. Auntie Vib met me in London and took me to Heybourne. I'd never seen her before. She only knew a little German, Uncle Bert knew none at all, and I didn't speak English or Danish. But I loved them, and I loved the farm. After I settled in, I had the time of my life."

His eyes were distant and his voice soft. "I thought I'd stay with Vib and Bert for ever. They didn't have children, and they wanted to adopt me. Then my name would really have been Roberts. My father had remarried, and I thought he'd forgotten me. But when I was thirteen, my stepmother lost a baby and couldn't have another. My father decided he wanted me back, and there was nothing Vib and Bert could do."

Eddy ran a hand through his hair. His face was tight with pain. "Going back to Berlin was hard. Other boys teased me. I had no friends. Then the Nazis came to power, and my father joined the party."

The words came pouring out of him. "When the war started, I went into a propaganda unit, because I spoke English. Anything seemed better than joining the army to shoot men I might have known at the village school. Then someone from the Abwehr approached me. They wanted to drop me in by parachute so I could report from East Anglia. I saw it as a way to come back to this country. I didn't intend to tell them anything. I planned to stay in London until the invasion, then go to Vib and Bert when Germany was in control and I was safe from arrest. But you said something that made me think Britain might still win, and I thought I could help. I could tell the Abwehr the defences were stronger than they are, and it might stop Hitler invading."

Now Mike felt ten times worse. Not only was he responsible for Eddy being caught, but he'd been responsible for him writing the letters that had caused all the trouble in the first place.

Carter coughed, stubbed out his cigarette on the bricks outside the window, and turned back into the room. "Where's your wireless? You wrote in your letter you were trying to fix it."

"That wasn't true," Eddy said. "The wireless was heavy – it weighed me down on the jump, and I was afraid I'd land too hard and break my legs. I dropped it just before I hit the ground. It broke in pieces, so I buried it."

"You didn't keep the cipher disc? Pity. Where did you come down?"

"In Essex." Eddy named a village. "In a field, near a … I don't know what it's called. A huge torch they shine in the sky to see the planes."

"A searchlight?" Carter said. "Lucky for you it didn't spot you, isn't it? All right. The Chief will want us to dig up the wireless, but that's for another day. Have you found the secret ink, Bernsey?"

Mike shook his head. Eddy made a move towards the edge of the bed.

"Stay where you are, Piglet," Carter said.

"It's in the floor," Eddy said.

"Under this rug, is it? Have a look, Bernsey."

Mike pushed back the rug, lifted a loose floorboard, and reached into the dusty recess beneath. He brought out a paper bag containing a bottle of clear liquid, a fountain pen, and a miniature book.

Carter took the book. "*Romeo and Juliet* – for your code? Was that the Abwehr's choice? Not exactly a happy story, is it? Gets you in the mood for the cyanide, I suppose. Are you sure you're not hiding that somewhere? We'd hate to lose you. Check his pockets, Bernsey. No, on second thoughts perhaps I'd better do it."

Eddy stood for Carter to search him. There was nothing in his pockets but a handkerchief. He didn't meet Mike's eyes. Mike's own arms hung by his sides as he watched. He'd never felt so powerless in his life.

Central England, 1941-45

Eddy was interned for the rest of the war. At first the Chief wouldn't let Mike see him. Then Eddy was moved to another camp where Mike could visit, but by then Mike had been transferred into a liaison role that took him first to Glasgow, then to Belfast, then to Italy after Mussolini fell. The Chief didn't want him in the unit any more. That stung, but he told himself he was happier away from the whispers.

There'd been a lot of whispers. Either Carter had guessed or Eddy had told the Chief about their time in London. Both, perhaps. Mike didn't blame Eddy. He had to tell the truth. His life was at stake.

Eddy grew thin in the camp, but no more than any other civilian. The whole country was thin by the end of the war. He didn't lose his smile, and he always seemed glad to see Mike. The second camp had a farm, and he said he'd rather work there than for Farmer Hawkey.

"They won't let me write to Auntie Vib," Eddy said the first time Mike saw him.

"You're an official secret. They'll want her to think you're still in Germany, and you wouldn't be able to write from there."

Eddy brushed this off. "Will you tell her I'm all right? Not where I am, only that I'm alive and well."

Mike didn't want to. He'd be breaking the rules, breaking the law. Frustration washed over him – frustration with Eddy and himself and the war. He didn't like secrets any more. He wanted things out in the open, including his own guilt.

"Do you understand what I did? I betrayed our friendship. I told my CO that I'd met you in London and knew you were going to Whitstow."

"I know." Eddy didn't look hurt or even surprised. Perhaps there was hope.

"Would you have done the same?"

"No. I'd have come secretly and advised my friend to surrender before he was arrested."

All the breath went out of Mike's lungs. His shoulders sagged and his sinuses throbbed. Why hadn't he thought of that? He could have taken a bicycle and found Eddy in a weekend. Things would have been easier for Eddy if he'd given himself up to the police; the Chief hadn't liked him punching Carter. And there would have been no questions about his relationship with Mike.

Eddy added, "But I'm not you. You have a clearer sense of right and wrong. I act more on feelings. Would you deceive your own country? I don't think you would, even if you thought its government was evil."

The question hit a sore spot. Mike had never been comfortable with what Eddy had done. From the German point of view, Eddy was a traitor. Certainly Mike would never betray his king and country – but then he believed his country was right. What if he'd been a German citizen? Would he have followed the rules, gone into the army, and fought for fascism? He hoped not. Opposed Hitler openly? He wasn't sure he'd have the courage. But he would never have been a spy. He'd met enough agents to know he didn't have the quality they all shared – what the Chief called "bare-faced cheek".

Then there was the wireless. He accepted that Eddy had to jettison it on his jump, if he thought it would injure him. But to *bury* it, leaving it to rust in a field? That shocked Mike. He'd have carried it anywhere himself, however badly broken, for the pleasure of fiddling with it until it worked again. He wouldn't discard a broken machine any more than he'd throw away a jigsaw puzzle because it was in a thousand pieces.

"We're so different," he said, despairing.

Eddy said gently, "We're different, but we can still be friends." He touched his fingers against his own lips in a quick, casual gesture. A kiss, or the nearest he could get to it with the guard watching.

Mike took a risk and went to Heybourne. He told Vibeke and Bert Roberts that Eddy was in a safe place. It was what Eddy would have done.

They never talked about their time in London, not in front of the camp guards.

Warwickshire, September 1945

"He's out with the livestock," Vibeke Roberts told Mike. "Set yourself down, will you, and I'll go and find him."

She looked thin, tired, and ten years older than when Mike had seen her in 1941. Bert had died just after VE day, knowing the war in Europe was won and Eddy would soon come home to Vibeke. Rules had relaxed, and Eddy had been able to write to them.

"I'll find him," Mike told her. "Just point me in the right direction." He'd arrived in England three days before. Two nights at his mother's, and now he was here. He didn't want any more delays. He wanted to go to Eddy.

He crossed the yard to the milking shed. Eddy's mouth fell open at the sight of him, and he leapt up, almost knocking over a full pail.

"You're home! When did they let you out?"

Mike laughed. "*I* wasn't in prison."

"You know what I mean – out of your service." Eddy came over and put a hand on Mike's shoulder. "I'm so happy to see you. How long can you stay?"

Mike's heart was pounding. He wanted to hug Eddy, but they were in full view of the house. He tried to keep his voice steady. "How long do you want me to stay?"

Eddy tipped his head a little to one side as if he were weighing Mike up. "Well, we have room for a lodger. But you won't want to be here very long, will you? You'll want a job with the BBC, or something like that."

Mike shook his head. "There are a lot more former wireless operators than the BBC can employ. I'm hoping to work for the GPO, putting in telephone lines and linking up exchanges in country areas like this."

Eddy came closer. "I'd like you to work near us. I'd like it a lot. You'd be a long way from your mother, though."

"A very long way," Mike agreed. "My mother's marrying the commanding officer of a US Air Force base, and they're retiring to Iowa."

Eddy's eyebrows disappeared up into his curls. "Isn't that more than her ration?"

"American men aren't rationed, apparently."

Eddy grinned. "Oh, then we must go there on our holidays."

Mike knew he was teasing, but it made him voice a question he'd never been able to ask on his visits or in their censored letters.

"Were there men in the camp?"

Eddy's expression became serious, and he met Mike's eyes. "None who mattered."

The relief made Mike's knees shake.

"Were there men in Italy?" Eddy asked.

"None who mattered." Mike brushed his lips with his fingers in the gesture that meant a kiss.

Eddy's eyes twinkled. He headed away round the corner of the shed, beckoning Mike to follow. "Come with me. The pigs are round by here, but they won't mind."

Author's Note

This story and its characters are my own invention, but I have situated them in the real world of the misinformation sent to Germany by British-controlled German spies in the Second World War. The Chief's faith in his team is adapted from opinions expressed in *The Double-Cross System* by J. C. Masterman, but the Chief is not meant to be Masterman or any real MI5 officer. For research I also read *Deceiving Hitler* by Terry Crowdy and *Agent Tate* by Tommy Jonason and Simon Olsson. Any mistakes are, of course, mine.

We Live Without a Future

Julie Bozza

The sitting room on the ground floor was placed low, snugly nestled into the ground, and it was luminous and green with living light. At times it seemed as if it were all one with the garden, the Monk's House garden tended with ruthless beneficence by Leonard. At other times the living room seemed as if it were a peaceful dell of water, hidden far beneath the bright surface flow of the river.

In times past the room had seemed the quietest of refuges. Now it was piled about with the books they had rescued from the wreckage of the house in Mecklenburgh Square. And no matter how often Virginia wiped and scrubbed at the books, they seemed always smothered in the black soft dust left behind by the bombing.

Was it cowardly to admit, Virginia wondered, that she had been pleased to be forced to abandon their home in London? She had always felt that all of life was to be found in London, and yet now – perhaps she was growing old – the quietness of Rodmell village, steeped in Sussex rusticity, induced a long trance of pleasure. Even the Messerschmitt aeroplane that had been shot down nearby looked like nothing more than a moth that had settled with its wings extended on the grassy slope of Mount Caburn.

There were days and days of nothing but peace, freedom, just Leonard and Virginia doing for themselves, and reading and writing and corresponding, and biting into the crisp luxury of pears from the garden with the juice running down their chins.

Then another plane would grind low overhead, with a humming and a sawing and a buzzing that was so loud it vibrated through her very marrow. If she and Leonard were out walking, they would hide under a tree or at the edge of a haystack, lying face-down with arms sheltering their heads. "I don't want to die yet," Virginia said to Leonard. Though there was something fine and clean about the idea of Leonard and Virginia – the Wolves, as she liked to call them – standing tall and fierce, hand in hand in the open, and being broken together.

The bombs dropped – some as near as Lewes – but never quite found them at Rodmell. It seemed only a matter of time. And if not the bombs, then the German invasion, which was always to happen in the next week or two, or maybe the week after that. Shipping was massing at French ports, the Channel had never seemed narrower, and of course the air raids were only a Prologue to make the English cower, and Act One would open with the German troops landing at Eastbourne. The last time that England was successfully invaded, Virginia mused, was so long ago that the landing place at Pevensey was now a mile inland, and so that wouldn't do at all.

It seemed almost fated. Although in September a gale rose and England was saved once more by Armada weather. Despite which, the invasion still seemed inevitable.

The Wolves' group of friends had mostly survived the Great War, and the Spanish War – though they had lost Julian in Spain, and Nessa was for ever changed by a mother's grief for her favourite son – but now this was too much. Not only the air raids, the bombs, the ghastly stories and rumours one heard … It was all another step beyond anything reasonable, anything that could be understood, that could be survived.

Before the rationing made it impossible, Leonard had stowed a full can of petrol in the garage. That was to be their end: going to sleep in the car, perhaps even at midday if it became necessary, with Leonard reading to her, his beloved measured voice reading to her, so that she need not focus on the untimely darkness nor the rumble of the engine.

What made it necessary for him was that Leonard was a Jew. What made it necessary for her was that Virginia could not live at all comfortably without him, not any more. She would fall into madness again, and with Leonard gone there would be no one to catch her. Not even Vanessa could care for her as Leonard did. And it was said time and again that the invaders would force the subjugated to give up their Jews, and so it would not only be the Germans coming for Leonard, but the English pointing the way. How could they want to live?

Vita visited from Sissinghurst in February, and said that she and Harold had made plans likewise. They each had a lethal pill, which Harold called a 'bare bodkin'. Vita took it from her handbag, to show Virginia, and they peered at it together.

"Harold knows he's been too outspoken, you see," Vita explained as she put the pill away. "Well, just as outspoken as he should be, for us – but too loud on the wrong side of the question for Herr Hitler." She gave the title mockingly, and then leaned near Virginia again to say with sincerity, "You and Leonard, too, of course. You've both made your views plain on this fascist nightmare Germany has succumbed to. But not me!" Vita laughed lightly. "I am sure they neither know nor care that I exist – but then Harold says there'll be much I'd rather avoid. Who wants to be occupied? The pain, the humiliation … not to mention the sheer tedium."

Vita laughed again, and Virginia could hardly help but smile despite the topic. "It isn't only the politics," Virginia said, "but that Leonard is a Jew."

A pat on the hand from Vita. "I do remember, my darling!"

"And all our friends … " They were on the sofa in the upstairs sitting room, drinking tea, and now Virginia put down her cup and lay back to rest her head, unable to support the thought. "I cannot imagine that any one of us will not be in danger. Except perhaps Vanessa, though she'll be tainted by association, and I suppose they will not like her living apart from Clive. But think of our men! A good half of them are buggers, and the Nazis despise homosexuals."

"I know," said Vita with a sympathetic sigh.

"Did you ever talk with Isherwood? Morgan's friend?" That wild boy Isherwood, just a slip of a thing with quicksilver eyes. He had been forced to leave Berlin in 1933 when Hitler and the Nazi party came into power. It had been quite the haven until then. There had been a growing sense of freedom, real freedom. "If even half the boy's tales are true – "

"I know, I know. Arrests. Interrogations. Concentration camps. Death." Vita paused, before saying in straightforward tones, "The latter does seem preferable, if a choice must be made."

Virginia also sighed, still musing on Isherwood. As the war loomed, he had travelled to America and comparative safety. Some accused him of running away, but after what he had seen in Berlin, one could hardly blame him for wanting to escape.

"You're thinking … " Vita began, her hand pushing closer to Virginia's where it lay on the sofa seat. "You're thinking that Herr Hitler will not like Sapphists, either, nor feminists."

Virginia turned her head to consider Vita, and let the assumption stand.

Vita continued tartly, "Nor anyone who's ready, willing and able to speak against him. What hope do any of us have?" Then she put down her empty cup, and patted the sofa cushion between them so that Virginia felt the slight vibration of it ripple through her. "Now, my lively little squirrel," Vita said, "come nearer and nestle."

And Virginia wanted nothing more in all the world than to nestle with this enchantress – but a slight archness in Vita's tone made her bristle, a slight smugness and a coquettish smile made Virginia feel ignorant and dowdy, when moments before she would have happily sunk into that offered embrace and never surfaced till morning. Was it Vita's occasional cluelessness or Virginia's nervousness most to blame?

"Oh, no," Vita murmured sorrowfully. "Now I've made you skittish."

Virginia huffed irritably – but rather than let that ruin this chance of a cuddle, she took a deep breath and dived in closer to Vita, and somehow in the woman's arms she transformed from a sharp-elbowed scarecrow to something supple and strong. Vita slowly, deliciously edged closer – surreptitiously, as if it weren't utterly obvious what she was about – until at last she stole a kiss, and they communed directly, honestly, mouth to mouth. For a few moments Virginia felt a tidal surge of passion deep below …

… but then it gently ebbed away again, and the two of them settled into a warm bundle that contained all the perfections that Virginia had ever craved.

Leonard found them like that some while later, when he came in from the garden, the soil still darkening the whorls of his finger-pads. He grunted a greeting, completely unsurprised. "We have more leeks growing than will ever be wanted at Lewes market. Do you want to take some home with you, Vita?"

"That would be marvellous, Leonard, thank you," Vita replied warmly, smoothly, not shifting her hold on his wife, nor reminding him of the bounteous gardens at Sissinghurst.

"Good." For a moment, Leonard's piercing blue gaze considered Virginia, but then when he had satisfied himself that she was as happy as she might be, he turned away muttering, "Letters to answer." A moment later he was in his study, quietly closing the door behind him to give them privacy.

A still moment passed, and then Vita gently asked, "How are you *really*, my darling?"

Virginia sighed … and resisted the urge to tense up into her regular posture. "Don't let's spoil things, dearest."

And Vita pressed a kiss to Virginia's hair, and let all the dreary things be. The peace lasted all the afternoon, and all evening, and when Virginia lay down that night alone in her narrow bed, she slept as soundly as if there were no such things as dreams.

Vita left the next day, though, and despite all Leonard's tenderly firm care of Virginia, she grew restless again. There was *Between the Acts* to rescue from mediocrity, if she possibly could, but she could not concentrate, could not even quiet her mind enough to read something entirely unrelated. Not that revising her work was ever easy, but the task felt particularly freighted now, the heaviest of the many things weighing her down.

Neither did it help that the birds began mocking her whenever she walked down through the garden to her writing lodge. "Skimble-skamble," one squawked. "Skimble-skamble."

The water meadows stretched from the foot of their garden away into the hazy distance, peacefully gleaming under the cool clear sunshine.

"Nothing's solid!" another bird shrieked.

"Very solid or very shifting?" quibbled its mate.

"Nothing's solid!"

"What's the Channel?" chirped another. "What's the Channel, if they mean to invade us? What's the Channel?"

And if Virginia couldn't settle, then poor Leonard couldn't settle either, and he couldn't work, not properly. Not that he ever complained, but the world was darker without the light of his formidable intellect shining upon it, while it could do very well without a trivial novel about a village play.

"Orts, scraps and fragments!" the neighbour's chickens clucked. "Orts, scraps and fragments!"

Eventually, inevitably, it all narrowed down to only one solution. She had tried it before, but this time she would succeed. She owed it to herself to succeed. And Leonard would be stronger without her distractions, and somehow it seemed possible that England would be stronger, too, that England might stand firm against the forces ranged against it, if only it could be sure of this fiercely intelligent Jew standing firm on English soil, staring across the sea at the Continent. He might have his hands in his pockets, but his stature was unbending, and his sharp blue eyes saw through everything.

That was enough. That was more than enough. And she was just getting in the way.

"The wheels scurred on the gravel … the wheels scurred … scurred … the wheels scurred."

Each stone that she put into her coat pockets lightened her burdens, and then the river welcomed her down into its darkness, and the salt water promised her rest in the endless peaceful energy of the ocean. True, she struggled for long painful moments – but she struggled against the struggle – and her will was stronger, and she calmed again.

Virginia drifted past …

Author's Note

Virginia Woolf's personal fears relating to a Nazi invasion of Britain were founded in reality. The *Sonderfahndungsliste G.B.* ('Special Most Wanted List, Great Britain', 1940) included the following entries in a list of British residents to be arrested:

[W] 115. Woolf, Leonhard [*sic*], 1880 geb., Schriftsteller, RSHA V1 G 1.
[W] 116. Woolf, Virginia, Schriftstellerin, RSHA V1 G.

This translates as them both being writers wanted by the Reich Main Security Office, Scientific Research department. Also included on the list were others of the Bloomsbury circle, such as E.M. Forster, Harold Nicolson and Lytton Strachey.

Virginia and Leonard agreed to kill themselves using their car in the garage, should an invasion be successful. In the event, fearing a recurrence of mental illness, Virginia drowned herself in the River Ouse near Rodmell on 28 March 1941.

The story title is taken from her diary entry of 26 January that same year.

A Life to Live

R.A. Padmos

The last three families on the Isle of Kinnon stepped onto the small ship that would bring them to the mainland. Their sons of fighting age were all in the army. Their daughters, in the narrow window of time between girlhood and marriage, worked in the munitions factories and on the farms in England. What remained were the very young and the old, and now they too left. "We'll be back before you know it," they said to the one staying behind, but he and they knew that would never happen. The small island community had barely survived the Great War, but Thomas Wilson didn't fool himself into thinking they could ever return to old times.

"Are you sure? It'll be lonely," the captain of the evacuation ship asked.

Thomas nodded while pointing at the lighthouse at the top of the hill. Although it no longer functioned, it was still the highest landmark for miles around.

The captain shook his head and grinned. "Can't imagine the Krauts risking their Stukas to bomb a handful of sheep."

Thomas shrugged. He had felt death in the eager hands of flames, in the greedy tug of waves dragging him down, his serge uniform becoming his grave. He had felt it all in the same moment, though he knew water and fire could not exist at the same time. He had said his farewells to the men he had fucked, the men he had fallen in love with, the men he had admired from afar. Not a word of goodbye for the island he had left, because he would not have returned anyway. He wasn't a fisherman by nature, though he would probably have become one if the war hadn't taken him away. And so he had left gladly.

But now he was back on the island, as alive as he was dead.

There had been this young man, this curious-about-the-world lad, walking for hours through the unfamiliar landscape of the French countryside painted in yellows and greens. Wondering what he would paint if he had been a painter or write if he had been a poet. He knew he was that man, but the memory had no meaning to him beyond the acknowledgement of the mere fact. There were other broken shards of what he managed to recollect, but they never formed a recognisable pattern. Sand under his feet, the sound of the Stukas and dying men, boats, big and small, bobbing up and down the water … he had no idea what to do with those images, because he was neither a painter nor a writer.

For more than a week, there was nothing but blessed solitude. Thomas performed his tasks of taking care of the small garden and the chickens, which formed, together with the small cottage, the main worldly inheritance that Mother Maeve had left behind after her death at the age of ninety-seven, now more than a year ago. He prepared his meals, washed and mended his clothes, and above all walked over every inch of the island, as if he expected something new to find.

After nine days, he was ready for a trip to the mainland to get new provisions. He didn't need much, but what he needed, he'd rather not do without. Fuel for his boat and lamp, sugar, salt, tea, perhaps a bit of pork or anything else than mutton or fish, fresh vegetables and fruit if they were to be had because the garden still missed its mistress's hands and refused to be as fruitful as Thomas knew it could be, but anything canned would be welcome. He was able to survive for a very long time on what the island and the sea provided – he was a man alone after all – but that didn't mean he didn't enjoy the occasional sugar in the occasional tea. Better not forget his ration book.

It surprised him how little pleasure he derived from seeing other people after more than a week of total solitude. He admitted he was lonely, but being among fellow humans didn't do much to change that feeling. As he went from shop to shop, he was thankful for his limp, because it made it easy to explain why he, an otherwise healthy-looking man in his twenties, wasn't in uniform. Most damage was invisible, and was the real reason the physician had looked him in the eyes, after a long stay in a military hospital, only to say, "Go home, the war is over for you." It wasn't quite the truth, but Thomas had understood the spirit in which it was meant. The owner of the grocery store and the man in the pub knew enough of how he had been when he left for France and how he had returned, to see him with a mixture of admiration and pity. He didn't particularly care for either, but he still accepted the half pint of bitter gratefully.

Old man Jones raised a glass in his direction. "Down with Hitler! Care for a game of chess?"

"I'm afraid the weather might become a bit rough later on … next time, perhaps?" It was a lie, told in a polite voice and with a genuine smile, but still a lie. He remembered the time when he would have jumped at a chance to play chess against a sharp opponent. Now all he wanted was to down his bitter and be alone again.

The nightmare was forgotten before he was fully awake, but it still kept him from falling asleep again. He tried, for what he guessed might be a few minutes, half an hour, only to finally give up and, like most nights, walk the short distance to the lighthouse and climb the stairs to the top. He didn't need any light, because he knew every stone, every irregularity.

He looked out, watching how the light of the stars and the moon glistened over the water. He listened to the sound of the waves breaking against the southern rocks, of a Spitfire transported from the factory to one of the military airfields … Why would the ATA ferry a plane in the middle of the night, when German bombers were active? And why did the Spitfire sound like a Heinkel? But if it was a Heinkel, then why was a German fighter plane so far up north? And why did that plane sound as if it was in deep trouble? He stared into the distance, but couldn't see a trace of any plane.

Perhaps he should give sleep another try. The war would go on, with or without him.

With the incident of the previous night already half forgotten – though he knew what he had heard, precisely because he remembered at least some of it, and dreams were always lost before he became even aware of them – he walked to the southernmost part of the island. The sea had been rougher than usual and, who knew, there might be something worthwhile waiting for him, like driftwood or a barrel of who knew what. But when he noticed the motionless figure, he realised immediately what he had found.

The downed German pilot was lying on his face, his arms widespread. Thomas had to do something, since there was no one else to do it for him, so he prodded the man's shoulder. "Hey … "

What did he expect? A reaction? Something else other than the utter silence of a man if not dead, then very close to dying? He turned the body because for some reason he had to see the man's face.

He was dead. He had to be, because no living human being could be this pale, this unmoving. Did he breathe? If so, Thomas found no proof of it. He guessed all he was able to do now was to get the German a bit further away from the waves, inform the authorities and place the whole matter in their hands.

So why was this the moment to remember his favourite childhood story, the one he had asked Mother Maeve to tell over and over again?

Once upon a time, there was an old woman on an island. All the people on the island were friends with the old woman because she always took care of them when they were ill. She had a small house with a garden, books to read and a cat to keep her company. But there was one thing she didn't have. You have to know, that a long, long time ago the old woman did have a man and a son to love. Every day, except on Sunday, they took a boat to catch fish because that was what all men on the island did. One day the sea didn't want to give the old woman's man and son back. For a long time the old woman was so lonely she thought she would never smile again. But then a great war broke out. A mother and her child had to flee over the sea, but the ship they travelled on sank. Fishermen from the island found the mother and her child. They could not save the mother, but they brought the child to the old woman because they could not believe she was not able to help this cold, still boy …

She had refused to give up on him, so why did he give up so easily on this stranger? On the other hand, he had been a child, hardly more than a baby, too young even to remember anything from his past except for a few images that were probably fantasies anyway. This pilot, this enemy, had fought to protect the planes that dropped bombs on cities. He might be one who had dived his Stuka into the mass of already beaten soldiers on the beach of Dunkirk. He, or any of his mates. Did it matter?

Now this enemy was the one who was beaten. Pale and silent.

"They brought you to me so I could prepare you for a decent burial. With these hands I have welcomed every child on this island for the past sixty years and I washed the dead for their last journey, but I simply knew you still had your life to live."

Perhaps it was for this reason that Thomas bent down over the pilot to get rid of his life-jacket. He touched his face, his chest. He had never known a man could be this cold and still be alive. Did he imagine the thud … silence … silence … silence … silence … thud … silence … ? Most likely he did, but it was enough to make up his mind. He would try to help.

This was the first time he hated the fact that he was alone on an island in a sea not easily navigated. How was he supposed to get a dead or dying man to the relative warmth of his house? Drag him over the sharp stones? Even if the Kraut had been lucky enough not to have broken a couple of bones when he hit the water, the rocks at least would make sure there would be little left of his uniform and the skin on his back. Thomas couldn't stop a chuckle. If he wanted to finish off an enemy, he might just as well take a big boulder and bash his head in, which would be a lot less exhausting. Because this dripping wet, ice cold, unmoving log on his shoulders was wearing him down fast. Perhaps that was why it was possible that someone built like a boy, and a slender one at that, started to weigh so heavily that after a couple of minutes Thomas wondered if he could make it to his home. Less than half a mile it was across Kinnon, a nice, albeit short, walk, but this felt like an unending trudge. The uneven terrain didn't help much either.

"Hard to imagine why they accepted you in the Wehrmacht. Didn't they laugh and ask if you were old enough to leave your mama? That's probably why they sent you to join the pilots, isn't it? Small and light can't hurt in that job. I knew a guy once – in the biblical sense, yes, so it's a good thing you probably have no idea what I'm saying or you could get me in as much trouble as I can get you in – you remind me of. When you first saw him, you would think you could blow him away by simply breathing on him, but when I touched him, I found out he had some good muscles on him."

He wasn't a talker at the best of times – none of the islanders were – but if talking helped him put one foot in front of the other in a rhythm that would enable him to bring the man he was carrying to the safety of a house, then that was what he would be doing.

"You better still be alive, or I'm making a fool of myself. If I manage to keep you from dying, I'm obliged to hand you over to the authorities. Don't worry, they have comfortable prison camps for pilots like you. I know there are enough men and women in English cities who have every reason to tear you to pieces with their bare hands, but we're not Nazis. I think I remember seeing one of yours shooting a couple of mine after they had already surrendered, back in France, but that part of my mind broke on the beach of Dunkirk, so … " He stood still for a few seconds to catch his breath.

"I should simply drop you, walk away and notify the mainland I found a properly dead German pilot. Or even better, I should have kicked you back into the sea and let the crabs eat you." But while he said those harsh words, his feet moved again in the direction of Mother Maeve's cottage, which was now his cottage. "The woman who raised me never cared who my real parents were and where they came from. I was a child that needed her help in a time of war and that was enough for her. They should have left me on that Dunkirk beach, but someone obviously thought it a good idea to rescue me. Most of my days I find it hard to be thankful to my fellow soldiers who risked their lives to save mine, but here I am … and here you are … "

He kicked the door further open, lowered the still unconscious pilot on the bed and for a short moment stood helplessly because he had no idea what to do. Then he remembered that the first rule was a simple one. Get them warm first and only then see what more they need.

Should he remove the clothes? Leave them on? How could wearing something this soaking wet do anything but make things worse?

Actually getting the wet uniform from the uncooperative body of a full-grown man without any help wasn't easy, to say the least. Performing that task while being exhausted from carrying that same man across the island made Thomas wonder if he had gone permanently mad. He wrestled too many too big buttons through too many too small holes, to remove soaking wet textile clinging to clammy skin. Bootlaces tangled into tangles within tangles. But he had to get those clothes off that man or his body would never have a chance to warm up again, and so he fought the good fight.

"You don't hear me and I guess you don't understand English anyway, so I can safely say I've happily shared a bed with much uglier guys than what I am looking at right now. However, it's obvious that cold doesn't do a man's pecker much good. It'll be fine once your temperature is above freezing." He chuckled. "Not that I expect to be ever lucky enough to get a peek. I know, you're a Kraut and I'm a Tommy, but my eyes are fine and you can't blame a man for his appetite."

He tried to remember if he should wrap the pilot naked in blankets or give him some clothes first. The experienced fishermen would know, Mother Maeve would certainly, but they were not there with him to give advice. A warm hand-knitted sweater made from the wool of local sheep … no, later perhaps, now he had to wrap him in a couple of blankets as quickly and as tightly as he could, and give his body a chance to warm up.

"I don't think I ever saw an islander woman or girl from the age of seven without a pair of knitting needles in her hands. Everything for a meal on the table and a bit of money in the pocket. This isn't a good place to live. Fishing is dangerous because the sea knows little mercy, the climate is unkind and the only way to make anything grow except for grass is to scrape up whatever fertile soil there is, collect it and make tiny vegetable gardens. Much of what they need has to come from the mainland, and if the weather is too rough, well, they have to do without. And you know what? They survived, generation after generation, but now I'm not so sure if they'll ever return." He made a helpless gesture as if he wanted to throw the useless thoughts far away. "It's just me now."

There he was, talking to a man without even knowing if he was going the last steps towards death, or the first towards life. What more could he do but sit next to the bed and eat his reheated and grown cold again stew. He observed the face of the pilot for a while, simply because it was the kind of face he considered pleasant to look at. In another time and place, had he met a man like this, he might have taken the risk and thrown out some subtle hints …

"Look at me, falling for a Kraut who hasn't even opened his eyes yet. You look like a blue-eyed kind of lad. Grey, perhaps … no, definitely blue." Who was he even talking to? "It's the loneliness. Not being alone as such, I can deal with that and enjoy it too. But knowing that there will never be someone for me, that's hard when I was so close to finding someone to be with. There are a lot of men in the army, and there are always a few like me among them. Perhaps even one … well, a man can dream … The point is, that I was no longer alone. Even being in the same room with a man I knew to be like me, at least in that aspect, meant everything. A Stuka put an end to that on the beach of Dunkirk. I'm damaged goods now."

Did the man move? Make a small sound? Let out an audible breath? Thomas wasn't sure if he saw or heard anything, until the pilot whispered, "Wo bin ich?"

"I don't speak German."

"England?"

Look at that, a Kraut who understood and spoke English.

"Closer to Scotland. How are you doing?"

"Cold, very, very cold." The German shivered, his teeth chattering.

"I believe you on your word." Thomas looked into the linen chest to see if there was yet another woollen blanket. "Here you are."

"I've been captured? Am I a prisoner of war? Who are you?" The man looked around. "Where are the others?"

"What others? There weren't any crewmates of yours to be seen."

"The Heinkel ... I was supposed to protect them. They were in trouble. Then I got hit and ... I'm not sure ... If I'm a prisoner, why am I in a civilian home? This is a home, isn't it? And who are you? Why aren't you wearing a uniform? I demand ... "

"Calm down. Do you really think I carried you all this way to harm you? In that case I could have spared myself the trouble and left you to rot at South Point, where I found you. This is the Isle of Kinnon, the most northern part of England or the most southern of Scotland on the east coast, depending on whom you ask, if you insist on knowing. My name is Thomas Wilson."

"You saved me?"

Thomas shrugged and walked to the stove to make tea. "Here's something hot to drink."

The stranger tried to sit up, but winced in pain. "My ribs."

"You better lie still then." Thomas helped the stranger to take a few sips of the tea. "I even put in some sugar."

"Thank you."

"Do you have a name?"

"It's in my identity booklet. Did I lose it?"

"I didn't look for it," Thomas admitted, though he didn't have the heart to say he didn't even care to look for the name of a man who was likely to die.

"My name is Paul Brühl, I'm from Mainz, and that's all I'm volunteering until I see a fellow soldier."

"I don't need to know anything from you. As for being a soldier ... "

"I'm sorry. I didn't mean it that way. Where were you wounded? I noticed you have a limp, and I bet that's not half of it."

"Dunkirk."

"That was ... "

"I know." Thomas didn't want to talk about something he only remembered in shreds of memory, and certainly not with a Kraut. "You get some rest."

Thomas looked a while longer at the sleeping man. "Blue eyes, I was right about that," was the last thing he thought before he dozed off himself.

The human body is nothing if not resilient, Thomas realised, when he saw how soon Paul was able to get out of bed with some help, then move around the cottage without even needing the support of the furniture and finally followed him around the island like an excessively enthusiastic puppy. They even climbed the lighthouse together, and while Thomas assumed the pilot wouldn't be overly impressed by how far he was able to see, Paul couldn't stop saying how beautiful it all was. "But the best thing on this island is right here, beside me," and he turned toward Thomas and kissed him.

It was easy enough for Thomas to accept that he had fallen in love and to bask in the unexpected, and perhaps undeserved, joy of simply being close to someone who made his heart beat faster. It wasn't even all that hard to allow Paul to love him back. Or perhaps it wasn't love as such – that was too big a word – but the comfortable ease of pleasant company and the thrill of sex with a man for whom he wasn't second best or make-do. A slow getting to know each other over endless talks, a growing friendship and then, finally, an admission of mutual attraction, might have been the right way to go about it, but war didn't afford such wasteful luxuries. No, better to grab with both hands what was available.

"Can I look at you?" Paul asked, the very night after he kissed Thomas for the first time, not invited but enthusiastically welcomed.

Thomas didn't pretend he had no idea what the other man meant, and he undressed to show all the scars and the burns. Fear and hope battling like equally strong angels.

"Your body reminds me of this island."

"Rough and unforgiving?"

"Does the way my body reacts to yours look like I'm not attracted to you?"

"Still ... "

"You almost died and I almost died. Can't we have at least whatever time we're able to steal from the war?" Paul smiled. "Come here." And when Thomas joined him on the bed, he placed his hand against his chest and said, "You have a soul of glass. And I don't want to be the one to break it."

"And yet you will."

Paul nodded in calm resignation. Then he kissed Thomas, because what else was there to say about what they both knew to be true?

Later, after the physical needs of their bodies had been thoroughly sated, Paul traced the lines of every scar on Thomas's body.

"Were you there, at Dunkirk?" Thomas asked.

Paul started to laugh. "You think they would have entrusted me with a Stuka back in those days? A single one of those planes was worth more than my life to them. No, I had to learn to fly on an old beast." He became quiet as if he realised something, then continued to talk. "That doesn't mean I wouldn't have attacked you if I had been a year or so older, a bit more experienced as a pilot. I wasn't the one that did this to you, I obviously couldn't be, but I could have been … "

"I know that. Just as I know I would have fought you if I had still been in the army." Thomas held the other man closer. "Who cares what I'm doing on this godforgotten island? They pity me, the half-mad man on a deserted island … the war is somewhere else, my darling."

"The war is everywhere."

"Let them continue without us."

"We have no choice. You have to tell the authorities what happened to the pilot of the downed Heinkel. Sooner or later, they are going to find out, or do you really believe no one will ever get the idea of taking a look at their home or their sheep? Or what if someone decides this piece of rock has a military purpose after all? Knowing the British, they will treat me like a human being, but they will punish you severely."

"I'll be alone again."

"We had five days. How many men like us are able to say they had a whole world of their own for nearly a week?"

"You came here to bring death." It was not meant as an accusation, because they lived in a time of war and both had played their role in the big machine that devoured men in such massive numbers and yet never seemed to be satisfied. "But this is worse."

"You have to take me to the mainland in the morning, so I can officially surrender."

"Aren't you supposed to do everything to avoid capture and return to the Reich?" The words sounded pitiful to his own ears.

"I've seen the sea here, and your boat. I'm not suicidal." Paul kissed him with a force that told Thomas he had no intention of dying any time soon. "If that makes me a deserter, then so be it. They want me to fight and die for them, but I'm not good enough as I am. Not a real man. It's the same here, isn't it? There's no place for us in this world."

"We have a whole island all to ourselves."

Paul clutched him in his arms. "Perhaps, one day, but not yet … Please, let this story end with as few tears as possible."

Thomas nodded. "I will." But that night he dreamed of a sea too rough for his little boat to cross to the mainland, and it was the best dream he ever had.

The Town of Titipu

Adam Fitzroy

Appell that morning was the usual cold, miserable shuffle – down a chilly stone spiral, out over frost-glazed cobbles and slowly, muttering, into ragged and disgruntled lines. Freddie Lyon, gloved hands in the pockets of his greatcoat, balaclava covering his mouth, could scarcely summon the energy to look around him; it was winter, Saxony, wartime – what was there to see, after all? – yet at his side Bob Eversleigh, Freddie's close friend and confederate in whatever scheme might be currently in contemplation, seemed awake and alert, almost bouncing on his toes, like an over-excited child on Christmas morning.

"Parcels," he said, half under his breath. "There are parcels today. I can feel it in my water!"

Freddie had heard something of the sort a time or two before. "I'll believe it when I see it," he replied dourly.

"Miserable bastard!"

"Too right. And that's 'Miserable bastard, sir!', by the way, Pilot Officer."

"Yes *sir*, sir," grinned Bob as the parade was called to order. Silence fell – and so, again, did the snow.

It was routine now. There were days when the prisoners would cheerfully play up their German guards – changing places in the ranks, taking off or putting on caps or spectacles, stamping their feet or otherwise behaving as awkwardly as they could – and days when they just wanted to get it over with and get back inside, to the stoves in their quarters. It depended, too, which Germans were taking the parade: whey-faced lads who fell over their own feet and blushed when they had to speak were always fair game, although they were few and far between these days; the grizzled older men with exhausted expressions who had replaced them were as eager as the prisoners not to be kept standing around on icy mornings, and sometimes rewarded good behaviour with small concessions. Cultivating these, a little at a time, was one of Freddie's regular pursuits.

This morning it was Hauptmann Vogel who took the parade;

businesslike but fair, he treated the prisoners with respect and demanded the same from them in return. Vogel did his job, no more and no less; he was not among those who sought to belittle and discomfort the men he was guarding. He waited patiently as his staff meticulously counted their charges, entering the tally into a book proffered to him by a Gefreiter.

"And there are four in sickbay," he added aloud. "That is quite correct. There will be a distribution of parcels in the canteen at eleven o'clock." Bob's elbow landed squarely in Freddie's ribs, his whispered "I told you so!" lost in the general murmur of approval. "Your Parcels Officer will be required to assist," continued Vogel, ignoring the hubbub. "He should report to my office at ten thirty precisely." Briskly he saluted the Senior British Officer. "Thank you, Group Captain. Good morning, gentlemen."

"Remain on parade," instructed Group Captain Fyffe as Vogel and his men made themselves scarce; within moments the courtyard was in sole possession of the British. "I have good news," he continued. "As you know, some months ago I wrote to the manager of the Savoy Theatre – who happens to be my brother-in-law – asking for any costumes and other materials they could spare to enable us to put on a show. I'm now informed by the Kommandant that two large crates have been received at the gatehouse and must be unpacked under German supervision this afternoon." He paused there to look around pointedly at some of the more adventurous officers, who could convert anything from a tank to a toothbrush to some nefarious purpose or another. On the whole the Group Captain preferred not to know about most of their activities, and he rarely issued prohibitions of any sort; this time, however, was different. "I want one thing clearly understood," he continued. "I've given my personal undertaking that none of these supplies will be used except for the purpose intended, and that nothing will leave the theatre without my written authorisation. Loss of theatre privileges, especially in winter, would be detrimental to everybody at Hohnbach, so I'll ask you kindly not to abuse my trust. Officer of the Day, please."

"Sir." A tall, fair man stepped forward, wearing his RAF greatcoat over a Fair Isle sweater.

"Ah, Squadron Leader – we'd better have two men to deal with the crates, I think; I'll leave you to organise that. Gentlemen."

Dormandy snapped off a muddled, woolly-gloved salute as Fyffe took his leave, then returned his attention to the assembled ranks. "Right, then – Gerry, you heard the officer, you're going to Vogel's office for the parcels. Freddie and Bob, you can unpack the crates; if there's any whisky in there, it's mine. Other business? No? Good, I'm late for breakfast at the Café de Paris. Dismiss." And he was almost swept away under thundering hooves as the entire contingent attempted to get through a single doorway and back up into its quarters at the same time.

"Café de Paris!" laughed Bob, as they jostled in the mêlée. "I don't think the Dodo even knows where he is, half the time."

"I wouldn't bet on that." Freddie's observations of Francis Dormandy dated from before their arrival at Hohnbach, officially designated Stalag Luft XI and at the present time solely the domain of the RAF; they'd travelled across Italy in the same batch of prisoners and stopped at the same transit camps, making the same ambitious but ultimately futile attempts to escape from them. "He probably did, you know, before the war – have breakfast at the Café de Paris, I mean. He was a journalist or something." But here they were parted by the crush and the conversation was not resumed, which was just as well; a night hiding with Dormandy in woodland above Vestone had unexpectedly become a night of physical intimacy, about which he had no intention whatever of informing Bob. Sex with a man hadn't been an entirely new experience to Freddie but the Dodo's approach had been completely unexpected – and so had the absence of any reaction to it since; neither of them had mentioned it again, in fact, and it had never been repeated. Freddie was still trying to decide how he felt about that.

Parcel distribution at Hohnbach was well-regulated. Unlike Red Cross parcels, which were pooled to share out later and hoarded as long as possible, individual parcels could – and did, within limits – contain almost anything; prisoners had been known to write to Harrods or Fortnum and Mason for tins of sardines, Oxford marmalade or Gentleman's Relish, but more usually family members sent books, scarves, gloves, socks, or other items not available in camp. A list of recipients was posted by the canteen door; people came and stared at it, and more than half wandered away again with shoulders drooping. The more fortunate queued to sign for their parcels, then carried them off with exclamations of delight.

"It's from my brother!" Freddie erupted into the dormitory he shared with eleven others. "I hope he's sent some wedding cake!"

"The farmer or the solicitor?" The Dodo's lofty expression mildly disapproved of anyone not actively engaged in fighting the war, Freddie's two stay-at-home brothers not excluded.

"The farmer – the solicitor's already married. And my other brother, the submarine commander, isn't really the type." Freddie met Dormandy's gaze across the narrow gap between their bunks.

"Oh?" The Dodo inspected his fingernails nonchalantly and shrugged. "Not the type to get married?"

"No," said Freddie. "Apparently he's got a 'chum'. Hoping there'll be a picture of them both in here, actually." He was busy breaking open the parcel. "Cigarettes!" he exclaimed. "Fifty Players, thank goodness! Two pairs of pyjamas … how did they manage that? Mustard … Old Salopians magazine … Here we are, wedding cake, squashed but smells all right. And photographs." He paused, running his eye across the wedding group. "Dark-haired chap with a beard looks suitably artistic, but my money's on this one." He pointed to a tall, thin-featured individual at the end of the back row. "He looks awkward; they haven't really known where to put him. Besides, look at the way Thomas is scowling! Well done, Harry, sneaking him in under Tom's nose like that – I bet it caused a riot!"

"Keep your voice down," Dormandy told him, almost without inflection. The hubbub in the room had been enough to cover the more indiscreet aspects of their conversation, but he still looked uncomfortable. "Your brother's illegal proclivities are none of my concern – it's nothing to be proud of, is it?"

Freddie's eyebrows lifted, and he returned his attention to the Dodo. "That's a matter of opinion. The law can sometimes be wrong, you know."

"It can. But right or wrong, it's still the law." This was argument for the sake of it, Freddie realised, because arguing was the way the Dodo kept a formidable intellect from atrophying in the confined conditions of a POW camp in the midst of a war that didn't look likely to end in the immediate future.

"True. Only German law says we shouldn't escape from here, and that isn't going to stop us trying!" Freddie could see he was making no headway, however. "Look," he offered amicably, "why don't we just have a cigarette and then I'll read my magazine?"

This produced the closest to a smile that the Dodo had managed all morning. "One of those?" It was a necessary clarification; the cigarettes available in the camp were small, and rumoured to be made from shredded army socks.

"One of these." Freddie broke the seal on the Players tin and offered up the contents.

"Thank you." They lit one each and smoked in appreciative silence for a while, until the Dodo added cautiously, "You know, I'm a grumpy old bugger sometimes." It was the closest he would ever get to an apology.

"I know. And not just 'sometimes'. Don't worry, I'm used to you, and it doesn't trouble me a bit."

Lunch was what the Germans called 'stew', although bearing a closer resemblance to soup, and would have been a cheerless occasion had four men in the dormitory not received parcels that morning; Freddie's mustard improved the flavour considerably, and there was the rare treat of a wrapped barley-sugar each for dessert. Afterwards Freddie and Bob made their way to the gatehouse, where they were clearly expected, passing the guard on the courtyard entrance and sauntering down the cobbled slope as if the temperature wasn't well below freezing. Prisoners rarely hurried anywhere; appearing relaxed was an act of passive resistance to captivity, and they also valued every opportunity to look around for chances to escape. Freddie did so now, casting an eye over the embankment which led to the river meadows, noting that an extra guard-tower had been added at the corner of the wire. Tentative plans which had centred on this potential route out of Hohnbach would now have to be set aside, he realised; their preparations had been overtaken by events. Not that much would go to waste: the civilian clothing they'd made would be put to use on another scheme, and until then everything was safely stored in the attic above the chapel where nobody would ever find it.

Freddie's thoughts about escaping, however, took second place to Bob's excitement. The man was almost vibrating with tension, his hands clasping and unclasping as he walked, and the smile on his face would have melted an iceberg.

"Groupie didn't mention what they were sending," he remarked almost randomly, as though they'd been in the middle of a conversation. "Didn't know, I suppose."

"Well, it's bound to be better than anything we can improvise here," Freddie told him, encouragingly.

At the gatehouse they were nodded in by one of the less charming guards. Beside the officer's desk stood two tea-chests, nailed shut, and behind the desk was Hauptmann Vogel himself.

"You have two hours, gentlemen; I suggest you not waste them. Müller, open the first crate."

The Gefreiter – clearly the only person Vogel trusted with the claw hammer and screwdriver – made short work of the task; pulling aside a layer of straw, he exposed the crate's contents to view. Underneath, interleaved with tissue paper that could not have been less than fifty or sixty years old, was something the colour of faded gold.

"Good grief." Freddie was unable to believe his eyes. "Is that ... Could that actually be ... silk?" Gefreiter Müller had continued his work, prising the lid from the second crate and revealing several mysterious packages which had a pungent smell. "Wigs ... greasepaint ... sheet music, everything we need."

"For what?" Bob was delving deeper, bringing out layer upon layer of coloured costumes well beyond the first flush of youth, their frayed hems and threadbare panels eloquent of a long and illustrious history.

"*The Mikado*. They've sent us everything we could possibly need to put on a production of *The Mikado!*"

"Really? *Really!*" Bob, apparently hypnotised by the pile of shabby lilac and ultramarine kimonos, the scarlet and sky-blue sashes, the wooden swords, the fans, seemed incapable of coherent communication; it was as if his mouth had gone on speaking while his brain was engaged elsewhere.

"Unfortunate that Japan happens to be on the other side in the war," mused Freddie. "It would be like trying to stage *Rosenkavalier* or *The Magic Flute* in London; nobody would want to know."

"Oh, but they're still doing that! And anyway it's like a panto, it's funny, who could possibly object?"

The list, thought Freddie, was a long one, and would begin with the Group Captain. On the other hand, he was the one who'd solicited the donation of costumes – and if there had been a particular reason for wanting to avoid Japanese ones no doubt he could have said so in his letter. He would have to be consulted before they went ahead, of course, but would perhaps take a lenient view of the project in the circumstances.

"We're a bit light on musicians, too," he continued, aware that to all intents and purposes he was speaking to himself. "One piano, one flute and one violin; we're hardly the D'Oyly Carte, are we?"

"No, more like the Oily Cart! No reason not to try it, though, is there?"

"We're also short of sopranos, although I suppose we can transpose everything down an octave or two."

"Or find people who can sing falsetto." Bob was rifling through the box of greasepaint: there were some new sticks, and even more part-used ones that were dry but could be revived with care. Clearly, when the Group Captain's plea for help had been received, someone had emptied out the contents of a long-forgotten backstage cupboard and shipped off everything but the mothballs.

"Well, I can't, for one," said Freddie, "but I'll be playing the piano anyway. That's the way it always seemed to end up at school." He had reached the bottom of his crate; it was lined with a sheet of newspaper bearing casualty lists from the Battle of the Somme.

"I can," replied Bob, and coming from a man with a burgeoning RAF moustache it was a distinctly incongruous assertion. "I was a treble in the church choir; I used to sing solos. My mother thought I was going to be another Ernest Lough – you know, 'O for the Wings of a Dove'?"

"Right, then, we'll put you down for Yum-Yum, assuming you can hit the top notes," Freddie told him decisively. "And the other two little maids can be baritones." Groupie had always been quite clear that it would be Freddie's job to direct whatever entertainment might emerge from the donated materials, and the picture was beginning to take shape in his mind already; with limited resources, it would have to be a halfway house between a straight production and a parody – which, when he came to think about it, was what *The Mikado* was anyway.

He was still mentally allocating roles when Hauptmann Vogel coughed as discreetly as any Belgravian butler and reminded them that they were supposed to be inventorying the contents of the two tea-chests. They settled down to do so under his tolerant supervisory gaze.

A week later, reasons for the German officer's forbearance began to reveal themselves. Freddie was alone in the theatre, under parole, with the piano in pieces; he had removed everything he could possibly remove and was now burrowing around inside the carcass, pausing occasionally to strike one of a set of tuning-forks and try to extract a note from the corresponding key. Unlike the one in the chapel, which had been used frequently and remained in good condition, this instrument had been neglected for quite some time before the British prisoners had arrived at Hohnbach. Freddie's limited tuning experience had never encompassed anything quite so badly awry as his present customer, and he'd been attending to it in stages since his arrival at the castle. Only when the retired music teacher who was the organist of the village church had been prevailed upon to donate a proper set of tuning implements – complete with fork, hammer and mutes – had he made appreciable progress, but not until Hauptmann Vogel made his leisurely patrol of the theatre had anyone gone so far as to remark upon an improvement.

"Flight Lieutenant Lyon, I think you are getting somewhere at last!" he exclaimed in amusement, stepping onto the stage.

Freddie straightened up and grinned at him. Very occasionally Vogel behaved like a real human being, and at such times it was difficult to remember he was supposed to be an enemy.

"Do you think so, Hauptmann?"

"Yes, indeed. In fact, if I may?"

Nonplussed at first, Freddie was not immediately certain what Vogel had in mind. However a simple gesture towards the piano and the unexpected removal of the German officer's cap indicated his intention. His hair was white, Freddie noticed with surprise, and combined with mild grey eyes and a somewhat weak mouth gave him a distinctly benevolent look; he might have been a cricket umpire or a genial grocer rather than the representative of an enemy power.

Freddie moved aside and shunted the worm-eaten piano stool back into position. "It won't sound right without the front on, of course," he murmured, but it was obvious Vogel knew that already.

"Well, then, we will give it the benefit of the doubt," he returned smoothly, his fingers finding the opening bars of what Freddie quickly recognised as Chopin's Nocturne in E-flat major.

Into the dusty first floor prison theatre, lit by panels of amber glass which gave onto an unforgiving winter sky, Hauptmann Werner Vogel of the Wehrmacht poured the liquid balm of music, his only audience an enraptured officer of the Royal Air Force. In later years, that would be one of Freddie Lyon's most compelling memories of his wartime service – the day one of his captors had cast aside the political differences between them and, briefly, paused in his duties to share a moment of transcendent joy. And most of the notes, Freddie was delighted to hear, sounded more or less true.

Afterwards Freddie gave Vogel a standing ovation; the Hauptmann, as though embarrassed by his minor act of insubordination, jammed his cap back onto his head and smiled awkwardly.

"You must have studied, Hauptmann, surely?"

"Oh yes, in Vienna – but that was a long time ago. And you, Flight Lieutenant? I have heard you playing in the chapel."

"Not to your standard, I'm afraid, but any saloon bar with a piano and I can play 'Roll out the Barrel'. I had a few lessons at school, but I'm mostly self-taught. Good enough for this place, though," Freddie added wistfully. "You, on the other hand … " He left the sentence unfinished. The inference that the Hauptmann's past had featured elegant recitals in chandeliered halls was irresistible, but that had been another life – and the life which had existed before Hohnbach was something nobody from either side cared to dwell upon in any detail. Neither that, nor the life that was to come.

"Well, this should remain our secret, I think," was the quiet suggestion from the German. "The Kommandant would perhaps not wholly approve, but he has gone to Leipzig for a meeting."

"I won't tell him, Hauptmann, if you don't," grinned Freddie, and was rewarded with a conspiratorial nod of the head from Vogel as he took his departure from the theatre.

Rehearsals began the following day. There was little or no need for an audition process: the little maids virtually chose themselves – beefy ex-rugby-playing types with formidable facial hair, who could produce the occasional comically squeaky high note – and beyond that the casting was of the 'any warm body will do' variety. Freddie's initial concern that the cast would outnumber the audience, however, was soon allayed; some fair-weather friends dropped out when it became clear that actual work was going to be required, one or two were loud in their disapproval of what could be construed as wearing women's clothing, and in the end he was left with a core group of players to cover the major roles and a couple of volunteers dedicated to constructing scenery and painting it. The Mikado, however, was proving something of a challenge; he had begun to contemplate playing the role himself, and had even considered asking if Hauptmann Vogel might stand in on the piano while he got up on stage to sing, but no matter how respectful relations between the Germans and their prisoners might be he could hardly imagine High Command on either side approving this particular request. Personally he was inclined to see this as an opportunity lost, but he quite understood their point.

In other respects, however, progress was rapid. After only a couple of individual rehearsals with Freddie, Bob could make quite a reasonable showing in 'The Sun Whose Rays' – although coaching the two carthorses through 'Braid the Raven Hair' was proving something of a trial. Squadron Leader Dormandy, however, had taken like a duck to water to the role of Ko-Ko and could frequently be discovered enumerating his 'little list' in turret stairwells, lavatories, store cupboards and a variety of other unlikely auditoria.

It was Bob Eversleigh, though, who seemed by far the most enthusiastic participant. Although he had been teased mercilessly about accepting the role of a romantic heroine, he had stood his ground and answered only that he expected to be rather good. He had then, in a quiet moment, secured permission to have Group Captain Fyffe's batman, Spalding – a cheerful Cockney who was a barber in civilian life – dispatch his moustache as professionally as possible for the duration, which had left him temporarily with baby-soft skin and a slight pink flush to his cheeks. Shortly after that, when the costumes had been brought to the camp theatre and installed in what would have to be the changing room behind the stage, he spent a whole morning selecting a kimono for the performance, eventually settling on a fuchsia-pink creation embellished with yellow roses. There was only one wig in anything like fit condition for a heroine and Spalding had undertaken to restore that to health, but the carthorses had elected to wear the dregs of the collection in all their tattered and lopsided glory. They had also been allocated the worst of the kimonos, which were to be held together with uniform braces, leather belts, and – in one case – a Free Foresters' cricket club tie. Bob regarded his little maids with something resembling sympathy;

they might be as comical and maladroit as they chose, but he made it abundantly clear that he intended to be elegant. He would be the principal boy, and they would be a clod-hopping chorus line of Widow Twankeys.

It was almost by accident that Freddie ended up casting Gerry in the role of the Mikado. Gerry, who would one day be a duke, was interested in a more literal form of escape than Freddie himself had in mind, but approached him suggesting what he diffidently referred to as a mutually beneficial arrangement.

"I'll sing for you," he offered, "if I can get a good look round the theatre in exchange."

This was uncharacteristic, except in the sense that Gerry was always looking for opportunities to examine areas of the castle previously unavailable to him; his excursions up chimneys and under floorboards elsewhere had often been the starting point for escape schemes, some of which had gone a long way towards succeeding before the Germans nipped them in the bud.

"I've never really heard you sing," was Freddie's immediate response. "You hardly seem to open your mouth in chapel." Which was not strictly fair; he had been aware of a sort of bass rumble that could have been anything, but there was no sort of projection involved which might lead him to think Gerry capable of reaching the back seat of a motor car – let alone the back row of an audience. "Can you actually hit the low notes?"

"In 'A More Humane Mikado'? I'd need to practise, but I should manage it all right. *Elliptical bi-hilliard balls*," Gerry bellowed, at a volume which made Freddie want to take a step backward. "*Elliptical bi-hilliard bawlllls.*"

"Good lord!" Coming from someone with such a small and slender frame, the magnificence of the voice was almost impossible to believe.

"I know." Gerry shrugged modestly. "Awful, isn't it? My Uncle Peter always tells me my voice is a foot taller than I am."

"Your voice, Gerry, belongs to a man of at least six-foot-six and built like Oliver Hardy," retorted Freddie, grinning. "Why do you never sing like that in chapel? No, don't answer that; I know." There were one or two strong singers who always seemed to dominate proceedings, and a few more who yodelled along cheerfully enough but couldn't carry a tune in a bucket. The whole thing was more like a chorus of cats than an act of worship, and as a result the hymn-singing was usually mercifully brief.

"Well, do I get the part?"

Freddie shrugged. "It's not as if I'm overwhelmed with applicants," he admitted. "Come to the next rehearsal and we'll run through the song properly. You can always have a look round while I'm working with other people."

"Done!" exclaimed Gerry, shaking Freddie's hand enthusiastically. "Good man!"

It was only after Gerry walked away, however, that Freddie began to wonder precisely what had been done, and to whom. Nevertheless from the next rehearsal, when Gerry turned up virtually word-perfect, the production began to take on a life of its own; actually having a Mikado for *The Mikado* gave it a coherence that no amount of warbling falsetto or comic patter could adequately supply, as if Gerry's casting had provided the piece of the puzzle that finally rendered the picture whole.

Hauptmann Vogel continued to take what Freddie had begun to consider a professional interest in the proceedings, and he often managed to ensure that he was on duty during the rehearsals. This did not noticeably hinder Gerry's surreptitious activities, as he was supported by one or two gentlemen of the chorus who kept a close eye on the movements of the Germans and were able to warn him if any looked like approaching too closely, but from time to time he cut it very fine indeed. Indeed, on one occasion, he was pulled out from under the stage with only seconds to spare; the boots of a patrol were already audible on the stairs. Covered in dust, Gerry reached automatically for the nearest disguise – one of the tattered 'maid' kimonos and wigs, and one of the pleated paper fans which he flourished flirtatiously in Gefreiter Müller's direction as he entered the room.

The humour of Gerry's instinctive reaction conveyed itself to everybody present, with the possible exception of Müller himself. Mildly affronted, but clearly willing to put this down to the well-known eccentricities of the British, Müller wandered around the theatre briefly. He checked that the tools and paint permitted for scenery construction were all still present, idly opened the lid of the piano and found it innocent of contraband, and eventually stood at the door saying, "You may carry on, gentlemen," as politely as if he had been Vogel himself. Vogel, however, with his clearer understanding of what the performance involved, would not have been fooled for a moment by Flight Lieutenant Bredon's impromptu performance as a little maid.

"Good God, Gerry, that was quick thinking," said the Dodo quietly as Müller's footsteps retreated towards the courtyard. "Bastard nearly got you that time!"

The general consensus was much the same, with murmurs of approval as Gerry divested himself of his borrowed plumage. There was one countervailing opinion, however, and it was expressed clearly and trenchantly from stage left, where Bob Eversleigh had been standing like a statue throughout the unexpected intervention.

"As a matter of fact, I think it's bloody selfish," he proclaimed. "You're putting all of us in danger. Remember what Groupie said about losing our theatre privileges? Some of us actually care about this sort of thing, you know!"

"Oh, don't be ridiculous, Bob!" Gerry was quick to defend himself, and his gentlemen of the chorus seemed more than willing to take up the cudgels on his behalf. "It's only a silly play! There are more important things to think about, like getting out of here and getting back to our units, for example."

"Silly?" Bob echoed, as though the meaning of the word eluded him. "It isn't silly at all. Don't you realise that this – theatre, art, music – is part of what we've been fighting for all this time?"

"What, your right to dress up in a frock and sing in a high voice?" Gerry, hands on hips, was shaking his head in disbelief. "You need to grow up; this isn't country house theatricals, man, this is a theatre of war!"

"That's enough." Idle and lethargic as he might appear, Dormandy's voice was more than strong enough to carry across a parade ground; the occasions when he asserted his rank were few and far between, but he was always listened to when he did. Listened to, and obeyed with alacrity. "Flight Lieutenant Bredon, Pilot Officer Eversleigh – kindly pull yourselves together, both of you; if I hear another word of this 'conversation', now or at any other time, I'll arrange to have you excluded from the theatre permanently. For now, I suggest you both find something else to do … away from here, please. Freddie, I'd like a word. Carry on," he added to the others, "and let's try to keep it civil, shall we?" And, as though a switch had been thrown, everyone was suddenly employed in some gainful occupation and conspicuously not arguing, and Bob and Gerry were on their way out of the theatre and back to their quarters.

"Sir," said Freddie respectfully, as he and the Dodo stepped over towards a quiet corner. It didn't hurt to remember occasionally that they were military personnel and subject to certain measures designed to regularise their conduct.

"It's all right, I know you weren't involved." Dormandy kept his voice low, his tone confidential. "Gerry's going to have to watch his step, though; Bob's right, he could put us all in danger with his antics. I'll talk to Groupie and see what he wants done about it, but in the meantime I want you to find out what's ruffling Bob's feathers. It's not like him to get upset over something as trivial as that."

"It isn't," conceded Freddie, "but I don't think it's trivial to him. He cares a lot about all this – the show, the costumes, the music. He's a different man when he's rehearsing."

The Dodo nodded his head slowly. "He'll talk to you," he said. "He thinks the sun shines out of your backside. Help him to calm down if you can; we're all in the same boat, missing our families and our freedom, and we all have to bear it as patiently as possible and not make things worse for each other. If it's a question of psychiatric help," he sniffed, expressing his opinion either of those who ministered to the mind diseased or those who found themselves in need of their ministry, "it'll have to wait for the next Red Cross visit, and that could be six months away. Let's see if we can manage without that, shall we?"

"Yes, sir."

"Good man. Now, do you want to rehearse my 'little list' this morning, or shall we leave it for another time?"

"Let's rehearse," replied Freddie quickly, "while I've got you, and before you think of somewhere else you have to be." And for the next half hour or so they pattered on cheerfully about pestilential nuisances, banjo serenaders, ladies from the provinces, apologetic statesmen, and a great many other unpleasant-sounding people who never would be missed; they'd none of 'em be missed.

Confident that the Dodo would deal with the Gerry end of the equation, Freddie looked out for a suitable opportunity of talking to Bob about the contretemps in the theatre. It presented some difficulty; Bob was remarkably evasive in the day or two that followed, and even when they were together in the same room – which was a significant proportion of the time – he seemed to have his nose permanently buried in a book or to be writing a letter home, and on those occasions Freddie decided against interrupting him. Next time they were in the theatre, however, it was for a final solo rehearsal and costume adjustments; with the hour of the performance nearing there were now only minor details to attend to and therefore they were alone, and luckily Bob appeared to be in a reflective mood.

"Will we do another, do you think?" He was in his underwear and studiously applying make-up to his immaculately-shaven face, delineating arched eyebrows and Cupid's bow lips.

"Another show? Maybe," replied Freddie. "When we've had a chance to recover, anyway. In the New Year. Not that these costumes would be much use for anything else."

"Oh, I don't know – there's *The Geisha. Madame Butterfly* would be a bit advanced, I'm afraid. *Aladdin*'s set in China." Bob's voice trailed off wistfully. "It seems a shame to have all these wonderful costumes here and not make full use of them, doesn't it?"

It was a point Freddie hadn't actually considered before. "I suppose we could cut them up and make them into something else," he suggested, vaguely. "Ballgowns for *Cinderella*?"

Bob almost shuddered. "I'd hate to think of them being cut up," he said, "but at least that would be better than putting them back in their crates and forgetting about them again, like they seem to have done at the Savoy. They must have had better ones, mustn't they, to be able to do that?"

"Yes. Or maybe these belonged to the pre-1914 company, and they lost so many people they decided it was better to start again from scratch." At this, the conversation lapsed for a moment; the reminder was ever-present that their fathers' generation had endured conflict on a global scale only some thirty years or so earlier, and a few of their more seasoned officers had actually seen service in both wars.

"Well, we should do justice to them, then, shouldn't we?" Bob said firmly. "Don't want to sully the glorious reputation of the Oily Cart!" The name had stuck; elaborate posters bearing it had been painted to advertise the performance. "Pass me the wig will you, Freddie, please?"

Freddie did so, and with determination Bob settled the elderly wig on his head; then he graciously permitted Freddie to help him into the layered costume. Lacking pictures to work from, utilising only the limited resources of memory, nobody was in any position to vouch for the accuracy of the ensemble as authentic Japanese apparel; however, as the carthorses would be disporting themselves in kimonos over uniform trousers a certain amount of artistic licence might be considered allowable. Some of the more damaged costumes had already been cannibalised to make under-kimonos and sashes but this had taken time; the Hohnbach escape tailors had not liked being diverted from their regular pursuits, and had only now completed their specialist contributions to the project.

"Your sash, madam," said Freddie, pulling a wide strip of sky-blue around Bob's waist and fastening it competently at the back. "You're done – not that a real Japanese person would recognise you, mind!"

"This has nothing to do with Japaneseness," said Bob, teetering delicately towards the piano. "And since they're busy bombing our lot over in the Pacific I don't much care whether they recognise me or not!" The distinction between the reality of the Japanese contribution to the war and the mock-Oriental fantasyland that was the town of Titipu was evidently clear in his mind.

"True." Freddie laughed. "You know, for what it's worth I think W.S. Gilbert would rather have enjoyed this situation! It's wonderfully topsy-turvy, isn't it? He loved turning things upside down and inside out. I think he'd have been amused to see a Pilot Officer in the RAF getting all dressed up to play Yum-Yum in the middle of a war. Not that he'd have had much idea what the RAF was all about – or this war, either, for that matter." But his bonhomie was falling on stony ground; Bob had become unaccountably silent, and was staring at his reflection intently in the flyspecked glass that served the artistes for a mirror.

"Difficult to believe that it will all be over soon," he said, after what had threatened to become an interminable pause.

"The war?" Freddie, watching Bob from the corner of his eye as he set out his sheet music, could hardly help noticing a subtle change in his tone of voice, a barely-conscious softening of his mannerisms, and it came to him with the force of a revelation that he was looking not at an actor inhabiting a character but at the person his friend might have been if the randomness of Fate had dealt with him differently – if, in fact, he had been born into another gender altogether.

"The show," confirmed Bob. And then, almost as if he was embarrassed about having to say it, he added painfully, "I really don't know how I'm going to give this up."

"The costume?"

"Yes." Again Bob waited, not elaborating further on his remark but also failing to meet Freddie's searching gaze. If he had brought himself to do so, however, he would have realised that confusion and compassion were currently disputing dominance over his friend's mild and amiable features.

"It means that much to you?"

Bob shook his head violently, displacing the antique wig to a lopsided angle. When he moved to adjust it, Freddie could see that his hands were trembling.

"Oh, it's not what you're thinking!" Bob exclaimed defensively. "I just like to … like to … Women's outfits are really a lot nicer than ours, Freddie – always softer and kinder to the touch, don't you think?" These last words emerged all at a rush, without as much as a vestige of punctuation between them.

Carefully Freddie reached out, slid his fingertips appreciatively over the silk of Bob's sleeve. "Definitely. Not quite as practical, though. Well, not this outfit, anyway. Not much use if you're trying to pilot a Wellington, for example."

"True. But I like wearing them anyway." A nervous little gulp of laughter, but still Bob's eyes remained averted. "You don't seem half as shocked as I thought you'd be," he conceded at last.

"No? Well, maybe that's because I'm not. I'm not saying I suspected it or anything," Freddie went on to add, "but I'm certainly not uncomfortable with knowing. In fact, I'm honoured to be trusted; I imagine it's something you usually keep quiet about?"

"Yes. People don't understand, on the whole; they think it's peculiar. And of course I thought I'd seen the last of it for the duration. Locked everything in a cabin trunk and stuffed it in the attic of my mother's house in Devon; if I don't survive I'm afraid she's got a nasty shock coming when she opens it!"

"Hope it doesn't give the poor old girl a heart attack, then," grinned Freddie, elaborately callous for effect, and was rewarded with a sidelong glance and a half-chuckle. "Got a good collection? Dresses? Underwear?"

"Shoes, coats," Bob added, nodding. "Nylons. Some of the girls at home would give their eye teeth for the things I've got stashed away – although they're all in large sizes, of course. I sometimes wonder if I look ridiculous, but then there's nobody to see me; I draw the curtains and I never answer the door. Being in prison isn't really that much different, now I think about it."

Which, in itself, Freddie thought, was a searing indictment of the many types of prisons people were accustomed to building for themselves and others, using bars of conventionality and blocks of public ridicule.

"Well it's something to look forward to, isn't it, after the war?" He was careful to make his tone as gentle and neutral as possible. "Getting home to all your wonderful clothes?"

"Yes, it is. If I knew when that would be. If I knew they'd be safe. If I knew we were going to win. If I knew I'd live through it, really."

This was unanswerable, of course, and Freddie let it go. "Well, we'll have to come up with some sort of plan for keeping this lot around then," he said instead. "Maybe not the make-up and the wigs, but some of the costumes perhaps. It's not as if we could potentially use them as escape supplies, after all – not unless we suddenly get a delegation of Imperial Japanese courtiers visiting or something. What about parasols for the summer?" he added, brightly. "Shirts or waistcoats, even? If everybody's got something out of the collection nobody's really going to take a lot of notice of what you personally may or may not be wearing – are they?"

This observation seemed to hit Bob like a bolt from the blue. "'If everyone is somebody then no one's anybody'?" he gasped in astonishment.

"Absolutely! Of course that's Gilbert and Sullivan as well – *The Gondoliers.*" Which brought with it the germ of an idea Freddie was at pains to push directly to the back of his mind; the thought of starting another show at this stage was almost too horrible to contemplate, but he supposed it might not hurt to write home and ask for the music anyway. Thomas was always very useful for that sort of thing: his middle brother was a difficult man with few – if any – redeeming qualities, but he fancied himself as musical and might well be able to lay his hands on a copy of the score.

"You do understand," Bob went on, turning awkwardly to face Freddie for the first time since his revelation, "I'm not queer. Well, not in the usual sense, anyway. This isn't all some transparent excuse to get my hands on a man. If that was what I wanted, there are other ways of going about it – I imagine, anyway. It isn't because I want to droop daintily onto the Dodo's manly bosom or anything, I can assure you of that."

Don't you? thought Freddie, surprised. *I do. I miss him about as much as you miss your frillies, which I suspect is a hell of a lot more than you're saying.* But he kept the sentiment resolutely to himself.

"That's all right," he said instead, "it takes all sorts. Now, shall we go over your solo again, Miss Yum-Yum?"

"Yes, if you like," returned Bob, as diffidently as if it was an offer he could take or leave alone, but the look of contentment in his eyes conveyed a different impression altogether. He was as happy as a man could be, given the situation he was in, and as far as Freddie was concerned that knowledge fully justified any slight disequilibrium he himself might have been subjected to; that meant nothing to him at all, as long as he was able to help and support his friend.

"And how are the rehearsals going, Flight Lieutenant Lyon?" The theatre was empty again, apart from Freddie himself, but somehow this time Hauptmann Vogel's arrival had taken him less by surprise. "The first performance will be on Friday, I think?"

"Friday evening," Freddie confirmed. "Dress rehearsal tomorrow. We're still having trouble with some of the lyrics and the fans keep falling apart, but I'm quite sure we'll be ready in time for the opening night."

"Good. I understand the Kommandant has invited several people from the village to be present: Herr Behringer the organist, for example, although he will no doubt have some difficulty with the stairs."

"Really?" Freddie was taken aback at the notion; the Kommandant was rather a distant figure, and apart from giving permission for the show to take place he had scarcely been concerned in it at all. "Nice of him to make the effort – Herr Behringer, I mean. He must be at least ninety!"

"Oh yes, I think so. But it is a special occasion, and perhaps he wants to see whether you have succeeded in tuning the piano correctly. I have of course assured him that you have, but he is most particular in such matters and would no doubt prefer to find out for himself."

"Good man," enthused Freddie. "I hope I'm half as stubborn as he is when I'm the same age!"

"I hope so too, Flight Lieutenant." The obvious corollary, that this would require him to survive the war, remained unspoken; however, Freddie had no difficulty detecting it in Vogel's tone, which encouraged him to take more of a liberty with the Hauptmann's habitual courtesy than he had ever been tempted to try before.

"Hauptmann, may I ask you a rather odd question?" he began.

"You may ask, Flight Lieutenant, but I do not guarantee that I will give you an answer."

Freddie nodded. "Fair enough. It's just that … " It was difficult to know how to phrase it tactfully, and without giving away too much private information. "I believe one or two members of my cast would be very sorry to see the costumes packed away again and never re-used. In view of the fact that they're all in rather poor condition – the costumes, that is, not the cast – I was wondering whether we might be able to get permission to cut them up and make them into ordinary clothing. Our uniforms are all looking a bit shabby anyway, and if people are wearing stuff they've had sent from home … " Aware that he could perhaps be accused of babbling, Freddie drew there to a somewhat embarrassed halt. "Well, perhaps it's a ridiculous idea," he conceded wryly.

Vogel was watching him with an amused expression – one that made Freddie wonder, in fact, what the man would be like if ever he stopped being a German officer and became instead the person he had presumably been before the war. They could have shared a drink together quite amiably, he decided. They would have had a considerable amount in common, and no doubt enjoyed each other's company.

"It is certainly an *unusual* idea," Vogel agreed, after a moment's thought. "But not utterly impossible, I believe. I shall introduce the subject to the Kommandant if an opportunity presents itself." He paused. "Would I be correct in thinking," he added, perhaps emboldened by Freddie's own cautious overture, "that there may be members of your cast who place a particular value on having the chance to wear female costumes?"

"Ah." This was so unexpected that for a moment Freddie struggled to form a sufficiently non-committal response, but eventually he managed to pull himself together enough to continue. "It would be a justifiable inference, Hauptmann, but I'm sure you don't expect me to be any more forthcoming on the subject than that." He would not have said half so much, either, if it had not been Vogel who asked the question.

"No indeed," Vogel nodded. "Your discretion does you credit, Flight Lieutenant Lyon. Escape in wartime may take many different forms, may it not?"

"It may, Hauptmann. And some of them, I'm bound to say, are considerably less dangerous than others."

"Quite so." And with this Vogel seemed to recollect his duty and bring to an end this unexpectedly confidential discourse. "Well, I shall look forward to the performance with enthusiasm; good music is all too rare a treat in these present constrained circumstances."

"I can't promise it'll be *good* music, Hauptmann," Freddie told him, laughing, "but it will certainly be loud, and there'll be plenty of it, and that will have to do. See you at the show on Friday, then?"

"Yes. On Friday."

And they were smiling at each other now, which was not at all strange because nothing was the way it was supposed to be in the town of Titipu, and men could be women and enemies friends if that was what they chose to be – and that, Freddie felt, was certainly something that would be well worth singing about.

A Cup of Tea

Sandra Lindsey

Robin trailed along the road home from school, just far enough behind the other boys to catch the drift of their conversation, not so close that he'd draw their attention to his presence. The grammar school they all attended stood at the top of the hill, and though the other boys usually peeled off from the group in ones or twos as the route to their homes diverged from the main road, today they stuck together. To judge by the chatter drifting back towards Robin, they were headed right down into the oldest part of town, keen to gawp at any damage caused by the sudden overnight storm. Robin, then, would be lumbered with their company all the way down to his home. He usually walked the last few yards in blissful absence of any fellow schoolboys, though he was never short of greetings from neighbours and friends of his parents on that stretch of the high street.

If the boys had ever bothered to offer real friendship, Robin could have satisfied much of their curiosity hours ago – he'd seen from his bedroom window the mess made by the river bursting its banks, and PC Davies had called in during breakfast to ask his mother about room availability if there was a need to call in outside help to alleviate the situation. Not that he'd caught any more of the morning's conversation than that. His mother had noticed him loitering in the doorway and chased him from the house as if all possibility of his success in life hinged on never being late for school.

"Cor!" exclaimed one of the boys as the group stopped abruptly and Robin nearly tripped over his toes making sure he didn't walk into them. "The whole street's underwater!"

"Hey, look! They've got the army in!" replied another.

All the boys – Robin included – looked in the direction the second boy pointed. A crocodile-line of khaki uniforms snaked from the back of a Bedford lorry, parked high and dry on the opposite side of the bridge, down towards and through the ankle-deep water of the crossing. Soldiers passed sandbags hand-to-hand along this line, and then to a second group of soldiers who placed each bag in position at the edge of the roadway. It looked to Robin a little like shutting the stable door after the horse had bolted, but he supposed there must be some logic behind the men's actions. Perhaps more rain was forecast tonight, and the sandbags were a defence against the situation worsening. Not much comfort to those whose homes had already been flooded, but – as the picture house newsreels kept reminding everyone – people in the cities had it far worse with the bombing and suchlike.

The other boys started moving again, arguing with each other whether they'd be in trouble if they asked the soldiers what was happening, and Robin wandered homewards in their wake. He knew he ought to get a move on and head straight back so he could complete his chores before five o'clock opening, but something drew him to linger. Besides, he thought, justifying his actions to himself, the pub would probably be quiet tonight since many of their regular patrons lived over in the other side of town, across the bridge. That hadn't always been the case, of course. People didn't like to walk too far for their pint, but when Mrs Withenshaw decided she couldn't cope on her own any longer and closed the White Hart for the duration, all of her regulars had decamped to the Green Dragon.

They were close to the soldiers now. Close enough to see the sweat on their skin and lines of weariness around their eyes. A corporal was directing the operation at this end, and he turned and flashed a smile in the direction of the clump of schoolboys.

"Come to help us, lads?" he asked with a laugh. Then added, "Best go home and change first if you do want to lend a hand – I don't want to catch flak for you grubbying up your school uniforms."

"Do you need our help?" one of the older boys asked.

The corporal glanced over his men, then walked closer to them so he could speak without shouting. "Honestly? No, we've plenty of men, and we're all trained how to do jobs like this. You're welcome to help a bit if you want, but … " He shrugged. "No real need for you to. Just watch and learn – or go home and have your tea."

The boys nodded and thanked him, and the corporal returned to his task. Robin lounged just out of their line of sight, in the alleyway beside Mr Clark the grocer's shop, and watched as, over the next five minutes, the boys gradually drifted away back up the hill. When the corporal next looked over in their direction, all the other boys had left and the corporal seemed to smile to himself, then suddenly look back at Robin, as if his continued presence hadn't immediately registered. A slight frown marring his handsome face, the corporal strode over to Robin's hiding place.

"Not want to go home, lad?" he asked, looking directly into Robin's eyes and seeming to demand absolute honesty in his answer.

"No, sir, not that." Robin bit his lip, but the corporal waited as if knowing there was something Robin was holding back. "I was just thinking, sir, that you've all been labouring like this for a while now and – well – has anyone offered you anything in return?"

One of the corporal's eyebrows climbed towards his hat. "Offered us what, lad?"

"A cup of tea. I'm sure my mum would if I asked – she might not even know you're here cos you can't see this street from our downstairs windows, but I'm sure she'd be out here offering everyone tea if she saw how hard you're working."

The corporal laughed. "All of us, lad? I doubt your ration would quite stretch far enough."

"No." Robin smiled. "Not off our ration – Mum runs the Green Dragon, round the corner there. I'm sure our regulars wouldn't begrudge us if we ran short later in the week because of making tea for you."

"A pub, you say?" The corporal thought for a moment, then strode back to his men, gave them some instructions, then returned to Robin's side. "Come on then, let's go ask your mum if she'll make tea for a bunch of weary soldiers labouring to protect your town from the ravages of your own river water."

Robin laughed, pretty sure the soldier intended him to be amused, and was gratified to hear a low chuckle in return.

Robin's mum, when they arrived in her kitchen, said of course she could make tea for a dozen or so soldiers, and would they like some carrot cake as well? Then she chased both man and boy out from under her feet with a strong suggestion that Robin show Corporal Walker through to the parlour and she would call them when everything was ready.

"Is it just you and your mum here?" Corporal Walker asked after an initial awkward pause.

"And my little sister Elsie, sir. Our Dad's a POW over ... somewhere over in Europe. I'm not very good at Geography."

The corporal laughed. "Me neither. I leave that sort of thing to the officers. But call me Frank, if you would, while we're sat in your home."

"All right … Frank. And thank you." He tried to stop himself from smiling. It seemed a boyish reaction to being treated as a man and invited to address someone older by his first name.

"Not at all." Frank smiled in a friendly sort of way. "I've got a younger brother. I'd guess you're about the same age – David, his name is, he turned thirteen last September – though I've barely seen him since I joined up in 39."

"Is he any good at Geography?" It seemed a stupid question as soon as he'd said it, but Frank chuckled so Robin supposed it was all right to have asked it.

"Do you know, I have no idea. All his letters to me seem to be more concerned with girls than with school. He's not at a grammar like you, Robin. No smart uniforms in the Walker family so far, none of us have got further than the village school. David's been trying to decide what he should do when he leaves, and seems more concerned with which line of work will attract most girls than whether he's actually suited to the trade or not! I suppose all boys think like that at some point though."

"Do they?" The words were out of Robin's mouth before he could stop them. Something about how easy it was to talk to Frank, or maybe because he was a stranger whose path would probably never cross Robin's again, but suddenly Robin wanted to quiz Frank with all his worries and concerns about how different he seemed to other boys he knew.

Frank's expression changed fractionally. Something about the width of his smile made him seem wary. There was a pause, in which Frank looked at Robin. Perhaps he was trying to work out what was going through Robin's mind, or what Robin meant by his question.

Robin hoped he wouldn't be asked what he meant. He wasn't sure he even knew what he was asking.

"Most do," Frank said eventually, his voice softer than before, "though for some boys it's not until they grow into men that girls – or rather, women – become important to them."

"And the others?" Robin asked, equally soft. "Are there some men who never care about women finding them attractive?"

"Yes, but … " Frank looked away and breathed deeply through his nose before turning back to finish his sentence, "do you know what the law says about men who are … not attracted to women?"

"I know the Bible says that men and women should marry and have children."

"That's what the law says too, pretty much. Well, they'll let you off the having children because some people can't and you can't judge people for the way God made them. But … Robin, this is something you shouldn't really talk about. Just asking can make people suspicious of you, ok? Do you understand?"

Robin nodded, unnerved by the soldier's earnestness, but sensing this was something important.

"Some men aren't attracted to women. Some men are attracted to other men. It's … well, in my view it's just the way God works, making us all different, but the law doesn't see things like that, and nor do most people. The law says that a man who is attracted to other men can be sent to prison, that he should be kept separate from society because he's wrong." He paused, and directed an intense look at Robin as if he could see whether his words had gone in. "Do you see the danger in asking about this, Robin?"

Robin nodded, and swallowed a sudden lump of fear. "Yes … Yes. Thank you. I'll … remember what you've said."

Frank laid his hand on Robin's forearm. "It's ok, Robin, I'm not judging you. You're a lad who needed a question answered, and if your dad were here he would likely already have helped you understand how things are." Frank gave his arm a gentle squeeze, then let go. "I wouldn't worry about such things until you're older anyway. Concentrate on your schoolwork. That'll be your ticket to building a life that suits you."

Robin found himself smiling back at Frank again, and the strange atmosphere grown out of his question dissipated. "I think I just heard Mum coming out of the kitchen. Shall we see if she's ready for us to help?"

Frank grinned and stood, smoothing down his uniform. "Good idea, Robin. Lead the way!"

Letters

Eleanor Musgrove

Bridget squinted into the dusk, but she couldn't see a thing beyond her immediate surroundings. Blackout. It was really something; even now, she wasn't quite used to it. The trees rustled at the edges of the churchyard, but she couldn't hear any other sound. The village was still. Bridget's mother would have gone spare if she'd seen her out after sundown, before the war, afraid she'd catch her death of cold. Things had changed a lot since those innocent days, and now her mother accepted that Bridget needed to walk off the strains of the day sometimes. Since she didn't get home from work very early in the evening, this was her only opportunity to get outside. Bridget's mother didn't know where she actually went, however, or how little walking she actually did. After all, the church was only just down the road from their house, and once she was there she rarely wandered anywhere else.

Turning back to the task at hand, Bridget reached out blindly until her hands brushed polished stone. This particular monument was younger than she was, but not by very much. Bridget felt as if it had always been there, despite her dim memory of a collection being taken to pay for it when she was just seven years old. That had been twenty years ago, and it had been longer still since she had seen her father. She pressed her hand against the stone, tracing the outline of the familiar words on its face.

THIS MONUMENT WAS ERECTED
BY PUBLIC SUBSCRIPTION
IN GRATEFUL AND EVER LOVING MEMORY
OF THE MEN OF HIGH RANWELL WHO FELL
IN THE GREAT WAR 1914-1918

GREATER LOVE HATH NO MAN THAN THIS
THAT A MAN LAY DOWN HIS LIFE
FOR HIS FRIENDS

There were only twelve names on the memorial, spaced around the remaining three faces, but they were twelve too many. High Ranwell was not a large village, and those losses were felt deeply. Bridget felt the pain of one soldier's absence more keenly than most. Taking her soft-bristled brush and the small bucket of water she'd brought, she shuffled around the step of the memorial, one hand on it to guide her way, until she reached her destination.

"Daddy," she said, and spoke no more. If her father could hear her, he would know all the things she longed to say – that she missed him, that she loved him, that she wished she could remember him more clearly – and if not, she would only make a fool of herself talking to a carved and polished stone. Bridget liked to believe that he could hear her. On braver days, she would come and talk at length, as if he were right there beside her, telling him all about her day. She had only been discovered once; but the vicar, barely more than a boy himself and local, too, had been in a position to understand better than most.

"Don't worry," he'd told her, "I talk to them, too. Graves, I mean. Of course, the person's not there. They're with Our Lord, in Heaven. But I like to think that they'd still be interested in what we were doing. I never got to talk to my father – my earthly father, that is – about all the things I wish I could tell him now. So talk away." He'd chuckled, kneeling for a moment to touch a name on the memorial. CPL. G. HUGHES. "You know, when I was younger, when I decided that this church was where I belonged, my predecessor taught me all about its history. Even recent history. And he told me that this plot was chosen for its privacy, so that the families of those soldiers who were gone could sit and spend time with their loved ones, however they wished to do so. He lost one of his sons, too, you know. Nobody will judge you for talking to a bit of stone, not around here." Then he'd stood, smiled at her reassuringly, and walked away.

"Daddy, I miss you," she whispered.

"Bridge."

She dropped the brush and leapt back from the stone, terrified, but soon realised that the voice was feminine, familiar, and several feet behind her. "Iris? You scared the life out of me!"

"Sorry – the battery in my torch is running out and heaven knows when

I'll get another. And I'm sorry I'm late, it's been one of those days."

"Isn't every day? Still, you can't go creeping up on people in dark graveyards. You'll give someone a funny turn one of these days." Bridget's heart was pounding, although that wasn't necessarily just from the shock.

"I said sorry. Have you got started?"

"Pulled a particularly daring dandelion from the base at the front, but that's all. I've been paying my respects."

"Good. I like to do my fair share. Evening, Pa. Gentlemen." Iris never seemed self-conscious about talking to the memorial as if it were a full company of men in a mess hall, rather than a block of stone carved into an ornate cross. Bridget supposed she must be used to addressing wards full of men, given her job, but then Iris had been talking to the memorial for as long as it had been standing, long before she'd become a nurse. That was just the way Iris was: self-assured and completely indifferent to other people's judgement. She'd talked to inanimate objects and animals more than she talked to people, when they'd been at school.

Iris seemed to materialise out of the darkness on the other side of the memorial, her features more clearly visible with every step until she was just a few inches from Bridget's face.

"I love the night of the new moon," she told her, and Bridget could just about make out the cheeky grin that always preceded trouble. "Nobody can see us." Then she leaned in and brushed her lips over Bridget's.

"Iris!" Bridget laughed as her best friend – her everything – pulled away. "We're at the *church*! In front of our fathers' memorial!"

"You say that every time," Iris told her, unrepentant, "and every time you kiss me back."

"Not true. Sometimes I kiss you first." Tonight, however, she settled for reciprocating the gesture before picking up her brush from where it had landed on the stepped base of the stone cross. "And now to take care of Dad and his friends." She set the bristles against the thin layer of dirt collecting in the indentation forming the letters of her father's name. RFN. A. BILLINGSLEY. Sometimes Bridget wondered if they tended the memorial too often. They didn't use the brushes every day, but they always rubbed the stone down with a cloth, trying to keep it clean. Today, a bird had left its own tribute atop the stone block that formed the base of the cross. They would get to it, but first there were names to be cleaned and buffed.

They would work their way down from there.

As they cleaned, weeded and generally tended to the memorial, the two girls talked about their day. They always did. It was nice having someone to confide in about the struggles of everyday life. Mothers could get so worried, after all, and neither girl wanted to cause any more stress.

"How was work?" Iris asked, and Bridget answered with a sigh and a shake of her head. "Six today, and they never get easier. It's awful."

"Anyone I know? No, sorry, I know. You can't talk about it. Careless talk costs lives, after all."

"Perhaps not lives in this case, but feelings. As it happens, though, nobody I recognised got a telegram today. So probably nobody you know, either. How about you? Was it a really bad one?"

"Mostly the usual. Trying to help people who've lost limbs, or senses, or who've taken leave of their senses entirely. But then a man arrived who … He'd been shot down, he had the most horrific burns, but he'd managed to make it almost home before the plane caught fire. He … we nearly saved him. He was only young, and he just wanted to see England one last time. And all the time, all I could think was that he could be my brother. I … I just couldn't bear it."

"How is William?" Bridget reached to touch Iris's hand, a small gesture of comfort. "Have you heard from him?"

"Not recently. His last letter came a week ago, I told you about it. Well, then, Billy had written them weeks apart but they both came together. I don't know what happened. I suppose there is a war on."

"There is indeed. And on behalf of the Post Office, I'd like to formally apologise for any inconvenience caused by the delay."

"It wasn't a telegram, Bridge. Thank God. They're never good news."

"I do deliver normal ones, too, you know. Nothing to do with the war. Rich people's sons writing home, businesses with urgent messages to exchange between branches."

"But not for people like us. People like us, you and me, it only says one thing."

"Perhaps." Bridget sighed. "And no reply required. I don't know if I hate that little mark on the envelope, or love it. The sight of it fills me with dread, but it's better than cheerfully asking if there'll be any reply and then watching someone's world fall apart."

"Hm. I think I'd rather know. We don't often get to brace ourselves for bad news like that, certainly not in my line of work. If I have to break bad news to one more ma who's come down from the back of beyond to see her boy safe in his hospital bed … " Iris trailed off, a haunted look in her eyes. Then she reached down, wrenched a dandelion out of the ground, and threw it violently aside. Bridget reached out and put an arm around her friend's shoulder.

"You're the strongest person I know, Iris. I couldn't do what you do. That's why you're the nurse and I'm the messenger girl."

"William's the strong one. Out there, flying aeroplanes – "

"I don't think he could do what you do, either." Bridget nudged her gently with an elbow. "Besides, your uniform wouldn't look half as good on him."

"Oh, behave." But Iris kissed her cheek, and held her close for a long moment. "Thank you, Bridge. You always make me feel better."

"And you do the same for me. Every time, Iris Parsons. Now, I think we're done. Say goodbye to your dad, and let's get home before the sun rises. I think I can spare you a little light from my torch."

Iris moved away, and Bridget knew, despite the darkness, that she was pressing her hand to the deeply-cut letters she loved so well. FUS. R. PARSONS.

"Goodnight, Pa."

"Goodnight, Mr Parsons. You'd be proud of your daughter, I know you would. We all are." Then Bridget turned and brushed her fingers over her own father's name. "I hope you're proud of me, Daddy. I'm doing my best."

"I'm sure he'd be very proud."

Bridget felt an arm being linked through her own, and Iris pressed a brief kiss to her lips, taking advantage of the rare opportunity to do so unobserved. "Goodnight, Mr Billingsley. I'll see Bridget home."

"So chivalrous when you're trying to impress my dad," Bridget teased, and Iris sighed happily as she rested her head on Bridget's shoulder for a moment.

"Maybe I just don't trust you not to fall down a hole in the dark, trying to save your batteries. Besides, Ma gave me a book to pass along to your mother, and I imagine she'll want to send one over in return. Easier if I come along and facilitate it myself."

"Well, if you insist. It's not as if I mind spending a few extra minutes with you."

The walk from the churchyard to Bridget's house was a short one, and once they were there it became obvious that Mrs Billingsley had been looking out for her daughter.

"There you are, Bridget. I didn't know you'd gone out, I was worried about you."

"Sorry, Mum. I went to meet Iris on a whim."

"Well, I'm sure I don't know what she was doing on a whim in the first place." Mrs Billingsley turned to Iris with a weary smile. "Cup of tea, dear?"

"Thanks, Mrs B, but I've got to get back. Ma'll have supper ready by now. She asked me to run a book over to you, though – if you're interested?" She held the book out and Mrs Billingsley took it, scanning its covers eagerly.

"Oh, I haven't read this one since I was barely more than a girl! I do enjoy it." She opened the front cover and set about reading it there and then, standing in the hallway.

Bridget cleared her throat when her mother turned the page. "Will there be any reply, madam?" It was half a habit and half a joke, at this point, to pretend she was at work to get her mother's attention. It worked; Mrs Billingsley looked up with a start before chuckling and hurrying back into the living room.

"Oh, sorry, dear. Please thank your mother for me, Iris, and give her … " She had emerged into the hallway again, and was looking around for something. "Ah!" She reached into her handbag, hanging from its usual hook in the hallway, and pulled out a small book Bridget recognised. Shakespeare's Sonnets, her mother's greatest treasure. "Would you lend her this, with my regards? But, er, please ask her to be very careful with it. It's … Arthur gave it to me."

"I'll make sure she is," Iris assured her, taking the book with both hands and wrapping it in her handkerchief before tucking it safely into her own bag. "I'll get it back to you as soon as possible."

"Thank you." Mrs Billingsley smiled gratefully and took a step backwards. "Well, I mustn't keep you."

Iris took the dismissal with good grace. "Good night, Mrs B. Night, Bridget." She held Bridget's gaze for a moment longer, then turned and disappeared into the night.

Bridget watched her go, then turned her attention to more pressing matters. "Come on, Mum. Let's go and sit down."

"Hm? Oh. Yes." Her mother had already been engrossed in the book again. She'd become a little vague, distracted, since war had broken out. It all made the pain of her husband's death feel closer to home again, more painful than it had been since Bridget had been an infant. Sometimes it seemed to Bridget as though her mother had just stepped back from the world altogether, always just out of reach. "Cup of tea?"

"I'll make it, Mum. Go and read your book."

"You're a good girl, Bridgie."

Bridget didn't feel like a good girl, sometimes. Everywhere she went, she brought fear. To some people, she brought the worst news they'd ever hear.

"No," Peggy James gasped, falling back against the door frame, telegram clutched tightly in one trembling hand. "No … no, there'll be … there's no reply." Then she stepped backwards and closed the door. Bridget had barely turned away before she heard the first sobs through the door. Bridget had been at school with Peggy and David, but now she had no words of comfort to offer as one old friend mourned the loss of the other. Even if she'd known what to say, it was against Post Office rules; she delivered the bad news, she stuck to her script, and she moved along. There were more telegrams to deliver, and letters besides, with one of the postmen laid up in bed for the week. Apparently Home Guard training exercises were more dangerous than she'd ever imagined, and there had been an unfortunate incident with a pitchfork. Thinking about what sort of tomfoolery the old men and spotty youths of the local area might have been getting up to helped take Bridget's mind off her old friend and the terrible news she was delivering day in and day out – but once her shift ended, the dark thoughts came crowding back in.

"I feel like the angel of death," she admitted later, as she and Iris sat beside the war memorial. It really didn't need tending to tonight, but they had met there all the same. Routine was important in times of crisis – whatever crumbs of routine one could keep in the midst of blackouts and airraids and two-hour queues for rations. Iris's shift had been an earlier one than usual today, so they'd met in the last dregs of daylight, sitting innocently on the steps of the memorial where nobody would suspect anything untoward.

"You're not the angel of death," Iris assured her, patting her hand in gentle reassurance. "You're just my messenger."

"Oh, not at all. You save lives all the time! That's all you do, day in and day out: help people."

"All right, perhaps not the angel of death – though there's plenty of it, and the doctor likes to get us poor nurses to break the news. But I *do* feel like the angel of *it isn't working* and *you'll never see again* and *the good news is we managed to save one leg*. Gangrene," she clarified, noticing Bridget's shocked expression. "They do patch them up before they send them home, but … well, things go wrong."

"Poor bloke."

"He took it quite well, actually. Not sure if it's really hit him yet. You know how men are, stiff upper lip and all that. You never know what they're thinking."

"Mm. Thank heavens you're a little more straightforward," Bridget teased, trying to cheer her friend up, but Iris seemed to have slipped into a more melancholy state of contemplation.

"Nothing about us is straightforward any more, is it?"

Bridget hesitated for a moment before shifting a little further away from Iris and turning to look at her properly, noticing as she did so that the sky was turning a gorgeous purple, the sun sinking below the horizon.

"Do you want to go back to being straightforward? To being friends and nothing more?" Her voice was barely more than a whisper, but she was afraid all the same – afraid of being overheard, of being understood by anyone passing by … afraid of Iris's answer.

"Hm? Oh! No." Iris caught her hand and squeezed it, sending a wave of relief flooding through Bridget's body. "Not for anything."

Bridget walked Iris to work, one bright morning in September. The days weren't getting too much shorter just yet, so they'd had glorious sunshine, the first autumn leaves tumbling through the breeze to catch on the fabric of Iris's cape and cling to Bridget's uniform hat as they walked. It was a beautiful day – made more beautiful by the fact that Bridget had only had to deliver one horrible telegram. She had a spring in her step all day long until, at last, she all but skipped into the office to check for anything she might need to deliver on the way home. She took the single envelope and her good mood evaporated. There was the telltale mark on the outside of the letter, indicating that she needn't wait for a reply. Then she scanned the address and turned pale.

"Are you quite well, Miss Billingsley?"

"Hm? Oh. Yes, quite well. Just ready for my bed, I think. I'll see that this is delivered with all haste."

"I believe it's on your way home, in any case?"

"It is. I'll see you in the morning, Mr Hewitt."

"Take care, Miss Billingsley."

Bridget set off on her bicycle with a wobble – she hadn't wobbled on the bicycle in a very long time, but her hands were trembling now, turning the bicycle left and right and throwing her off balance. She righted herself, and made the journey to her destination without conscious thought, a familiar route to a familiar place. The next thing she knew, she was slowing down as she entered High Ranwell, trying to delay the inevitable. Slower and slower she went, until at last she coasted the last few yards to the right gate.

Stick to the script, Bridget, she told herself crossly as she forced herself to walk stiffly up the path. *Just stick to the script and get it over with.* She knocked on the door and waited.

"Bridge!" Iris looked so pleased to see her, Bridget could hardly stand it. "What are you doing here?" Then Iris seemed to register Bridget's pale expression, the envelope in her hands, and her face fell. "No."

GPO protocol was clear. Bridget was supposed to ask for the addressee, then hand over the telegram with her standard greeting, and leave without a fuss. What she did instead was hold it out and wait, trembling, as Iris cried out for her mother in a panic. Mrs Parsons' eyes lit up when she saw her, and then the reality of the situation hit home. Still Bridget held out the envelope, feeling like the lowest of the low. It felt as if she was betraying these people she loved, and who loved her; they all knew that telegram didn't say anything good. Mrs Parsons unfolded it and scanned it anxiously.

"Missing in action. Letter to follow." She looked up into Bridget's eyes. "No reply." Then, as calm as you like, she walked back inside and began clattering around in the kitchen. Bridget was surprised by her composure, but then she'd seen Mrs Parsons upset before and she usually retreated to her pots and pans while she processed the information.

Iris, however, was more direct.

"No ... William – "

"He could still – I mean, he's probably still – missing doesn't mean – " But Bridget's feeble attempts at comfort fell on deaf ears.

"But if his plane went down ... He could be d- Oh, God." Iris stumbled backwards, into the house, then reached out for Bridget. Bridget hesitated for a fraction of a second – *protocol* – before moving forwards to wrap her arms around her love. The door swung closed behind them.

Buttercup

Jay Lewis Taylor

To hear us grumble, you'd never have known we were all back safe from shepherding another Atlantic convoy, with no more than a torpedo dent in *Alceste*'s bottom; but there's nothing like being home with restrictions on leave to make a ship miserable. Commander Farren had no leave either, but then he could afford to pay for Mrs Commander's first-class ticket and install her in something cosy five minutes away, so *he* got to sleep ashore. In a bed.

June, twelve weeks' refit ahead of us, and only Liverpool and hammocks to spend it in. Life was shaping up to be dull as ditchwater until Chaplain the Rev. Harold Shorthouse, RN, had his very bright idea.

We were on the third game of uckers that week (ask no questions, but it's a cross between human ludo and outright war) when he stuck his head round the mess door and said, "Any of you lads sing?"

"Smudge does," Taff Evans said – the bastard, dropping me in it like that – and there was a mutter of agreement.

"You're the Welshman," I told him. "You can damn well sing too, boyo. Anyway, why, padre?"

"Thought we could do a bit of amusing the troops," the Rev. Shorthouse said, coming right in to the mess.

I grabbed a chair for him. "Pull up a bollard. What sort of thing?"

"Thanks, AB Smith." He sat down, broke open a pack of cigarettes, and handed them round the others when I shook my head. "I thought Gilbert and Sullivan, maybe. A couple of the officers are willing."

"Not going to be beat by the Wardroom," Taff said. "What say, lads?"

There was a general kerfuffle of agreement and disagreement, punctuated by the occasional "Can't sing for toffee, me."

"All right, all right," the chaplain said eventually, laughing. "Singers form fours to port, audience form a confused heap to starboard."

We got ourselves sorted out in the end. You'd think a man would know whether he can sing, but – not this lot. And then the Rev. said: "Who's the smallest?"

Taff coughed. He was pointing at me. So were several other people.

"*Oh* no," I said. "No you don't."

But it was too late.

"It's all right for you," I said to Taff later. "You're singing one of the crew. I'm bloody Josephine."

"Ah, stop dripping, Smudge," he said. "All those sisters, cousins and aunts in the same boat, so to speak – and at least we're all young 'uns. Spare a thought for him that's singing Buttercup, why don't you?"

That was Lieutenant Christopher Hall, RNVR, who had not long joined the ship. Rumour had it that in civvy life he was a hotel manager's son with a half-share in a fleet of yachts. It turned out later that he had a half-share in one yacht, which he had sailed to Dunkirk and back twice during Operation Dynamo, but what we knew for certain was that he could navigate blindfold and was a dead shot. If he minded being constantly joshed about having the Volunteer Reserve wavy instead of straight braid on his sleeves he didn't say, and most importantly he could sing, although his Buttercup sounded as if she'd been swigging gin and smoking blue-liners since cradle days.

"Couldn't you pitch a little higher, Lieutenant?" the chaplain asked once, to be answered with, "Saving myself for the right moment, Rev." Shorthouse didn't look terribly pleased, although I saw Lieutenant Hall talking to him later that evening and they were both smiling; so I reckoned that was one problem solved.

The other problem was … well, the other problem *might* have been the hero, Ralph Rackstraw, played by Danny O'Shea, or Rick as he was inevitably called. Rick and I had been oppos together as Boys Second Class, and he had made it to Leading Hand already despite being a year younger than me. Not that much of a surprise: he was better behaved in public, and cleverer at doing the right thing in front of an officer's nose, which is the way to get noticed.

No, the *real* problem was Lieutenant Wilkins, who was singing Dick Dead-Eye and taking the part of villain rather too seriously. He never had liked me, and now he was calling me Jo (not Josephine, which would have been a step too far for an officer) whenever he gave me an order, which was a damn sight too often.

"Want me to deck him one, accidental on purpose, Smudge?" Rick offered. "I could do it during the scene when he interrupts our escape."

"What, and get yourself trooped? Nah. I can bear it. Thanks for the offer, all the same." I thumped him on the shoulder and went off to learn some more lines.

In our earliest rehearsals we stood in line and sang like a choir in pews. It took a few days for the chaplain to persuade one of the sub-lieutenants to volunteer to block the staging, after which we could start acting and moving. That night, Lieutenant Hall at last stopped saving himself for the moment. He began his lines as usual, and then slid his voice up the scale to alto, where he held it for the rest of the rehearsal and some bloody long notes.

When he closed his mouth at the end of his first song there was a stunned silence, then applause. Rick muttered, "Talk about the Wavy Navy – the bloke was practically undulating. Are they all like that in the Reserves?"

"Who knows?" I answered. "Wonder what Chief McDonald thinks about it."

Chief Petty Officer McDonald was singing Captain Corcoran, and therefore 'my' father, who ends up with Buttercup, mostly on account of he was the only baritone who had what the padre called a 'lyric' voice. I don't know much about acting, but I could tell that he wasn't comfortable; still, he remembered his lines and got them out clearly. Also, he was the only baritone who was the right size for *Alceste*'s real captain's spare uniform, which Commander Farren had agreed to lend. That was fine until the great reveal when the Captain is demoted; McDonald could go back to his own rig, but Commander Farren's jacket would have fitted two of Rick.

"But isn't he supposed to have been exchanged with me when we were babies?" Rick asked the padre. "So we should be the same age. And then Josephine's marrying a bloke old enough to be her father."

"Don't blame me, blame Gilbert," the Rev. Shorthouse said. "You just have to run with these things, lads."

"Well, *I* think Gilbert was a dirty old man," Rick muttered, and stared at his script as if he'd like to swat the author with it.

Lieutenant Hall was our major benefactor when it came to props. His family home wasn't far off, and they had a history of amateur theatricals, so

137

that he was forever sending out for pasteboard cannon and the like. There was an absolute ban, hallelujah, on wearing frocks, what with material being on the ration and the Rev. being less easy-going about what we wore than whether we smoked or gambled. Ship's crew wore their usual rig, while those of us who were pretending to be girls or ladies wore our blue working dress, number eights as we'd say, with ribbons round our heads thanks to Lieutenant Hall's sisters. He, as Buttercup, wore a set of rating's number eights too large for him, with a wide belt to give him something like a figure. Once a scarf was tied round his head he looked exactly like a particular type of factory worker.

We were about halfway through rehearsals when Rick O'Shea came up to me one day and said, "Smudge, I need a word, private-like."

I looked round. We were on the foredeck, and it wasn't our watch. "Nobody here."

He scuffed his feet. "I got a problem."

"Oh, aye?" I propped my elbows on the guard rail.

"It's Lieutenant Wilkins," Rick said miserably. "He told me, he's got a bet on with someone that I'll kiss you on-stage at the end of the show. You know we haven't even made to look like we do it yet."

"I'm assuming you don't want to?" I had a fair tally against Lieutenant Wilkins already; this was going to be another deep notch in it.

"Of course I don't!" His smile shook a little. "Dare say you don't either."

I did not have to stop and think. "No, I do not. So what's the trouble?"

"Says he'll share his winnings with me." Rick seemed to be counting his bootlace eyelets.

I snorted. "You'll kiss me for tuppence?"

"Sixpence," he said. "Don't look at me like that, Smudge. I could do with a bit to send home, what with me mam not being too well. But I don't like it, and I wish he hadn't, and I want him not to."

Overhead a seagull squawked as if it was laughing. The sun was bright, and the air smelt of salt and coal dust: HMS *Wild Goose*, tied up astern of us, had been coaling ship that morning.

I said, "Who's he got this bet with?"

"He didn't say, and I wasn't going to ask. It'll be another officer, won't it?" Rick looked at me, forehead creased with unaccustomed thought. "Wilkins won't talk to a rating if he can help it. So we need another officer to find out for us."

"You're right, there." I put my own brain to work. "Reckon I'll try Lieutenant Hall. He's not so anchor-faced as the rest of the mob."

"You?" Rick said. "Should be me. It's my problem."

"You've got enough on your plate. Leave it to me." The bells sounded, and I jumped. "Christ, that's my watch. See you."

The thing about being in the seaman branch instead of being a stoker or tiffy is that you might be anywhere on the ship, which has its advantages when you're looking for someone. I lay in wait for Lieutenant Hall at the foot of the ladder up to the chart-room, and when he arrived took a deep breath and said, "Excuse me, sir, I wonder if I might ask a favour?"

He looked at me, a bit startled-like, but not snooty like some of them are. "Fire away, lad – AB Smith isn't it?"

"That's right, sir. Smudge Smith."

He laughed. "Is there a Smith that isn't Smudge? What do your parents call you?"

"Artie, sir. Short for Arthur." I was actually Arthur Brian, but I wasn't going to tell him that. I'd had all the AB jokes I wanted to hear in one lifetime.

"Very well, AB. What's the favour?"

"It's for LH O'Shea, sir, really. Lieutenant Wilkins – " I nearly stopped there. Even in the shadow cast by *Alceste*'s superstructure I could see the twist of Lieutenant Hall's mouth. "Lieutenant Wilkins told him he has a bet on about him – about Rick O'Shea that is, sir – with someone. And Rick wants to know who the someone might be, so he can ask him to stop it. If you get my drift."

"I get it very well, thank you, AB," he said. "Could LH O'Shea not do the asking?"

"He's worried, sir. His mother's not well. And to be honest I've got more nerve than he has."

Lieutenant Hall smiled, a curve of his mouth that set deep creases into his face; a rather long face it was, with dark brows. "I see. I'll do my best, and if I find out I'll let you know."

"Thank you, sir." And I went back to what I should have been doing.

A couple of days later, passing me in the gangway, Lieutenant Hall stopped me briefly and said, "What you wanted to know, AB. Surgeon Commander Burnett."

"What?" That was a surprise. "I mean – thank you, sir."

"Think nothing of it. And yes, that's what I said too." He smiled briefly, and walked on.

Rather than bother Rick, I took myself along to the sick-bay the next morning and put myself in the queue for aspirin, no.9 solution, and other unmentionable things. There weren't many of us, and I let the others go first in the hope of not being hurried or interrupted.

When I closed the door behind me Doc Burnett said, "You're looking remarkably healthy to be visiting me, AB."

"Come to sell you a ticket for *Pinafore*, sir."

"No, thanks. I loathe Gilbert and Sullivan. I suppose it's for charity?"

"Red Cross, sir."

"Here you are, then." He handed over half a crown, but I stayed where I was. After a moment, he said, "*Is* there something else, AB Smith?"

I took a moment to remind myself that I had more nerve than Rick. "Excuse me if I'm speaking out of turn," I said, "but LH O'Shea isn't happy about being the subject of a bet. Neither am I, to be honest."

"Ah. And how does either of you know about the bet? For interest's sake." He picked up a scalpel, and began to use the point of it, blunt edge on, to clean his fingernails.

"Lieutenant Wilkins told LH O'Shea, and O'Shea told me. Because he wants Lieutenant Wilkins to win, needing the money. Lieutenant Wilkins promised to share."

"Did he now?" The surgeon commander glanced up at me. "I wonder why Lieutenant Wilkins dislikes you so much."

"You think he does, sir?" I wasn't being quite honest, there: 'hated my guts' would have been nearer the truth, but it wasn't the done thing to say so.

Doc Burnett said, "Hah. I did hear one of his more inspired efforts. 'Call that a salute? I've seen better hands on a clock.' Very droll. Not right, of course, you seem to salute as well as anyone does on this floating bedlam."

"Thank you, sir. I think."

He laughed outright. "So if I share my winnings with you, what will you do? I have twice the amount on you getting your way as he does on LH

O'Shea getting his way, if that helps you to decide."

I shrugged. "So if I split my half of your winnings with him, LH O'Shea won't be any worse off."

"The boy has a brain," Burnett said. "Long may he continue to use it. Just *don't* let me hear you whistling any of those tunes. Right?"

"Aye, aye, sir." And I went off, trying not to whistle.

By now we were rehearsing whole acts at a time, and most of us had our scripts down. Tonight the padre wanted us to put more polish on the beginning of Act One, and I was ready and waiting in what passed for the wings of our stage.

Buttercup was fluttering her eyelashes outrageously at Captain Corcoran. "*Ah, I know too well / The anguish of a heart that loves but vainly!*"

And for a moment I wondered if perhaps –

If perhaps Lieutenant Hall was fluttering his eyelashes outrageously at Chief Petty Officer McDonald.

Which, of course, had to be the purest figment of my imagination; certainly purer than anywhere else my imagination wanted to take me. I shook my head, which made for a suitably pensive effect, and went on stage.

Opening night came round at last. We gave two performances on board, to allow different watches the chance to come and see us, and on the following days a performance at the two nearest church halls, one C of E and one RC. Then, at Lieutenant Hall's father's particular request, two more, matinee and evening, at Hall Court, his family place which had been requisitioned as an officers' convalescent home for the duration, apart from one wing where the family continued to live.

That was a day, and then some. We were fed lunch beforehand, and tea and stickies after the matinee, and then had an hour to wander round before the evening performance. It had rained all day, but although there were still dark clouds overhead they had lifted from the western horizon. The grounds were lit up as if the sun was a golden searchlight, picking out ship's singers and 'up' patients mingling on the patio.

The lawns below had been given over to vegetable beds, and beyond the patio's low zigzag hedges Hall senior was booming away about how the pasture was running wild without the cattle to graze it, and how high he'd had to fence the lawns to stop the deer getting at the vegetables.

I looked across to where the meadows were speckled all over with flowers, white and red and yellow. They were bounded by a brick wall, almost high enough to hide the bus that chugged along the road beyond, its painted roof like the top of a huge beetle scuttling past. A deer bounded into view as if she'd come up from under the wall, paused to let the fawn that was with her catch up, and walked slowly on, flicking her ears like signal flags.

"You would never have known she was there," someone said beside me, marvelling. Chief McDonald, looking as neat as ever, his face maybe softened a little by the sunlight.

"The ground dips towards the stream," Lieutenant Hall said, on the other side of him. "You can get onto the estate through the door in the wall by Alderbeck chapel, where the bus stop is, and work your way along the foot of the wall almost as far as the house before anyone sees you."

"Oh, aye," Chief McDonald said as if he wasn't much interested. Presently he strolled away, leaving me and Lieutenant Hall there together.

"All well, AB?" the lieutenant asked.

"Yes, thank you, sir." I turned round to face the house, and found myself being stared at by a trio of girls. Lieutenant Hall waved. "Sisters," he said. "Add in cousins and aunts, and I have more than Sir Joseph Porter does aboard *Pinafore*."

"Prettier than the crew of *Alceste*," I said, and then wondered if I should have said that to their brother.

The lieutenant laughed. "So I should think. Did you ever solve the problem of that bet?"

I went on watching the girls. "Not altogether, but I have had an idea. Do you think the young lady would lend me her parasol?"

"Helen? I'll make sure she does." He got to his feet and sauntered over to them; and presently came back, with Helen and the parasol. "In return for being able to touch your collar for luck," he said, seriously but with a glimmer of laughter in his eyes, "Helen will be very pleased to lend the parasol. Off you go, love."

He meant Helen, I hoped, not me; but I didn't have much time to think about it because, as well as taking the edge of my collar between her fingers, Helen leaned forward and kissed me plumb on the lips, which was startling, but a bloody nice surprise for someone who was as the song says 'only a poor AB'. When she had gone I found myself parasol in one hand and the other hand to my lips; Lieutenant Hall had discreetly turned his back.

"Phew!" I said, not having meant to say anything, but too surprised to stay quiet.

There was a pause while I registered that the lieutenant's shoulders were shaking.

"Beg pardon, sir."

He turned round again, amusement still bright in his eyes. "None needed. She's a hussy. Mind what you do with that weapon tonight. Two of us will be right behind you as usual, and I don't want Chief McDonald damaged."

"No worries, sir," I said. "I'll have it open in front of me. Ah – if Lieutenant Wilkins or Surgeon Commander Burnett asks, please tell him I didn't kiss LH O'Shea behind it. Because I'm not going to, and the doc says he'll give me his winnings."

"I see." He looked down at me, his face all at once sober, and the frown lines back on his forehead. "Very well, AB. I'm glad you're not fighting for the other side; you're too devious for me."

"I'm not keeping them, sir! It's so LH O'Shea can send a postal order to his mother. She's not been able to work for a bit."

"Indeed? Then I forgive you both," he said lightly. "I may even make a contribution."

Somewhere a clock chimed the hour. "Green room time," Lieutenant Hall said. "Once more unto the breach, AB." And we went indoors for the last performance.

It went like a dream. Rick and I ran the last number with me sitting on his knee as usual, and I opened the parasol at exactly the right time. Rick was giggling so much that it probably looked convincingly as if he *had* kissed me behind it, once I furled it away again.

What nobody saw, except me, was what happened behind us.

Because I was sitting down my eyes were at waist level, shall we say, with the couple behind us, Buttercup and Corcoran. When the parasol was safely open, one of Buttercup's hands slid well below Queensberry Rules level and squeezed. I fully expected Corcoran to revert to Chief McDonald and wallop him one, never mind the penalty for striking an officer, but what happened … what happened was, he braced himself on one leg, and made a single determined movement of the other. Again, I'd expected a yelp and double-up in response, but instead Lieutenant Hall let loose a dirty, throaty chuckle, almost drowned in the applause after the padre hammered the last chord down on the piano.

Returning to *Alceste*'s battleship grey was almost a pleasure. Returning to Lieutenant Wilkins, sour-faced and eagle-eyed for derelictions of duty, was not; and after one more salute not snappy enough for him, I was back at the sick-bay.

Doc Burnett sighed. "What is it this time, AB?"

I showed him the toothbrush I was holding. "I've been told off to clean the sick-bay floor with this. I think Lieutenant Wilkins isn't too pleased he lost his bet."

"And so is determined to make life miserable for us both." He regarded the bulkhead behind his desk as if it had a particularly nasty fungal infection. "Well, seeing as losing Lieutenant Wilkins a bet isn't exactly prejudicial to good order and naval discipline, you can forget that."

"What, sir?"

"The floor is already clean, in the best traditions of naval hygiene. Also, I outrank him."

All the same, I knelt down in the corner and started scrubbing. "He always checks the toothbrush."

"I know. Take this one and show it him. I'll rough up the one you've got there." The doc held out something that looked as if it had been used for cleaning flues.

"Really, sir?"

"Really. Medical details are confidential, as Lieutenant Wilkins should have known before he had his bright idea, and I'm not sending you out to stand in the gangway every time I have a patient."

I stood up. We swapped toothbrushes.

"Besides," Doc Burnett said, "I don't like bullies. Talking of the bet, I presume you shared *your* winnings?"

"I did, sir," I said. "Well, I gave them all to Rick, actually." Lieutenant Hall had made a contribution, but I thought that had better be confidential too.

"Good. Now go and steal some zeds somewhere and leave me in peace. If Lieutenant Wilkins comes looking for you I shall tell him I've sent you ashore after a bulb for the dead-light."

"I'd never fall for that one, sir, and he'll know it."

The doc grunted. "You're right. Something for my stores, then. Enough, young Smith. Just get the hell out of here, because I have work to do."

"Yes, sir. Thank you, sir." And out I got, plotting how to catch some sleep without being found in any of the obvious places, such as my hammock.

Every ship has one: the odd-shaped, unregarded compartment where lost oilskins come to die, and where such things as long weights, red oil for the port light and tartan paint might be kept, supposing they existed. In *Alceste*'s case it was the place behind the mess flat where the mats for PT training were stored, piled high to tantalise us with forbidden comfort on the way to our hammocks at the end of the middle watch.

There was a partition most of the way across to keep the pile of mats from sliding, a gap wide enough to let the compartment door swing, and that was it. I closed the door cautiously behind me and scrambled round the end of the partition. I considered unlacing my boots, but if I had to get down in a hurry I would need them. It was quick enough work to climb up the mats and lie down. Then I closed my eyes, shook all my *Pinafore*-related worries from me, and dozed off, despite the smell of rubber and dust.

If I were the snoring type, there would be no more to tell, but the long and the short of it is that I don't snore and that, therefore, the men who came in to the compartment next never realised I was there. The first I knew that *they* were there was the clunk of the door opening, which gave me just enough time to lie as flat as possible and get my nose out of the dust.

The door shut.

For a moment there was silence.

"Did you get my note?" That was Lieutenant Hall.

"I did, sir." A voice with a Scots burr: Chief McDonald.

"Well?"

"You asked for a few minutes of my time in case there was anything you could do for me," Chief McDonald said. "I would not be quite sure of your meaning, sir."

"Not after where I put my hand last week, and what you did in return?" Lieutenant Hall said, his voice light and a little mocking. "I think you know what I mean. You are, after all, still here."

"Very well, then, I know it, and a more stupid thing I cannot imagine."

McDonald drew his breath in sharply. "I apologise. I should not call an officer stupid. That was remiss of me."

"What would I gain from reporting you, when you're right?" Lieutenant Hall said. "Is there an answer?"

Anyone else might have shuffled his feet. From Chief McDonald there was total silence; and then he said, "As you say, I am still here. Sir."

"Then: shall I meet you at the door by Alderbeck?" the lieutenant said. "When we both have leave."

"That seems as good an idea as any, under the circumstances, sir."

Lieutenant Hall actually laughed. "One more thing. Enough of the sir. My name is Christopher."

The silence stretched out until I could almost hear it creaking. My nose was tickling dreadfully; any moment now I was going to sneeze.

"*Christopher*," Chief McDonald said, like he was swearing. The silence fell again, and eventually he said, "Will there be anything else, sir?"

"You know what I'd like. And what's your name?"

"Donald. But you can call me Mac like everyone else does." There was a rustle and a bit of a thud, a metallic thud, like a body being pushed against a steel door at close quarters. Lieutenant Hall let out an odd noise, startled but pleased together, and then there was silence. Almost.

I did not look. Of course I did not look. I lay as still as I could and tried not even to breathe because, let's be honest, it was going to be as embarrassing as hell for me to be discovered lurking there, let alone for them to realise that I had heard everything.

The tannoy went off with the call for the afternoon watch. I wasn't due on till the first dog, so I could stay where I was, but McDonald took a deep breath and said, "That's mine. Got to go."

"Of course." Lieutenant Hall said breathlessly. "Later. And thank you. I'll … I'll wait until the leave lists go up, shall I?"

Dead silence.

"Yes," Chief McDonald said.

The door opened, and clanged closed. For a few minutes there was no noise on my side of it except for Hall's fast, light breathing; and then he too took a deep breath, opened the door and went out.

I sneezed, wriggled off the gym mats like a worm off a hook, made sure I had the toothbrush, and retreated full speed astern.

There was no way I was going to gossip about what I had seen, but after a day or two I needed to ask advice from *someone*. I was fairly sure the chaplain would not approve at all; so I went to Surgeon Commander Burnett in the sick-bay again. At this rate my mates were going to think I had some unmentionable disease.

"Sir? Can I ask something? Confidential-like."

Doc Burnett's eyebrows made a bid to reach his hairline. "Yes. By all means ask, but be quick about it."

Now it came to it, I couldn't look him in the face. "Um. Well. I just – Doc, what do you think about two blokes kissing?" I looked at him just in time to see the eyebrows back to normal.

"Better than shooting each other," he said. "You're not the subject of *another* bet, are you?"

"No, sir. Not at all. I just – wondered."

"What I thought about it? Why?" He had been writing; now he wiped the ink from his pen, and set it back on its tray.

"Well – about what people do think, generally."

"Generally," he answered, with a sour twist to his mouth, "people don't think at all. There are so many worse things going on in the world today that two men could coat themselves in margarine and wrestle naked, and I'd think it was a better idea than not. But people, they would disagree."

I could have just said thank you and left. But … "But what should I do?"

"Do? Why, nothing, unless someone was being hurt."

"But it was – "

He raised a hand. "I *do not want to know*, AB Smith. If I know, I shall have to do something about it. You've asked, I've answered, so out with you. *Now*."

"Aye, aye, sir. Thank you, sir." And I went.

A while after that, finally – *finally* – the leave lists were posted. I had five days allocated, which meant three because it was a day's journey in each direction, and of those three days most would be taken up with the five aunts and uncles that Mum would want me to visit if I showed my nose at her place, or else none of them would speak to her for weeks. I was still dithering about what to do that evening, when I found Rick huddled in a corner of the mess, the picture of misery.

"Here, what's up, mate?"

"I thought I was going to be on the list for leave," he said, "and I'm not."

"Same for half the others, isn't it?"

"Yes, but I was hoping to get home given that me mam's poorly. Not so bad that they'll send me home on compassionate grounds, *of course*," he added bitterly.

I looked at him for a minute, to check he wasn't having me on: after sleeping in the hammock next to his for two years I knew his little tricks. But this wasn't one of them. "Your folks are in Stockport, aren't they?"

"Yes."

"Well, look here," I told him, "I got five days and much use they are to me, having to get to Truro. We'll go to the drafty and get it changed over."

And that was that – one happy Rick on leave, and me relieved not to be doing the family rounds, and maybe my reward stored up for later, if there is any justice in this world.

When Saturday came round I was harbour watch for the afternoon, which means stationed at the top of the gangplank keeping an eye on passers-by and doing the courtesies whenever officers came or went. I was Taff's relief, and he was in such a hurry to get to his run ashore that we hardly exchanged a word.

The ship was half empty, as quiet as a turkey farm after Christmas. The weather was glorious, but not scorching, with a nice fresh breeze off the Irish Sea to keep me cool. About half an hour before four bells of the dogwatch, which is to say half past four land time, Chief McDonald hove into view. He marched across the quayside, arms swinging, paused at the foot of the brow to adjust his cap, and strode up the gangway whistling. I snapped him a salute, and he responded in kind.

"Afternoon, Chief."

"Afternoon, AB. Lieutenant Wilkins having an effect on your salutes, I see." And he actually smiled.

"If you say so, Chief." Between relief at not getting my head bitten off, and surprise at the smile, I couldn't think what else to say, so ended up staring at his retreating back. And then staring some more.

Chief McDonald, the smartest man on the ship, had come back on board with a grass stain on the left elbow of his jacket. And, showing under the back edge of his cap, something that looked suspiciously like petals. Long, white petals of the tall daisies that you find among meadow grass; as if someone had made a daisy chain and put it on his head, before he forgot about it and put his cap on again.

I resumed my proper sentry stance and stared along the guard-rail, hoping my face looked as wooden as it ought to.

Maybe twenty minutes later, Lieutenant Hall returned.

I saluted.

Lieutenant Hall saluted back.

"Had a good afternoon, sir?"

"Excellent, thank you," he said. "A little tedious for you, isn't it?"

"Not so as I mind, thank you, sir. I'm glad you had a good time."

He smiled, not looking at me. "Yes, I enjoyed myself. Well, back on board, eh, AB?" For a moment he turned his head, looking over his shoulder; and I saw, as he stepped forward –

"Sir," I said, maybe a little too urgently. "Sir."

He turned back. "What is it?"

"You, er, there's a buttercup behind your ear, sir." There had been buttercups among the tall white daisies in the meadow.

"Oh." He reached up, brought his hand down again, and stared at the flower between his fingers as if he hadn't expected to find it there. Then he looked at me, questioning.

"Chief McDonald had daisies," I said, without stopping to think.

He blushed. I mean, I've never seen anything like it, he went scarlet. A moment later, his face went dead white, with his lips pressed together, and a look in his eyes that I hope never to see in anyone's eyes again. He was afraid.

Afraid of me.

For a moment I could only stare back at him. "I – it's all right, sir," I said at last. "I'm glad you had a good afternoon. Very glad."

He nodded. "Thank you," he said, in a voice so dry and hoarse that it was hard to believe he had ever sung.

"Ah, *damn*," I said, sending protocol flying in every direction. "Wish I'd kept my big mouth shut."

He smiled, lopsided. "So do I. Let's pretend you did."

"Let's," I said. "Don't worry, sir."

The smile shifted into a real grin. "What, never?" The so-and-so was quoting bloody *Pinafore*.

I grinned back, and did the same. "Hardly ever!"

Lieutenant Hall laughed out loud, slipped the buttercup into his breast pocket, and went below.

Between Friends

Sandra Lindsey

There had been plenty of time for second thoughts – and third, fourth, fifth, probably thoughts numbering into their thousands – on the voyage upriver. The old steamer, oft-derided, but faithful still, had chugged her steady way upstream, ceaseless in her efforts thanks to the servitude of Carlos and his shipmates, the men who fed her firebox, polished her pipes, and monitored her gauges and dials.

Steering clear of those aboard whose passage had been paid for by the government in their so-called Battle for Rubber, and being a stranger to the regular crew, Carlos kept mostly to himself in the weeks between bidding farewell to his old life – and Marcos – at Belém docks, and stepping ashore once more in Manaus. Back into what seemed a previous life.

He hadn't needed to return. By the time he reached his ultimate destination and began his compulsory service in the military, this side-trip would be counted as no different from his previous two years hopping from ship to ship with Marcos, working their way up and down the coast of Brazil, seeing as many towns, as many girls, and as much of each other as they could without falling under the notice of the law. Yes, he hadn't needed to return – except that he did. He had left things wrongly here, the folly and fears of youth grasping, clenching at his chest, and tearing him away with never a word sent back to say he even lived, let alone thrived, outside the forest. Guilt, not fear, now clawed at him, and had joined with other, stronger emotions and deeper desires to pull him back upriver.

Still, he thought as he shifted the bag slung over his shoulder, settling its weight more comfortably for his walk through the daytime heat and humidity of the city's streets, at least he'd come in person to apologise, and with gifts he'd bought with greatest care. And he knew the boats' timetables now. If he found no welcome where he headed, he could leave by noon tomorrow.

It was strange to see the changes war had brought to this enclave of civilisation. Wharves which had seemed half-empty when he'd last arrived were now full and bustling with scurrying folk. Languages and accents mingled, creating a cacophony to rival that of the wildlife on the seringal where he'd grown up. Tired of people jostling round, seeking space to order his thoughts, he headed inland from the river front, to the wide spacious boulevards of the city centre he recalled.

Once there he paused, finding again the city busier than he recalled. He wondered if his memory served him right. Had it always been like this and he'd forgotten? Some buildings seemed to have sustained recent damage – had the anti-German protests reported in the news spread even to here? Not that he'd be surprised by such feelings flaring up: if he'd been on land, not at sea, last August when the news struck of the five passenger ships lost within two days, he'd have been at the forefront of the mob with whatever weapon he found to hand. One of the ships lost had been his a scant two weeks before its loss. He and Marcos had clung together in a single berth that night, for once not caring if they were caught.

That winter night, with the sudden shock of attack on civilian shipping of an officially neutral nation, had seemed at the time an emotional low point unlikely to return, but slowly over the months since, creeping dread had grown until the constant wondering "what if – ?" had been a clamouring inside his head. That was when he'd decided to stop dodging, stop playing, and accept his responsibility as a man and citizen. He stood now, quiet and alone in the midst of the city, and gazed at the grand elegance of the Teatro des Amazonas. Its beauty and pomposity still taught a lesson in what luxuries wealth could bring to the unlikeliest of places. Though it seemed to have become infested with Americans, their white skin making them more visible than most among the Brazilian crowd, the building still took his breath away, as it had the first time he'd arrived and Dr Fernandes walked with him through the streets, teaching him the way from place to place, and showing the city's sights to him when he'd been but a wide-eyed upriver boy.

Dr Fernandes. Quite. His thoughts as nicely gathered as he could hope for, Carlos hoisted his bag once more and set off in the direction of the house he'd once had the privilege of calling home.

At last, after a few unnerving wrong turns and doublings-back, he turned into the street he sought and felt a sudden wash of relief that the doctor's sign still hung in its expected place. He hadn't realised, amongst his nerves, that he'd been worried the doctor might have moved. Keeping his pace to a gentle stroll he took his time to observe the house as he approached. Freshly painted, the pillars and doorway were picked out now in yellow against the white walls. Five years ago, he'd painted them pale blue. It had been the first task the doctor gave him on their arrival and, whilst paintwork rarely stayed pristine long in the city's humid air, he later suspected it had been given him to do in order to introduce him to the neighbours. Dr Fernandes had always had a way of giving things extra meaning and value like that, even when Carlos first met him during the doctor's inspection tour of conditions on the seringals. Carlos had admired the doctor's learning before any of his other charms.

Feeling someone's gaze fall on him from across the street, he realised he should dawdle no longer lest the watcher assume him to be a trouble-maker. Feet before the door, he raised his hand and knocked.

Silence.

Carlos waited, counting down a minute, then knocked again, louder this time, the sharp rat-a-tat-tat seeming loud enough to echo down the street, and Carlos stood there feeling far more conspicuous than he was used to.

Footsteps sounded inside the house. Leather-soled shoes on tiled floor. The doctor had always dressed and behaved as a perfect gentleman. Carlos had time for only a quick glance down at his attire: rough-cut, well worn cotton clothes and grubby canvas shoes, before the door opened and anything he'd planned to say vanished from his mind.

"Can I help you?" the doctor asked.

He hadn't seemed to have aged a day. Thick dark hair, close-cropped, framed his fine-featured face. The doctor had always seemed unaware of his beauty, which only increased Carlos's desire to trace his fingertips along the doctor's cheekbones, to feel the sudden change from smooth dark skin to tight curled hair …

Carlos took a breath to calm his nerves, raised a shaky-feeling smile and said, "Hello, Dr Fernandes. I'm sorry it took me so long to return."

The doctor looked at him – peered, really. Carlos struggled not to fidget like a child or shuffle his ill-shod feet.

"Carlos?" the doctor asked at last, and the relief Carlos felt made his small smile vanish into a broad grin, at which the doctor smiled back, opening his arms and crying "Carlos!" as though he were the Bible's prodigal son.

"Come in, come in." The doctor stepped back to allow him space to enter the hallway with its neat row of foldaway wooden chairs for waiting patients. Carlos heard the door close behind him and then he was being ushered further into the house, avoiding the front room where the doctor held his surgery, and into the neat but sparsely furnished kitchen where the evening light poured in through the back window.

"Come, sit," urged the doctor, as much the generous host as Carlos remembered, "I was just preparing dinner. Have you eaten? No? Will you join me?" He paused then, and his smile grew rueful. "It might not be as large a meal as we've enjoyed in the past, with the food shortages, but it will be so much more enjoyable than any meal I've eaten for a good long while, thanks to your company."

"My thanks." Carlos couldn't have shaken the smile from his face if he'd tried, and he dug one hand into the bag he'd placed at his feet. "Here – it's not food but it should help wash down the meal."

The doctor paused in his food preparation and took the bottle which Carlos held out. "Wine? A generous gift indeed. You have grown worldly-wise since leaving the forest."

Carlos laughed a little nervously, unsure if the comment was intended as a barb. "It is but a token," he said, "and the start of an apology. And, truthfully, such things are not as difficult to come by as they were before."

"Ah. The influence of our American friends."

Ever the diplomat as necessitated by his profession, the doctor's tone gave nothing of his own feelings away on the matter of American assistance, so Carlos simply said again, "I am sorry."

The doctor looked at him, his eyebrows raised in question.

"Sorry for leaving as I did," Carlos elaborated, "and sorry for never sending word. I … It was ill-done of me, Doctor."

"Luiz," the doctor corrected with a smile and wave of one hand. "You're a grown man now, Carlos. If I address you by your first name, you should do likewise to me. Thank you for your apology, but do not worry yourself further on the matter. What is done is done. You are here now, and well, and I am thankful for both those things. Open that bottle, pour us each a glass, and tell me where you've been."

Carlos smiled again and settled more comfortably in his seat after doing as the doctor – Luiz – bade him. Description of his journeys up and down the coast, discussion of the towns and cities he'd seen, and of the changes he'd observed on his return, took them through dinner, until they sat with empty plates, playing with their nearly-empty glasses, putting off the end of their meal. Carlos upended the bottle over Luiz's glass, and they both laughed at its continuing to be empty. Suddenly, Luiz lifted his wine glass and tipped it fully back rather than sipping as he had throughout the meal. His glass empty, he stood, his smile brighter than before though it somehow no longer seemed to reach his eyes.

"Do you have somewhere to stay tonight?"

Carlos shook his head, wondering if he was about to be ejected from the house, and wishing he'd dared to raise the topic before darkness had fallen.

"Stay here? Your old room's free." Luiz's smile seemed less forced at the enthusiasm with which Carlos accepted his offer. "The bed's not made though. Come through and help me find the sheets."

Carlos tossed down his wine, collected his bag from the floor, and followed Luiz into the well-remembered room.

Luiz had already found the sheets – neatly folded in the chest of drawers – so Carlos simply helped draw and smooth them over the thin mattress. When done, he sat on the bed and the doctor turned and walked towards the door. Carlos stopped him with his name.

Watching him with guarded gaze, Luiz recrossed the room to sit near him on the bed, a careful space of air between their bodies, but his attention given unequivocally to Carlos.

"I won't be here for long," Carlos said, "I'll leave first light if you wish, but I'll be heading for the army, which may mean leaving for war and – I didn't want to go without saying what I ran away from telling you four years ago."

"You don't have – "

"I know." Carlos smiled, and reached out tentatively to place his fingertips on the back of Luiz's hand. "I shouldn't have left as I did and, having done so, I should have made sure to send you word – to let you know at least that I still lived. Why else did you teach me my letters, if not to help with such things?" He paused, but Luiz smiled and gave a slight nod, so he plunged back into his confession. "I left because I didn't know what else to do. I hadn't known, and had been seeking another way – or some means to tell you – for over a year, since almost the time we met. But I was still a youth and, in your eyes, too much a boy for me to ask you to consider me a man. I felt I had to leave, to become a man, before I could broach the topic with you."

His words lapsed, and this time the silence stretched long enough that Luiz broke it.

"Whatever troubles you, I am sure it will seem less terrible once spoken aloud." He turned his hand over and gave Carlos's fingers a friendly squeeze. It seemed the trigger to shoot the younger man's troubles from his lips.

"I love you."

Luiz didn't gasp, as Carlos thought he might, but he did freeze, his hand still wrapped round Carlos's work-rough fingertips.

"I know it's wrong," Carlos said. "Every priest I've ever met tells us man is made to be with woman, and I've done that, but … I've also been with men, and liked that too. Do you despise me for a sinner?"

"No. Never. You know my thoughts about the church – about the way our nation's built. You've heard me speak often enough that you know I skirt the edges of the law. But this … Carlos, my dear, beautiful, courageous boy, I do not deserve your love. Not in the way you offer it. If you sin, then so do I, and for far worse crimes than you. I am old and insignificant, left alone as long as I remain here out of sight and mind of those who ought to welcome me as equal."

"You're not old!" Indignant rage at Luiz's dismissal of himself displaced the words he'd meant to say. "Older than me, certainly, but less than forty still, and I am over twenty now. There's many a man takes a woman as wife with much greater age gap than our fifteen years."

"You want a wife?" Luiz's eyes grew wide, flickering as if reading thoughts which sped through his mind.

"No." Carlos spoke firmly and placed his free hand over Luiz's, preventing him from breaking their hold on each other. "No, I don't want a wife. And I don't want just any man either. I want you, Dr Luiz Fernandes, just as you are."

"But I … " Luiz's look grew more concerned and he tried to pull his hand from Carlos's firm but gentle grip.

"I know," Carlos said, then checked himself and smiled, "or at least, I think I know, from guesses here and there. I may be wrong, and if so, I hope that you'll forgive me my error." He paused. Luiz's gaze had steadied, focused all on him, watching and waiting to hear what he had to say.

"You say your crime is worse than mine, but I say no. Society is in the wrong, not you. You are yourself, unashamedly so, and should you be censured for choosing not to lead the life others deemed you ought?" He paused again, watching the words he'd spent hours formulating be heard and understood, then told the doctor he'd brought another gift and released his hand to draw it from his bag.

Luiz received the narrow wooden box with a question in his eyes.

Carlos swallowed, hoping to quench his nerves, and nodded. "It is a gift, from friend to friend. I hope you take no insult from it."

A look of curiosity grew on Luiz's face and he kept his gaze focused on Carlos as he opened the box. Then he looked down and gasped. A moment passed before he spoke, and when he did it was accompanied by him lifting the object from its nest of tissue paper, and holding it almost reverently with fingertips alone. "A consuelo? An intimate gift indeed between friends."

Carlos found his throat felt suddenly dry. "But not too much from friend who hopes to become lover?"

Silence, poised between assent and refusal, greeted his offer. Carlos's heartbeat seemed to pulse stronger through his body than ever before. "There's more," he said at last, wanting this strange moment to end however it might, "another part to the gift, under the paper."

Luiz's eyebrows rose once more, but he placed the rubber dildo on the bed between them and delved into the box, quickly finding and withdrawing the leather and metal harness Carlos had chosen and wrapped up weeks before.

Luiz turned the harness this way and that, inspecting its design and occasionally glancing at the dildo on the bed. At last, he dropped his hands – and the harness – to his lap. "It seems you are more observant, or better at guessing, than most people," he said at last. "What do you want of me?"

"I would hope my gift, and what I said before, suggests what I would like from you," Carlos replied. Desire, long held in check, rose in his breast as he spoke. "But I know you to be a gentleman, so if you do not wish the same, I will leave you to enjoy them in any way you like."

"I … You surprise me. Can you wait – and stay – a day or so, for my answer?"

Carlos smiled and lifted one of Luiz's hands to his lips, bending his head and pressing a delicate kiss to his knuckles. "I've waited years to ask you. It's only fair to give you time to answer."

Luiz lifted his hand from Carlos's light hold and laid it against Carlos's cheek. Holding his gaze until he got too close, he leaned in and returned the kiss with a brush of lips on lips.

"You'll have your answer before you leave for war," he promised, "but for now I'll bid you good night and sweet dreams."

"Good night, Luiz. I love you."

Luiz stood, carefully cradling his gifts in his arms. "And I you, Carlos, which is what gives me pause. Desire? Lust? They are easy to understand, and easy to answer. Love requires more care. Good night."

Author's Note

Did you know that the Second World War caused a brief resurgence of the Amazonian rubber industry when Japan gained control of Malaysia? I didn't, until I started researching outside the British/Eurocentric history I learned at school. The Brazilian 'rubber soldiers' don't feature quite as much in the story I ended up writing as I initially envisaged, but I recommend reading about them if you're at all interested in how nations' histories are linked through global commerce.

From Air to There

Michelle Peart

Spring 1944

Peering through the small square window to my side, I stared, not for the first time in my twenty years, at a bright white cobweb, which held the night sky to ransom. The tubular interior of the Dakota burst with light, which bounced around the warplane's ribs like charged fireflies. Turning back, I tried to make out the faces of my brothers in the dark and freezing fuselage, which got colder the higher we flew. Three men had flown nine missions each and were considered the elite – perhaps because they weren't dead yet. But all in this plane, including me, would die for their country and today was probably the day we would make that sacrifice. Lit briefly as the tracers flashed by, Slugger fiddled around in his pocket for what I presumed was his silver crucifix. Nipper placed his hand over the chest pocket on his heavy jacket where he kept a letter from his sweetheart, and Wide-Fred, so called because he was twice the girth of all us skinny lads, readjusted the straps on his parachute, which only just about circled his broad chest. Sitting next to my friends, and with their hands firmly clasped, were three young chaps, their pale flawless faces raised to the roof in contemplation. I didn't rate their chances. I didn't rate mine.

The constant flickers from the tracer bullets lighting the glass next to me were giving me an eye-headache and the urge to move away was strong, but we were lined up in jumping order and I'd never have dared disobey my sergeant, Wide-Fred.

The plane lurched to the right as the pilot, Jock, heaved his beloved Dakota away from whatever was making its way to destroy us. I hoisted my heavy parachute rig back onto my shoulders – it had a habit of slipping off which I tried to ignore – and placed a hand protectively over the hip pocket in my trousers. Paper folds nestled in the pocket protected his photograph. Looking handsome in his Sunday best with his chest puffed out and blond hair mop tumbling to one side – he could never control it and I'd tried many times to slick it into a neat wave like mine, but he'd gently pushed my hand away saying it summed up his personality.

"Eh, Puppet. That your sweet'art's photograph?" Slugger shouted and pointed at my hand covering the pocket. It was so loud in the fuselage with the engine noises that we either didn't talk or yelled at one another, which was exhausting. Slug had nicknamed me Puppet during our first airborne assault. He said I could control the parachute like a puppeteer controlled his marionette. He wasn't wrong. I seemed to have an instinctive flair, which was odd considering I was a carpenter's boy who'd never seen a plane, never mind a parachute. "Let's see," he added and held out a large hand.

How did I reply to the man with nine kids and a lovely but worn-out wife? "Ah, Slug," I said, "you don't wanna see the milkman." Everyone laughed, but it was true, my darling Bert was the milkman.

A deafening crack-crack-crack rattled the plane's body and, as the noise echoed around my skull, the aircraft rolled to the left and the chaps tumbled off their benches. I jammed my feet against a ridge on the floor and wrapped my fingers around a metal upright.

"Fucking 'ell. Port engine's out." Jock's disembodied voice bellowed from behind the pilot's partition. Smoke filtered into the fuselage like steam from a hot bath and the plane dropped her nose as we all clung on.

"Fuck. Fuck. Not a flamer but the hydraulics are gone. It's not. Gonna. Be long," Jock spluttered. "Get out. Move."

Now? It wasn't time to go. Our mission was to hold a ridge overlooking the River Rhine and to provide support to the ground troops who needed to cross the river before moving on. We weren't over the designated drop area and I knew that because suicidal as our division was, even we wouldn't drop through tracer lines.

Wide-Fred leaped up and tugged at the arched door to my side. It didn't budge. He yanked again, throwing all his bulk at the door and then looked at me and panted, "Help. Puppet!"

I leaped up and encased Fred's hands with mine. Pulling together, the door screeched open and Hell invaded uninvited. Throat-clogging smoke from the destroyed engine, the screech of the bullets, and the deep oranges and bright whites of the Germans' arsenal, filled the inside of our crippled plane as if it were Bonfire Night.

Slugger, Nipper, Fred and the three young ones all clipped their release cords onto the rail that ran above the door.

"Wait!" Jock yelled. "Let me get 'er level." Jock's struggle with the controls was clear from his loud grunts and curses. The Dakota levelled but she'd dropped altitude. The lights from the ground were closer than before. "Bale. Bale. Bale," Jock ordered.

Slug threw himself into the furious sky followed by Nipper, then Fred, and then the young 'uns behind him. Through the open door and with the wind flapping the parachute straps into my face, their flash-lit bodies disappeared into uncertain futures, and then the plane started to turn like the hands of a clock.

"Jock!" I yelled over the din and rush of air. "Come on."

"I'll keep 'er steady while you jump," he shouted back, "then I'm with you."

I clipped onto the rail and inched my toes over the lip. The Dakota rolled, Jock shouted unknown words, and I slipped into the nightmare's mouth.

I was a fly spinning in a fire cobweb. My canopy was now open but how it wasn't riddled with bullet holes I had no idea. Maybe God was with me. No, God wasn't with men like me, or so Reverend Matthew says.

My eyes watered and my throat dried. I had to get out of the acrid smoke. Yanking the parachute's right riser, I twisted my body in the same direction just in time to watch the Dakota, and brave Jock, take a screaming nosedive. I cried out his name, over and over, knowing that my voice would never reach his ears. Twisting my face away and screwing my eyes shut I waited for the explosion that signalled Jock's turn to line up at the Pearly Gates. It came a few seconds later.

Dropping my head, I searched for an unlit area to aim for. To my right was, I guessed, farmland; I pulled the chute riser and drifted towards it. Then the expected happened – my rig shook in a hail of bullets. I was surprised I'd lasted this long. Without warning I was no longer floating, I was falling and spinning in a stomach-and-heart turned-to-soup way. In the dark, was the ground a hundred feet away or a thousand? I closed my eyes and pictured Bert's face to take me into my last moments.

My rig caught and I came to an abrupt back-jarring halt swinging like a pendulum between the branches of a tree. There was just enough time to slow my breathing before I was falling again and then hitting something hard. My legs crumpled first, they bent to one side and folded behind me, and then my chest smacked down and my head bounced like a ball on the uneven surface.

I rested for a moment, battling for breath, and focusing on my broken body. Then I started to slide. Head first with my twisted body following, I slithered and shuddered on the ridged slope for a few seconds, but it felt like a lifetime as my confused brain tried to make sense of where I was, and why I was sliding. I couldn't reach for anything to stop me as my hands were tied in the chute's cords. Then there was nothing but air.

I slapped soft ground, and wet sludge coated my face and hands before I passed out.

Coming to, I blinked into the weak sun that warmed my face and chest, and everything hurt, even my ears. I'd spilled in a tangled heap and every limb was stiff. I untangled myself with care and corrected my limbs to appear more human-shaped again. Dropping my head back into the wet sludge I stared for a long moment at the sky. It was blue fading to orange, with long misty clouds creeping across it. It was as if last night had never happened. Lifting my head, I surveyed my surroundings. The slope I'd landed on was a barn's red tiled roof in French occupied territory. Below the roof was an old stone building with a row of green painted doors that led into animal pens. As I drew myself into a sitting position, an eye-watering rancid smell hit me. I'm a farmer's son, I knew the smell of pigs. Great, a pig-sty, luckily its occupants seemed long gone, or long eaten.

I untangled the chute from my limbs and unclipped the harness from my body. However, the movement sent pain pulsing from my leg and down to my toes. I tugged my trouser leg up and blew a long breath. My knee was bloody and swollen to three times its size.

Still attached to the roof was the chute's nylon canopy, so I yanked it down and gathered it over my freezing body. I needed to stay warm whilst I focused on my next step. Where were Slug and Nip? And Fred? Did they make it? Was Fred's wife now a widow? And his children without a father? I shook the thoughts from my head and replaced them with instinct. I needed to get out of the cold mud and find protection from the enemy.

Lugging my battered body and the canopy, I crawled to the open door of the pen and was relieved to see a dry and straw-strewn interior. Squashing myself into the corner furthest away from the door, I took off my helmet and cloaked myself with the nylon, and then calculated that the food in my pocketed waist belt would last me a few days.

Hobnailed boots sounded on cobbles, lit every nerve, and stiffened every muscle. Accompanying the footsteps were an out-of-tune whistle and broken humming.

"Déjeuner. Déjeuner," a bright voice called followed by a sound like pebbles in a bucket.

I pressed back into the crumbling wall and held my breath. There was no guarantee a Frenchman would be a friendly man.

"Déjeuner. Déjeuner," the voice said again but this time fainter. I released the breath, wiped the sweat from my brow, and rifled through the scant training I'd been taught for a down in occupied territory. First was survival, which included food, water, shelter, and first aid. Okay, I had the food and shelter but not water or first aid. Second, was resisting any enemy. Well, I had no obvious enemy yet, only a whistling French farmhand, who could be a collaborator. And the third was escape; that was going to be the tricky part with my damaged knee but I had to make every effort to do so. No Germans or their allies would procure any information from me; I'd rather die first.

Rifling through my pockets I pulled out a box of hard sweets and popped one in my mouth. I wasn't hungry enough yet for the corned beef and biscuits, I'd save them for emergencies. I hatched a plan to recover just enough to limp out of the farm, find a group from the Resistance, and, if God were with me or not, go home.

I pulled Bert's letter and photograph from my pocket. We'd met early one misty spring morning in a narrow back lane outside the village. He was on his way back to the dairy with empty milk bottles rattling on his milk float and I was skulking in the hedgerows. He'd stopped and stared at me for a long moment before saying, "Birdwatching?"

"Aye," I'd replied.

"Have you spotted a dunnock?" Bert said and hopped off his float to join me.

"It's the last on my list." I'd pulled out a battered notebook from an equally scruffy satchel. "See." I showed him my British birds list; all but one had a tick placed next to their names.

Bert sat next to me with his back against the prickly hawthorn, looked me in the eye, and said, "It's on my list also." There didn't seem the need for any more words so we'd sat in silence for an hour with the occasional pointed finger, and watched the sun rise. We didn't spot the elusive dunnock, but it didn't matter.

Bert had placed a hand on my leg to help him stand and a lightning bolt shot up through my spine at the contact. Bert looked at his hand in surprise; perhaps he'd felt it too? He said, "Same time tomorrow?"

I'd nodded because I had no words.

We'd spent that spring and summer meeting up with my father's old field glasses slung round my neck, but very quickly the birds weren't important. We wandered the fields and woodlands, shared the field glasses, ate meat loaf washed down with lemonade, and talked about life. Sometimes we walked hand-in-hand or with our arms wrapped around each other's waist. Sometimes we paused to feel the sun on our faces and kiss in the shadows of the trees. And sometimes his fingers would work their way under my shirt and make my skin prickle to his touch. I loved him, and he me.

He's dead now.

I found out in a letter from my mother, who'd overheard old Mrs Woolston gossiping at the post office. My mother had written in her perfect calligraphic handwriting … *that lovely young milkman you were friendly with has been killed, apparently died outright as his tank took a direct hit.* Only twenty-one words, the same amount as the years he'd been alive, but they broke me in two.

A long creaking sound broke me from my reverie. The gate to the pen. I stuffed Bert's photo and letter back into my pocket and held my breath. Squelchy footsteps in the mud, snuffles, rattling bucket, and soft French words followed. The pigs were back … and their keeper. Then a large pig, black with a white band around its shoulder, joined me in the little hut. It stopped as its tiny black eyes spotted me, raised its snout in the air, and headed straight for my rations belt. Little bastard. I whacked it with the flat of my hand, but it towered over me and, ignoring the injured foreigner, it continued to probe its filthy nose into my belt.

"Fuck off," I shouted in the animal's face and then froze with horror.

The bastard pig's owner called, "Qui est là?"

No. No. No. Stupid. Stupid. Stupid.

A human shape filled the doorway and as the farmhand spotted me, the bucket flew into the air and he fled the pen, splattering through the mud as he went.

Well, I didn't expect that. In the dark, did he think I was a German? Perhaps he wasn't aware I was injured. I half-crawled my way to the door and for the first time saw my surroundings. In front of the pigsty was an open structure with a rusty corrugated roof, wooden legs, and a drunken lean. Beneath and arranged as if on display, were battered vehicles. All had lost their original shine, and some their wheels, but I guessed they had once been expensive. To my right, a tractor, in the same state as the cars, and a crumbling farmhouse peeked out from behind the car barn with the same roof as the pig houses, and faded green shutters. Strewn all around the farmyard were … A loud clang reverberated inside my head.

I came to, focused my swimming vision, winced at my throbbing head, and stared at the young chap kneeling in front of me. "What did you hit me with? The fucking tractor?" I quipped and glanced around. I was back in the pen with my hands bound behind my back. My feet were free but I wasn't able to run anywhere.

The farmhand raised his face to the ceiling and frowned as if searching for the words. "Non. A boo-ket," he said and pointed towards a discarded pig bucket as if I needed clarification. "English? American?"

"English," I replied and then chastised myself for giving away the information.

"Ah." He stood and placed his hands on his hips. "Good for you."

Good for me? Did that mean I'd landed in the farm of a collaborator and he was going to shoot me? I scanned my waist belt for my rifle. It was gone, so I searched for my dagger. It was also missing.

Needing time to think and formulate a plan, I kept him talking. "Good for me? Why?"

"I am your man."

Oh, I wasn't sure about that. "You speak English well. Where did you learn?"

"I speak a little."

Why do the French always say 'a little' when they have a whole vocabulary at their disposal? I could say hello, goodbye, where's the railway station, and a few other words.

"Parlez-vous français?" the chap asked.

"Un peu." I shuffled on the spot, and winced as pain from my knee pulsed up my leg.

"You are damaged." He knelt again by my side. "I will help." He placed a hand on my leg; the contact made me shudder just as Bert's first touch had.

I must have a fever. Then, for the first time, I really looked at him. He had brown hair that looked as if it'd been cut with shears … whilst drunk; a pleasant tanned face, and wore a dirty white shirt under brown dungarees which were tucked into boots that looked far too big for his skinny frame.

"Resistance?" I assumed a collaborator would've arrested me by now.

He hauled me onto my feet. "Come. No more pig caca. I take you to bed."

"B-ed?" Granted, he had an attractive face and pleasant demeanour, but I think there were more pressing matters. "Erm, thanks, um, maybe another time?" I offered him a smile.

The farmhand stopped and looked me right in the eye. "Non. Non. For your recovery."

"Oh." Now I felt stupid.

"Henri," Henri said as he dragged me out into the sunlight.

"Puppet. Pleased to meet you." And I was. It was lucky I'd fallen onto Henri's pig-sty.

"Pou-pet?"

"Puppet."

"Puppet," Henri repeated and scowled.

"It's a nickname," I said.

"You stole the name? There are better English names to steal I think," Henri replied.

"No … " I shook my head. "Doesn't matter."

Still bound but ably supported by Henri's arm, I limped across the yard towards the low stone farmhouse next to the derelict barn. "Why do you have all the old cars?"

Henri paused and stared at the crumbling vehicles. "They were my Papa's." He heaved me back up into his arms and continued, "Now. They are mine."

As we approached the green door, it struck me that there might be other people in the house … maybe Fred, or Slugger, or someone else. "Have you seen others like me?"

"I see many things drop from the sky – people, avions, and weapons, but only you landed on my ferme." He hauled me into his house.

The dim room was sparse with a slab floor, table, two chairs, a sink hanging off the wall, and an open fire with dying embers, but it was spotlessly clean with a scent of candle wax and flowery curtains at the small window.

"Here." Henri plonked me onto a chair and went to fill a cup with water. As he passed it to me, I asked again. "Resistance?"

Henri paused before saying, "I am with the Dutch-Paris. We smuggle documents but also smuggle people like airmen. You, mon ami, were lucky to land on my pigsty."

"I'm not sure lucky is correct, I've lost all my friends in one night." After taking a drink, I placed the glass on the table and made to stand. "I've never heard of the Dutch-Paris."

"Then we have kept the secret."

"So you're Dutch?"

"Non, français." Henri placed a hand under my elbow and led me to a narrow staircase that twisted away from the corner of the room. "Can you climb?"

"I think so." But every step shot threads of pain down to my toes, made my head spin, and squeezed my eyes shut.

The only door on the landing had a curved top. Henri squeezed past me and opened it into a small bedroom that resembled the interior of an upside-down wooden boat. Inside, its sloping roof demanded that we shuffle with bent heads. The smell of pigs made me do a quick check around the room. Perhaps Henri kept one in his house, hiding it from hungry locals; everyone knew the Germans kept the French people submissive by starvation.

There was no pig. Or much else for that matter. An oversized brass-framed bed sat against the only straight wall, piled high with mismatched blankets and cushions. Next to it, a chair pretended to be a bedside table, and on the floor were neat piles of clothes – presumably Henri's.

"Here." Henri led me to the bed, turned me to face him, and held my gaze for a second before untying my bound hands and then unclipping my utility belt and dropping it to the floor. He then edged round me and deftly undid the flap on my Denison, unbuttoned the smock, and slipped it off my shoulders. There was a pause before he undid and discarded my heavy battledress with ease and chucked it into a corner. I had a feeling I wasn't the first paratrooper he'd undressed … or the last. He left me in my vest, drawers, and regulation socks and then stood back to admire either his undressing prowess or me. "Lie on the bed, I will darn your knee," he

168

commanded.

Hoping that he wasn't going to actually darn my knee, I lay on the soft mattress as Henri disappeared from the room then reappeared with a clump of tiny white flowers, green leaves, two water bowls and strips of white material. With an old, and I hoped clean, towel, he wiped away the blood. There was a deep laceration in the skin; Henri cleaned the wound with one bowl of water then soaked the flowers and leaves in the other bowl before screwing the wet mush into a ball and smearing it onto the wound. He used long rhythmic strokes moving up and down my leg further than was needed. I let my head flop back onto the pillow, closed my eyes, and crossed my hands over the front of my drawers. Henri cleared his throat, brought his stroking to a regretful end, and presented the longest needle I'd ever seen; from it hung a long thread.

"What is that for?" I asked but knew the answer.

"Lie still."

I'd never been darned before but it was a surprisingly pleasant experience. I felt no pain, the pale grey flower mush had numbed my skin, and Henri's deft fingers were soothing. "You pray for no dirty wound," Henri said and bound my knee tightly with the material. "You are not safe here."

"I'm guessing you have regular visitors?"

"My ferme is on the escape route and the Germans suspect me."

"You're playing a dangerous game."

"The war forced me to play." As he stood, the mattress undulated like the sea. "I will get eat." He left through the half-door.

Within a few minutes the door opened again, this time a stern-looking chap with a folding camera entered. He indicated that I should get up and stand against the plain wall. I obliged and as he pointed the camera at me, I looked straight down the lens. The stranger took my picture and disappeared within a minute. Who was he? How did he know I was here? Why had he taken my photograph? I resolved to ask Henri when he returned.

Above the bed was a tiny window with the same floral curtains as downstairs. Outside, the sky was a pale blue with white wisps drifting across its expanse. Only God knew why such atrocities were happening under such beauty. I crawled back into bed and drifted off, and when I awoke it was dark and I was starving. By the bed, Henri had left bread, cheese, and cloudy juice. I heaved myself up and ate as if it were my last meal before the gallows, which it might have been. The door creaked open and half-lit in candlelight Henri poked his head round. "Okay?"

"Yes, I am, thank you." And I was. "Who was the chap who took my photograph?"

"The only man I know with a camera."

"Why did he take my picture?"

"You will see. We will move when the sun awakes." Henri turned.

"Where are you sleeping tonight?" I called after him. Of course, the fact I had his bed concerned me; but I would've enjoyed his company. My division were all married with children or eagerly trying for children. I was different and that made the world a lonely place.

Henri strolled up to the bed and studied me before saying, "On the chaise downstairs."

"Right. Yes." I smoothed the bedsheets and felt my cheeks burn. Maybe I'd read him wrong. Maybe getting into bed with me was one risk too far in this dangerous country.

"Goodnight, Pou-pet." The only light left with him as he shut the door.

The sound of clanking linked tracks and engines growling as if in pain filled my ears and shook me from my sleep. I twisted and heaved myself up on the metal bed-frame to peer through the small window. In the dawn light, I could just see a line of Panzers followed by a troop carrier as they rattled their way along the narrow road towards Henri's farm.

Thinking fast, I rolled out of bed and onto my good leg, gathered my clothes and equipment, hopped to the bedroom door and collided with Henri who had panic etched on his young face.

"Quickly," he urged, took me by the arm, and dragging me down the stairs two at a time. We fled across the cobbled yard with adrenaline keeping me upright and quick, and shot into the abandoned barn. Henri pulled me towards the back where an old wheel-less truck rested on bricks. He threw off the green tarpaulin that enveloped its high-sided flatbed, yanked down the back door, and bundled me onto the cold metal floor. The stink of engine oil and mildew made me cough and I was immediately scolded by Henri. "If you like life. You will not breathe." Then he fastened down the tarpaulin and disappeared. I was alone with only an old tyre and my heartbeat for company.

Arranging myself along the truck side for support, I wriggled into my clothes, and waited. And waited. And waited. An occasional German voice shouted instructions, a pig squealed, and engines coughed into life and then died.

Then an old rough voice, like that of a commander said, "Sie besitzen die Autos?"

"Oui, les voitures sont à moi," Henri answered.

"Deutsch," the German barked.

"I do not speak German," Henri replied.

"It will soon be your mother tongue." Footsteps came closer to the truck. "I will have these cars when we win the war. My brother is a collector." There was a dull banging noise and vibration as, I presumed, the German kicked a tyre.

"I show you the Citroën? It is a rare B14." Henri was trying to move him away from my hiding place because the red Citroen rested in the barn's furthest corner. Then the taupe shifted. Calloused fingers emerged above my head and cigar smoke drifted into the flatbed. I stopped breathing as every muscle in my body tightened, the hairs lifted on my nape, and my heart flew into my throat.

"Where are the wheels?" the German asked.

"On another voiture. Please. Come. See the Citroën. Your brother will be pleased with his prize." Henri's tone was sarcastic, not that the German detected it. Footsteps and chatter moved away from the truck. My body released its grip, shuddered for a moment, and I had a sudden desire to flee. Throughout the day, my knee, still wrapped, had continued to improve but I wasn't sure it would support a dash into enemy territory.

The light from the green taupe above my head faded, marking the end of the day. I was cold, stiff, and hungry in the silent barn, then I heard Henri – his footsteps were so much lighter than heavy German boots were.

The door creaked open, the tarpaulin rippled as Henri flicked it back a little, and then he crawled in next to me pulling a large bag behind him. The flatbed sides allowed him to sit up with his neck bent. "Are you okay?" he whispered.

"Yes, I'm alive and that's got to be good." I shifted up onto my elbows and watched Henri rifle around in the bag and pull out two thick woollen blankets, a cob loaf, four boiled eggs, and a British Army issue water bottle.

"Here." He passed me a cover and then two eggs and the torn end of the cob. I covered my cold legs with the coarse blanket and ate the eggs in two bites. "We must speak quietly, the Germans are in my maison and drunk on Papa's wine, but still danger." Henri drew a blanket around his shoulders, scrunched the bag up as a pillow, and settled down next to me. The lines on his face and his calloused hands said he'd had a hard life for a young soul, and I could only imagine what it was like to live in a conquered land. My life was rough enough as a British paratrooper, risking my life every day, but I felt Henri's occupied life was tougher. "Tell me about you. How old are you?" he said.

"Twenty. And I'm just an ordinary chap who happens to jump from Dakotas."

"Not ordinary."

"Is anybody normal any more? How old are you?"

"Nineteen." Henri fiddled with the hem of his blanket.

"Why are you alone?"

"My parents were taken by, um, how do you say, tuberculose."

"Tuberculosis?"

"Yes, that. A year ago. They died within a month of each other." Henri sighed. "We have no médicament, no doctors, no one helped."

"I'm sorry."

"I buried them on the hill behind the house." Henri paused before saying, "Not good idea, now I feel they spy on me with frowns." He then laughed because, I believe, it was preferable to crying.

"Why frowns?"

"Ma chambre sees the hill. I forget to fasten curtains … "

"How many airmen have you had in this farm?"

"Airmen? Deux or trois. But many men need my help."

"And services … "

Henri kicked me on my good leg. "Only a few have had … services."

"I'm one in a long line then?"

"Monsieur Pou-pet. Do you want to be one?"

Fuck. Did I say that aloud?

"Um … "

Henri politely changed the subject. "Why do you jump out of avion?"

"I was a soldier in the army and a good one at that. I saw a poster in my barracks requesting volunteers, and longing for the damn war to end I thought the airborne division was the way forward, so I applied. They made sure I was right in the head and then trained me hard. And here I am." I waved my hand around. "In the back of a French truck."

"You are the best amongst men?"

"Yeah, I can control a chute and that earns me respect."

"Puppet … What is your proper name?"

"It's Colin."

Henri giggled. "Cul-in? Cul? Your name means arse en français."

"No! Colin. Col."

"I like it." Henri smiled.

I smiled back. "Do you have someone to help with the farm, Henri? Siblings perhaps?"

"What is sibling?"

"Frère? Sœur?" I said remembering my basic French and wishing to impress Henri, which surprised me, I hadn't wanted to impress anyone since Bert.

"One older brother. Working the land made him big and strong. The Germans took him." Henri paused. "I do not know where. I think … Frenchmen that Germans think are danger are sent to a labour camp or shot." Henri pulled his blanket closer. "I hope to see him again."

I reached out and placed my hand on Henri's arm; it was cold. "I'm sorry, Henri."

He shook his head before saying, "What will you do after war, Monsieur Cul-in?"

I could see that Henri was going to like using my real name. "If I'm still alive then I don't know because I expect to die. So if I am still breathing then I'll perhaps follow in my father's footsteps and be a carpenter or something ordinary like that."

"You are not ordinary, Monsieur Cul-in."

The way Henri managed to put a naughty twist onto my name was very cute. "No, I suppose I'm not." I stretched out my leg and shuffled my cul.

"Will you stay in army?"

"No. The military want me when they need fighters but after the war it will all go back to how it was."

"Was?"

"People … like me … are needed now in wartime but we will be rejected after the war. And if Germany wins … God help me."

"And me," Henri murmured.

"I'm afraid I need to pee," I said, breaking the moment.

"Here." Henri searched in his bag and then threw me a metal container with a narrow neck. He turned away as I used the vessel. "We will move in morning," he said to himself.

"Okay." I wished to move, of course I did. Occupied France was a dangerous place for a British airman and I yearned to get back to my division, to get back to my mates and show them that finding your way home could be done. Nevertheless, a part of me wondered about staying with Henri on his farm and forgetting about this wretched war.

Henri shuffled down the flatbed. "Sleep. It will prepare you for long journey home," he said before slipping into the dark. I missed his presence instantly.

The morning broke with engines roaring, barked instructions, loud chatter, and metal tracks chewing up the dirt road. I held my breath and waited until the noise faded into the distance. Half an hour or so later the tarpaulin peeled back like the lid of a sardine tin and I, the only sardine, squinted into the light. Henri, in dark-coloured travel clothes and a beret, with a leather rucksack and a walking stick, smiled at me.

"It is time." My limbs were stiff with cold as I struggled out. Henri passed me a plain shirt, brown wool jacket, and grey slacks. "Quick," he said, "change into these." I did as he asked and passed Henri my uniform, which he bundled into the truck's engine bay. Then he passed me a card which stated that I had a mental affliction. That would explain any problems I had with communication. It also read that my name was François Bertram and that I was born in 1922 – a good guess on Henri's part. In the top corner was the photograph of my face that had been taken earlier in the bedroom, and marked in the bottom left was a round stamp and an official-looking signature scrawled across it.

"Where the hell did you get this?" I waved it in Henri's face.

"From a good forger who learned in prison."

Not wishing to know any more, I held my arms out and did a twirl. "Okay. Do I look like a Frenchman?"

"You must not fool," Henri scolded.

My cheeks burned. I wasn't used to being told off, I normally gave out any dressings-down that were needed, but my life depended on Henri; so I said to the dirt floor, "Yes, of course, sorry."

"We will make our way over the Alps to the exchange point." He made it sound so simple. "Along the way we will meet people who will help."

"There's a children's game in England called pass the parcel. I feel like the parcel."

"Oui. You are the parcel."

"You're all risking your lives for me. Why?"

"You win the war and we get our country back."

"How many times have you made this trip?"

"More than is lucky."

I was well aware of the danger he was putting himself in. Downed airmen were slung in a POW camp but, if the rumours about the Resistance were true, death came as a blessed relief for them.

We marched away from the little farm and spent two days shadowing hedgerows, using them for cover and shelter from persistent spring showers. When we reached a gap in the green wall Henri would peek round the leaves, whisper, "Now," and dash with me across to the relative safety of the other side.

My back hurt from tramping bent over and my neck ached from constantly turning my head whenever I heard the slightest rustle or crack. I was a nervous wreck and we were only on day two. I'd heard stories of men taking nineteen months to return to Britain. That's nearly two years. I was sure that if it took me that long to get home my life would never be the same again. And I wouldn't be alone; many people would be damaged by this war. Ace paratrooper or Home Guard, it made no difference.

A robin's haunting whistle stopped me mid-stride. The song took me straight back to Bert and our perfect summer in the cornfields and woodlands of home. Would I ever see my village again?

Henri, sensing that I'd stopped, turned, and hissed, "What is it?"

"A robin."

"What?"

"A bird."

Henri scowled at me. Why? Maybe he thought I wasn't scared enough. I wasn't at the moment; however, Henri's face told me I was going to be very afraid before I finally escaped – or died.

"Sorry." Rolling my neck, I hunched my wet pack back onto my shoulders, placed one muddy boot in front of the other and continued my bent trek.

As the light faded, we ventured out into an open field. Using the natural lie of the land we kept hidden from the small lane that ran parallel to the field. Then a tiny village, folded into a valley, appeared in front of us.

I'd been squatting alone in a hedge for more time than my sore knee cared for when Henri came scurrying back. "How you say? The coast is clear," he said.

"No Germans?"

"Non, the propriétaire de l'auberge said he will feed us and bed us."

I opened my mouth to comment on Henri's turn of phrase but decided against it and simply said, "Good."

Nobody turned to face us as we entered the cramped auberge; it was as if the drinkers desired no knowledge of our presence, which was fine by me. We found a round table near the fire to dry ourselves and I set down my weary bones on the hard chair. The propriétaire brought us beer in dull tankards and dumped them onto the table causing the liquid to slosh over the rims. A wiry old woman plonked metal plates loaded with bread and blue cheese on the table and then scuttled away, her eyes never leaving the floor. I glanced around the room at the locals, shifted on my chair, crossed my arms, and then uncrossed them.

"Stop it," Henri hissed.

"What?" I whispered, but I knew what.

"Eat. Drink. Then we will bed."

Then we will bed. Bed. I needed release, a distraction from my situation, maybe Henri would be up for a quick shuffle? I shook my head. No, no, concentrate, man, I scowled at myself but couldn't stop thoughts of writhing naked bodies and creaking beds rampaging around my head. I was dog-tired, and … a little scared at my situation.

"Pou-pet?"

"Um?"

"Eat." Henri shoved the plate towards me. I obliged, even devouring the sock-tasting cheese the French find so appealing.

The candlelit attic room had a bare board floor and small round holes in its tiled roof. A breeze played with the frayed curtains at the lone window and in the corner was one leaning wooden bed.

"Faut quitter avant que le jour se lève," the propriétaire growled and slammed the door behind him. Something about leaving before day, I presumed.

"He is frightened," Henri said and threw himself onto the bed; it swung alarmingly, creaked loudly, and chucked a million dust motes into the candlelight. Henri stretched his arms above his head.

"And I sleep where?"

Henri propped up onto his elbows and considered me for a long moment before saying, "With me."

"Um, there's no room, I'll, um, sleep on the floor." I spun on the spot like a dog before settling down to sleep.

"You do not trust me?"

I didn't trust myself. "Um."

"Then you. In here." Henri crawled under the one frayed blanket, nudged up against the wall, and indicated that I join him.

I kicked off my boots and climbed into the bed; as expected, it creaked loudly which only served to fuel my imagination. I lay so far on the edge that only one arse cheek was on the mattress. Henri took my shoulder and rolled me back so I was staring at the holed ceiling flickering in the light from the tiny flames. "You need proper rest." His body heat warmed my side, his breath tickled my cheek, and his hand rested on my shoulder. "Sleep, Pou-pet." I closed my eyes.

Heavy footsteps on the wooden floor woke me in a heart-stopping instant. The propriétaire regarded us embraced in the small bed for a moment before saying, "Il y a une camionnette en dehors. Dépêchez-vous."

We gathered our things, pulled on our boots, and followed him to a back door. A pale blue van waited, engine running, on the lane behind the pub. The driver, who looked about twelve, maintained a steely gaze on the road ahead and a firm grip on the wheel. Henri opened the back doors and we climbed in.

Henri closed the doors behind him and we set off at a rattling speed beyond the van's capabilities. "Where are we going?"

"A la gare," Henri replied.

"A train? Henri, is that wise?"

"It is fastest way. I have done many times. Do not worry, Pou-pet. I will guide you."

Easy for him to say, he was a proper Frenchman; I was a downed enemy paratrooper posing as a Frenchman, who didn't speak the language, or even know where I was.

The ride to the station was bumpy and the van smelled of chicken shit. Henri exchanged information with the unsociable driver, but I said very little the whole journey and mainly held on to the front seats, trying to avoid a bruised tail bone.

"Nous sommes arrivés," the driver said.

"Follow me." Henri slid out of the van and I followed. We were in a narrow tree-lined lane to the side of the station. Henri straightened up, smoothed his clothing, turned to look at me, and then nodded. I nodded to show that I was ready. However, I wasn't. My heart was so loud I'm sure Henri could hear it.

We casually walked towards the station, not knowing if this would be the place where it all came crashing down. There were so many hurdles – the ticket office, exposure on the platform, the guards, any Germans, the people on the train, my false papers, the … the list was endless.

Henri bought tickets and we made it through onto the only platform with only a bored glance from the boy behind the counter, but the platform was packed. This could be a good thing – lost in the crowd – or bad – more German guards on duty.

It was bad. A line of Germans stood along the platform checking identity cards. Before we'd entered the station Henri had said, don't even try to speak, so I knocked his arm and nodded towards the guards. Henri pulled me into the crowd.

We managed to slip past the platform guards and find two seats together, with a chap's cul in my face as he stood in front of me. The train was standing room only and stank of engine oil, smoke, and sweat. Henri had given me a newspaper, so I held it up to my face and pretended to read the French news as the train clicker-clacked and swayed beneath me. The journey to – I'd forgotten where, was about two hours long, Henri had said. It was going to be the longest two hours of my life. I 'read' the paper and glanced at the passing countryside and villages. After a while, I settled back into my lumpy seat and let my shoulders droop a little and my head loll. The German word, Papiere, echoed loudly around the carriage.

"Relax," Henri murmured. He folded up his newspaper, placed it on his knee, and pulled out his identity card. I copied him. The German, a large grey looming figure, thrust his hand into Henri's face, and barked, "Papiere." Henri passed his card over without a word, the German thumbed it, turned it over, and stared at Henri. "Was ist Ihr Geschäft?"

"Visite à papa malade," Henri replied in French, whatever that meant. The man threw Henri's card back at him and held out his hand for mine. I passed it over and with all my willpower held the German's stare.

The man read the card and bellowed, "Was ist Ihr Geschäft?"

I didn't reply. How could I? I couldn't speak German or French. I was an Englishman on a German-occupied French train. Fuck.

"Was ist Ihr Geschäft?" he repeated with spite in his voice.

Silence. From the whole carriage.

"Il est sous ma responsabilité," Henri replied. "Il a une affliction et est muet. Il ne peut pas être laissé seul."

There was a long painful moment before the German handed me back my card. "Danke," he said. I opened my mouth and the English words "You're welcome" were on the tip of my tongue but something, some guardian angel, made me snort a reply instead. The German laughed and moved on. If I could've crapped myself there and then I would've and it was a battle to stop bile rising in my throat. I felt Henri slip down into his seat as I concentrated on the blurry trees through the window.

We arrived at a station with a clear view of the mountains. "Come." Henri dragged me out of the railway station, into a back lane, and from there into another field. We squatted down behind a hawthorn hedge. "How is it you say? Fuck me?" Henri blew a long breath.

Well. Yes. I would have liked to actually, but I replied, "Aye," instead.

"I have a place to stay."

"Where?"

"You will see." Henri winked.

It was still light when we reached the place. A brothel. We couldn't walk in full view through its doors so we waited in a nearby wood for dusk. Henri was quiet and brooding.

"Penny for them?" I asked.

"Penny for what?"

"Your thoughts."

"Oh. This is where I lost a man," Henri said.

"Lost?"

"Yes. A pilot. He bedded a girl and in passion cried out in English. I told him to stay away from girls."

"Then?"

"Girl ran to the madam. Madam tied up naked English man. Germans paraded him in the street." Henri stared at me. "Do not bed girl."

"Um, Henri, not much chance of that."

"Good," he said.

Was that *good* so I don't risk getting caught? Or *good* because he craves me for himself? Shut up, Puppet.

The room the madam gave us was small, dim, and painted red with one huge bed set in the centre. She'd winked at Henri as we'd entered the brothel and spoken in French. He had blushed and shaken his head; she chuckled and twirled her full skirt as she flounced out of the room. The room was warm but smelt of cheap perfume and rubber. The whole house groaned with the sounds of passion and the room next to us was no exception. The high-pitched whimpers coming from there made me shuffle on the spot and cough.

"Why here, Henri?"

"The Germans do not check brothels as regularly as hotels. Probably German next door." He indicated with his thumb. Well, that was just great. Henri locked the door and slid a bolt across. Any other time I would've been celebrating – nice-looking chap, big bed, the night ahead. But I would've rather been anywhere but here. There was a soft knock on the door. Not German, I reckoned, they would have battered the door. Henri opened it a crack so bread and milk could be passed through. "Merci," he whispered and bolted the door again.

After eating, I lay on the soft bed with my knees drawn up to my chest, fully clothed but desiring to be naked with Henri. The bed dipped as he crawled behind me, slipped his arm around my waist, and pulled me towards him. His hipbones stuck into my arse as he pushed his knees behind mine causing my body to curve away from him. I knitted my fingers with his and then let sleep take me.

About a day, Henri had said, twenty-four hours to walk to a town at the foot of the Alps and then to freedom. But before relative safety we had a bridge to cross, the only surviving one across a wide deep river and heavily guarded by German sentries. But, as Henri had said, laughing at his own joke, we'll cross that bridge when we come to it. First, we had to avoid capture through the fields and lanes between here and there. My knee gave me an odd twinge occasionally but mostly it didn't show in my thoughts. In fact, Henri loomed larger. We rested for a few hours in a dip by an old oak tree, nestled amongst roots as big as my arm, but most of the time we trudged in the shadows.

From our vantage point on a hill above the river, we observed the patrols pace the narrow wooden bridge – the thin brown line which would take me closer to freedom.

"The only way to do this is to be brave," Henri said.

"Brave?"

"Locals allowed to cross bridge with papers. We have papers."

"The right papers?"

"Papers are papers. Courage in their face, Puppet. Less think. More go." He strode towards the stony goat track that ran down to the bridge. I had nothing to lose; if I was caught I'd spend the rest of the war in a camp. I could have lived in the shadows on Henri's farm but I was a paratrooper and a valuable one and I was needed. Straightening my back and steeling my gaze, I followed a step behind Henri.

We stood with our heels on the dirt path and our toes on the bridge's wooden planks. "Papiere!" a German shouted and barrelled towards us. Good God, they liked their own importance in someone else's land. I held my ground even though my whole being ached to turn and run.

Henri took a step forward. "Guten Tag," he said and handed his card to the red-faced man.

"Zweck?" he demanded whilst he examined the card.

"Visite à papa malade," Henri repeated.

"Und Sie?" The German pointed at me.

"Il est sous ma responsabilité," Henri replied. "Il a une affliction et est muet. Il ne peut pas être laissé seul." As the German stared at me, I was sure he could see my heart beating in my throat and the sweat forming on my forehead. Henri took another step forward. "Mon papa est malade. Allez. Rapide." Then there was a kerfuffle at the other end of the bridge: a man was on his back flailing his arms with a guard straddling him. Our German thrust Henri's card back at him, turned, and ran towards the skirmish.

"Quick," Henri said under his breath and we walked as fast, but as controlledly, as we could past the downed man – whom I silently thanked – the patrols, and into the hills on the other side.

The French Alps spread out like a row of jagged teeth and, even in spring, white crowns topped their peaks. "Now where?"

"An old path. It will lead to Suisse."

"Old?" I repeated.

"Overgrown, steep, and unused, except by the Resistance and goats."

The light was fading. "I'm guessing we walk through the night?"

"A little. But dangerous path. There is a cave we can sleep. Then continue at first light." Henri's eyes were dark-ringed, his shoulders drooped, and his beret skew-whiff. He was taking a huge risk for me, as for all the others he'd helped. I briefly wondered who was feeding the pigs in his absence.

The path's start was steep with little natural platforms in the rock that were useful as steps; sometimes the path required handholds as well. And it was narrow, about the width of a goat, with a sheer drop into a steep-sided valley to my right. Clearly, I didn't have a problem with heights but here, if you fell, with no chute, it was a certain death.

After an hour of knee-burning scrambling, the path levelled out and the surface became littered with little round stones and gravel – perfect for propelling feet along and then off the side. I stood tall and trailed my fingers along the rock face to anchor me in the dark. In the distance and lit by a bright moon, the path stretched ahead like a grey serpent winding itself around the mountain. Henri, in front, suddenly stopped. "It is here."

"What?"

"The cave. Here we will stay until dawn." He disappeared off the path like a magician's assistant.

"Henri?"

"Here," his call echoed.

Taking a few more steps, I saw a black slit in the rock that was as tall as a man and twice as wide. I hesitated for a moment before going inside; the cave was bone-numbingly cold and smelled of damp. Henri was on the floor, a lone candle already lit next to him, and slices of bread fanned out on a red spotted handkerchief. In that moment, I loved his doggedness, his bravery, his humour, his kindness, his jaunty beret, his face, and his mouth. I loved the cave, the candle, and the funny handkerchief. I loved him.

In the flickering light, I sat down in silence, wanting this moment to last. Henri passed me a slice of bread. "Déjeuner," he said with a smile.

I took it, said, "Thank you, kind sir," and bowed.

Henri laughed. "If God is with us. It is not long now."

"What happens when we reach the end of the path?"

"Luca will be there to meet us."

"Luca?"

"Oui, my Suisse handover."

"Pass the parcel."

Henri looked at his feet. "Oui."

"Will you be okay?"

Henri shrugged. "Are any of us okay, Mr Cul-in?"

Soon Henri's soft snores filled the cave. I was sure he could've slept on the front line. I spent an uncomfortable and freezing night with stones jabbing into my back, but I couldn't sleep anyway. I desperately sought to return to England, to fight once more for my country, but I also wanted to stay with Henri: with his pigs, flowery curtains, rusty cars, and dangerous work.

First light brought yellow sunshine that shone a line through the cave entrance, lit Henri, and made him glow. He stirred and murmured, "It is time."

The path, crumbled away in places, overgrown in others, led us through the mountains, then hills, and finally, as we were losing the light again, onto grassy lowlands. Henri led me towards a large clump of stumpy trees and bushes and we hid amongst the twisted branches, waiting for Luca.

A whistle, high like a bird's, rang out.

Henri whistled a reply.

A man surfaced beside us, I made to bolt, but Henri caught my arm. "Luca," he said.

Luca, wide shouldered with a weather-beaten face, replied in English, "Henri. Is this him?"

Henri nodded and then everything moved quickly as he bundled me towards the man. Luca took my wrist and pulled with some urgency. Uncaring whether he overheard, I asked Henri, "Will I ever see you again?"

Henri gave Luca a glance before replying, "I would really like that, Mr Cul-in."

"Then I will come back for you, Henri, I promise."

"Then I will stay alive for you." Henri turned and melted into the shadows.

Winter 1945

The farmhouse looked the same, the cars still rotted in the barn, the truck on bricks still waited, and the pigs smelled, but somehow it felt different – lighter, brighter, freer. I knocked on the faded green door, smoothed my blazer, and pulled my scarf tighter.

I'd showed up on a whim with no idea if Henri was still alive, or if he still lived at the farm, or if he wanted to see me. A year is a long time but a war year is an eternity. No answer. I knocked again and peered through the kitchen window. Nothing. As I turned, a rattle of pellets in a bucket filled the morning air.

"Déjeuner, déjeuner," Henri called.

Time stopped and rewound. I stood still, unbreathing, until his eye caught mine … then the bucket dropped with a clatter. Henri ran and launched himself at me, circled my waist and neck with his long limbs, propelling me back into the wall of the house. I knotted my hands under his backside and laughed.

"Mr Cul-in! You are alive."

"And you."

Needing no more words, Henri kissed my neck, took my hand, and then opened the green door.

This paratrooper was going to keep his feet firmly on the ground from now on; the thought of tending to this land, and to the needs of the farmhand, was very appealing indeed.

We're Out of Hero Fabric

Andrea Demetrius

Before dawn, on the morning of August 23, 1944, Camil registered a change in the air. A musty whiff, just a tad cool enough to make it noticeable, sneaked beneath his bedroom door.

His heart skipped a beat.

But a reluctant glance at the clock put a swift end to his hopes. It was just the old housekeeper sent in to check up on him.

He made himself remain in bed for a few more moments: to erase the longing from his mind, or to delude himself that, any moment now, the doorknob would turn, and some other person would enter his rooms.

But, of course, over the years, he'd cultivated his reflective nature too well to be able to go back, or to make good use of any kind of pretence for long.

With a weary sigh, he admitted defeat. He was, had been for a while – hours, or maybe two months, the last two years? – all too wide awake.

Camil got up, raised his chin in a defiant challenge to the air above him – or maybe to the direction of the royal palace – aware of the whimsical ritual he'd fallen into, but too stubborn to part with it, and he whispered to himself, once, "Perhaps this is the day".

He shook himself, afterwards.

He owed Sebastian a reply to his letter, anyway. It had been on his desk for more than a week already.

Sebastian couldn't easily spare the time, or the resources, to send word from whatever part of France he'd lately managed to find his way to, so Camil should have attended to the correspondence post-haste.

Camil had attempted, unsuccessfully, to justify his failure toward his friend. One such justification lay in the fact that he'd made a habit of keeping an eye on Sebastian's properties. The newly assigned 'owners' of the house seemed, at least, to take proper care of it; but sadly, the situation at the once-renowned gentlemen's outfitters hadn't changed one bit in the year since it had been broken into. There was no sign of anybody willing to step in, not even to ensure its proper protection to avoid further weather damage. People dared not even let themselves be seen walking near places such as this.

As for Camil's lack of involvement, well, ever since the war broke out, he had had to accept the knowledge that the world hadn't given birth yet to the tailor capable of making the hero battledress that would suit him.

Thus, in the absence of new happenings of enough worth to be passed along, Camil had put off writing back.

It stood to reason that, after Sebastian had to flee abroad, and the subsequent limitation of their correspondence, what with the crafty way they had to bend every word and Sebastian's ever-changing return address, Camil had to deliberate carefully over what once had been such a quotidian, almost careless endeavour.

It was a quite valid argument, all told.

Despite that, there had been far less of an upheaval or lasting scrutiny concerning his friend's whereabouts than any of them had expected, considering that Sebastian was known to have participated in reunions in Paris and Brussels ever since 1934.

There had been questions, of course, and Camil had been warned, but ultimately he supposed he hadn't been deemed to fit the type the Green Shirts had hunted for back then.

It had been staggering to realise that even people who adopted the theory of purification by death, and were not at all inclined to ask questions or have doubts before rushing to inflict their opinion on others, had so easily dismissed him from their sights.

On the other hand, after being revealed as inadequate even as prey, Camil had found a kind of thrill in maintaining his correspondence with Sebastian in these circumstances.

What, for Camil, had been a simple matter of much-needed, personal contact with a dear friend far from home, had for the militia read as proof of involvement with a treasonous partisan, and even their customary greetings had been suspected of some kind of subversive, rebellious undertones. But, the threat to his life now gone, Camil was left feeling as if they were engaging in one of those wicked pranks they used to play as kids, back in the days when things were easy, back in the days before his accident happened, putting an end to their carefree happiness.

Which made his delay in putting pen to paper even more mystifying, he supposed.

186

Of course, these days, it was harder to lie to oneself. The war was steadily stripping away all his pretences and illusions. For example, Camil would once have had no qualms in proclaiming that his preoccupation extended, without question, to the fate of all the Jewish men and their families, and not just to those of his inner circle, as Sebastian was.

But his character thus revealed, his awareness of his true nature imprinted into his every thought, Camil could no longer deny he was a different man today, the veneer of the proud intellectual individual he'd once been having been slowly washed away in the years since he had parted ways with his friends.

This morning, like many others before, Camil shied away from looking too closely at one particular corner of his rooms.

He'd renounced the pursuit of what had previously been his guiding light. His idea of a society relying on intellectuals organised in professional guilds, Plato's aristocracy of the wise brought to life. Camil's old issues of 'Intellectual Work' remained, gathering dust and seen out of the corner of his eye every waking hour he had to spend in here. He barely remembered the times when he would peruse them feverishly in search of that one morsel absolutely vital to his personal enlightenment, so consumed by eagerness and so convinced that this was the only way he could better himself as a human being.

Camil faltered before leaving his rooms.

Despite his wide-awake, constant, and obsessive analysis of self, on days like today when he was plagued by insomnia and walked around feeling stripped to his flesh and bones – days like every day had been ever since the news came in June that an Allied invasion had indeed occurred in France – it seemed as if Camil's mind was still wholly able to trick him. To fail him. To let animal instincts, feelings, overpower whatever remained of what once had been subjected only to the most objective mental processes.

This morning, he could not escape the realisation that he had constructed a screen from his, all too real otherwise, preoccupation with Sebastian's possible opinion of the changes that had occurred in Camil.

What's more, his friend's safety wasn't hanging in the balance because of Camil's tardy response to his letter. Camil's guilt and self-recriminations were out of proportion to that specific, and sadly, all too real fault.

But there was a vital part of Camil's self that was at stake these days.

And because of it, Camil was trying hard to avoid dissecting his most recent actions. Camil had gambled away his one chance to step up in society, to become the kind of man his father had probably given up on him ever becoming. To act as the saviour of his family. To be the honest journalist he was supposed to be.

And, of course, the means he had used, the cards he had held spoke only of his complete lack of scruples.

But still, if applied more rightly, if he had subsumed them to a more noble motive, their use might have been somewhat mitigated. His debasement could have served an honourable purpose, fulfilled a filial duty, proved his familial loyalty, or his professional integrity.

And even so, there was not a drop of shame, of remorse, to be found in Camil. His only thought was on the success of his gamble.

Bucharest was unquiet: the Allies had been winning in Italy ever since spring, and the summer had also brought a new offensive front all the way from France's own shores. But even more alarming, because of sheer proximity, was the threat of the Red Army, rapidly closing in on Romania's borders, having already occupied Belorussia and Ukraine.

And there had already been confirmation of prisoners taken on the Eastern front.

Apostol had not been on any of the lists. Camil had checked, again and again. The wounded reports. And the missing reports.

The lists of the dead.

He had checked.

It was proof, he supposed.

But writing in hand, or not, Camil couldn't shake the haunting feeling that time was running short for Apostol.

Each day, the pressure grew. On the streets, in the salons, at the clubs. Camil had felt that he needed to do something. It had been as simple as that, in the end. At long last, the time for action had come for him too.

At this point in life, wasn't Camil eons away from the person whose existence expressed itself only in meandering, reflective verses? Two years back, before he had decided to answer the call to arms, Apostol had courteously endured the last of that stubborn individual who had been so determined to remain on his chosen path. Soon after their parting, cracks started to appear, veritable holes torn out of the fabric of Camil's existence, and he realised he was outgrowing the theatre world as his sole, chosen medium of experiencing life.

These days, his existence needed a great deal more active participation and involvement than the stage could provide for him.

It seemed as if Camil had reached, at long last, the same standards which directed the life of his fellow men.

He could almost grasp what Apostol had tried to explain, why he'd chosen to join the army: the need to be involved, to be a part of, to respond to some visceral instinct propelling him to be out with the other men, to personally contribute to the defence of their country.

Almost.

There had been a year of neutrality, followed by a hasty alliance with Germany when the Soviets occupied part of the north-eastern territory. If it had not been for Apostol's and Sebastian's direct involvement, the war would not have meant much to Camil beyond the reality of its heavy material costs, the rationing, and the increase in inflation and poverty.

But soon the whole country had become an open battle front, with change in the air. Shaken out of their stupor by the real terror of becoming crushed between the two parts of the conflict, people had put aside their fear of the Green Shirt militia. There were more public protests by the day. More sabotages. People were vociferously demanding the urgent negotiation of an armistice to remove the country from the war, if not to turn the arms outright against the Germans.

And now Camil too found himself caught up in the considerable force of his countrymen's turmoil.

However, he could not deny that there was an element of animal hysteria taking hold of the population, and of him too, or that the cause for this was the nearness and the undeniable reality of the Anglo-American bombardments of the oil camps just west of the capital.

Camil had been suddenly gripped by the idea that this was not the time for Apostol to be far away from home, away on the Eastern front fighting Russians.

Things were all too real and terrible, as they hadn't been two years before, and Camil had spent his days since June on the brink of exhaustion, waiting breathlessly for news from the battlefront. From Apostol, really.

Which, of course, made Camil perfectly aware that his current existential anguish wasn't caused by the sudden emergence of some kind of patriotic feeling inside him. Or any other type of noble sentiment of elevating nature.

The entire world was holding its breath, ready for the balance of war to tip one way or the other. And Camil, who, for once, was in step with his peers, held his own breath, too. But there was no illusion left to blind his eyes. The war had shown him the truth. He cared with all his heart, yes, that much was true, but his care was reserved only for his personal circle.

"Perhaps this is the day," he repeated daily, like a condemned man waiting in his cell for redemption.

And perhaps, once news of Apostol came, Camil would also be able to rise up again.

Certainly, he couldn't imagine falling any lower, lying at the bottom of the ladder as he now was.

Stela, forever self-conscious it seemed, but still managing to give a chiding tilt to her jaw, planted herself in his path to the front door. Camil found a smile for the grey hairs that spoke of her long presence in his life.

"Shall I start cooking lunch? It's looking to be another dog day, today. Better come home early on, before it gets really hot. You work too much." She might have said that.

Or he might have read the meaning straight from her brain, thanks to frequent repetition of this speech.

He shook his head, and tried to murmur, "Not today, no."

He couldn't bear staying at home, and waiting, by day too. Nights were long enough as it was.

And of course, Camil did have his newspaper column, and the daily information gathering to get his head round, too. However 'beneath a man of his age and status', or typically 'dilettante' as a form of employment his activities might seem to others.

It had all ended up serving him well, hadn't it?

Without his 'connections' to certain night circles, he wouldn't have collected all those pertinent facts about the habits of certain 'personalities' of the social and political sphere. Without his choice of a profession, Camil would not have had the necessary weight to influence any of those 'men of the moment' either.

He was somewhat ashamed, yes. And he still had a price to pay.

But if this made it possible for Apostol to avoid becoming a prisoner of this war – or, God forbid, an even worse fate – then Camil would take his shame, and bear it without a word of complaint, for the rest of his life. There would be no room for regrets, because it would all have been more than worth it.

Pity, he could never tell his father that he was right. It seemed that Camil was unfit to be an heir, after all. He was far from agreeing that the cursed accident had incapacitated him for assuming his gentlemanly responsibilities in the eyes of society, but he could now understand his father's position better.

By noon, Camil's tour amongst the awakening theatre world was coming to an end. Late night events collected, a half-written article already fixed in mind, Camil made a last stop by the outdoor coffee house he normally frequented for the too-loose speech, and even more revealing demeanour, of the politicians du jour and their acolytes.

The coffee house was tucked behind the royal palace. Its patrons were as discreet as a cocotte, and had the same motivation too. They were driven by the need to have their faces publicly recognisable in pursuit of higher favour, and they resorted to dropping hints of significant events and names to show off their importance.

The more 'sensitive' a matter, the more they seemed ready to burst at the seams with the need to tell of it. It was especially tempting when they were presented with the seemingly ideal recipient: a deaf journalist, renowned for the fact that his scribbling never ventured outside the mundane. But at least he was no longer confined only to the art scene. Camil was someone of no real political and social consequence, true, but he wasn't exactly a nobody, either. His fame came half from his family name and half from pity.

Camil didn't linger too long today, though.

It was too hot, and it was not as if he had any appetite, anyway. Besides, the nervous energy stoking the already weather-charged air contributed to chasing him out of the door almost before he had set his cane inside it.

After the long night he had had, Camil was truly in need of a place less neurosis-inducing than this one. In all honesty, that was a hard order to fulfil during these last months.

Of course, the presence of the aide of a certain Secretary of State also had its share in Camil's decision to head back home. From the way the man was taking refuge in the leafy corners of the rooms, signalling his disposition to rendezvous with those willing to share his news, Camil was better off far away from him.

He was determined to dig in his heels, and withhold his part of the deal until he had proof that the devil had indeed carried out his part of the bargain first.

He'd been noticed, he knew, but then he honestly couldn't tell if he was being hailed by his name, could he?

It had been thirty-five days.

By the time Camil returned home he was much wearier than when he'd left. But he had delivered the article, and he had survived another day among people who, preoccupied and distracted, constantly bumped into him. He had also suffered an impatient shove that almost provoked him into putting his cane to good traditional use, but he'd managed to restrain himself just in time.

People were jumpy, as if deadly aircraft lurked behind every cloud and every shadow on the pavement was a menace to them.

Camil understood. Hell, he even shared in their fears sometimes. Still, he was grateful to reach the sanctuary of his home today. On the way back he had almost hallucinated about that pitcher of cold water Stela usually left behind for him. So much so that he had even decided to indulge her and serve himself a portion of that sour cherry jam she had always been so proud of. She would appreciate it. She had worked hard to gather every speck of sugar available to produce a few of her usual preserves.

Spotting his doorman outside, and taking to the shadows of the old tree guarding the entrance, Camil waved him off, set to head in without delay. He didn't avert his head quickly enough, though, and was signalled that there was a visitor waiting for him in the garden.

Abruptly invigorated, Camil ran, breathless, to the back of the house. By the time he barged into the cooler space, like the impatient child he had once been, his head caught up with him, arguing strongly with his foolish heart which told him that Apostol was waiting for him.

Apostol would have let himself be seen already. He would not have remained hidden behind the greenery when he knew how much Camil longed to see him back, safe and sound.

Nonetheless, Camil continued to run.

When he finally arrived, unfit for company, out of breath and dizzy, one look sufficed to send plummeting any lasting, stubborn hope he had had left.

Disappointment had barely time to settle, when dread of another kind spurred him to his feet again. Hastily, he re-gathered his wits, readying himself to face the man pacing furiously up and down the grassy path. Camil's father.

"Finally! Couldn't you at least keep civilised visiting hours, inconsiderate child?" his father shouted.

Camil actually heard him.

Long acquainted with the features scowling at him, Camil would have supplied the words by rote, anyway, but, for some reason, this particular tone of his father's when shouted soundly in his face like this, never failed to penetrate the fog of his hearing. Camil had never been able to determine his exact feelings on this matter, but neither could he stop himself from greedily drinking in the sound.

Going upstairs – his father vainly protested the courtesy, but the man always refused to lower his voice when speaking with his son – Camil's heart chose to climb down with each step up they took. He would have liked to take the easy path of offence at the obvious scorn displayed, but the unusual visit combined with real anxiety beneath the older, but otherwise almost identical, features, told him this was a conversation that would not bode well for him.

A growing, deeply unsettling inkling of what might have brought his father to his door, on top of the man's aversion to catering for his eldest son's 'affectations', thus forgetting himself and talking without turning his head toward Camil, made their side-by-side conversation into an even more strained and incomplete exchange than usual.

"Have you any news? You must have heard … " His father closed his eyes at the slip.

Camil's increasing worries didn't stop him from wanting to ask how many more years needed to pass, if fifteen were obviously not enough, for his father to stop tripping over Camil's infirmity in this way.

"The King asked the Brigadier General to come to the palace at noon, today. The General was supposed to leave this morning on a visit to the battlefront, so he was held back. And I've also heard – " This time his father raised his eyes to the skies, as if in prayer for patience.

The man had, early on, declared it a real nuisance to attempt any kind of meaningful conversation with his son, and had since then preferred to keep his distance.

"The whole Cabinet, in fact, was summoned for an unscheduled meeting," his father continued, testament to the importance of his breaking his habit, and seeking out Camil.

If only it wasn't for what Camil was now almost convinced would fix the breach between them for eternity.

"An unannounced Crown Council. What could be the meaning of this? Are we abandoning the war? Will there be an armistice? You must know something – you say you're a journalist now. What have you heard? You do have responsibilities toward your family, I hope you remember this. We must know the terms. We need to prepare. If we're going to turn against the Germans, it would mean that rights to the oil refineries would revert back to us – well, what's left of them, now that the Allies seem determined to bomb them all out. Which can't be, of course. Hitting the supply, yes, that I understand, but it must only be intended as a measure for pressuring us into changing sides. They can't continue long with this bombing business, I'm sure. After all, the English and the Americans both owned quite a substantial share of them, before this whole war affair started. They must be aware of what an irreparable loss this all could be. For all of us. This is about business, after all."

His father stopped then, the words slowly catching up with him. At a loss all of a sudden, the old man looked away.

This one time, Camil preferred it so.

Camil dredged up a social smile, for himself more than anything.

His family oil investments. Camil had been twelve when he went to accompany his father on a tour of the refineries. A recent purchaser's unalloyed enthusiasm was Camil's last memory of that day.

Long after the explosion, after Camil's denials, bargaining, and crying had brought him no more than a begrudging acceptance that the verdict on his deafness wasn't going to change miraculously no matter what he did, Camil had come to regret that that exploratory visit continued to remain so clear and perfect in his mind, when other, much more important things were slowly fading away. Like the laughter of his younger sisters. Or the voice of his mother.

It had seemed like a curse that he could remember perfectly well the timbre of his father's proud voice that day, the wonder in his voice when he introduced his heir to what he'd deemed the future of their family. But it seemed even more unfair that with each of their subsequent encounters that damned memory, instead of losing power to the intervening years, only became even more vivid. More real. It was a total curse. Good and wrong at the same time.

It also served now to wash away all remnant of the goodwill that the cultivated distance between father and son had preserved for them over the years.

Because Camil would never know Apostol's voice. His way of saying even the most banal of things. He would never be sure if those complex emotions a human being experienced through life were what seemed to be reflected back at him sometimes in the warmth of his friend's features. Or on those of his mother and sisters. At the theatre, or at the opera. Or even on those strangers he encountered on the streets and among whom he found it so cumbersome to navigate his way.

"I reviewed last night at the National Theatre, Father," Camil said, heart hardening with the remembrance of his many regrets.

"The National Theatre. I'll never understand why you insist on going to these productions you can't even – anyway, it's that cabaret singer you should go after, she is well in with the Germans, I've heard … "

The man continued unsuccessfully in this vein for quite some time.

Camil armed himself with every regret about his deafness between 1929 and now to steel himself better in the face of what he had to do; to be able to stay upright and bear his father's inevitable rebuff when he proved once more a disappointment to the man, and to his family.

When Camil denied his father's request, he saw a remaining, feeble hope die in the old man's eyes, and he almost broke and gave in. His father had come to him for help, after all. He had found in himself enough faith to make this effort toward his son.

Once left alone, Camil fell against his favourite chair by the street window and tried to put a stop to the thoughts spinning inside his head, all but threatening to drown him, no longer content to be kept at bay.

Ever since the day he had decided to bargain with the Secretary of State's aide he had been constantly trying to avoid connecting certain dots, put a name to his actions. Trying not even to think about the responsibilities to his family, about which his father had just reminded him.

Because his father was right. Camil should have thought of his family's future, put them first, as he had been taught to do. As he so vividly remembered being told in that dreadful day of visits to the refineries. How it was supposed to be his duty as a man, and a son.

Of course, he could argue that his family most definitely would not become destitute because of this, either.

But still, he had weighted his family's failure to thrive and prosper against much more complex, but wholly personal, some would even say base, feelings.

The day he had met the panicked gaze of one particular Secretary of State in the bedroom of a half-naked actress, Camil realised that he held a powerful card, a game-changing card, in his hands. The choice had been made in a split second and, once he made it, Camil felt as if part of his soul had returned. He had left the actress's rooms determined to ensure that the other part of his soul returned home safe and sound.

All his life, after the accident, Camil had felt nothing more than a shadow. Perpetually scurrying at the edge of the crowds, never quite managing to connect with the rest of the world, never quite touching. He had always been close enough to brush by, but just that one step too far away.

Then, one day, one person had reached back to him. That one connection had never faltered; and more, through that communication, this person had not only tied Camil to him, but through him to the rest of the people too.

Of course, Camil had gambled away the card that had fallen in his hands. There was but one choice to make, and that was to choose action over endless debate about what was the best choice. A man's life. A family's future. Both were important. One could use criterion upon criterion to determine the right order, and probably never definitely settle the matter, and while Camil's mind loved a good intellectual conundrum, this time he made his choice in the blink of an eye. "Perhaps this is the day," Camil repeated, searching the face of every passer-by under his window.

Late afternoon, the doorman came upstairs. Face perspiring, shouting loud enough for Camil to catch a stray word or two.

The army is on the streets!

"The Germans?" Camil asked, heart pounding.

He hadn't taken into account that this might happen before Apostol returned.

"They're attacking us? What are you saying?" Camil asked again.

There wasn't a strong German presence in the country. About 600,000 soldiers and officers, he had been told. Also, the bulk of the army was maintaining the South-Eastern front line, on the Ukrainian border. They weren't supposed to be in the city.

Camil had taken careful consideration of the few troops present in the capital, of the obvious numeric disadvantage they would have in the event of an uprising, but mostly, since military strategy wasn't a strong point of his, he'd kept an eye on the German officers mingling in society circles. They displayed only confidence in their presence being welcome, even when wild rumours – though Camil had managed to confirm a few as accurate over the time – constantly flew about the city of secret meetings and talks about forcing the Brigadier General to step down, about overthrowing the entire government. Everybody speculated on who the members of the shadow Cabinet actually were, and no one doubted its existence.

Of all this, the Germans seemed unaware. Just last night, for example, six of the seven German generals in the capital had attended the soirée at –

Camil came back to the present only to gather that his caretaker seemed not to have said much except, "I don't know. Something bad is happening."

Camil dismissed the man, sending him back to his family, as he would be no help because of his worry for them.

For a brief moment, he considered going out to see for himself the truth on the streets. It didn't make sense for the Germans to snuff out this weeks-long open secret of a coup d'état out of the blue.

And Camil had already set his plans in motion. He had thought that he had taken everything into account. But he had not expected the Germans to turn against them.

Moments passed, and, of course, no one came to bring him news. The street was eerily silent even to his damaged ears.

He agonised about this possibility that a handful of Germans, previously so disconnected from the country's political landscape, was now standing in the way of what had seemed such a fait accompli that very morning. The fate of the country had been all set. The signs had all been there. Hadn't his father said that the King had asked the Brigadier General to attend on him at the palace?

Dark was falling when Camil felt vibrations shaking the building's walls.

He had been staring out of the street windows for what had seemed an eternity, but he had not seen any explosions to signal that fighting was taking place, as he had been warned could happen. So maybe he was only imagining the world trembling around him.

He couldn't tell any more.

And he couldn't hear anything.

People had been abuzz all over the city for weeks now, recounting again and again how they had all heard the aerial bombardments taking place kilometres away from the capital. Camil had drunk in every morsel he could get his hands on, wanting to be prepared, to be able to read the signs for himself once the time came.

And now the world was quieter than ever before.

Whole, fierce battles could be happening only streets away from his home, and Camil was more alone than ever. Cut off. Forgotten.

Camil let his eye fall on the radio receiver his father had given him with an admonition to keep practising his hearing, so as not to set himself further apart from the world by isolating himself and worsening his condition; as if there was a choice to be had in this.

He'd thought it a cruel joke at first. Then he had come to accept that the old man simply could not admit that his son's hearing would not come back, no matter how much exposure he 'practised'. It wasn't his father's raised voice that he 'heard', as much as reading the visual clues from the few who bothered to pay attention and offer him conversation. For that to happen Camil needed somebody's presence in front of him, not a featureless contraption.

He took a second, longer glance at the apparatus, shaking in impotence.

Information was literally at his fingertips.

He just couldn't hear it!

A rare rage overtook him and he moved with intent toward the wireless set, only to suddenly have the apparatus jump up – shake? – on the table it had been resting upon.

Camil froze.

A beat later, he let out a breathless laugh. "I'm losing my mind."

The words served to focus him, to push aside the wave of instinct that had been threatening to carry him under; and that was when the realisation struck.

Camil stopped breathing for a moment.

He turned, slowly, chest tight, burning. A few footsteps and he stood before his open window, not yet daring to open his eyes and look down.

Behind his eyelids he replayed, over and over, the image of a piece of bark from the aging tree guarding the entrance to his house. It had come to rest incongruously on the furniture, stark brown against Stela's white macramé.

Apostol had taken it into his head to saw off the old branches, claiming he was doing it for Camil's sake. His friend feared that one day a chunk would break off, and Camil would be too absorbed in dreaming about his poems to notice something amiss, until it was too late and the thing fell on top of him.

Camil ran straight downstairs, not a single moment wasted in looking out of window to confirm his suspicions.

If his mind was playing tricks on him, so be it.

It would still be worth it. Because maybe Apostol was really waiting downstairs, waiting for Camil to notice him …

Camil ran faster.

The front door opened somehow, and earthquake tremors threw him off his feet.

He was safely caught, though, in strong, familiar arms. The smell was all wrong, but he knew, oh, how well he knew this person!

"Are we being attacked? Apostol! Is this what a bombardment feels like?" Camil asked idiotically. Then, too relieved to wait for an answer, he buried his head in Apostol's shoulder. "Apostol," he repeated. "Did you feel it? Doesn't matter now, I guess. Do come inside."

And for some reason, Camil couldn't stop himself babbling.

But Apostol didn't loosen his hold, either; more, he kept pressing Camil's face against his jacket. He might have been talking – Camil's cheek registered what felt like tiny tremors of his chest – and this uncharacteristic behaviour on Apostol's part baffled him.

It took him a moment longer to recognise what the shaking actually was.

He lifted his face, eager to drink in the laughter he was sure he would encounter on those beloved features.

Apostol looked down at him, eyes soft, worn-down, his cheeks too thin. "Camil," Apostol's smiling lips said.

Camil swore his brain recognised every single letter of the word.

"Sorry it's so late." His friend did not look very apologetic, and Camil smiled back at him, happy to have him here, at last.

"It's not late at all," he was quick to reassure. "Come inside, though. I think the world has gone mad out there."

"Feels like it, yes. I thought I'd never arrive. I've been on the road for days." Apostol glanced down at his clothes. "Do pardon my appearance. I would have gone to a hotel first, but I fear things aren't looking good tonight in the city. I chose to come straight to you."

Camil's chest tightened again. He took Apostol's elbow, prompting the man to start walking. "There's nothing to excuse. There are actual fights in the streets, then?"

Apostol looked at him. "I didn't see any. But I've been stopped and told to get indoors. My orders … Camil. I also come to see you tonight because I fear, despite my orders, that I should present myself to the nearest command post and – "

"No."

Camil couldn't maintain eye contact with that too earnest, but oh-so-tired gaze. He pushed Apostol toward the staircase.

"Come, wash, eat something. We'll talk later." Or never at all would be much better.

Apostol granted him his wish, but Camil knew well that stubborn jaw. Apostol's decision was already made.

Camil could keep at it, he supposed, hoping to wear the man down, bring him to his way of thinking. But Camil wasn't his father.

So, instead, he just smiled at Apostol. The man was here now, and that was all that mattered at the moment.

"You should at least make time to pay a visit to Ecaterina's. They're in town," Camil said.

"I know they're here. She wrote to me. And just in time too. They were already on their way by the time I received these strange orders to return. I'm ordered to stand down until some later, undisclosed date." Apostol scrutinised Camil.

Camil looked away. "Ecaterina sent me a note too," he said, rushing in, not wanting in any way to talk about those orders. "Asking me to mediate and obtain her an audience with the War Secretary – "

"You shouldn't have!"

Camil bit his lips. "You're going to marry her. She has a right to interfere, especially since her whole family's future rests upon your marriage. You accepted this commission and went to war hoping to improve your station in life. Hoping to offer her a much better position." Staring Apostol in the eye, he tried to joke, to dispel some of the awful tension between them. "The Cabinet offices are full of wives and mothers pleading for their men, these days, Apostol. Her coming to me made me feel part of some kind of modern ménage. It's la mode du jour in the city, you could say."

Apostol grimaced and looked away, shoulders sagging. "I am sorry." His lips, his whole dejected mien shouted the words loud and clear.

"I have never been against her place in your life, Apostol. I introduced her to you."

Ecaterina had needed to marry, but she was not especially inclined to marry Apostol himself. And she had known Camil since infancy, her family having been neighbours to his mother's country house.

"I meant it as an amusing anecdote, anyway," he continued. "I'm part of the trend these days, isn't it great? My father strove all his life for me to belong. But let me tell you, wives and mothers may constantly be in the waiting rooms arguing for a spare moment to be granted to them, but the mistresses? Well, the mistresses are all inside the offices, using the direct, if backstage, entrance."

"Don't talk like that! Please."

"Do you still have room to pretend, Apostol? I'm glad. This blasted war has stripped me of all my trivial, frivolous layers. I no longer have the luxury to claim being hurt in my amour propre. I got Ecaterina the audience she wanted. She wouldn't have been able even to cross the threshold to the outer rooms, and you know it. So you should be grateful, and not angry as you look now. You must be aware of what those women are offering in exchange for nothing but an empty promise. Ecaterina did well in coming to me. She has no idea of the real world. Not really. So you will thank her prettily for having thought of you when you next see her."

Apostol's clenched fists shook at his sides for a moment, as he stood there, head down. He looked up. "Of course I'm going to thank her. Yes."

Then he pointed to his dusty, wrinkled clothes.

"You know where everything is," Camil said in answer to his tacit request.

After Apostol left to change, Camil let out a long breath. It seemed he would never have to lie, after all. He would be able to lay it all at Ecaterina's feet, and even be mostly truthful. He'd manoeuvred hard to put the idea in her great-aunt's head. They spent altogether too much time at their country house, and had become too afraid to push at boundaries.

But sadly, Ecaterina's audience won her nothing but a thinly-veiled offer to bed the Secretary, and Camil had to step in more obviously. Of course, later they had agreed to forget that the event had ever occurred, and never bring it up again.

"You look much better," he was quick to say when Apostol returned. "Want me to search the pantry for something else than whatever is on the table?" Where was that jar of cherry jam? He never had got around to eating from it, had he?

"This will do for now. It's not as if you've eaten much of anything. You're nothing but bones. I fear I've cracked one of those pointy ribs of yours just now." Apostol's eyes wrinkled in a smile.

"You say that every time we spend some time apart."

"Maybe because it's all too true. You never take sufficient care of yourself, Camil."

"Stela's coming over every other day."

"Is she now? How did you win your father's favour?"

Camil snorted. "This war's been all about favours, didn't you know?" *Merde*. He shouldn't wander back to paths best left forgotten.

"Speaking of war. Let me turn on the wireless. It's quite a stormy night out there, and ... " Apostol methodically chewed the old hard cheese and washed it all down with wine.

Camil held his tongue, hoping Apostol would not start again about the orders.

"I know you don't approve," Apostol continued. "No, you never had to say anything." He sighed. "And now Ecaterina has put me in her debt even more. Will you tell me who I have to thank apart from you?"

Camil didn't answer him.

It did little to slow Apostol down, of course. "I can't stay, don't you see, Camil? Not if things are happening out there. The Soviets pushed us so far back this week … They took Moldavia again, they breached our lines in only two days, Camil. Two days. That's why it took me so long to arrive. I kept being turned around. I really cannot account for these orders I got – "

Camil's good intentions went out of the window. "I can't believe you're so eager to throw yourself back into that hell!"

To judge by his posture, Apostol wasn't surprised at all by his outburst. So he went on.

"Apostol, I saw the lists of dead, the list of prisoners. I read every single bit of news from the front. I'm all too aware of what is happening. People are dying. People are hurt! And the ones who escaped and came back? I went and visited them. I saw what was left of them. It's not even about the physical damage and loss; you're aware how well I know that one can adapt and live impaired. But the look in their eyes!"

He turned away; couldn't bear to see again the images his mind had stored, and, sometimes, outright invented for him, replacing, in what had become his worst nightmare, the bodies of those lying in bed with the body of his Apostol.

"Apostol, about those men." He needed to make the other understand. "Even if they could be returned to perfect condition with the help of some miraculous medicine, I fear they will never be the same. They are lost souls. I couldn't bear to look at them. I pity them, and I mourn them at the same time. But I can't, I simply can't let you go again into that nightmare." *Knowing that, even if you'll be returned to me, a part of you will be lost.*

It was not an easy entreaty, imposing his will on another man like this. But Camil was willing to stoop to it, anyway.

Then Apostol was suddenly there, blessed soul, engulfing him in his arms again. And maybe Camil didn't deserve his affection, or his infinite patience, but he would never turn away from it, either.

Of course Camil gripped him back, holding him fast to his chest, vowing never again to let go of him. It was a futile promise, and he didn't bother to hide his sniffle in Apostol's jacket.

"I'm sorry," Apostol pulled his head back to say.

As if he had anything to apologise for.

Apostol's eyes were filling with tears too, although his palms were softly holding Camil's face upturned toward him. This forced Camil to acknowledge Apostol's decision lurking in the pained depths of his eyes. In spite of it, Camil couldn't close his eyes in denial, not if it meant losing these precious moments with this man who was rooted so inexplicably deep in his heart. He couldn't do it, not even if the whole German artillery were to fire at the roof.

"You make no sense to me, you know," Camil whispered, mostly to himself. There was no rational explanation for his feelings for this man. The most he could do was to accept them, and deal with the reality of them the best way he knew how.

"I can't do you justice," he continued bitterly. "Compared to you, I … Well. Forget my cowardly display just now. I will support you the best I can. I'm proud of you. I did once admire all these heroic, extraordinary traits some men seem to possess. Men just like you. I think you've read my thoughts in a poem. Or three. I read one to you when we first met, I think." Camil chuckled, ignoring how forced his cheerfulness was. "And, rest assured, when you go back, your family and Ecaterina's will continue to be well and safe under my – "

Apostol kissed him.

A long, deep kiss Camil let himself drown in, losing all awareness of self.

"I'm no hero, either," Apostol told him some time later. "It's not about bravery." He was trying to explain once more to Camil. "It's about fear, actually. I just can't let them go on without me. We've been brought together by terror. We pulled each other from the brink of the most mindless animal behaviour. I am thankful I mostly can't even remember how brutally we all reacted, sometimes. I fear for them. My fear for the men under my command kept me from losing my mind. For giving in to my own fear. I constantly wanted to run away. Some of the men gave in. We – I had to bring them back. Although I felt the same urge as them. To run, and run, and run. To never stop running. I should have felt ashamed of myself, but … I can't leave them behind. You can't imagine how it is. I don't want you to know. And it's not right by you, to make you wait still, and I know I should not ask you again. But I can't stay."

And maybe Camil had been deluded, after all, to think that his plans would ever work, considering the moral fibre of this man.

"You're more heroic than you'll ever know," he said instead. "And a manipulative bastard to boot. I would have fought you tooth and nail if you had got on your high horse again and talked to me about having a duty to restore the territory the Soviets took from us – "

Apostol kissed his hair. A tired but relieved chuckle vibrated on Camil's skin for a while, until Apostol pulled back.

"As manipulative as you were, telling me of Ecaterina's many efforts to bring me back home?" he asked, mouth twitching. At least he wasn't seriously displeased.

Camil smiled back. *If you only knew!*

"You're plotting something." Apostol groaned playfully and tightened his grip on Camil, only managing to make the latter smile more broadly.

They kissed again.

"Oh. Wait a moment."

Camil scowled at the interruption.

"The King's on the wireless. Why would he? – It's ten at night!"

Camil's heart became weightless then, mad hope soaring through him, making him sway on his feet behind Apostol who was gaping at the blasted apparatus.

If this was what Camil thought it was, he would never again say a word against the wireless set. Maybe he would even send his belated thanks to his father for the gift.

He embraced Apostol from behind, content, for once, to wait for the news to be transmitted to him. Moments like this should be precious and were definitely worth whatever price the world chose to put on them.

Camil could read Apostol's reactions to the announcement in every vibration of his body. Could feel the fondness the man had for him in the unconscious way he had of resting his fingers upon Camil's intertwined hands, or in the way he leaned slightly back into Camil's arms. These were moments of perfect communication between them. Moments which pushed the world to one side, and Camil could feel, here, in the cocoon of the two of them, how he finally fitted in with someone, in this place, in this moment, at this man's side.

Besides, he wanted to really savour their reunion since, finally, his plan seemed to be coming to a head. It looked as though Camil had played the right cards, after all.

He hid a satisfied smile in Apostol's shoulders.

"We're out of the war against the Allies," Apostol told him. "We'll join the coalition against Germany. A new Cabinet has been appointed … "

Camil read the confirmation of his hopes on Apostol's lips, and nodded. It was the most he could do. With a relieved breath, he kissed Apostol, and welcomed him home.

"But I still have to go."

The words left Apostol's mouth while their kiss was still on their lips.

Camil didn't stop to choose his words with care this time. "The war is over, Apostol. Let it be over. You did your part."

There was no way Camil would accept Apostol's decision now. Things had changed. Different circumstances needed different responses, and Apostol was too close to see it.

"The war is not over." Apostol set his jaw stubbornly. "The German artillery will soon respond to – "

"Your war is over, Apostol. Don't you see? We had a purpose when all of this began. You called it your duty as a citizen to help bring back our eastern territory. That's the call you answered. The game has changed now. The territory is still lost, but it looks as if we will no longer fight to get it back from the Soviets either. The men in your command are long since prisoners of the Red Army. They're no longer your concern. If you go and request a posting now, they will send you west, not back to the east. You'll be joining the Soviets you've spent almost two years fighting! How is this still your war? The rules have changed, you have to adapt your game, or you'll play a losing hand from the start."

"What are you saying? Do you really think that my purpose is now fulfilled? So I should retire? My duty is the same, Camil. I took this commission. I swore to follow orders. It doesn't matter that things have now changed."

Camil shook his head. "You weren't going to play the duty card, didn't we agree upon this? Didn't you just say you're no legendary hero, obeying his King's every word? You said your loyalty was of a more personal kind. I thought the main reason you went to war was for material and social gain for you and your future family. I supported that argument." Camil saw no reason to restrain his tongue.

"I thought you ascribed to the professional intellectual guild theory?" Apostol threw back at him. "Wasn't the ability to accept a different argument considered the basis of any discourse? Weren't you professing to despise dilettantes and the histrionics of those who didn't know how to accept an opposing view?"

Camil smiled, all teeth. "I long since renounced those pretentious ideas. I'm acknowledging my cowardly nature now, and only the most basic of wants and needs. I'm a brute."

Apostol closed his eyes. "I'll never believe that of you. I know you too well." He touched Camil's hand. "I know you will accept my decision," he said. "I don't care about the words you use to now redefine yourself, Camil. I would always stand by your side. And no matter how harsh your words, I will never doubt that you will stand by mine, whether you agree or not. That's just the man you are."

Camil bit his lip. He wanted to shake some sense, or sense of preservation, into the idealistic fool.

"I'm a changed man. I'm not sure there's any integrity left in me."

"What are you saying?" Apostol asked sceptically.

"I'm talking about this war! The political decision throwing us one way or the other, is wholly removed from the reach of our influence, but its impact reaches deep to every individual. How can you suffer it and not change? More to the point, how can you honestly conceive of going to High Command right now, and asking to be sent to the front again? How can you be that hero you were supposed to be, do your duty by your men, to your country, when within a few hours your enemies have become your allies, and vice versa? You spent two years fighting the Russians, Apostol, and now you're supposed to follow them, follow their orders?"

Camil breathed out, and shook his head when Apostol made to speak. "I can't bear being rendered useless by a decision, and event, not of my own making. You know that." He looked his friend in the eye. "Apostol, you are given the chance to make your choice now. Those orders can end your commission for good. You went to war to restore our territory. We've lost. The game is over. The King renounced that course of action. Now, there's a new game on the table. You don't have to keep playing. It's another war altogether and you have to make your decision anew. You can choose to stay at home. It's an honourable choice."

Apostol pressed their foreheads together, closing off their means of communication. Camil waited him out.

When they made eye contact again, even before reading his lips, Camil knew he hadn't managed to change the other man's mind.

"For a renegade intellectual, that was quite an impassioned argument. But, as I said, I'm not going back because I am honourable, I'm going back because my one wish when I was there was to come back to you. And it has been granted to me. There was nothing more keeping me alive some days than thinking about our future life, the one you pictured for us: we settle Ecaterina in the country as she desires, and you and I ... But, Camil, although that is my most cherished wish, and I would not have turned back for anything in the world once I received the orders to march back to the capital, because it meant I was to see you again, I ... I felt the worst man on earth."

Apostol closed his eyes. "I felt ashamed of myself. I need to go back. Redeem myself by standing next to my men. No intellectual discourse about choices, political structure and individual rights, principles of social duty and allegorical heroism will change the fact that I know in my flesh and blood that this war is fought by men like you and me. I fear I will not rest easy by your side if I don't go back to them."

Apostol kissed Camil's brow. "I may have started on this path for other reasons, as you reminded me, but I have my place now, out there. With those men. And so it will be until the war is really over. For all of us."

Camil sniffed. "Sometimes I hate you so much."

"You don't," Apostol said. "Just as I'll never hate you, either." Another press of his lips. "You'll wait for me?"

"I do hate you now, just a bit, for such a stupid question."

Apostol grinned. "Did I hurt your amour propre by questioning your loyalty? Thought you got rid of your integrity, and all of that."

"Do not be so sure of yourself. You should ask Sebastian once all of this is over. Is over again, I mean. By your definition of 'over'," Camil could not resist adding.

Apostol smiled. "Did you have news? How is he? Your last letter mentioned you were awaiting word from him. You sounded pretty worried."

"He wrote to me, so that means he was well at the time. Didn't mention any offensive from France, which is telling in some kind of way I have no idea how to interpret. I've been an awful friend to him, though, since we're speaking of integrity. Although he's God knows where and doing who knows what, he still takes the time to write and reassure me that he's alive and well. In exchange, I, who do nothing but write about theatre and the social scene all day, couldn't spare him the same consideration and answer his letter promptly!"

"You fear for him constantly, and he knows it. That's why he keeps in touch."

But I feared for you more, these last weeks. How's that for integrity of character?

"He's a better friend than I deserve," was what Camil said instead.

"You're very hard on yourself tonight. Has something else happened? Something more personal? Did you father send you one of his encouraging notes?"

"He came by, actually. Asking for a favour. I had to refuse him."

"Ah." Apostol's thumb pressed hard into Camil's chin. "He cares for you. He'll get over it soon enough."

"We'll see," was all he could reply.

It had been worth it. Even if Apostol ended up going back to the battlefront he had at least been given a choice, a real one, and he'd decided still to follow his path.

Camil gathered his friend in his arms. This made it all worth it too.

"I have to go," Apostol reminded him.

"Surely it can wait until morning. No one will miss you. You're not even expected, I'm sure."

It would be quite a surprise for a certain Secretary to receive him, actually. The understanding had been that the orders for recall were just a step nearer complete retirement.

"They are fighting already, Camil. It feels wrong to delay."

Camil sighed."You need rest. You said yourself that you had to take a detour on your way in. You're tired. You won't be much use tonight if you're asleep on your feet."

By morning the worst of the fighting would be over, hopefully. A few days, they said. Camil had asked around, hypothetical questions from a letters man, and quite a few condescending gentlemen had been all too happy to make their predictions known to him. A petty part of him wanted to go and renegotiate his agreement with a certain Secretary of State, to make the man pay for Camil's having such a stubborn friend.

"In the morning, then," Apostol said, relenting. "I'll leave some notes for you to convey on my behalf?"

Camil nodded, and tried to forget all about the Secretary. For the moment, at least. Maybe it was better to keep up his part of the bargain, anyway, and grant the man the newspaper articles he so wanted. It wasn't as if someone would actually believe the Secretary had been secretly acting on behalf of the Soviet agenda all this time. The Communist Party numbered a few thousand members, all told. They had hardly any influence at all.

It was too transparent a move to claim a previous allegiance now that the Red Army was on their doorstep. Perhaps Camil felt petty enough to allow a few new dents in his reputation in return for the disbelief and mockery that his claims on behalf of the Secretary would be met with. The man was mad for engaging in such a wild, impossible scheme.

"It can all wait for the morning, though," Camil agreed aloud, and without looking, he shut the window, and retired for the night.

Camil might not have held the winning card on this game-changing day, after all. But he didn't feel as if he had lost, either. Especially not right then, with Apostol back in his arms, and the world silent, far away from them.

See

Adam Fitzroy

A bright morning, cool, clear, the sun just showing behind the trees; it would be warm later, but for now there was something fresh, invigorating and secretive about being alone with the sky, the lake, and the whisper of the breeze. Bare feet padded across clipped damp grass, over a wide concrete path which was already beginning to warm up, and along the old boards of a jetty worn silken smooth by years of use. This was where the wealthier officers kept their boats, little sailing dinghies in which – when the weather was good and no other business pressed – they could amuse themselves by skimming across the glassy surface of the water like insects, with no particular direction or purpose in mind but pleasure.

Those who did not have the resources to acquire their own boat and have it transported to the lake, however, could swim as often as they wished to. Indeed, for some, it was required; there were men here, recovering from injuries, whose bodies would benefit from a course of vigorous exercise – and, into the bargain, more than a few who had overindulged at the table and been instructed to lose their excess weight as quickly as they could.

These men were a menace. They clustered in the shallows talking, laughing, complaining, some of them smoking, making it difficult for anyone who took swimming seriously to get in or out of the water at all. A man who intended to swim the length of the lake before breakfast, therefore – and particularly if he intended to swim it naked – was obliged to get up early, wrap himself in a bathrobe, collect a towel, and wander down to the end of the jetty almost before the sun had risen. For such a man, however, the rewards were plentiful: a clear path to the lake, a fresh and undisturbed surface through which to dive, and then an hour or so when the only sounds were the cries of the birds and plash of his own rhythmic movements. Elsewhere there was turmoil – guns, bombs, roaring engines, chattering machinery – but here there was sanctuary. Here, for a short time anyway, he could be at peace.

So it was today: a perfect slow glide from the end of the jetty, an almost soundless dive, and then the cold caress of the water. He stayed beneath the surface as long as possible, moving languidly, before rolling onto his back and finning up gradually into the light, content simply to float with his nose and eyes above the meniscus but his ears below. Small, otter-like undulations of hands and feet kept him moving, the sky a rotating kaleidoscope of grey and lilac beneath which shone the rose-gold of the early sun. He watched it avidly, as if he could drink in its beauty, absorb it through his skin, keep it within himself against the imperfect times to follow. As a child he had never wanted to come out of the sea; he would have swum all day if he'd been allowed to, but he had vivid recollections of his mother pursuing him down the beach – daintily clad in a pale silk dress and delicate shoes of dyed kid – calling to him urgently.

"Ingolf! Ingolf! Come back in now, or your father will be angry!"

Even at four or five he had known which of them his father would be angry with, though, and it had not been him. He had used that knowledge, played up the poor woman mercilessly, got his own selfish way more times than he could count, but it hadn't lasted. One day his mother had simply not been there: his father had installed a mistress in her place, and Ingolf had been sent away to school. That was where he had learned that swimming was what soothed him whenever he was troubled – and that was also where he had learned what being troubled was.

Around the curve, where the lake narrowed, there was an island upon which, some fifty years earlier, the rich owners of the estate had built an elaborate octagonal summer house in a confused architectural style resembling nothing so much as a Chinese pavilion. Here they had lunched in considerable comfort and dined by candlelight, conveyed there in their own little flat-bottomed riverboat powered by steam; there were old photographs on the walls of the castle showing girls, with improbable quantities of piled-up hair and pettish little lap-dogs, graciously accepting the homage of mustachioed men in high collars and summer-striped suits. Here they had drunk champagne and eaten cold chicken and strawberries. Here they had read and sketched and flirted while their servants moved noiselessly in the background, as little regarded as the insects scuttling away beneath their footsteps.

Then there had been a war, and families had risen and fallen. The girls with piled-up hair had become sour-faced matrons or widows; the young men with moustaches were in their graves; the riverboat had burned and sunk years ago, and the summer house was left to the mercy of the woodworm and the weather. Those who visited it now would row out, or swim if they could. There were no more elaborate picnics on the island, but a litter of beer bottles proved that there was still the occasional bacchanalian revel enjoyed there from time to time.

In a strong, easy stroke the distance to the island vanished. It had often been Ingolf's destination, where he had picked his way carefully up the shallow beach and lounged for a few minutes drawing warmth from the pale old boards of the verandah. Perhaps once a week, during his assignment here, he had made this little pilgrimage, paying his respects to the shades of the departed. Or, at least, so he had told himself, and so he would have said to anyone who had ever questioned him about it. But nobody had. Nobody cared what an unimportant clerk chose to do with his time, particularly when everybody else was asleep.

And there had never been anybody else here, either, until today.

It was a moment or two after he had hauled himself out of the water before Ingolf realised what was different this time; shaking his head, clearing the water from his ears, he was at first too preoccupied to notice any change. Then, slowly, it became apparent that somebody was smoking nearby.

"Don't worry," a calm voice told him. To judge from its direction the man it belonged to must be sitting in the sunshine on the verandah. "I don't bite."

"No, neither do I." And then Ingolf paused, because what he said next could potentially be the cause of consternation. "I should warn you," he began, "that I'm naked."

"That's all right," was the good-humoured response, "so am I." And the tone was so quiet and encouraging that Ingolf's heart flipped over sideways and began to oscillate violently in his ribcage; he was sure it must be audible for miles around.

Recollecting himself at last he stumbled forward, one hand automatically finding the support post of the roof, leaning from it so that only the top part of his body would be visible around the angle. Friendly or not, the other man – whoever he might be – deserved better than to be intruded upon without appropriate modesty; good manners alone decreed as much.

"Good morning," said Ingolf.

"Good morning. Don't be shy; come and have a cigarette."

The man on the verandah was younger than Ingolf by a decade or so, and a very different physical type; where Ingolf was tall, thin and studious-looking, this man was shorter, more robust, a boxer or a football player perhaps. He sat on the verandah with his back to the other support post, one bare leg thrust out in front of him and the other drawn up with his hand resting on it, a cigarette dangling loosely between his fingers. He had a wide, fair face, short-cropped pale hair, and a smile whose brilliance rivalled the sun's.

"Thank you." Emboldened both by the other man's welcome and his nakedness Ingolf stepped out from the shelter of the building. "Did you swim here? I didn't see a boat."

"Yes. Oh, the cigarettes, you mean? They were here already … and the matches, too. Somebody left them in the hut." Belatedly Ingolf realised that the door, usually padlocked, was now open – and that the man on the verandah had a small key on a cord around his neck. "I have friends who sometimes use the building," he explained, off-handedly.

"Really?" Accepting a cigarette from the offered tin, Ingolf crouched and allowed his host to light it for him. He was close enough now to notice that the stranger had golden hairs on his arms and legs as well as an abundance on his chest; and that he had three toes missing on his left foot.

"Frostbite," the man explained briefly. "Norway, my boot split. You?"

"Oh. Pleurisy." A long, slow pull on the cigarette. He had been warned, of course, that he should give up smoking, but really there were few pleasures available these days that were neither illegal nor prohibitively expensive; smoking was the last luxury that remained to him. "But also I work here. My name is Ingolf."

"Heinz." Solemnly they shook hands. "I don't want to know anything else about you, though; you understand why?"

"Yes." And for a moment they watched each other smoking, and it was all peaceable enough. "Have you been here before?"

"To the island? Yes, with my friends. In better times, of course. But the place has always had something of a reputation."

"So I've heard." It was the same reputation that certain bars in Berlin still enjoyed, or the occasional *Zum Wilden Hirsch* or *Vier Jahre zeiten* in a rural area where nobody cared too much. The information whispered along from man to man in moments of quiet, but only when each man was sure of the other. When he knew he was not dealing with a Gestapo agent. When he was certain he would not end up on a pink list somewhere, or randomly executed to suit the whim of some senior officer with an axe to grind.

There was a long silence. "Nobody knows I'm here," said Heinz, after a while, grinding out his cigarette.

"Nor me." Ingolf took another deep lungful of smoke, then stared at the rest of his cigarette with genuine regret; he had not tasted anything as good in months, perhaps years.

"Oh, by all means finish it first," Heinz told him, accommodatingly. "Some experiences should not be wasted, after all. I could perhaps send you a few, as a comradely gesture?"

Ingolf did not remind the man that he had only just refused to know anything about him beyond his first name. "Perhaps not," he said instead, "but it's a generous offer."

"Oh, I can be very generous." And there was a wickedness in Heinz's eyes now, and something unutterably thrilling about the way he licked his lips, and Ingolf's eyebrows rose in astonishment. "If you'll let me."

One last, wistful drag of the cigarette, over too soon, alas, but better that than none at all.

"Yes," said Ingolf, crushing the final embers on the deck of the verandah. "I'll let you."

Heinz moved closer, and Ingolf shut his eyes and felt the warmth of sunshine on his skin.

"Will you be here tomorrow?" asked Heinz, later, and the note of hope in his voice was unmistakable.

Ingolf shook his head slowly. "I've been transferred," he said. "This is my last day. There's a new general taking over, and he's bringing in his own staff."

"Oh, yes, I'd heard something about that." There was a long, contemplative silence. "Curse all generals and their stupid staff – that's very short-sighted of him!"

"Perhaps. But it isn't wise to say so."

"No. Except that in this case I think I might get away with it." Heinz sighed. "It's a shame, though; I suspect we'd do quite well together, under other circumstances. I wish there'd been a chance to find out."

"Of course. But nothing will ever be safe for men like ourselves as long as this war lasts – and afterwards, it could be even worse."

"Afterwards. If we survive it."

"Yes." But there was nothing more to say now, and the longer they remained here together the greater the risk of discovery. "Will you leave first, or shall I?"

"You, I think," said Heinz. "If you don't mind?"

"Not at all. And thank you." Ingolf stood up. To his surprise Heinz did so too, and was half a head shorter than he was. He moved awkwardly, supporting himself on the railing of the verandah, putting his damaged foot down carefully. "Will that cause you problems in your work?" asked Ingolf, sympathetically.

"This? No, I'm getting used to it. I've had some special boots made with padding inside, and when I'm wearing those you'd never know there was anything wrong with my feet. I'm considered fit for duty, anyway, which is why … " But Heinz stopped there. "Well, I can do my job. And very few people ever see me naked."

"Then I'll consider it even more of a privilege," replied Ingolf, politely. "Goodbye."

"Wait." Heinz relinquished the support of the railing, reaching out both arms. "Friends embrace," he said, as though reminding Ingolf of one of the finer points of military etiquette.

Ingolf let himself be pulled into a warm hug, savouring the texture of the man's skin, and without thinking about it at all he dropped a gentle kiss onto Heinz's cheek – realising only afterwards how unwise and inappropriate an action it might have been.

"That's enough, or I shall never want to let you go," said Heinz, extracting himself carefully and half turning away so as not to meet his gaze. Ingolf allowed himself a moment to appreciate the play of sunlight on the fair skin of Heinz's shoulder, before emphatically averting his eyes and stepping back carefully across the beach into the water.

He didn't look back. He knew he couldn't. Mustn't.

Still, he knew he wanted to.

The morning paled after that, as how could it not? Ingolf walked through his duties respectfully enough, filed his last documents, covered up his typewriter, handed everything over to his successor, and then returned to his room to pack. His bathrobe and towel were still damp.

At noon there was a parade to welcome the incoming general, and Ingolf formed up on the square with all the other members of the castle staff to watch the man arriving. The general stepped out of a gleaming Mercedes saluting sharply, seemingly quite satisfied with the welcome he'd received, and took a moment to stare all around him as though surveying the measure of his new domain. If he was looking for anything or anyone in particular, however, he did not seem to find them, and soon he recollected himself and marched briskly into the castle at the head of a train of obsequious acolytes.

He had been absolutely correct, thought Ingolf.

When he had his boots on, one would never have imagined there was anything wrong with his feet.

Across a Thousand Miles

Barry Brennessel

The coin sparkled against the turquoise sky.

I tilted back my head to meet the American's gaze. He towered over me. He smiled, the scratches along his left cheek still wet with blood.

"In appreciation. A gift," Hê Jing said from behind me as the American handed me the coin.

My little brother whined, stomped his feet, demanded his turn to hold it.

"Hsü Xiong!" my mother called out. "Stop causing such a scene!"

Xiong never followed my mother's orders.

I asked Hê Jing – who'd been a friend of my father's since their boyhood – to translate the words for me. "Liberty". "In God We Trust". "The United States of America". "One Dime". He learned English at the mission in Shangrao.

Arguments ensued after that, between the American pilot, my father, and Hê Jing. The front of the coin was a Roman god, the American said. Hê Jing insisted it was a woman, since the other two American coins he'd seen had women on them. Women named Liberty. My father said the back of the coin depicted a column. Hê Jing said it was a bundle of sticks bound together. Soon, Hê Jing put up his hands, explaining first in Chang-Du, then in English, that his mouth was too parched to continue, since he'd been required to translate all the words that were being bandied about.

I thought the American dime was the most beautiful coin I'd ever seen. The pilot said I could keep it.

The Americans were found near the coast. Adults always pretended to have all the answers, but the stories as to how these pilots ended up on our shores, and how they'd been transported to the city, were as varied as the elders' accounts of heroic deeds they performed during the last several wars.

My brother continued to shout for the chance to hold the coin. I couldn't imagine that I was quite so childish at eight years old. Now that I was fifteen, I felt mature. In fact, I'd been told by relatives and shopkeepers and the teacher I had before the current war that my temperament and inquisitiveness exceeded that of people twice my age. My mother cautioned me to not let these observations go to my head. So I didn't. Much.

After some debate (truthfully, very little) I decided it wasn't a good idea for Xiong to get his little hands on the gift from the straw-haired American with his sky-blue eyes, and a name I couldn't pronounce. My brother lost things. Or hid them and pretended they vanished. Whether or not the face on the coin was a god or a woman, the American had given it to me. It was special. I couldn't take risks.

I did have to show it to Guanyu though. He would agree with me. This silver coin was truly a work of art.

"It's a work of art," Guanyu agreed. I knew he would.

We sat on the banks of the Ganjiang River, our feet dipped in the murky water.

While Guanyu studied the coin, I studied his profile, especially his lips, so much fuller than other boys'. The feelings I'd had lately were so … perplexing. A flutter in my heart when Guanyu moved a certain way, with poise I'd never possess. Tingling in my whole body when his fingers grazed my arm. A flushed face when our eyes held each other's gaze a few seconds longer than what seemed normal. I thought of him at night. I thought of him at sunrise. I sprinted along the streets to meet him in the afternoons. While I still could.

My father let me know that my freedom was nearing its end. The war was intensifying. Some in the city were saying the presence of the American pilots wasn't the good-luck omen people were making it out to be.

"What did he look like? The pilot who gave you the coin," Guanyu asked.

I shrugged. "I don't know. Western. Yellow hair. Ocean eyes."

"Tall?"

"Yes."

"Broad shoulders?"

"Yes."

"Muscles?"

"Yes."

Silence, save the river splashing against a rock.

I suppressed a smirk. Guanyu, I could see, was doing the same.

We said so much then, without saying anything.

I didn't dare press the subject any further. But how I longed to ask Guanyu, "Do your palms sweat, too, whenever you stare at me? Does your heart beat more quickly when we lock eyes?"

"Hsü Bao!" my mother shouted when I walked through the door at dusk.

"Hsü Bao!" my brother echoed.

"You can't do this any more," my mother continued, taking hold of Xiong's arm and nudging him out of her way. "Do you understand?"

I did, in a way. But the Japanese weren't actively patrolling around us. Yet. My thinking was that we should relish the freedom while we had the chance. And deep down, I felt the Japanese couldn't last. They didn't belong in China. Eventually China would rear up and expel them in one mighty battle worthy of an epic mythological tale.

"When your father gets home, we'll have a chat. Believe me."

My brother pursed his lips in satisfaction. He was sure to bring up the coin in the family discussion.

It seemed to me there were far more important things to worry about. How long would the American pilots be in our city? Were more coming? Where would they stay?

There was another topic on my mind, too.

Guanyu.

Did he mean for our legs to stay pressed together when we sat on the banks of the river? I tried to remember the number of times our hands touched. Nine. I was sure it was nine. And I categorised the number of times I caught him staring at me. Six, total. Four times he was embarrassed. Twice, he had a sweet, shy smile with a dash of daring. (He caught me staring at him twelve times. I was red-faced each time as I quickly looked away.)

"I'm hungry," Xiong complained.

"We'll wait for your father."

My father eventually came home two hours late from working in the fields. He paced about, his breathing heavy. This was not a good sign for me. His agitation opened the door to the possibility he would channel his sour mood into raising the relevance of what I considered very minor transgressions. After all, if he was late, why wasn't it acceptable for me to be a little late from my time with Guanyu? As for my brother and the coin, couldn't my father see that Xiong wanted everything? I was simply teaching him that he couldn't have all he wanted in life.

Father's tone was quiet but intense. Drops of sweat trickled down his forehead. This wasn't normal.

He huddled with my mother in a corner. I knew well enough not to go near. Yet I couldn't help tiptoeing toward them. I crouched down on the floor, behind a tall vase, in the hope I could pick out a word or two.

Planes. Raids. Japan. There were a few other words I heard, but these three provided me with all I needed to know. I had figured out why the American pilots had shown up on our shores.

Did this mean more Americans? The thought of bashing Japan made me tingle inside a little. But it also tied my stomach in knots. I wanted to tell Guanyu immediately. I wanted to hear his perspective.

The Japanese killed his grandfather.

My grandfather was Japanese.

Guanyu didn't hate me for this.

Guanyu didn't call me 'impure' as the other boys did.

My grandfather, though he died many years ago, made it necessary for my father to work two jobs: farming, and proving his loyalty to Chiang Kai-shek.

The politics were so complex.

My mother said it felt like wearing leaden shoes and walking on already cracked eggshells.

The next morning I met Guanyu at the river.

He took a yellowed, torn map from his pocket and carefully unfolded it.

"I marked Shangrao. See? We'll start there. Then head to Běipíng. From there, we'll cross into Mongolia. Then Russia."

We had a plan. A plan for the future. We were determined to visit every nation. It would probably take us years and years, and the stupid wars spreading all over threatened to cause us major delays. In the meantime, there was no reason we couldn't start plotting our route.

"We have to start in Shangrao," Guanyu insisted. "I want to see the mission." I was fine with this. I wasn't concerned where we started. Or ended. As long as it was just the two of us on this grand journey.

I didn't dare mention now about what I'd overheard my father saying the night before. There was already too much bad news in places like Nanking and Chongqing. Awful, awful stories that some people talked about too much, and other people pretended didn't happen at all.

"Hê Jing has been reciting things from his notes," Guanyu said. "My mother likes to listen to him."

"The Christian stories?"

Guanyu nodded. Hê Jing had been reading Bible stories to my father for years. My father called it nonsense, but in more polite terms.

"Do you believe them?" I asked.

Guanyu searched the sky. "I don't know. I wonder about things. I think … I think some of the stories seem impossible. But some of them are so beautiful. And … there could be someone up there watching over us."

"He's not doing a very good job," I said.

"You sound like my father."

"I sound like my own father."

Guanyu continued to search the sky. I followed his gaze. He was watching a cloud drifting past.

"I do want to visit the mission, though," Guanyu said. "Hê Jing said it's one of the most beautiful buildings he's ever seen."

"Then we can definitely start our journey there."

"Imagine the journey those American pilots have been on," Guanyu said, "soaring through the air. Across a thousand miles. That will be us. On trains. On ships. Maybe even on a plane one day. From Shangrao to Běipíng to … everywhere."

After a time I didn't hear words. Only Guanyu's voice. Speech transformed into a symphony. His eyes, his smile, the motion of his hands, the way his left leg bobbed up and down …

I felt this overwhelming urge to touch him. For our bodies to be intertwined.

"Bao?"

My face burned. I looked up.

"Were you even listening?"

I looked at the ground. "Mostly."

"So do you think there are?"

"Are what?"

Guanyu rolled his eyes. "Many trains in Africa. You weren't listening."

"We'll just have to find out."

Guanyu nodded. He studied Africa on his map. "We'll have to learn French and English."

"Hê Jing can teach us English. We can learn French in Paris."

Guanyu smiled. "Many, many weeks in Paris."

Many, many weeks with Guanyu.

The sun sank low on the horizon. Orange ribbons of reflected sunlight swirled in tiny whirlpools at the edges of the river.

His gaze was on me. I sensed it.

I froze.

I didn't want to embarrass him. Even more, I wanted him to keep staring at me, for in my mind it meant … maybe, just maybe … he really did feel the same about me as I him. Was it possible?

"What were you thinking about?" he asked me.

My chest pounded.

"You don't have to tell me," he said.

I can't tell you, I thought, but I want to tell you.

Guanyu stood. He looked out over the water. In whispers he said, "I had a dream last night."

"What kind of dream?"

He was silent. His silhouetted form stood motionless.

I rose. I walked over next to him.

"We were hiding," he said softly, "from the other boys at school."

"Where?"

"The old storage house near the bridge. It was dark. And damp. It smelled like earth."

"Why were we hiding?"

From the corner of my eye I saw him glance at me. I kept my gaze on the lights that had come on across the river.

Guanyu bent down. He picked up a small stone. He threw it. The reflection of the city lights shook and my eyes blurred as I tried to stay focused on it.

Guanyu suddenly turned and sprinted along a path parallel to the river.

"Guanyu?"

I took off after him. He had always been able to run faster than me, but this time he stumbled over a branch and fell to his knees. He rolled onto his side.

I came up to him before he had a chance to right himself. I fell down beside him and pressed my hand on his arm.

He was out of breath.

"What are you doing?" I said, trying to catch my own breath.

"I can't pretend any more."

"Pretend what?"

He covered his face with his hands. He let out a moan. He pounded his heels against the ground.

"Are you having an attack?"

He reached up and took hold of my shirt. He pulled me toward him.

We gazed into each other's eyes.

My throat went dry. Drops of sweat rolled down my face. I was paralysed. Then Guanyu lifted his head just an inch more. And … our lips met.

I'd always imagined it might be like a flash of light exploding in the sky, or a wave crashing against the shore.

But the kiss felt as blissful as a breeze sweeping through a field, stalks of grain subtly changing colour as they rippled in arcs.

Guanyu pulled away. He sat up on his knees. He started to say something, but only guttural sounds came out. Ahh … uhhh … ahhh. He shook his head. Then, he jumped to his feet and became an Olympic sprinter once more, and disappeared into the darkness.

I returned home. My heart hadn't yet calmed down. Guanyu told me he'd had a dream; now I felt I was in one. I didn't know what was real any more.

"You're late," Xiong said.

I looked around. "Where are Mama and Papa?"

"At a meeting."

"Meeting?"

Xiong marched over. He held up a whistle. "You weren't the only one to get a gift."

The whistle was scratched and rusted. "Where did you get it?"

"From an American pilot."

"Did he really give it to you?"

"I don't steal things!" Xiong shouted, his eyes narrowed.

I elbowed him away from me. "What meeting are you talking about?"

"The pilots are leaving. Papa said they have to move in darkness."

I rarely trusted what my brother told me. Yet somehow this seemed mostly true. It didn't make sense to me that these pilots would spend much time in our city. They had battles to fight.

Xiong tried to blow the whistle. Breath and squeaks were the best he could do.

I sat down in a corner of the room. I touched my finger to my lips.

"They told me I was old enough to stay by myself for a little while," Xiong said, sitting down next to me. "But you'll still be in trouble when they get home for being so late. Unless – "

"Forget it," I said. "You're not getting my coin."

Xiong dropped the whistle to the floor. "It doesn't even work."

My little brother went on about the injustices of life.

All I could think about was … kissing. Guanyu and I had kissed. What … what did it all mean? What happens next? "What happens next?" I actually said it out loud.

"Next? After what?" Xiong asked.

I closed my eyes. I smiled. I took deep breaths. I was still in a dream.

"You're a very strange brother to have," Xiong said, picking up his whistle. He stood and marched into the next room, all breath and squeak.

We sat against a large rock. We were partially hidden as dusk fell and the first stars appeared. Though we were on the fringes of the city, anyone could have seen us.

I didn't care. My heart beat so quickly as I held Guanyu against me. His fingers gently stroked my arm, up and down, in small circles, in zigzags. Every angle. No spot untouched, palm to shoulder.

I couldn't deny twinges of panic, imagining someone reporting to my parents that their son was embracing another boy.

The first time that other boys at school teased me about the Japanese blood coursing through me, Guanyu asked me why I cared what others thought of me. I didn't have a good answer. But I knew entire civilizations had been brought down because of what some people thought of other people.

Guanyu said it had been months. "Months of wanting to tell you. Wondering. Convincing myself you like me the same way I like you. Then thinking it was impossible. Crazy. That if I told you, you would hate me.

Never speak to me again."

I admitted to him the same thought patterns. But that I'd had so many visions both in my sleep, and when I was fully awake, that somehow, in some way, we would end up just like this, him in my arms, his head on my shoulder.

We were very serious about our journey. The journey we would make a reality. In many ways, though, I realised that this journey we'd started planning stood for something else, too. The journey of us. Something for Guanyu and me that the rest of the world wouldn't have a say in.

"Symbolic," Guanyu said.

I nodded. I thought of the coin. Full of symbolism. But worth something in its existence.

"I have to leave soon," Guanyu whispered.

"Me too."

We decided if we wanted to keep having our meetings by the river, we should keep our parents happy by not returning home late.

It was an acceptable trade-off.

But our goodbyes felt worse and worse each time.

Xiong was crying when I returned home. He sat on the floor, his right leg bent at the knee. His skin was scraped and bloodied.

"What happened?"

My mother knelt next to him. She dabbed the wound with a wet cloth.

"Never mind!" my father said. He was pacing the room, his eyes darting about. There were a million things on his mind.

"A little scrape, that's all," my mother whispered.

"They called me Japanese!" my brother said, between sobs, his eyes red and puffy.

He got on my nerves so often. My heart broke a little, though, seeing him in pain like this.

I looked away. I tried not to notice my father, pacing pacing pacing. I tried to block out my brother's cries.

I reached into my pocket. I clutched the dime. What was I going to do with it? What value did it hold for me? Especially now that the most confusing yet wonderful thing had happened to me?

I slid out the coin. I grasped Xiong's hand. I pressed the cool metal into his palm.

"Really?" Xiong said, his face bright despite the tears and quivering lips.

"Really," I said. "You take good care of it."

My mother stared at me, her eyes soft. She silently thanked me.

The next day felt wonderfully vibrant. Full of colours, sounds, scents: the blossoms on the trees, the rustle of grass in the gentle springtime breeze. A peaceful sensation, the first in a long while, unlike so many days of late. As we sat next to each other on the riverbank, our bodies pressed together, all the questions and doubts and fears had vanished. Now I knew what it meant to be this close to Guanyu.

The map rested on his lap. In the night he'd marked more routes of our future voyage: Pacific islands; South America; big cities like New York and London. He made the trek sound so achievable, and the paths logical. He made notes about gathering timetables for steamships and trains. He'd pointed out places where hiking would be a challenge but well worth the effort.

The fingers of his left hand brushed across Siam. The fingers of his right hand were interlaced with mine.

Just as I squeezed tighter, we heard the voice. A woman. We both panicked. Was she yelling at us? Two boys sitting so close together? Out in the open?

Guanyu pulled away first. He sat up, the map clutched tightly in his hand.

I turned and saw the woman. She stumbled. There were two boys behind her, younger than Xiong.

She yelled at us.

"Run! Run! Run!"

Others appeared. Old men, helped by younger women. More children.

Guanyu stood. The map fell to the ground.

"Japanese!" a young woman shouted. Was she looking at me? I thought of Xiong's scraped knee.

Guanyu ran over to two women who looked like twins.

I rose. I retrieved the map, folded it carefully, and tucked it into my pocket.

Guanyu raced back over, his eyes welling with tears.

I clutched his arm. "What? What is it? What's happening?"

It took him several moments to find his voice. I grew impatient, panicked. I shook him. "Ch'en Guanyu!"

"Those American pilots," he stammered. "They bombed Kobe. Osaka. The Japanese are seeking revenge. House to house … going house to house … anyone who helped … "

Guanyu doubled over. I helped him to the ground. He was heaving. I placed my hand between his shoulders to try to calm him, steady him. I searched about, and located the twins. I ran after them.

"What's happening?" I asked, my own voice now almost gone.

"Just run!" one of the twins shouted.

"They shot them dead," the other twin whispered. "All of them. Right in front of us. I told him not to take those stupid American gloves. Why did he take them?" She sounded more and more delirious. She searched the sky, her eyes red and her entire body trembling. "The gloves proved nothing!" she screamed. Her sister jerked her forward and they hurried away from the river and into a thick grove of trees.

My mind raced. Images bled together. Then, like a faraway object coming into focus, it started to make sense. American gloves. Something a pilot must have given away. Like so many other things. Just like the dime. And the whistle. Both of which now belonged to Xiong. If the Japanese found them at our house …

"Ch'en Guanyu!" I shouted.

He was curled up on the ground. He seemed as delirious as the twin. I'd never seen him like this before. A lump formed in my throat. My stomach was in knots. I ran to him, and knelt down.

I had no idea what to do. What to say. What were our options?

People were fleeing. We'd been told people had been shot. What about our families? My father would be in the fields on the other side of town. My mother would be home with Xiong. Guanyu's father … I didn't know where he worked! And his mother … probably home. Were they safe? Had our houses been searched?

"I don't know what to do," I whispered as I rested my forehead on Guanyu's arm. I felt his body shake.

Guanyu stirred. He rolled to his side. He sat up, and wiped tears from his face. His voice was stronger. "We have to go see. Don't we? We have to check on them."

I knew he meant our families. I froze, until I felt his hand grasp my wrist. Then I nodded. What else could we do? How could we flee, and leave our families behind? Then again, how could we go back into the city if the Japanese were killing people?

"There's no good choice," Guanyu said, as though he'd read my mind.

I tried to push images out of my head. I just couldn't stop thinking about Xiong. If the Japanese searched our house, and found the coin and the whistle …

Guanyu gasped. He scrambled to his feet, and raced up the path toward a girl, all of five or six years old. She was crying. Guanyu bent down and said something to her. She answered him. Guanyu stood up, arched his back, and threw up his arms, toward the sky, the vibrant blue now so dim.

He turned toward me. His voice cracked as he let out a wail. "They took her!" he shouted. "They took my mother!"

In that instant, my world split apart. I spotted Hê Jing in the distance. I saw Guanyu running toward me. I heard people calling out, telling us not to stay near the river, that it was too dangerous. I saw Xiong, on Hê Jing's back, his arm soaked with blood.

Guanyu embraced me with such force, I almost fell backward. When I regained my balance, I put my arms around him and pulled him to me. He stared into my eyes. He kissed me, passionately, longingly. My head swirled.

He pulled away. He stroked my cheek.

"We'll find each other again," he said, through tears, and then turned and ran faster than I'd ever seen him run.

"Brother!" Xiong called out. Hê Jing made his way over to me, nearly falling. He tried to balance the weight of Xiong on his back.

Flesh had been torn from my brother's arm. Hê Jing could barely breathe. He fell forward. Xiong ran to me and buried his face against my ribs.

"Go," Hê Jing whispered. "Both of you go. Just go."

"Mama and Papa?" I said.

Hê Jing closed his eyes. He shook his head. He waved us on. "Keep your brother safe."

I took hold of Xiong's hand. The hand attached to the arm that hadn't been shredded. I ran, tugging him behind me. He called out, but his words were a jumble. I couldn't carry him the way Hê Jing had. I wasn't strong enough. But Xiong needed to be strong now. He needed to stay with me as we went far away. Far away from the Japanese monsters. We had to keep running, running, running so fast that I wouldn't have time to think about my parents. About Guanyu. About the end of China.

But I couldn't stop the words sounding in my head.

We'll find each other again.

They grew louder and louder as I felt Xiong fall to the ground.

We'll find each other again.

Xiong lay on his right side, the way he often slept, when I would stare at him, feeling so ashamed I'd been short with him, losing my temper, losing my patience, wishing I were an only child.

We'll find each other again.

I kissed Xiong's cheek. As I had so many times before, as he dreamt, only now I didn't feel his breath, or hear the slight wheezing sound he always made, especially in springtime, the same sound as my father.

We'll find each other again.

If I could make it to Shangrao, I knew I'd find Guanyu. That was our plan. Shangrao to Běipíng, then on to Mongolia and Russia, and then to everywhere.

For a few moments, I forgot the sting in my eyes. The queasiness in my stomach. The ache in my chest.

Because I knew across a thousand miles, I would find him.

I would find Ch'en Guanyu.

The only precious thing I had left.

Wild Flowers

JL Merrow

I see her the third day in, a dozen or so women along from me on the bucket chain. We're clearing a site just off Unter den Linden, and I can't think why I haven't noticed her before. Maybe it's just that the sun hasn't shone until today, lighting up her wavy blonde hair and making it stand out like a gold coin in a coal scuttle. Not that any of us see much gold, or coal either for that matter, these dark times. The Tiergarten is a sad wasteland, its trees long since gone for fuel.

She's younger than I am, maybe 20, with rosy freshness in her cheeks, and wears a sackcloth apron over her pretty green dress, the colour of new leaves after rain. I look down at my old grey frock, made greyer by brick dust, and frown. She smiles a lot as she works, and chats to the women around her. One time, she catches my eye and I smile back at her, my face feeling odd, as if it's forgotten how this works. I look away in embarrassment. Ruth, I hear her name is, from one of the old women who sit chipping mortar off bricks with a pickaxe so that they can be used again. Berlin will be a phoenix, rising from its own ashes.

And there are so many ashes.

Ruth won't remember the times before the devil took our country and our people's hearts, not as I do. So many clubs, like the Dorian Gray and the Topp-Keller, where you could buy a drink and watch handsome women singing in drag, and where pretty boys picked up foreigners for love and money. Berlin was beautiful then, gleaming white and red and gold. Now, the pretty boys are all dead and the clubs long since closed down or destroyed. I had a lover then, Anna, with cornflower eyes and wide, red lips that laughed and swore and kissed me with equal abandon. When she was killed in the bombings of 43, I thought my heart died with her.

Is it disloyal of me, to be glad to find some part of it still lives?

The next day, I put on my good dress, the scarlet one people tell me puts colour in my cheeks. It's too good for work, but what am I saving it for, after all? It still fits me. I've always been scrawny, even in the pre-war times when bread was there to be bought any time we chose, and butter not a luxury.

Frau Müller from my building, whose husband was a teacher who came back from the war with no legs and only one arm and slit his own throat the first time they let him have a razor, tells me she's heard they're asking two hundred marks for a kilo of butter on the black market. A fantasy, when we earn seventy pfennigs an hour. If you'd told me in 1933 that one day I'd dream of fresh, crusty white bread, warm from the baker's oven and spread thickly with creamy yellow butter that melts to golden as you watch, I'd have laughed. But then I laughed a lot in those days.

My walk to work takes me through the Brandenburger Tor, that great symbol of peace. Today, it's pockmarked with bullet holes and scarred from shrapnel, and the quadriga on top is a mangled ruin. The horses are nothing more than twisted scrap, only one head still recognisable of the four.

Anna would have sighed and said, *Poor creatures, it isn't fair that they should suffer too.* I would have laughed at her fancy, and put my arm in hers.

A Red Army soldier stares at me as I pass by the six-metre tall picture of Stalin, his name written underneath in Cyrillic, and I duck my head. Maybe the scarlet dress wasn't a good idea, after all. Soldiers are everywhere in Berlin. They leave graffiti scrawled in their foreign tongues upon our battered, broken walls, as if they hadn't left enough of a mark already. Elsewhere I've seen a notice, the colour of blood, that tells us the Red Army don't hate us, that they respect the rights of the German folk. Tell that to Ilse, her face hard and her belly big with some Russian soldier's bastard, a souvenir of their triumphant capture of our city and our nation.

I was luckier, if you can call that luck. But I don't think of that time any more.

We women, though: we pay for a man's arrogance and greed. For his inhumanity, although it shocks me so; what we hear about the work camps – can it really be true? I don't want to believe my fellow Germans could do these things – and yet, I've seen so much evidence of what war can do to honour, to decency. I see men on the street now, the ones who have come home, and I wonder, were they the ones to round up the pretty boys I used to know, and the Jews, and the gypsies, and do all those terrible things?

We pay now, with our empty bellies and our aching backs, our blistered hands and our lungs filled with dust. With our broken hearts. There is always the thought: Could I have done more? Back in the thirties, as a professional woman, back when there was such a thing, could I have spoken out, changed minds, before the eyes of the nation narrowed to slits too fine to admit bare humanity? Too late now, with *Kinder und Küche* barked out at me so often it rings in my ears even yet, for all that I have no children and there's precious little food to cook. There was a third K, the *Kirche* the Kaiser so generously allowed us, but the National Socialists didn't care for that one, and now his namesake church on the Kurfürstendamm is a jagged, hollow tooth tearing into an empty sky. God doesn't live there any more, if he ever did.

Ilse raises her pickaxe in greeting as I reach the site. She's joined the old women now, her belly too big for clambering on rubble. "A special occasion?" she asks, eyeing my scarlet dress.

"Yes," I tell her. "The sun is shining, and we're alive to see it. How are your children?"

"See for yourself." She nods to one side, and I see Erich hammering in cobbles while little Hans, too young to help, squats barefoot by his side. "I had a letter from Franz," Ilse says, and then pauses, her hand in the small of her back. "He thinks they'll let him come home soon."

"Have you told him?" No need to say about what. He won't be the only man coming home to a little cuckoo. Although there are more, of course, who won't come home at all.

"Not yet."

"Franz is a good man," I tell her, although I've never met him. He's a prisoner of war somewhere in England. They give him good food, Ilse says, but make him work on a farm. He misses the city. Ilse hasn't told him how little of it is left. "He'll understand."

"Two more months," she says, and turns to look at her sons again. "It will take longer than that, won't it, before he's home?"

I'm not sure why she says that, but it's not my business to pry. I rest a hand on her shoulder and go to take my place in the line. It's a beautiful day, the skies a perfect azure as if no harm could ever come from them.

"Today would be a wonderful day for a swim," the woman next to me says, as we pass the buckets of rubble hand to hand. "I used to love trips out to the Wannsee before the war. My friend from the department store and I would take a picnic and our bathing suits, and lie out in the sun and pretend not to notice the men looking at us. Unless they were very handsome, of course." She laughs, and I see that half her teeth are missing. Her face is thin and lined under her chequered headscarf and I think she's forty or so. It's hard to tell. "I don't think any men would look at me now, do you?"

"Nonsense," I say gallantly. "If I were a man, I'd look at you."

"Only to ask who left that bag of bones there!" She laughs again, a raucous, rasping sound like too many cigarettes, although I've never seen her smoke. "I'm Lili," she says, "Like Lili Marleen." She offers me her hand. I stare at it for a moment, expecting a bucket, then catch myself, feeling foolish.

"Henny," I tell her as I clasp her dry, roughened hand in mine. "And do you still wait under the lantern for your young soldier?"

She shakes her head, still smiling. "I've waited for so many young soldiers. None of them ever returned. And you?"

"My young man fell in the early years," I say, a practised lie become bitter all-but-truth.

Lili nods, a comradely acknowledgement of shared sorrow, and passes the next bucket. I wonder if those young soldiers were her lovers or her sons. Maybe both.

I lost so many friends during the war. So many of them, I don't know if they lived or died. Felice, the ballet dancer with dark eyes and a sharp wit, because she was a Jew. Gerda, the writer, who had a good heart for all she made my head ache with her rhetoric, because she was outspoken and a troublemaker. They took them away, to Ravensbrück and to Bergen-Belsen, and I never heard from them again.

It haunts me: did they break her spirit, brave, fierce Gerda? Did they force her to become a whore, as other women like us were forced? A woman who would not bear children for the Führer had to be corrected, after all.

And Anna, my Anna, who smoked too much and drank too much, and kept me awake half the night with her kisses. There are days when I could weep to remember the taste of good wine on my lover's lips. I didn't get to kiss her, the night she died. She was late for her shift at the hospital, and she had to run.

She still didn't get there in time.

When work is over for the day, I straighten my back and stretch weary arms. Today was a good day. The sun shone, nobody was hurt when the building we worked on shifted and settled, although the women standing closest looked like ghosts from all the dust, and Lili (who I can't help but think of as a battle-weary Lili Marleen, Lale Andersen's sultry, knowing voice ringing in my head) gave me two cigarettes she got from a soldier. A cigarette is a precious thing, these days – they say you can buy a car with a few packs of American cigarettes, although they don't say where you'd get the petrol.

These are not American cigarettes, but precious, nonetheless. They're safe in my pocket as I start the walk back to my room in the British Sector, where Frau Müller will be cooking whatever she can scrape together from our rations and a widow's smile. Maybe more than a smile, but she doesn't seem unhappy so I don't ask. Perhaps I'll give her one of my cigarettes. Or perhaps I'll smoke them both myself, and remember how Anna tasted after she'd been smoking. I find myself heartened by the thought; isn't that odd?

As I walk through the Brandenburger Tor, leaving the Red Army behind me for the day, a flash of gold catches my eye, burnished copper in the setting sun. I turn.

"Hello! I don't think we've met?" Ruth says, and smiles at me. Her teeth are white and perfect, except for one little crooked one that hides its face behind another, like a shy teenage girl at her first dance. Her lips are full and pink, and her eyes aren't cornflower, they're green, like her dress. "This is my way home too. I like your frock. We need some colour, in these grey surroundings, don't we?"

"Sometimes the greyness overwhelms me," I find myself blurting out. "Our beautiful city. How can we ever start to build again, when so much has been destroyed?"

"One brick at a time," she tells me, and she links her arm in mine. She's taken off her apron and our dresses are bright in contrast, scarlet against green, like wild flowers blooming in a summer meadow. "One brick at a time."

I offer her a cigarette, and as the match flares red and gold, I almost think for a moment I can see the phoenix rise.

Author's Note

This story is dedicated to the Trümmerfrauen of Berlin, the "women of the rubble" who, in the face of their country's crushing defeat and the loss of so many of their loved ones, laboured to clear the many, many bombsites of the almost flattened city to enable rebuilding to begin.

Acknowledgements

With grateful thanks to Petra Howard, Sandra Lindsey, Astrid Ohletz, Annika Buehrmann, Angelika Ranger, Julia & Sage Marlowe.

Better to Die

Charlie Cochrane

One of my earliest memories is of running around like a mad thing in the local Hampshire woods, almost going arse over tip into a massive hole. Dad said a German bomb had made it, thirty-odd years before, where the crew had ditched their remaining bombs before turning for home after attacking the docks. That had been one spring night in 1942, and Dad said he remembered it clearly. He'd been fifteen, and scared shitless sitting in the air-raid shelter. One of his pals from school had dropped dead through fright during an air raid only the month before.

War leaves its mark, on land and in minds.

The war graves in the local churchyard didn't have such an immediate impact on me. We'd walk through there, me and Mum, taking the short cut home from school. *Tell me about this one, Mum. Where did he fight? How did he die?*

I must have driven her mad, but kids want to know, don't they?

Corporal J.L. Williams, Army Cyclist Corps, the headstone by the yew tree. Private C.P. Lloyd, Manchester Regiment, the grubby white stone by the hedge, nineteen when he died. Mum said he'd been killed at the Somme, on the very first morning, in the very first wave. At least, that's what she told me. I must have been a blood-thirsty little oik, because I remember pestering her about what it had been like for the soldiers. In the end, she got me some books from the library, and reading them was when I began to grow up. The first time you discover that your mother lied to you about who'd died where and about what war was really like.

Captain H.R. Gore-Davis, Royal Leicestershire Regiment, the green-tinged stone by the path, was my favourite. One day Mum suggested we come down with paper and crayons and do rubbings of all three stones. After a few botched efforts, and a bit of help, I had three pictures of the regimental badges to put on my bedroom wall. I always liked the Captain's best.

Gore-Davis was a puzzle, though. He'd died in 1953, which was after Korea, and Mum said he'd probably died in a terrible accident during training. It seemed the best explanation at the time.

Even when I was at secondary school and didn't need to take the shortcut, I went to visit the graves, and not just on Remembrance Sunday, which was the only time anybody else seemed to bother with them. Even when I was home from medical school for the holidays, I still paid my respects to the lads, walking Mum's old Labrador through the graveyard and telling him about my heroes, as Mum had told me.

You can talk to your dog and nobody thinks you're mad.

By then I'd found out a bit about Gore-Davis, although not why he'd been buried there, because the family – a well to do lot, what Mum would have called 'old money' – were based in Wales. That fact came from Debrett's, and some Welsh history books the librarian in the town library tracked down for me. She'd also suggested trying the local university, as it had a microfilm archive of old newspapers. I was poking about in the wartime editions looking for the Leicestershires when I came across Gore-Davis's name. He'd been with the regiment out in the Far East; the paper had a notice of his promotion to lieutenant. I had no idea how he'd ended up buried in our village.

By a coincidence, my great-uncle had served in World War Two, out in Burma, with the Chindits, though it would have been stretching things to hope Great Uncle Frank had known *my* captain.

Frank was the black sheep of the family. He'd lived in our village until I was five and my fondest memories of the man were the stories he regaled us with. Snakes in the jungle so thin they'd slip through the eyelets of your boots, Gurkha soldiers as hard as adamant that you thanked God were on your side and not the other. Never anything about the fighting, though; he kept that close to his chest.

I'll never forget the dirty great Gurkha kukri Frank kept on his wall. Mum had kittens when he got it down and let me hold it, but I treated it with respect. Didn't so much as nick my fingers.

"Jamie," Frank used to say, "when you take a kukri out of its scabbard, it has to taste blood before it can go back again. That's why I took this out and keep it out, so it doesn't need satisfying again. My fighting days are long gone. You can have it when I'm gone."

"You'll never go," I'd said, secretly delighted that I'd get the thing one day.

"Better to die than to be a coward," he'd replied, enigmatically. Later I found that had been the motto of the Gurkha Rifles, but I was sure there was more to what he was saying than just that.

Frank moved away not long after, and our side of the family lost touch with him. I suspected Dad knew where he'd gone but he wouldn't even let anyone send Frank so much as a Christmas card. When I was twelve Dad sat me down and told me I was old enough to know the truth: war was hard, and Frank had suffered the worst of it. He'd seen some dreadful things, done some dreadful things, and he found it difficult to live with himself. Dad reckoned Frank had come home with something like shell shock so he acted loopy at times. It was safer for all of us not to be near him when things turned bad.

That changed my mind about being a squaddie – I was going to save lives, not take them. Going off to Bart's meant I stopped grave visiting, although I tried to keep up an interest in browsing war books, although *that* stopped when I discovered sex. No healthy, testosterone-laden medical student was going to stay at home with 'Merry Christmas Mr. Lawrence' when he could be out getting his leg over. Notice I didn't say "when I discovered girls" and you'll get the picture.

Time moved on. The dog died during my second year at Bart's and Mum didn't have the heart to get a replacement, so we didn't even have an excuse to walk past the war graves when home. Then, in my third year, Dad had a massive heart attack; after the funeral nobody fancied hanging round graveyards any more. By the time I'd finished medical school I hardly ever thought about 'my lads', except for wearing a poppy each November, and my last year had proved so busy I didn't have time to think about *anything* except work, eating, sleeping and the occasional bit of sex. My boyfriend had given me the push because he reckoned he never saw me, so I was footloose, fancy free and fond of hitting the scene with a vengeance.

Captain H. R. Gore-Davis came back into my life when I had a break between medical school and starting my houseman post. Most blokes would have spent a few weeks on an island in the Med, overindulging in sea, sand and sex, but I was tired of burning the candle at both ends and decided to spend a few days researching my old soldier. Because that's the kind of wild, crazy guy I am.

I stayed up in London, intending to work my way through some military history, but first I had to drop in to the medical school library to return some books. There was this stunning bloke lurking around the psychiatric racks, so I reckoned I should lurk there too. We got talking, and it turned out he'd studied psychology, and was following that up with a master's degree in children's development. Just the sort of thing to really impress your mother when you take a boyfriend home for the first time, but that was getting ahead of myself. We'd only exchanged names, let alone phone numbers. He – Ben – was trying to find some stuff about the influences on gender and sexuality in teenagers so I offered to help him look. While we were rummaging through a set of journals, I spotted a name which brought me up with a start.

"What's up?" Ben sounded so concerned, I must have turned white. I'd certainly jumped. "Someone walked over your grave?"

"Not *my* grave." I pointed a shaking finger at the page. "Gore-Davis. That bloke's buried in my local churchyard. I had no idea I'd find him in the *British Journal of Psychiatry*."

"Sounds like we should have a look at the article. You. I mean *you* should look at it." He was dead cute to start with, but the blush turned him drop-dead gorgeous.

"Fancy a coffee? We can read the journal at the same time."

"No fear. That librarian's a dragon. She'd flay us alive if we spilled coffee on anything." Ben, smiling, looked at the open page. "We'll read in here in one of the carrels. I suspect you'll need a coffee afterwards."

"Why?"

"Look at the title of the article. You won't like it."

I looked. I didn't like it. 'Treatment of homosexuality in the 1950s: Capt. H.R. Gore-Davis.' "What the fuck?"

"Don't ask me. I've never come across the article before." He took my arm. "Let's go and find out the worst."

I should have thought I'd hit the jackpot, squeezed into a carrel with a knockout bloke, but all I wanted to do was read that article. It started with giving some background on the state of the law back then, but I wanted to skip over that: old news. I bided my time, though, letting Ben read at his own rate. We soon got on to my man, with details about his glowing war service. I knew about the Military Cross and the DSO, but hadn't realised what he'd been decorated for. I wasn't surprised to read he'd captured a machine gun nest and held it while his men reached safety. My man was bound to be a hero, wasn't he?

The vicarious pride I felt in his achievements soon disappeared when I got into the article proper. Gore-Davis was on leave. Arrested in the 1950s equivalent of a gay bar, and found himself in court. The army tried to hush it all up, but there had been a limit to what they could do. Given the choice of prison or medical treatment, he'd taken the option a lot of people would have gone for.

Medical treatment.

"Bloody hell." Ben ran his slim fingers through his hair. "I wonder if it was aversion therapy?"

"We'll soon find out." Even those fingers couldn't distract me from the text. It hadn't been aversion therapy, but what people call chemical castration, the sort of thing they still used on sex offenders. I jabbed the page. "Bastards. I bet nobody during the war was bothered about who he liked to shag on leave. That counts for nothing in the jungle."

I stopped, suddenly aware that I'd let my gob run on. And I'd assumed that Ben was at least sympathetic; for all I knew he was a raving queer-hater. But he was smiling sympathetically, and clapping my shoulder, and it was all okay. "Maybe we should ditch that coffee and go for a drink afterwards. This can't have a happy ending."

"Good idea."

The arrest and trial were dated 1953, the year Gore-Davis had died. I wondered, fleetingly, whether he'd killed himself, but the truth was even worse. Officially he'd had a massive pulmonary embolism – so died of natural causes – but the article doubted that view. The authors believed his death had been brought on by his treatment, suspicions having been raised not long after, but nothing had ever been proven because nobody wanted to dig too deeply. He'd only just turned thirty-five.

"Doesn't it make your blood boil? Fit and healthy bloke, snuffed out like a light. Hey, are you all right?" Ben leaned over to stick his hand on my forehead. "You're all clammy."

"Is it any surprise, reading this sort of stuff? He was a hero." He was *my* hero. Why hadn't the stupid bastards treating him made sure he wasn't at risk taking the drug? Why have such a stupid fucking law in the first place?

"I guess being a hero was no defence."

"What do you mean by that?"

"All I meant was that he couldn't have offered up his medals in court as proof of character. People wouldn't have given a shit." Ben shrugged; he did that very attractively, but I was in no mood for flirting.

"It's not fair. Not – sorry, I'll be back." During one of my stints in the casualty department, I'd seen a young squaddie, Gore-Davis's age, rushed into casualty with a heart attack, and dying before we'd even got to work on him. The sudden memory, hitting my gastric system, sent me racing out of the carrel and into the loo to lose my dinner down it. When I came back, suitably cleaned up, Ben served up sympathy, but we couldn't unread what we'd read and I couldn't unlearn what I'd just learned.

"I didn't think it would be so hard to take," Ben said, rubbing my clammy back. He'd returned the journal to the shelf – if the librarian would kill us for getting coffee on it, how would she feel about puke? "It's a horrible case study."

"He's not a case study, he's a bloke. *Was* a bloke. Somebody's son, somebody's boyfriend. My Howell. I mean Rhys." That had been a shock, too, finding out that he preferred to go by his middle name. The fact I'd been thinking of the bloke by the wrong name all these years felt like a kick in the stomach. There was no way whoever had written the article had any right to know more about my soldier than *I* did. I needed that drink. "Come on. I'll buy you a pint."

Over drinks in a local bar, we went through the whole "Where are you from, what are you studying?" thing which led naturally into me telling him why I was interested in Gore-Davis. Ben took it all in, asking the odd question and fixing me with his dark, seductive eyes. "He clearly wasn't local, given what it said in the journal. Does anybody come and look after his grave? Or are his family too ashamed?"

"I bet the family were told he'd died from natural causes. Everything swept under the carpet, with a discreet announcement in *The Times* and no fuss. I've read that announcement – no indication of what had gone on."

"I suppose that's how it was in those days." Ben rubbed his forehead. "Ironic, don't you think? You being obsessed with this guy's grave and it turns out that not only was he gay, but it was the doctors who killed him."

"Ironic? Is that what you're calling it? Shouldn't the word be murder?"

"Probably." Ben grinned. Come-to-bed smile to match the come-to-bed eyes. "I meant the coincidence was ironic, or something. The connections to you. Like fate wanted you to link up or something. Tell me to shut up if I'm talking crap."

That was food for thought. "I don't know. It's spooky. Like the whole thing about why he's buried in our churchyard when he seems to have no local connections." All too much for a mind addling after a pint of beer on an empty stomach. "Fancy something to eat?"

"Do I ever. Stomach thinks my throat's been cut."

That was the day my life changed, in more ways than one. A burger, more beers, followed by a session in my bed, and Ben making sure I had his number and he mine. The next morning when I woke I knew something significant had happened. I'd dreamed about Rhys, meeting him in a bar in Brighton of all places, the captain drowning his sorrows and me, enthralled, hanging on every word. Not that I could remember the details of what he'd said once I was awake, but the feeling lingered, like the prickling memory of a burn when the skin's healed.

I couldn't get him – and what had happened to him in the name of so-called justice – out of my head. Nothing I could do about it, though. I lay, staring at the ceiling, dreaming up mad ideas like raising a petition to have him pardoned or calling for a public enquiry. Perhaps the doctors who treated him would still be alive and I could have them brought up before the General Medical Council, but what would any of it achieve apart from making me feel that I was doing something? The still, small voice of reason – surprisingly active seeing how muzzy the rest of my brain felt – kept saying it wasn't my fight, and that maybe the rest of the Gore-Davis family wouldn't want the story to be resurrected.

I expected the feeling of hopeless frustration would pass but it took its time. Ben and I started going out, relationship developing nicely, as I eased into my house officer role, with a view to eventually specialising in paediatrics, but Rhys wouldn't go away. I kept seeing reminders of him everywhere – a documentary about the Chindits on the telly, a letter in a magazine about a petition to pardon some other poor sod who'd been caught up in a crackdown on gay blokes back in the benighted fifties, an article in the *BMJ* about historical medical practices that had fallen little short of torture.

Some days almost anything could trigger a batch of Rhys thoughts – even Ben noticed I was growing edgier, although he put it down to the strain of work. I'd never been an obsessive, never had a particular bee in my bonnet, but now Rhys was buzzing around my head like an insect I could hear but couldn't swat. Then the dreams started.

At first they were like that one I'd had back home, Rhys crying on my shoulder over a pint or three. Soon he was bending my sleeping ear every night, or rising to tell me off for not having done something, although I never found out what it was I'd left undone. Always vivid, always too real for comfort, those dreams rapidly became interspersed with nightmares. Rhys in casualty, with me trying to save him and failing, always failing. Rhys's funeral and everyone accusing *me* of having left him to die.

I'd wake exhausted, or shouting out in the night. Ben was wonderful – at first – soothing me back to sleep any way he could, but even his fortitude ran dry. He rarely spent the night at mine, so I took the hint and made sure I didn't sleep over at his, unless it was on the settee. He wouldn't be able to hear me from there.

Sometimes I could go a whole week of dreamless sleep, which meant I could recharge my physical and emotional batteries, but then the things would be back, with a vengeance.

"Get help," Ben said to me, after one particularly bad night. "This isn't doing you any good."

Those words stung me into action. I made an appointment to see my GP, nearly chickened out, but went along anyway. I held out little hope that he'd be able to do anything other than give me some benzodiazepines and I wasn't sure I wanted to spend my life half off my face. But the doctor trotted out the usual stuff to explain the condition: overwork, strain, the need for a break.

I *did* have leave booked – a week in a villa in the sunshine, my first break with Ben – and by the time it came I was desperate. At first it seemed like the strategy had worked, three dreamless nights and glorious days in between, spent on the beach or in the sea and doing very little. Except maybe falling in love. We even slept in the same bed.

That changed, the fourth night, when Rhys reappeared, perching on the bedstead and asking where I'd been. He said he was lonely, he needed me, why was I playing around with some other bloke? I woke in a muck sweat, sure I'd shouted loud enough to wake Ben, but he was still sleeping, even breaths coming from an unlined, carefree face.

I fetched a glass of water, went out onto the balcony and tried to clear my mind, but it wouldn't be cleared, thoughts piling in on me. I turned, glancing through the glass of the balcony door to see Ben sitting on the side of the bed.

Only, as I realised – and dropped my drink in the process – Ben was still asleep where I'd left him, and someone else was sitting there. Rhys. The vivid sensation of water scattering over my bare feet woke me for real. I was dry, and still in bed.

"What's up?" Ben, next to me, croaky-voiced, touched my shoulder.

"Oh God," I groaned.

"The dream's come back?"

"I don't know." I tried to explain what had happened, as senseless as it sounded. The vividness of the dream within the dream or whatever it was.

"Shall I make you some tea?" Ben offered.

"No!" Too loud, too sharp. I had to play this light. "No. It'll remind me of the glass and the water."

"Okay if I make myself one?"

"Go ahead." I listened to him pottering around in the apartment kitchen, but the usually comforting domestic sounds held no consolation and the bed felt too empty. I got up to watch Ben from the door, noting the intense look of concentration, the effort he was putting in to being brave. Enough to break the hardest heart. "Ben, tell me if this isn't working. I'd understand."

"Is this the polite way of giving me the heave-ho?"

"Not unless you want it to be. I just can't bear you having to endure more than it's fair to ask."

He looked at me, holding his empty mug and just weighing his words, until I wanted to scream at him.

"It's hard," he said, eventually. "You mean the world to me and I hate seeing you suffer. I don't want to walk away."

"There's a 'but' coming, isn't there?"

"There's several." He smiled. "But you need proper help. But you can't carry on like this. But I feel so helpless."

Conversation stopper. It seemed like neither of us could trust ourselves to say anything more, so we sat watching middle-of-the-night TV, like a pair of old codgers with insomnia.

That's when things began to cool, just as they'd got properly heated. We were still crazy about each other but there was a hard knot of … something which sat between us, the elephant in the room. Or the soldier on the side of the bed. We saw each other, Ben and I, but less frequently, and sex couldn't make up for whatever had gone wrong with the rest of the relationship. I visited my GP again but he was worse than useless and I couldn't afford to see a consultant privately.

And still the dreams came, dreams from which I'd half wake and imagine Rhys sitting at the foot of the bed, smiling, until I shut my eyes, reopened them and in so doing made him disappear. The storylines of my dreams had changed, too. No longer was I the villain – now I was standing up to testify as a character witness in court, or managing to work the medical miracle that saved his life. The knight in shining armour, rather than the man with the cape and the moustache.

As the dreams became less distressing, life steadied again. Work was less stressful, I no longer dreaded going to sleep, so Ben started staying the night again. Until I realised the nights he stayed were the nights the dreams turned dark again. As though dream-Rhys was jealous of my time.

Ben wasn't over the moon about having some sort of incubus as a rival for my attention. In the end, it was a case of choosing between him and Rhys, which was no more than Hobson's choice. I could decide when I saw Ben; Rhys selected when *he* visited. And once Ben was pretty well off the scene again, Rhys's visits intensified. No longer could I just shut my eyes and open them again, working the miracle and making him disappear. He'd still be there, at the end of my bed, talking and smiling, until I walked out of the room and came back again. I worried whether a time would come when that strategy would cease to work, when I couldn't make him disappear no matter what I tried.

Was Rhys a waking dream? A hallucination? A ghost? How the fuck did I know?

The inevitable came one morning, when he didn't go. I'd been in and out of the room three times, splashed my face with cold water, slapped myself – any and everything to try to rouse my senses, break the dream, but the result was the same. Rhys wasn't on the bed this time, but standing by the window, looking out over the rooftops. He turned, with a devastatingly handsome smile, and said, "London doesn't change, does it? Not really. Not at heart."

"No," I replied, disorientated. "Did you … come here often?"

"You make it sound like a dance hall. Not often enough. At times, it felt as much like home as anywhere did."

"Where *was* home?"

He turned back to the window. "Just outside Shrewsbury. At least, that's where my family lived."

I sat on the bed, wondering why I was making small talk with either a hallucination or a ghost. Bending down to fish my slippers out from under the bed, I started shivering and had to put my head in my hands, trying to work out whether I'd just gone mad.

"If you're from Shrewsbury, why are you buried in my local churchyard?" I think I asked the question because silence felt so scary, but when I looked up to receive his answer, he'd disappeared. Either my brain had shaken off the phantasm or the ghost had become fed up with my interrogation.

Whatever the truth, it wasn't the sort of experience I rushed into sharing, not unless I wanted to find myself carted off to have my head examined. But I needed to tell somebody. I got back in touch with Ben, seeing as he'd been in from the start and had reached the point where very little was going to shock him. He was surprisingly pragmatic. I think he preferred dealing with a spectre to having to put up with my nightmares. There was no great romantic reunion. Well, to be absolutely accurate, there was, but it didn't become anything permanent. Rhys saw to that.

Ben, in one of the few conversations we were having at the time, suggested I had a priest round to discuss an exorcism. That might have been an idea when it all kicked off, but I was getting less spooked the more it went on. Rhys was becoming as normal a presence as the morning DJ on the radio, or one of the faces in the pictures on the pinboard in the kitchen. I was convinced he wasn't going to hurt me; he just wanted to be part of my life.

Turns out Ben had worked that out long before I did. His unanswerable question to me was whether I wanted a real live boyfriend or some phantom who came round and discussed the war, and life in London after that. I couldn't find a logical response. I hadn't chosen Rhys – he'd chosen me.

I kept asking Rhys why he'd been buried in our village, but he kept turning the question back on me. Didn't I know why? He certainly seemed aggrieved – if ghosts felt aggrieved – at his grave not having been tended, but he wouldn't tell me more than that.

Surprisingly, he wasn't aggrieved at how he'd been treated. I'd have been screaming blue murder, railing against the fucking injustice of it all, but he just shrugged and reminded me I had to remember the times. Remember the prevailing attitudes. He'd played with fire, he'd got burned. If one of his men done the same, Rhys would have hauled him over the coals.

Clearly this wasn't a case of "Hamlet, revenge!", so why should the ghost walk now?

"I need you to do something," he said one morning, perched in his usual place on the windowsill. "Find someone for me. But I can't tell you who. You'll have to work it out."

"Thanks a bundle." I stirred my tea, having gone back to taking sugar in it. "Not even a little clue?"

"He's an old mate."

"By 'mate' do you mean 'lover'?"

"Of course I do." He looked out over the rooftops again. "He lived in Hampshire. He'd be … oh, seventy now."

I wondered why Rhys couldn't have gone and found his old paramour, but I could guess the answer. A sudden reappearance might have been enough to frighten the poor bloke to death.

"I could try to find him, if you'd give me enough information."

"Not allowed to say. Orders." He stood up straight, as though on parade, a movement which usually preceded his disappearing.

"And what am I supposed to do if I ever did find him?" Tell him you're haunting me and would he like to have his share of the burden?

"Just tell him I'm sorry. Better to die than to be a coward." Rhys rubbed his cuff over his face. "I was a fool. For not keeping my head below the parapet. For not keeping it in my trousers."

"Plenty of us need to apologise for that," I said, immediately regretting it. Times *had* changed. The stakes were higher back then. But here came the tricky bit. "If I do find whoever it is, how do I explain how I've got a message to tell? It's not like you and I could have met at any point."

"Say you found an old letter or something, addressed to him. Those sorts of things are always turning up, aren't they? Your vicar was absent-minded and stuffed it among some old hymn books."

"You think he'll believe that?"

I didn't get an answer – Rhys was gone, leaving me with what seemed an insoluble problem. He was far too fond of disappearing when asked awkward questions; I wondered if his lover had found him the same, forty years previously.

After that, I just about managed to get through a day's work without killing anyone, because half of my mind was always on the challenge I'd been set. Where to start? Regimental records, court reports, old electoral rolls for Hampshire? Two o'clock in the morning, when I'd not had a wink of sleep, I had my road to Damascus moment. Rhys had assumed I'd know why he was buried in our village, that I would be able to find his lover without any clues from him, Rhys had fought in the Far East … and Rhys had said "Better to die than to be a coward."

Which was the Gurkha motto.

The connection had to be Frank.

I phoned Mum as early as was decent, demanding that she give me Great-Uncle Frank's address. I didn't let her drag the reason out of me, just insisted it was important. Turned out he was only in Wiltshire; I was free the next Saturday, so I'd head down there then. I thought about asking – more likely begging – Ben to come along with me, but in the end I decided this fence had to be taken alone.

Frank's new home, in a little village that must have reminded him of ours, turned out to be a pleasant semi-detached house on the main street. A street I walked three times up and down before I decided I had to choose between going home, ringing the bell, or getting arrested for loitering. I did the second.

I guess Mum had pre-warned Frank of my arrival, because he greeted me with a huge grin and an unexpected hug; he'd never been one for the touchy-feely stuff. He was still sprightly, dapper, with a full thatch of white hair and a neatly trimmed white beard. I only hoped I'd look as good at seventy-odd. I accepted his offer of tea and biscuits, then kept smiling my best doctor's bedside manner smile while we caught up with family news. He said he was sorry he'd lost touch, but things had got too much for him.

"They'd have called it shell shock fifty years ago. What's the modern term? Stress disorder?"

"Something like that."

"I couldn't trust myself. Remember that old kukri of mine?"

"Yes. I've been wondering where it was." Certainly not in the pride of place on the wall it used to have.

"I reached the point I worried that I'd get it down and run amok." He shut his eyes and took a deep breath. "Does it sound loony that I'd rather have that happen among strangers and not risk hurting you and your mother?"

"Not loony at all." I could understand the strange logic. "Did you get medical help?"

"Yes. As you'll have guessed from the fact I'm here and not in prison." He chuckled, looking just the way he'd looked when I was a boy. "So, what's this visit about? I'm not so daft as to think it's just about catching up. You could have done that down the phone."

"You always saw through me. Even when I thought I'd covered all my tracks." Memories of nicking biscuits and getting a slap on the backside for it flooded back. "I'm afraid this is going to sound totally stupid."

Frank gave me one of his long, searching looks. "Try me."

"Remember I was obsessed with the war graves in the churchyard?"

"Ye-es." Was I imagining that he'd turned a shade paler?

"Rhys Gore-Davis. Did you know him?"

"Know him?" Frank chuckled, although it sounded forced. "Yes, I did. Biblical sense and all. "That's why he's buried there – the old vicar was sympathetic."

"Ah. Right." I tried to look surprised, but acting isn't my strongest suit.

"Funnily enough, I've been dreaming about Rhys," he added. I didn't have to act surprised at that; I almost dropped my cup. "Just these last few months. I thought it was my age, starting to live in the past. I think about him a lot during the day, too. Miss the daft old bugger. Missed him for nigh on forty years."

I pretended I hadn't noticed the tears he brushed away. "I had no idea."

"Of course you didn't. Not the sort of thing we used to trumpet about. Probably can't trumpet it much now, even though we're supposed to be so enlightened. You and your Ben would know that."

I nodded, dumbstruck. Mum must have been keeping in touch with him all this time, and he must have already known much of what we'd been supposedly catching up on earlier – I certainly hadn't mentioned Ben to him by name.

"It's a bloody shame when you can't be yourself," he continued. "Anyway, what's this about Rhys?"

"I think he misses you." No point in making up some story about long lost letters. Better the truth.

Frank gave me the sort of look patients give you when you're a medical student and they don't think you know what you're doing. "What do you mean, he misses me? He's dead."

"I know. Thing is, I've been dreaming about him, too."

He started, as though a sharp pinprick of shock had hit him. "Never. You're joking."

"God's honest truth. Not just dreams. It's … like I said, it's odd. If someone else told me this story, I'd think they'd taken leave of their senses. But it's true, every word of it. You can ask Ben."

"I'll trust you. You're a doctor." He smiled; maybe one madman naturally understood another.

I explained the whole thing, from the revelations in the library to the challenge phantom Rhys had set me. By the time I'd reached the early morning windowsill conversations, the words were tumbling out of me, as if it was the most natural thing in the world to talk to ghosts. Frank followed the story carefully, riding the twists and turns in the tale and asking astute questions, making me elaborate on the bits which clearly meant a lot to him. The bits about Rhys himself.

Was he looking well? if ghosts could look well. I told Frank that I supposed he did, but not having seen him in life I had nothing to make a comparison with.

"Wait a moment." Frank eased himself slowly from his chair and walked over to an old-fashioned bureau, from which he took a silver-framed photo. "This is him."

"Oh, yes," I said, studying the picture. "Yes, he looks much the same. God, he was handsome."

"Knocked me off my feet." Frank rummaged in his pocket for a hankie, then wiped his eyes. Slumping back into his chair, he suddenly looked every year of his age. "I wonder why he didn't come and see *me*? I wouldn't have turned him away."

"I have no idea. I asked, but he does have a habit of not answering questions."

"He's not changed, then." Frank's smile was tired and rueful. "Slippery as an eel when he wanted to be, our Rhys. My Rhys."

Don't let him cry. I'm not good with tears at the best of times, and old men in tears, whether relatives or patients or whatever, I have no idea how to cope with. But he was an old soldier and he kept his upper lip stiff.

"So, what did the silly bugger say?" Frank asked, when he eventually came back from wherever his thoughts had taken him.

I got out my notepad, so he could have it verbatim. "He said 'better to die than be a coward', which was what led me to take a punt on you being the mystery man."

"The old Gurkha motto. Although neither of us were cowards. Not *out there*."

"Yeah, I've been thinking about that. Did he speak to you around the time of the court case?"

"No. We were," he searched for the words, "temporarily estranged. Which became permanent. Why?"

"I wondered if he was saying he'd been a coward, accepting the treatment. Whether he should have opted for prison."

"And whether in dying he regained his valour?" Frank shrugged. "Ask your Ben. He's the psychiatrist."

"Psychologist. Not quite the same. But yes, I'll ask him." I consulted my notes. "Anyway, Rhys had a message for you. 'Tell him I'm sorry for being an idiot. For not keeping my head below the parapet. For not keeping it in my trousers.'"

Frank gulped. "Really? That's what I should have said to him."

"Sorry?"

"*I* should have apologised for being an idiot. Then we'd have been together as usual. I'd been a fool. The lure of the Horse Guards. Never could resist a man in uniform. Rhys found out and we argued. He'd never have gone to that bar otherwise. Not in his nature, the daft sod."

Which was the point where I learned that all you had to do for an old man in tears was give him a hug.

There were no further early morning conversations with an old soldier perched on a windowsill. Not in my flat, anyway – maybe he'd relocated to Wiltshire, although Frank never mentioned them. There was one more dream, though. A parade ground, with Rhys giving me a salute, a smile and a quiet order to dismiss.

I visit Frank every month. He shows me his old photos or we play chess, although I still have no idea what he did with the kukri. Threw it in the river, maybe. He's trying to get me back together with Ben, but that's a bit early to know which way it'll go. Not an easy road to walk: we know each other too well and too little.

Every November I still wear my poppy and put a tenner in the British Legion tin. It's not enough – none of it's enough – but that's love. And war.

About the Contributors

Julie Bozza (*We Live Without a Future*) is an English-Australian hybrid who is fuelled by espresso, calmed by knitting, unreasonably excited by photography, and madly in love with Amy Adams and John Keats.

Find Julie on her blog **juliebozza.com**, Twitter **twitter.com/juliebozza** and Goodreads **goodreads.com/juliebozza**.

Barry Brennessel (*Across a Thousand Miles*) is the author of novels *Tinseltown* and *The Celestial*, which were Lambda Literary Award finalists. *The Celestial* won the Gold Medal in the 2012 ForeWord Book of the Year Awards. His story collection *Sideways Down the Sky* was a Ferro-Grumley Award finalist. Several of his screenplays have been finalists and prize winners in various competitions, including the Rhode Island International Film Festival, Writers Digest Annual, the Arch and Bruce Brown Foundation, American Zoetrope, Launch Pad Feature Screenplay Competition, and Scriptapalooza.

Charlie Cochrane (*Better to Die*) couldn't be trusted to do any of her jobs of choice – like managing a rugby team – so she writes. Her mystery novels include the Edwardian era Cambridge Fellows series, and the contemporary Lindenshaw Mysteries.

A member of the Romantic Novelists' Association, Mystery People and International Thriller Writers Inc, Charlie regularly appears at literary festivals and at reader and author conferences with The Deadly Dames.

Andrea Demetrius (*We're out of Hero Fabric*) lives on the island of eternal spring, or so the brochure says. She's far from being able to confirm that statement, though, since more often than not there's 'just one last book' to finish first.

Adam Fitzroy (*The Town of Titipu, See*) is an imaginist, purveyor of tall tales and UK resident who has been successfully spinning male-male romances either part-time or full-time since the 1980s, and has a particular interest in examining the conflicting demands of love and duty.

Elin Gregory (*Extraordinary Duties*) lives in South Wales and works in a museum in a castle on the site of a Roman fort. No wonder, then, that she writes not only about historical subjects, but also about modern men who change shape at will, and echoes of the past that can be heard in the present. There are always new works on the go; she is currently writing a sequel to *Eleventh Hour* and the next book in her Pemberland series while also reading up on WW2, the Dark Ages and the Romans.

Sandra Lindsey (*A Cup of Tea, Between Friends*) lives in the mountains of Mid-Wales with her husband, cats and chickens. You'll probably hear as much about them as about her writing if you follow her on Twitter (**@SLindseyWales**) or Facebook (**Sandra Lindsey**), and her Instagram (**@sandralindseywales**) is mostly pictures of her garden.

Sandra loves reading, writing and discussing stories, finding them a route to seeing the world from different viewpoints and understanding other experiences. Manifold Press published her novel *Under Leaden Skies*, also set during the Second World War, and she contributed to the Press's Austen-themed anthology *A Certain Persuasion*.

JL Merrow (*Wild Flowers*) is that rare beast, an English person who refuses to drink tea. She writes (mostly) contemporary gay romance and mysteries, and is frequently accused of humour. Her novel *Slam!* won the 2013 Rainbow Award for Best LGBT Romantic Comedy, and several of her books have been EPIC Awards finalists, including *Muscling Through*, *Relief Valve* (the Plumber's Mate Mysteries) and *To Love a Traitor*.

JL Merrow is a member of the Romantic Novelists' Association, International Thriller Writers, Verulam Writers and the UK GLBTQ Fiction Meet organising team.

Find JL Merrow online at her blog **jlmerrow.com**, on Twitter as **@jlmerrow**, and on Facebook at **facebook.com/jl.merrow**.

Heloise Mezen (editor) has been immersed in words ever since she learned to read, which was before she went to school. Under another name she had her moment of glory twenty years ago when her second book was shortlisted for the Guardian Children's Fiction Prize, and nowadays she contributes to the ... *and other Oxford Stories* series **oxpens.co.uk/anthologies**. She works as a (possibly the only) rare books librarian for the Royal Navy, and enjoys researching her family (Mezen is her great-grandmother's maiden name) and eating too much chocolate.

Eleanor Musgrove (*The Boy Left Behind, Letters*) was born in a seaside town on the south coast of England and sometimes feels as if she's lived almost everywhere else since. She has always aspired to be an author and, in 2016, achieved her dream of getting a novel published. With *Submerge* on the shelves, she is now working on several other projects and hopes to release something new soon.

R.A. Padmos (*A Life to Live*) says: I am, in no particular order: woman, writer, in a relationship with my wife since 1981 (though we had to wait until 2001 until we could actually get married), mother of two grown sons, owner of cats (I can pretend, can't I?), reader and a lot more. My background in social history might be obvious from the kind of stories I tell, though I do not shy away from more contemporary themes.

F.M. Parkinson (proofreader) lives in the West Country of England and has had a career in Cataloguing, dealing with many different types of items including archaeological aerial photographs, books and journals, archival documents and museum artefacts.

Writing for pleasure and sharing stories with friends has been a fascinating pastime for some thirty years. She is the author of historical romance *The Walled Garden*.

Michelle Peart (*From Air to Here*) says: After a working life as a graphic designer and a lifetime of devouring books I began to write. I completed four advanced writing courses and passed all with distinction. Apart from my debut novel, *To the Left of Your North Star*, I have written various short stories and enjoy writing my blog, The Copper River *thecopperriver.wordpress.com*. My spare time is spent with my family, painting sets at my local Amateur Dramatics group, or in the wilds with my camera. Find me at **@shellpeart**.

Eric Ravilious (cover image) – artist, engraver and designer – was born in London in 1903, and won a scholarship to the Royal College of Art aged 19. When war broke out in 1939 he had been married for fourteen years, and was appointed as an official war artist, ranked honorary Captain in the Royal Marines. In September 1942 he was posted to Iceland, where he joined the crew of a plane searching for a missing aircraft. That plane too disappeared, and he has no known grave; he is commemorated on the Chatham Naval Memorial.

Megan Reddaway (*The Man Who Loved Pigs*) has been entertained by fictional characters acting out their stories in her head for as long as she can remember. She has worked as a secretary, driver, waitress, and flower-seller, among other things, but she always has a story bubbling away at the same time. She lives in England. For more stories from Megan, visit her website: **meganreddaway.com**

Jay Lewis Taylor (*An Affirming Flame, Buttercup*) is almost entirely English and, accordingly, drinks a great deal of tea. His books explore the lives of people on the margins in one way or another, and the power of love and language to break down the barriers between them. Manifold Press has published *Dance of Stone, The Peacock's Eye, Across Your Dreams* (2016 Rainbow Award Best Historical) and its sequel *Break of Another Day*, as well as two stories in their previous anthology, *Pride of Poppies*.

Manifold Press

Life in all the colours of the rainbow

For **Readers**: LGBTQ+ fiction and romance with strong storylines from acclaimed authors. A variety of intriguing locations – set in the past, present or future – sometimes with a supernatural twist. Our focus is always on the characters and the story.

For **Authors**: We are always happy to consider high-quality new projects from aspiring and established writers.

Our 'regular' novels are now joined by the **Espresso Shots** imprint for novellas and our **New Adult** line. Visit our website to discover more!

ManifoldPress.co.uk

Printed in Great Britain
by Amazon

47269627R00153